W9-CCA-732

JOE FLAHERTY

TinWife

SIMON AND SCHUSTER New York

Designed by Karolina Harris
Manufactured in the United States of America

3   5   7   9   10   8   6   4   2

Library of Congress Cataloging in Publication Data
Flaherty, Joe
Tin wife.

I. Title.
PS3556.L28T5   1983   813'.54   83-20112
ISBN 0-671-47280-1

For my daughter, Siobhan Flaherty—a dazzling new bit of business who will set the world on its ear.

.   .   .

And for my wife, Jeanine Johnson Flaherty, who once upon a time, like the good ship Rachel, plucked a floundering orphan from an all-encompassing sea.

ACKNOWLEDGMENTS

During a sad season a chorus of loved ones whack-rolled this tenuous enterprise. The perverse delight in this is that Manhattan is renowned as the capital of chilliness. So much for the smart money. I shan't name all those who helped, since many of my friends are writers who know the sleazy excitement of seeing their names in print. These are the friends who supplied everything from unasked-for finances to lusted-after laughter at bedside. They are the same men and women who shared at my table, who touted me at race tracks, who kept back the dark night of the soul at the Lion's Head. And be there more to come, we will kick it around again on a celestial turf.

I would, though, like to cite those outside my intimate orbit. Ed Koch and Dan Wolf opened doors for me. Behind one of those doors was Maureen Jordan Lindie with her gracious and ministering hands. Then there was Stanley Bosworth, headmaster of St. Ann's Episcopal School in Brooklyn, whose heart proved larger than his infamous polysyllabic patter.

Of course, there is my family, my mother Maggie and brothers Doc, Bill, and Gene, and foremost, my son Liam, who proved wise and courageous beyond his years. Indeed, such conduct in Caesar's court would have brought the deserving accolade of noble.

But one person must be singled out, Karen Schnitzler Hitzig, the only agent I've ever had. Karen's profession evokes vile images. But to view Karen as a typical agent would be akin to calling Bill Veeck one of the Lords of Baseball.

—Joe Flaherty
August 6, 1983
New York City

*S*ISSY SULLIVAN reached sanctuary. It wasn't perfect, but it was the best she could do. The running water helped to drown them out, and there was the steam. Their jackhammer voices were dissipated by the elements and the security of the locked bathroom door. And the steam. It annexed them to another plane. The agony was muted, if not removed entirely. A bit like Purgatory. A nice Catholic thought, that.

"What is she doing in there?"

"Boiling herself. She'll come out looking like a beet. I don't know how many rolls of Sanitas she ruined at home with those damn boiling baths. It used to peel right off the walls. If I told her once, I told her a million times. But not her. She thought money grew on trees. She's her father's daughter. He treated her like the Queen of Sheba."

"Ah, the young ones. They think everything comes easy."

Sissy turned on the water with more force. Their voices, tempered by an Irish lilt, still cut through the seams in the door. Musical razor blades.

"The Queen of Sheba." "Lana Turner." "Wally Simpson." And on and on. She had heard her mother's baptismal litany as long as she could remember. The Irish were great with names. Fey nicknames or putdowns. Her mother, Nellie McKenna, could hold her own with the best. No Nonsense Nellie. She prided herself on that. What had Sissy's father said? "The woman's charm is municipal. She has a nose for sewer contracts."

Sissy laughed at the memory. That was the measure of his charm. Despite all he had done, she could still laugh—even now, years after his death. His lousy, ugly death. Michael "Mickey" McKenna was still getting laughs from the wings. That would please the ass off him, she thought.

Rivulets of water ran down her cheeks. Not unlike him, she pretended they were something else. The steam. She was her father's daughter.

"Well, I hope she isn't all day about it. They say the Mayor will probably be there," said the other voice. Or was it her mother's? No, it was Eddie's mother's. The whine earmarked it. Every octave was a station of the cross.

"I'll put a move on her, Mrs. Sullivan," her mother said. "Sissy! Sissy! It's gettin' late, and Mr. and Mrs. Sullivan are here." Twenty years related by marriage, and it was still "Mr. and Mrs." The social graces were staggering.

"Soon," boomed the daughter through the door, terrifying herself with the perfect harmony. Oh, no—never her mother's daughter.

She slid deeper into the water, hoping to steal a few more minutes before facing them. Her raft of pubic hair floated to the top. She used to pretend it was the black hair of a child growing inside her. "Tippy," she'd called it. Then when Eddie buried his face there, he used to say it was like pulling a watch cap over his ears. Her husband once gave it numerous raves. "The Black Shield of Falworth," he had dubbed it, from a movie in which Tony Curtis had played a renegade knight. Had any of them, her included, ever gotten their heads out of the fifties? Damn! Her brain was running off. Not today. Hold it together, Theresa.

"I'm telling you, the Pope himself could be waiting, and she'd take her own sweet time. Sissy! SISSY! We're not going to a ball. The Mayor isn't going to smell you."

"Screw you, Mother dear," she mouthed into the steam.

"We'll never get to Manhattan on time, Mrs. McKenna. How do we get there anyway? Where *is* City Hall?" her mother-in-law whined.

"Through the Cumberland Pass, you dumb old bitch," Sissy mumbled. "Fifty years in the country, and she can't find her way out of her own parish." This, too, evaporated in the bathroom steam.

"Leave the girl be. The day will be trying enough for her," said a male voice, tentatively breaching the female monopoly.

Her mother-in-law repelled Sissy's ally. "You just go in the living room and finish your tea. You're sweating so much, your shirt is pasted to you. And try and get some toast into you. You were so late, you ate nothing at all last night."

Sissy turned off the water and heard the scratching of a chair on the kitchen floor and the faint rattle of a cup and saucer. Christy must have had another long night. She'd better get out there before they ate her father-in-law alive. She listened to his shuffling retreat.

As she drained the tub, she heard her mother, "Well, about time." Old lady Sullivan delivered one of her patented sighs. Another cross to bear. Catherine had the franchise on maternal grief. The McDonald's of misery. She alone thought Lee Harvey Oswald had climbed the stairs of the Texas School Book Depository solely to break Rose Kennedy's heart.

Sissy toweled herself vigorously, bringing a glow to her body. Not bad for forty-four, she thought, as she surveyed herself in the bathroom mirror. The breasts sagged a bit, but what could she expect after two kids? Besides, they had always been too big. But the legs and ass had held pretty well. Especially the legs— they were her aces, though there were stretch marks now at the top. Combat ribbons of domestic bliss.

She brushed her teeth and gargled with mouthwash. There would be a lot of ceremonial pecking today. She let the cold water run till it was ice, then filled the sink with it and submerged her face, holding it under for fifteen seconds. She repeated this a half dozen times until the water tightened her skin. Freeze over the crow's feet. She bundled herself into a floor-length terrycloth robe. She was ready to greet her family.

Sissy opened the door and walked the few feet through the foyer to the kitchen. Her mother and mother-in-law were sitting at the Formica kitchen table, nursing mugs of tea. Domestic Irish sacramental wine, Mickey had called it. The two of them were turned out. Flowered dresses, paste pearls, proper small hats and gloves lying at rest atop their handbags. And their hair was done, permanents touched for the high occasion with a blue rinse. They always looked their best for solemn occasions. At weddings and christenings they were too involved for special grooming. After all, they might be called on to wipe a dish or boil water for tea. Solemnity brought out the style. Like stately old lionesses, they were granted the role of sentry at life's sad events. Given a wake for a popular local, every hairdresser in Flatbush had an economic surge.

Sissy perfunctorily kissed each on the cheek, being ever so careful not to disturb the taut curls on their heads, an unnecessary consideration, since a blackjack couldn't move them. "Hi, Nellie. How are you, Catherine? I won't be long."

The two women merely nodded. It wasn't that they were angry about her tardiness, it was her greeting that disturbed them. Years ago, she had started to withhold from them the demanded "Mom," and they never forgave her. In normal circumstances it was bad enough, but on a day such as this! The girl had no sense of propriety, never mind occasion.

She watched their gloom with satisfaction. Moral loansharks being denied their vig. If Eddie were here, they would be beaming. Eddie not only would Mom them, but offer flirtatious remarks about their hair and clothes. Dry foreplay was the way to win them. But then again, they would be hurt if they knew Eddie had called every old blowser in a bar Mom and the men, depending on their ages, Unc or Sweetheart. In a way, it wasn't phony. It came from the heart. Eddie was terrified of being disliked by anyone he encountered. It was odd he'd become a cop. Willy Loman "on the job."

"Where's Pa . . . Christy?" she asked, her tipped hand not unnoticed by the women.

"In the living room," his wife answered. "Sissy, maybe you can do something with him? When I talk to him, it's like talking to a stone wall."

"What's the matter, Catherine?"

"He hasn't had a bite to eat today, and as far as I know, he had no dinner wherever he was last night."

Sissy pulled her robe away from her skin in mock discomfort. "It's probably the weather. Nobody has an appetite."

"John Jameson's has more to do with it than August," Catherine shot back.

"Oh, you'll never get her to chime in against the men. She was her father's lawyer," Nellie sniped.

She glared at her mother and altered her tone of voice. It became what Nellie called "uppity." "Nellie, get me a cup of coffee."

Her mother scampered for the pot. Sissy felt sleazy when she pulled this. She knew her mother had never cast off the yoke she bore from years of "living out" as a domestic when she was a young greenhorn. It was easy to intimidate people with history. She disgusted herself, so she dropped her voice and winked conspiratorially at the two women. "I'll get some toast into him." Even the syntax bowed to them. She wondered how long ago she had mastered manipulation. She remembered sneaking up behind her father and kissing his bald spot, the one he spent strategic sessions in the bathroom each morning trying to disguise. Had she come out of the womb a hustler? That was too depressing to contemplate.

She made Christy's toast, buttered it, then layered it with strawberry jam. She knew the ritual well. Replace the sugar in the blood. She put the toast on a plate and went into the living room. God, he was gray. A picket fence of sickly sweat ran across his upper lip. "How's it going, Dad?" she said, as she kissed his forehead.

"I've had better mornings," he replied, with the grin of a prankish boy. "About twenty thousand of them."

She laughed at the bravado. Take the cigarette instead of the blindfold. If you can't handle it—whatever—laugh at it. And if the laughter is a Roman sword on which you impale yourself, so much the better. It was so typically Mick.

"Have some toast. It will make you feel better."

"I don't think I could get it down. It's a rocky road down there."

"You've been going at it a little heavy lately, Christy."

"Please, Theresa, not a sermon from you. I got one from the Mount this morning."

She kissed him on the forehead again. The gesture was part conciliatory, but more a thank you for calling her Theresa. He was the only one in the family who did. She hated "Sissy," but when you grew up an only daughter, they tried to neuter you quickly. Convert a child into a maiden aunt. Nobody would try to play it fast and loose with the "Sissys" of the world.

"No preaching. I just worry about you. I lost a father that way, and you're the only distinguished old beau I've got left."

He softened. If all men were gray and impotent, her life would have been a cakewalk.

"Ah, don't you go to worrying, child. You have woes of your own. I thought the vice squad was going to break down the bathroom door."

She loved the banter and rejoined, "What they don't realize is that if you grow up in a railroad flat, the bathroom is the presidential suite."

He perked up a bit. "Locked doors are against their religion. The only reason they allow them is that bodily functions are a greater sin."

For a moment she was taken aback by his pungent observation. She tended to forget that he, like everyone else in this culture (or was it a lack of it?), sublimated himself, masked his mind. The inspiration for that bodily function crack was singsonging in the kitchen. One should get a plenary indulgence for sleeping with Catherine. But that, like everything else important except money, was left unsaid. The commandment was to come off "regular." Ideas consigned you to the Irish Elba, the baptism, "oddball."

"I just don't want another Mickey on my hands."

"God, I miss his laughter. Ah-h. It's just that I have too much time on my hands since retirement, Theresa. I'm not very good at supermarket intrigue or checkers at the Golden Age Center in Prospect Park. At least the bars have some life in them. And some young people, too. Spending your time with walking obituary columns gets you down. God, you never realize how long a day is till you don't have a job."

Tears welled in her eyes. It was part anger. At times like these she remembered her class. He was sixty-eight and useless. A retired maintenance man for the Transit Authority. Just another slob who worked with his mitts. What was forgotten was that he had a mind—a mind tough enough to represent his union for twenty years. This unassuming ghost had helped forge tough contracts with those who were bent on bilking him and his kind out of every nickel. Now he was relegated to "golden" circles. Every political hack thinks the old are lusting to be checkers experts, macramé weavers, and retired commodores out on fishing boats in Sheepshead Bay. Nobody listens, Sissy thought.

She rose and winked. "I'm going to freshen your tea, but I

want to see that toast disappear." She didn't need to elaborate. She went to the kitchen, took the boiling kettle, and added hot water to the tepid tea, leaving the cup two inches short. "He's doing fine," she threw out for public consumption. Then, faking confusion, she added, "Where the hell is my hair dryer?" She walked into the TV room with the cup and saucer in hand, went to the bar, and topped the steaming tea with Irish whiskey.

She hated this room with its gaudy decor, a loud red leatherette bar and frosted mirror. A gilt spiderweb. And the pictures. Eddie in his uniform, and Billy looking manly in his Marine dress blues. Goddamn uniforms—she hated them. Both of them, gone. She jammed the rolled collar of the robe in her mouth to stifle the incipient sobs. She thought about sipping Christy's tea, then rejected the thought. That might get her rolling. Not today, Theresa. If it was to be anything, it would be Valium.

She stared at the pictures on the back bar while she tried to compose herself. Her glowing wedding picture. Was it ever that right? The sad part was that it had been. She glanced at the framed photo of jaunty Eddie and Sal, posing in their uniforms outside the Police Academy the day they received their metallic diplomas, their shields, their beloved tin. Sal, Eddie's partner, his "sweetheart." Did Eddie know about his sweetheart? She panicked. She was losing it. She left the tea on the bar and went to the bathroom and gulped ten mg of Valium.

She didn't know if the drug took immediately, but she had an illusion of calm. Was she becoming pill dependent, as her doctor had warned could happen? Forget it. The brain, at least, was centering. The kaleidoscopic connections stopped.

She returned to the hated room, picked up the tea, and stared at the picture of her son. Maybe it wasn't anyone's fault. When Billy died in Vietnam, Eddie crumbled. He was the one who had insisted Billy "should be part of it." A Marine like his old man in Korea. What a mad legacy! He was proud to hand that down! Do men have any sanity at all? she wondered. If death wore a skirt, she would be the hottest number on the block.

This was sentimental slop. It had gone bad long before that. She should have known when Eddie built this bar. A nice, beer-swilling kid building a mafioso whorehouse off his living room. No, he had been changed for a long time, and she was just too dumb, no, too frightened, or maybe too coy to accept it. She went along with the lie. But it wasn't all Christian charity. She liked the idea of living, for once, without a budget. Where did she think the money had come from—the tooth fairy?

She fled the room. Christy was waiting with all the patience he could muster. He took the cup and drained it half away. Color started to rise in his face, and he picked up a piece of toast. "A deal's a deal."

"Sip the rest of it until you get the toast down."

"Theresa, my little flower," he said, smiling. The plasma had taken hold. "Where's Eileen?"

"Upstairs, dressing. I'm going up to do the same."

He reached into his pocket and took five dollars from a crumpled wad. "Give her this from Granpa. To buy a record or something."

"Pops."

"Come on, now. Give it to her. She'll have to earn it soon enough."

Sissy took it. She didn't have the heart to refuse. His last vestige of manhood was giving money to his grandchild.

Christy taken care of, she made her way up the carpeted stairs to Eileen's room. Her bare feet caressed the depth of the pile. Where had she kidded herself the money for that came from? And the bar, and the four television sets—the color ones in the bar and the living room and the black and white portables in her bedroom and Eileen's? Five, really, but Billy's room was off limits. She had to get around to that soon. It had been two years now. If she wasn't careful, she'd be the caretaker of a shrine. Soon. Enough on her mind today.

But she couldn't let the incriminating decor alone. The schlocky Italian Provincial peppered throughout the house. And the marble cherub soapdishes in the downstairs and upstairs bathrooms. Fat, decadent little bastards holding up bars of soap. Diminutive bagmen. The whole house was a castle of corruption.

Eileen's door was open. The girl was sitting on her bed in her underwear, reading a book. *Franny & Zooey*. Sissy had put her onto Salinger. Books had gotten Sissy through a lot in life, and she was pleased her daughter had her appetite for them. They were closets to hide in in a prying world. Billy had never read. Well, the *Daily News* and various sports magazines. His father was the same. They bitched they couldn't sit still that long. That should have been a clue. There was something wrong when people needed motion all the time.

"Hey, how goes it?"

The girl looked up and uncrossed her legs. Sissy noticed the fullness of her figure. She hadn't been that developed at seventeen. The great blossoming of American nutrition. Kids were being fed out of existence.

"Okay," the girl answered.

"How's the book?"

"Weird."

"Weird?" Sissy queried, arching her eyebrows.

"You know what I mean. He doesn't write like a man."

"That's why I recommended it. That's a good observation."

"I'd like to read more of him."

Sissy approached her daughter and hugged her. "You can read to your heart's content in college."

Eileen turned sullen. Sissy hated that in her. The child's facial censure. She felt like slapping her, but it would be a self-directed blow. She could hear the voices of the nuns: "Take that look off your face before I knock it off."

"What's wrong, Eileen?"

"Well, do you really think I should go to college? I don't know if I'm smart enough. You know what I mean."

"No, I don't. And stop repeating 'you know what I mean.' You're a bright young woman (Sissy paused mentally—those feminist sessions had gotten something across woman, not girl), and you'll do great at school."

Eileen grew deliberately younger. "I don't know," she mumbled. "Not many of the other girls are going to college. Besides, with Dad . . . you know what I mean, we could use the money."

Sissy bristled. "I don't give a damn what your classmates are doing. What are you going to do—go through life with your classmates? That only happens in June Allyson movies."

"June who?"

Oh, shit, the vaunted generation gap. "It doesn't matter. Some drip from the fifties. And let me worry about the money. I'll get a job, and with your father's pension we'll be all right."

"Well, the nuns were talking about the good job market. We had recruiters from companies coming around the school."

"Forget the nuns. All they think about is work. Just because they ended up drudges, they think everyone else should."

The girl rose from the bed and pulled herself up to her full height. She had half a head on Sissy. Her eyes were flashing, and when she pointed her finger at her mother, Sissy momentarily cowered, recalling Eddie.

"Daddy said St. Agnes was one of the finest schools in Brooklyn, and I'm not sure he was so hot on me going to college."

So that was it. Not religious loyalty, but daddy. It was endless. Sure, daddy wasn't strong on college. Keep them little girls. Sewn up brains and sewn up hymens. What had Eddie joked (joked, ha!), that Sissy was trying to turn Eileen into an egghead, like herself? And what had Mickey said to Sissy when she wanted to study fashion design? "Leave that to the la-de-dahs. I'm not going to have any child of mine mincing, even if she is a girl." Mickey's compromise was to send her to Katherine Gibbs secretarial school. The pantheon of Irish class. And did he ever brag about the tuition price! Dollars made everything quality. Especially if you had to borrow them. The loan book added suffering. An economic altar lily.

"Eileen, honey. St. Agnes is fine as far as it goes. But preparing you for a job isn't the only reason to get an education. Money will come later. You're young. Try to enjoy your life. You know we have an appointment at Columbia after the ceremony. I realize you're nervous, but give it a try. Okay? I'm sure Daddy would be proud of the first Sullivan to graduate from college. You know he would be proud." Was she lying in her teeth?

"You think so?" the girl said more amicably.

Sissy gave it her best laugh. "I know so and you know so. He was so proud of you, and you know how he loved ceremonies. To see you walking down the aisle in a cap and gown would bust his brass buttons."

Eileen hugged her and fell into a tough-guy imitation of Eddie: "Yeah, that's her, the kid's mine. That's my rabbit at the top of her class. It's in the blood, Sullivan all the way."

It was an uncanny parody. Sissy's eyes teared through the laughter. "And Eileen, remember Dad's favorite expression, 'Give it a shot.'"

"Okay, Mom. I'll give it a shot."

Sissy threw a playful left hook at her, completing Eddie's reincarnation. Eileen's eyes filled. "Come on," Sissy said. "Let's get ready. Those old hens in the kitchen are sitting on a griddle."

"Oh, Mommy, you're terrible."

"So I've been told. So I've been told."

"Mom, is today going to be gross?"

Gross. It drove her mad. Damn expressions. But she had to be fair. In her day everything was "putrid." "No, it's not going to be *gross*," she chided. "It's going to be fine. Your father and some other cops are going to be honored. The Mayor will be there. It will be a lovely day. And I have a secret for you."

"What?"

"Don't mention it downstairs, but your daddy could be promoted posthumously to lieutenant."

"Lieutenant? He was only plainclothes. Why?"

"Those who know say it's because he was working on a big drug case when he died, and the Commissioner and Mayor might want to honor him."

"What does it mean? To us, I mean."

"It means a lovely honor, for one thing, and that we could be getting a lieutenant's pension. So, young lady, get those worries about money out of your head."

"Oh, mom. The Mayor!"

"Yes, the Mayor."

"Mommy, all my clothes are so gross."

"No, they're not. Wear your white linen suit. It's a perfect day for it."

"But Mom, a suit for the Mayor? It's . . ."

"I know, gross." Sissy walked to Eileen's bureau and took her writing tablet and a magic marker. She sketched quickly, finished, and handed the pad to Eileen. "How's this, Cinderella?"

Sissy had sketched an elaborate ballgown on the pad, replete with ruffles, flourishes, and bows. "Oh, Mom, if only I could."

"For graduation from Columbia. I'm going to crank up that sewing machine of mine and design you a whole college wardrobe."

"That's bribery."

"I know it."

"You should design clothes, Mom. You're so super."

"Someday, Eileen. Meanwhile, you worry about today, and I'll take care of Yves St. Laurent in the future."

"It's going to be a great day, Mom?"

"Great."

"The Mayor?"

"For sure."

"Mom, will you be all right? You know, at the ceremony?"

Never show vulnerability. Even the innocent throw it up to you. "I'll be fine, Eileen. I'm very calm. The only thing that will drive me crazy is one more 'gross.' "

"Mom, I didn't say crazy."

Sissy laughed. "I know you didn't. Your mother lacks diplomacy. A crude old Brooklyn broad."

"Just don't get upset, all right?"

"A veritable cucumber in August."

"Wow! They really thought that much of Dad?"

"Everyone who ever met him did, dear." She kissed the child. "Now get your gorgeous Irish butt into that linen suit."

"Mom, you are crude."

"You betcha," Sissy said, as she flounced toward the door, wiggling her backside.

Eileen howled in delight. "Mother, you're gr . . ."

Sissy turned and crossed her eyes. "Do you want your mother to wig out?"

Eileen was now full of merriment. "Wow! A lieutenant."

"It's still a rumor, mind you. But a hot one. I'll be back in fifteen minutes, dressed, and I expect to find you the same way."

"Then Dad's a . . . a hero?"

"Yes, honey, a hero."

Sissy went to her own room, her duty done. Christy's shakes had abated, and Eddie was elevated to hero. It continued. She was still powdering and diapering men.

Sissy dressed for the weather. Instead of nylon panties, she chose a pair in white cotton. Her duff would be on one chair or another all day, and she didn't want a rash. Besides, cotton always gave her a sense of security. Nylon was too wispy to house privates. She remembered the panties Eddie had given her for their honeymoon—the ones labeled with the days of the week. There was no rest day then. Double time, triple time, around the clock. Not long after Eileen's birth, he had slacked off. Sissy didn't know if it was her maternal role or the pressures of the job that hounded him. After Billy's death, you needed a court order to get

him to perform. Now her desire was basic cotton. You're getting
back to your peasant roots, Sissy girl. Soon it will be gunnysacks.

She hooked on a white bra. She had to get some new ones. The
cups looked like overflowing biscuit tins. Then her moment came.
She lay back on her bed and luxuriously pulled on her pantyhose,
an act that had given her pleasure since she was a girl, since the
first time she knew her legs were something special. The boys
used to say she had them right up to her ass.

Her ritual was an imitation of fornication. She pushed each leg
into the smooth openings ever so slowly, pausing at intervals
when she encountered an obstruction, then penetrating with more
force, moving deeper until she hit bottom, where she would move
her toes around in sensuous triumph. When Eddie did that to
her with his penis, he had called it "spooning the bottom of the
cake bowl."

She extended both legs into the air as she stretched and
smoothed the pantyhose. They were still there—right up to her
duff. She knew this was her vanity, but she didn't care. As a girl,
she had kept scrapbooks of actresses with great legs and compared hers against theirs. Grable, Dietrich, Ann Miller, Cyd
Charisse, Gretchen Wyler, even a nonentity like Julie Adams.
Adams, a fifties flash in the pan, was anointed with LePage's glue
just because she had the rep of fitting Grable's leg measurements
perfectly. Did Julie, now in obscurity, know she had a fifties arti-
fact as an admirer? Sha Na Na.

Sissy giggled. The Valium had taken hold, maybe too much.
She allowed her legs to drop straight out across the bed, rearranging the L of her body. She shoved off the bed with the
palms of her hands and moved to her dressing table, where she
applied makeup, a touch of blusher and a hint of pale lipstick.
Even when she was younger, she had shunned heavy lipstick—
only tough broads went in for the scarlet smear. Jesus, they'd
looked like victims of Jack the Ripper. Eddie used to say that if
one of them gave you head, you'd look like you bought it in the
balls.

But the eye makeup was different. Here, her hand was a little
too heavy and she knew it. But she had purple eyes, Liz Taylor
eyes . . . Jesus, she sounded like a seed catalogue for *Silver
Screen*. But it was true. They *were* violet, not dark blue. And
with a liberal application of light lavender eye shadow, they

glowed, and did they ever play off her jet-black hair! Amethysts on a black velvet display cloth. Hedda herself could have said it no better.

Her hair was a problem. She couldn't wear it down straight in the new fashion. Her body had too many circles: her hips, her breasts. Straight down, her hair flattened her body, and she looked like a johnny pump. A classic Celtic body dilemma. So she piled it high on her head in an old-fashioned upsweep, attempting to elongate her frame. Besides, it wasn't coal black anymore. There were wisps of gray—webs—like the bar mirror. But she wouldn't dye it. That would be cheating, like wearing falsies. And she had earned those strands. She snorted. Nellie and Catherine would appreciate that sentiment: "Well, if you went through what I went through, you'd have gray hair, too." Thatta daughter, Sissy, retirement in Calvary Village is right up the road.

Her shoes were another bow to the past. She wouldn't be caught dead in those fashionable squat heels. They were for charwomen's legs. She still had a reserve of stiletto-heeled pumps in good condition. She stepped into a pair and backed away from her mirror for a long shot of the backs of her calves. Dynamite!

Now for the ceremonial weeds. Her basic black shift? Even with what she was floating, that was a little much. After the last decade with Eddie, black could get her indicted for fraud. Ah, aquamarine, for a summer day. She'd always loved that color. Not too loud, not quite green (no phony Irishness), but muted and cool. She slinked into the dress and caressed away the wrinkles. The vision in the mirror pleased her. A tall, sexy sherbet.

She debated jewelry. In her jewelry box she spotted the pin Eddie had given her, a miniature replica of his badge. No, that was . . . gross? Like hell it was. Milk them for sympathy, the Mayor included.

The other piece was staring up at her from the box. She hadn't touched it since . . . since God knows when. Her engagement ring. She picked it up with trepidation and fingered it. She then did a very strange thing. Sissy Sullivan placed the ring in her mouth, and when the taste of salt flooded her tongue, her regal eyes rained purple.

*I*T COULD HARDLY have been described as a whirlwind affair. Sissy got Eddie with staying power. Plenty of girls had been in line before her (indeed, had better shots), but they had blown it. She assumed they'd let Eddie have his way (women were always easy for him). After their marriage, he had intimated as much in an offhanded way, never spelling it out. The code had it the real stuff only went down in the confessional. He just dropped hints, hoping to get her goat. But she had the ring. In cop lingo, that was the bottom line.

His innuendos were probably more exciting than the reality. Having his own way meant some stolen tit or the big payoff, a hand job (*la dolce vita* in the Eisenhower years). As far as Sissy knew, all her friends had gone to their bridal beds virgins. It was smart politics over mindless passion. The few who "put out" became notorious. "Cunt," they were labeled. The fifties, what a time to grow up.

It wasn't that Sissy wasn't tempted. She was ready enough. Many a night she'd humped her pillow into submission. That was fun—a banquet. The pillow was capped by the head of her choice, whoever of an evening had worked her into a beery flush on a dance floor. But cleverness kept her intact. It was easy to read men. Even the ones who were worthwhile.

And no denying it, Eddie was a catch. The local variety maybe, but she knew no other. It wasn't for his potential (nobody gazed into a crystal ball) but for what he was. Handsome, and Sissy never discounted that. Even later, after she'd gone to feminist meetings and worked to "raise her consciousness," she'd had trouble relating to men who weren't sensual. Oh, she loved spending time with them—they weren't threatening and they listened. That was a breakthrough—not being dismissed automatically. Though sometimes she wondered if attentiveness wasn't just another gambit to pull off her pants. Her mother was right, she would question a saint. But these men without bodies were like lying in the sun to her. A passive, secure pleasure. They never moved her to thoughts of action.

Eddie was the opposite. He was beautifully proportioned. Not in the old, hokey, beefcake way, though he would rate. In a symmetrical sense. He had pleasing hands and feet, large but not coarse. So many of the Irish had brutal extremities. You could trace their dour history through their hands. And his being blond topped it. He bounced off her blackness like a light in a coal mine.

But it was more than that. Everything about him was nifty. The way he moved or tossed a football on a beach, his glide on a dance floor. He was shellac on the rough grain of her existence.

He also carried clothes better than any woman she had ever known. Not just suits or his uniform (in that, he was capable of wiling his way into a biddy's will) but in his casual wear, which he transformed into a uniform. At the beach (he was always summer to her) he wore boxer swim trunks, white or tan, with a form-fitting bush jacket starched to attention by the Chinese laundry and topped by a strategically crumpled fatigue cap. The sand that sullied others only enhanced the blond curly hair on his legs. Festive angel hair. The summer she read Fitzgerald, he immediately became Dick Diver.

And there were other niceties. He had such good table manners. Unlike the other Irish she knew, he ate slowly, not as if the famine was closing in. His speech was much the same. He wasn't a hotshot wiseass who thought conversation consisted of one-liners. Sex-ridden machine guns. And he always noticed when a girl made a stylish effort and paid a cogent compliment. "Your feet look like Leslie Caron's in those ballerina slippers." Not much now. But then it was a league ahead of the asininity you usually got.

When he was sad, he would tell you so, unlike the others who would steamroll their hurt with a layer of hot epithets. They considered the confession of pain the province of skirts. Sissy often listened, and he liked that in her. She gently joked him out of his moods and played "pal" and cheerleader, never designing woman. And when she had put him back together and assured him his dreams were around the corner, and he wasn't becoming a wastrel with his sporadic hell-raising, he would go off renewed to pursue another girl. Usually, a little simp who looked like nun's droppings. He would always have an attraction for those "just put me in your pocket" types.

But she never complained or chastised him about it when they next met, and he liked that. His tactlessness was between her and the towel when she dried her tears in the bathroom at home. She knew she could outlast those Lilliputians he could bend to his will. So the Kleenex never came out in public and certainly not in private with him. Sissy knew how to campaign—she was in for the long haul.

The timidity of the knock on the bedroom door told Sissy it was her mother. Eileen would just have barged in. And why not? Since Eddie no longer shared her bed, what did Sissy have to hide? Stirrings from the subconscious didn't creak bedsprings. Even her own daughter didn't think Sissy's privacy was valid without a man.

The tap was repeated, fainter this time. It sounded like a kitten begging to get into a room. "Come in, it's open," Sissy invited.

Nellie peered in the door. "I was just up visiting my granddaughter, and I thought I'd drop in and see how you were doing."

Inwardly, Sissy bristled. Was the visit to Eileen a ruse to check her out? God knows what Nellie and Catherine had been speculating she was doing in her room. Morosely parading in her wedding gown?

"Lord, she's getting to be a looker," Nellie said.

It sounded sincere. Maybe Nellie's trip upstairs was prompted by grandmotherly love. It wasn't such a farfetched tale, it was just that Sissy never gave Nellie the nod on a close one. She tried to make amends for her suspicion.

"She comes from a good line," Sissy said. "Her looks didn't come from the wind."

"Yes, you were a pretty child," Nellie agreed.

"And I didn't get it from the wind either," Sissy observed.

"Well, you didn't get it from me," said Nellie without a trace of self-pity in her voice. "That was your father's department."

"Don't sell yourself short," Sissy said, smiling.

Nellie didn't respond. They were not at ease when wooing. Those weren't love notes they had thrown across the barricades all these years.

Nellie decided to concentrate on Eileen. "Well, wherever she got the looks, she'll outshine the whole lot of us."

"She reminds me of her father," Sissy said, deciding diplomatically to remove Eileen's beauty from her genes, too.

"Yes, she does," said Nellie wistfully. "I know it's odd to say about a man, but when you and Eddie were dating, he was almost pretty. I often thought if he was a girl he'd make a beautiful bride."

Sissy was taken aback by her mother's perception. She motioned Nellie to sit in a cane rocker by the window while she continued with her makeup.

Almost longingly, Nellie settled into the chair. How many times had Sissy promised to get her such a chair, for how many anniversaries, birthdays, Mother's Days? Bad enough that as a daughter she was an emotional welcher, but this, too?

"Yes, I guess you could say he was pretty then," Sissy commented, as Nellie absentmindedly rocked, staring out the window into the street. The window and the street, the designated neighborhood female vista.

Sissy thought of the clichéd scene in so many movies—the ingenue on a Manhattan penthouse terrace with the producer (was it always William Powell?). "Someday, my dear, all this will be yours." Something had gotten lost in the Brooklyn translation.

"No guess about it," said Nellie from the rocker. "When he came into a room, he turned more heads than most women."

Yes, Sissy mused to herself, that was true, but it wasn't the asset Nellie thought it was. His good looks made him vulnerable. Sissy had learned that lookers of either sex were easy to maneuver. They built their church on the flimsiest of foundations, and somewhere down deep inside they knew it. They could sense the lurking mountebank in the cellar under the cosmetic layers. It always came too easy for them. Not just sex, that was a small part of it. But everything. Their physical arsenals, supported by social graces, turned others into doormen.

Sissy had picked that up from Mickey, a shoeshine-and-smile

boy himself. Yes, her father was a regular seminar if you wanted
to matriculate in con or street smarts. Mickey could have had
his pick of the litter, but he chose her mother for marriage. Nellie
was as plain and as exciting as mashed potatoes. As substantial,
too—that was her trump. That was unfair. Why was she so hard
on her mother? Probably because Nellie hadn't warned her.

That was only partially true, as were the slurs on Nellie's looks.
In fact, her mother had moments of beauty. When you caught
her in repose with her grandchildren, or when she was baking. Her
innocent skin (which looked as if it had never been licked or
stretched by a man) radiated a restful beauty.

But this was still not giving her her due. Sissy recalled when
Nellie danced the Irish dances with her white skin flushed, her
black hair glistening with sweat, and her dark blue eyes flashing;
she was sensual—it was like a glimpse of an uncharted star from
another galaxy. And Sissy had to admit her coloring was her
mother's, even though schematically she fixed her mother's eyes
as dark blue. Another partial truth. Her fullness of chest and her
legs, especially her prized legs, were also Nellie's, certainly not
Mickey's. Mickey had stork's legs, and she suspected his in-
sistence on pajamas (in an airless railroad flat) had had more to
do with vanity than fastidiousness.

But the girl, the colleen, in Nellie was evident only when she
danced. Her youth had died somewhere back in County Wicklow,
or was it on the boat coming over, or in the hellish kitchens of
"the Yanks" before marriage rescued her from the domestic
drudgery of others. Since Mickey's death, that choked-down bile
had begun to spew forth sporadically. The nightmarish trip across
the Atlantic at sixteen, the relatives at the dock to receive her
with a domestic post at a doctor's home secured (passage wasn't
raised for sight-seeing), and her first Dantesque trip on a subway,
where she was separated from her cousin who exited at the station before, thinking Nellie was in tow. And the ensuing madness—an uncontrollable Nellie attempting to traverse the catwalk
back to the last stop, her cousin's exit, only to be subdued by a
cop, a Mick at that, who mocked the "greenhorn" for the sport of
the Yank passengers and to reinforce his own Americanization.
Sissy vowed to do better by her.

"He was a very graceful man," said Nellie, not turning her
head from the window. Sissy wondered if Nellie expected to find
anything new out there. She knew better. It wasn't the new

Nellie was looking for, but the way it once was. Could these drab streets ever have been as enchanting as the old remembered them? Christ, if you believed them, you'd believe Brooklyn was landscaped by Currier & Ives.

"Yes, he was a nice athlete," Sissy said.

"Oh, not only that," Nellie responded. "Plenty of them were good at sports. It was the way he moved. It was nice having him around you. He relaxed you. Like looking at a fish tank in a doctor's office. And he was a corking dancer."

A fish tank. Sissy shook her head. She was always amazed at the metaphors the Irish concocted to sublimate sexuality.

"He was smooth on a dance floor all right," she agreed. In an attempt to lighten it up, she added, "Your granddaughter says he was hopelessly out-of-date, though."

"Well, you wouldn't call that stuff they do dancing, would you? That madhouse stuff? Well, you know what I mean," Nellie added apologetically.

Sissy looked over and saw her mother biting her bottom lip. Poor Nellie. Sissy's short foray with a nervous condition had reduced her mother's already limited vocabulary.

"It's certainly wild," Sissy said cheerfully.

"Well, I guess it's all right for the young ones," Nellie conceded. "There's no harm in it. But I can't see the joy in it either. I guess I'm out-of-date, too. Just give me my Irish dances. And Eddie could dance those better than those born there. I loved to get up with him."

"Yes, he could," Sissy admitted. He also could do an Italian or a Jewish folk turn. Weddings were Eddie's metier. The old ladies were never neglected. Regardless of race, color, or creed, Eddie gave them all a spin. He was like Geritol laced with Spanish fly.

"He reminded me of my father in that way," Nellie said.

"What?" asked Sissy, confused by the entrance of a new player.

"My father," Nellie reiterated, still looking out the window. "They were a lot alike. Both of them were great fun, and they had that way with people. My father was a grand dancer himself."

Oh, lord, thought Sissy. She knew what was coming. She had heard it so often since Mickey died she could punctuate the lament. Why did special occasions always have this effect?

Plungers to unblock the shit of memory. It was hopeless to try to stop it. Anyway, she didn't have the heart.

"You know, my father never wanted me to come here," Nellie said. "He cried for days before I left. They gave me a coming-over party the night before I left—food, fiddles, the townspeople dancin' to beat the band, and he wouldn't come out of his room. That's how heartsick he was. The next morning he couldn't bring himself to see me off at the boat. He called me into his room and cried for a half hour and told me it wasn't his idea. A small, graceful, gentle man. He said my mother wanted it, and what could he do? He didn't want it, and I didn't want it. I never wanted to leave Ireland. We never saw each other again, and he never got over it. His letters were full of it. He died six years before I was able to afford to go back. I saved all his letters. Only *his* letters.

"Oh, my mother believed all that junk about America's streets being paved with gold. Gold, my arse (as strong as Nellie ever got)! I went from milking cows and cleaning pig slops to cleaning other people's slops. And believe me, many times the pigs were cleaner. Money, money, money, that's all they're interested in over there. Like it grew on trees, like you never had to pick up a mop or a rag to get it.

"Those fine houses I worked in? They fed their dogs better than the help. They counted every little scrap in the icebox like you would steal it. Well, I never touched a thing. I could feed myself, thank you. And your own kind were no better. After I was here seven months and sent home nearly every cent I made— I didn't buy myself as much as a hairpin—there was a County Wicklow dance up on 96th Street. So I took five dollars, five mind you, and bought this hat I had my eye on for months. My aunt, your great-aunt Mary, that old barge—God forgive me for talkin' about the dead—wrote my mother and told her I was living it up in America instead of sending home money for my brother Martin's passage. Can you imagine it? After seven months, five dollars!

"And I might add I paid back every single cent of my own passage to my Aunt Mary, that witch. God forgive my tongue. I brought out my brother, and he did well at the Telephone Company and bought his own house and everything, more than me and your father could ever afford, and I never seen a cent of his passage. Though I didn't do it for that reason, he was welcome to it, and more. And you know, my mother wrote back to my aunt that she had permission to chastise me, and she beat me with her husband's belt. I cried for a week, but I never wrote my father about it. He never touched me in his life, and the news would have killed him.

"That's your great America for you. I often curse the day I set foot on this shore. And believe me, Sissy, that's one of the reasons—and the Lord knows I had plenty of cause—why I never hit you."

Sissy could see Nellie was fighting to hold back her tears. She began to rock more rapidly, her neck arched over the curve of the rocker back, her eyes on the ceiling. It was as though she was trying to force the tears from where they had sprung. Sissy saw it wasn't going to work.

On the forward thrust of the rocker Nellie sprang up. "I think I could use another cup of tea," she said. "I'm only holding you up anyway."

"You're not," said Sissy. "We have time."

Nellie wanted to bolt from the room. "Can I bring you a cup? Oh, I forgot, it's coffee you like."

For one of the rare times in dealing with her mother, Sissy let her heart rule her head. "I think tea would be better for my stomach today. Why don't you bring up a couple of cups and sit with me while I dress?"

Sissy's unaccustomed kindness only brought Nellie's tears closer. "I won't be a minute," she said, as she scampered, head down, toward the door.

Like all the emotionally charged scenes Sissy had had with her mother throughout the years, this one had exhausted her. She could feel the sickening fatigue. Misery was more constant than happiness. Hurt had staying power.

Sissy went to the rocker Nellie had vacated and slumped into it. Though Eddie had bought the rocker for her when Billy was born—to nurse the boy—she had never felt it was her own. To nurse the child. In retrospect, the tableaux of early love mortified her. Pet names, special songs and places, outrageous sex talk over the phone, and madonnas in rockers. The curse of passion— attitudes were mistaken for philosophy.

To her the rocker would always be Eddie's. Maybe that's why Sissy never bought Nellie a duplicate. Sissy had risen from her bed for feedings in those early years, but it was Eddie who had sat sentry over Billy when he was a baby. Sissy would wake at odd hours of the night from the discomfort of her milk-laden breasts to find Eddie missing from their bed. He would be sitting in the rocker, peering at Billy in the crib. Out of tact and love, Sissy would do no more than silently spy.

She would watch Eddie get out the rocker and bend over the crib to check Billy's breathing. It was worse when Billy had congestion. Eddie would jostle the child slightly or tickle his hand until Billy stirred. Then he would go back and sit down or stand outside the open bedroom door and smoke a cigarette. He would never smoke in the same room with the child. By the time Eileen arrived, he had abandoned that amenity. Among others.

Somewhere in the whiff of gossip Eddie had heard of crib death. He quizzed the pediatrician about it, and neither the doctor's assurance that it was a rarity nor the fact that Billy showed no signs of vulnerability placated Eddie. It was he who had insisted that Billy's crib be placed in their room. Sissy wanted Billy in his own room from the beginning (all the books said it was healthier), but Eddie wouldn't budge. At the pediatrician's office he lied. He frequently dropped references to "the baby's room." His warning glances at Sissy were superfluous. She would no more have betrayed him than she would have confronted him about his nightly vigils in the rocker. She began to grasp child love. It was odd, she thought, that there were no impassioned sonnets on the subject, since it made sexual love look selfish and picayune. The Catholics knew what they were doing when they chose a babe in swaddling clothes.

They didn't move Billy into his own room until he was a robust eight months old. And it was only Sissy's kidding Eddie that expedited the move. Good-natured needling—"God, the kid kept me awake all night with his reading light on"—but Eddie got the point and finally succumbed with an embarrassed grin.

The wait had its pluses. Sissy was too miserable during the pregnancy, and Eddie too nervous, to prepare a baby's room. During those eight months they elaborately festooned one of the house's small bedrooms for Billy. Eddie did all the basic work— plastering, painting, scraping the floor—while Sissy took charge of the filigree. She chose furniture and carpet (a black and white penguin pattern to go with the sunshine-yellow walls) and hung a variety of mobiles. When Eddie questioned the number of mobiles, she explained they would pique the child's curiosity and exercise his eyes. "What are we raising—a Peeping Tom?" he'd joked. Back then, she didn't see that as cop humor.

Best of all, Eddie encouraged Sissy to use her drawing talents. He brought home comic books (mostly Disney), and Sissy painted cartoon characters around the room. Her taste ran to the sentimental—Bambi, Dumbo, Mickey Mouse, Cinderella's Fairy Godmother. Though Eddie cheered her on, he thought the room was getting "too girlish." He insisted Sissy paint Lampwyck, Pinocchio's tough cigar-smoking chum, on one of the walls. As Billy grew, his room was repainted many times. At each painting another character disappeared (the Fairy Godmother first). In time all were gone save Lampwyck. He was still puffing his stogie when Billy left for Vietnam. Men knew their own genes well.

Eddie had been so helpful then. Of course, he preferred to do the showy things, like strolling with Billy around the neighborhood, especially on Sundays. But he did his fair share of chores, too, stopping only at bathing Billy (he was frightened) and preparing formula. Sissy teased him that he should master it all if he was to become a complete parent. He took that badly. He was truly hurt. "That's not fair," he said. "You've been in training for this all your life. I wouldn't put you down if you couldn't make it through Marine boot camp. That's my strong suit."

To Eddie, that was logic. To Sissy's latterday feminist crowd, it was social preconditioning. Either way, Sissy never longed for the armed services. She even hated war movies. War movies and Westerns. *From Here to Eternity* didn't count.

Even when Billy was finally ensconced in his own room, Sissy occasionally would wake and find Eddie and the rocker missing. She knew where they were. She didn't know, though, when Eddie's vigils finally stopped. Perhaps when Billy became mobile. She now wondered if she had missed the paranoia within Eddie's solicitousness, the cop paranoia that life was endlessly menacing. The jungle was just around the bend, whether it was new people, new places, new styles, new music, new ideas, or accidental crib death. Maybe Eddie had seen crib death as part of the scheming streets? Or maybe his vigils had been a distant self-mourning for the sweet, gentle, open boy she'd married?

Sissy rose from the rocker and returned to her vanity table. In the mirror her smeared face looked like a milkman's note left out in the rain. Nellie. Eddie. Every soul who lived could mount a defense. If she was going to get to that ceremony, she'd better begin again.

Furious with herself, Sissy opened a jar of face cream, scooped out a glob with her middle three fingers, and slapped it on her face. She angrily spread the cream over the marred surface, while she checked the mirror image. What a sight! Emmett Kelly in drag. She had better get herself together. If she was weeping now, what would she be like later when they pulled out all the stops—the flags, the bunting, "family man," "hero," "our boys in blue," the Commissioner, the Mayor, and some holy man from the Ubiquitous Savior, a preacher of all philosophies (an odd Jew or Protestant might be among the honorees). Bad enough that the gathering would need water wings when Nellie and Catherine got going, nobody needed her to add to the bilge level. Maybe she should have taken some of Christy's tea. Oh, that was bullshit! With booze, she could work up a crying jag for Peter Rabbit.

Why wouldn't her mind hold still, focus? She had fought this problem ever since that wild period. But that was so brief. What? A little more than six weeks. Yet her brain remained like a collapsed umbrella, random spokes jutting out. She could live with it, but it took will. Force the center to hold, Sissy.

Under her ministrations her face was making a comeback. Nothing irreparable. The terrain still could be tilled. Where was she before Nellie stole in? Come on, dammit, get back to it. This was unfair, the present was always being mugged by memory. Her brain was as worthless as her childhood music box, all it could evoke was memory. What was it? Male. Eddie. Eddie and Mickey. That was it—looks, jealousy, and sex. Good. Sex was safe. What had once obsessed her was not even a threat anymore.

That was the strangest part of it. How could something that had once made her life revolve now be so meaningless? She was sure it wasn't lying dormant, waiting to be revived in a better time by a better partner. No, it was dead, and she didn't even mourn her copulating corpse. Perhaps it was age? Over forty. As the politicians say, maybe she had just shifted her priorities.

But it couldn't simply be age. Other women were still into it. She'd never had illusions sex would be the same now as when she was a girl, a bride. She knew it would calm down, perhaps become sedately graceful with age, but she'd never expected it to disappear. Not back then when she couldn't get enough. It was impossible to look at a room in the house or at a piece of furniture that had fornicating possibilities without remembering how she and Eddie had utilized them. The positions and the orifices! Standard between the legs, her on top (that excited the male in her), her legs hanging off chairs, the sides of beds, the kitchen table one night when they had half-drunkenly played doctor. Even the bathroom wasn't immune—in the tub, standing, laid out awash in bath oil, on the shag carpet on the floor. And backwards, her favorite, when he was deepest, pulling the mane of her hair as if he were riding a horse.

It took her only two weeks of marriage to discover her myriad possibilities. She pitied his single channel of pleasure. What a diverse thing it was to be a woman. She had cradled his member between her breasts, French style; inserted him playfully in her ear and up her nostril, under her armpit, in her vagina, and up her backside, enduring the initial pain till the pleasure began. And of course, her mouth, his favorite, the obsession of men. To her, it was the most boring. Like nibbling the eraser of her pencil in school. She didn't like the dull, hard, dead feeling. It was only in the beginning she liked it, when he was small, and she could feel him expanding inside the chamber of her mouth. That was power. She loved the thought of it, that she could transform another human with her devices, render him to her will. Sissy had found her sexual equivalent in Shakespeare. She ruled her magical island as Prospero ruled his.

In those days Sissy could do it all. She was ahead of her time, a veritable Cuisinart. Where were her gyrations now? It wasn't age, it was the limited return on her investment that had deadened it. She had poured too much of herself into sex to have the ultimate payoff come up empty. She had reached the point where she set aside the years of early dividends and considered only the tangible balance. In the end, sex failed her considerable energies in much the way the Church had.

She supposed it was her fault. She should have been more realistic. But that wasn't her nature. Whether it was the Church, her relationship with Mickey, her movie star scrapbooks, Eddie, or sex, she pushed too much of herself into the pot. Perhaps she never got over the idea of salvation, something to bail her out. She liked to brag that she was a "romantic." That was all fine and good in cometic youth, but after forty it became ludicrous.

Scott Fitzgerald was sad testimony to that. Keep dragging that fey luggage through the years, and you start to find merit in the likes of Sheilah Graham.

But there was something to be said for illusion. The feeling of specialness she got by removing herself from reality, from predestined life, was always seductive. Catholicism had once given her that. In retrospect, she didn't know if the Church itself believed in all that folderol it ushered forth, or whether the hierarchy was merely hip enough to realize the depth of day-to-day disenchantment. You'd never go broke betting against life.

Sissy had always been a sucker for show and ceremony. The liturgy of the mass never meant anything to her, but the intoned Latin, the incense, the bells, the body being transformed into a prim wafer (which could be served with tea on one of Fitzgerald's blue lawns) was another matter. When she felt grungy, there was confession. She missed that. That internal scrubbing down, the little old lady on the Dutch Cleanser can scouring away all the childhood impurities that gathered in her soul, the vestibule to her heart. Disobedience, cheating on exams at school, impure thoughts, and sinful fingers under the bedcovers. All whisked away in the eternal foam of sanctifying grace. It was crazy, but she had always felt lighter, physically lighter, after leaving confession. Another illusion? Then why had she always run with joy when she left the church after performing her penance?

Mickey wooed her with ceremony, too. He had made her feel as special as the Church had. A special daughter, unlike the other girls in the neighborhood. The other kids weren't damned, they were like the Protestants and Jews vis-a-vis the Church, merely unfortunate because they were denied a special blessing. After all, when other children were saddled with conventional pets, dogs and cats, Mickey bought her a duck which she paraded around Flatbush on a green leash. "Danny O'Drake," he had baptized it. How often she had been told she looked like a girl out of an old painting when she paraded Danny. She lorded it over the other kids with that duck.

Sissy made a face at herself in the mirror. No denying it, as a kid she'd been a bit of a shit.

She probably could foist that off on Mickey, but she had made an effort to dispel self-deception (her own command, plus doctor's orders). She had merrily complied with Mickey's malarkey. As he used to say to her with a conspiratorial wink, "We're in cahoots on this." It applied, she now recalled, to all enterprises that would prove detrimental to her mother, who epitomized the outside world. But dammit, he *was* different from other fathers (she noticed lately she failed to add her old standard "and better"). Unlike other fathers, he had never treated her as an annoying past due bill to beery lust. His gifts to her were special, and she wasn't nuisance baggage he grudgingly carted about. He would bring her into the bar where he worked, place her up on the piano, and they would sing duets to the delight (and the dollar bills—nobody would dare insult Mickey's kid with change) of his cronies. He'd taught her the old songs and she'd never forgotten them. In truth, they were the only songs she still cared about.

The knock on the door was so loud it startled Sissy out of her reverie. Surely, it couldn't be Nellie.

"Who is it?"

"Mom."

Sissy was exasperated. "Well, come in. You don't have to knock every time you leave the room."

"I can't. My hands are full."

Sissy went to the door and opened it. Nellie was standing there with two cups of tea. So that was it. She had rapped the door with her foot.

"Oh," Sissy said. "I'm sorry. I forgot. The tea."

"Well, let me set it down. It's hot."

"Just put mine on the dressing table."

"Won't it stain?"

"It wouldn't make any difference," Sissy said. "It's hardly new."

Nellie set Sissy's cup down and returned with her own to the rocker. "I'm sorry I carried on a bit before," she apologized. "You've got enough of your own troubles."

"It's okay."

"It's just that days like this set you to thinking."

"I know what you mean."

"I guess that's part of growing old. Occasions make you think of those who aren't here anymore. Not that this isn't an occasion we could all do without. I mean, it would be grand if Eddie was . . . well, you know what I mean."

"Sure, Mom."

"You know. Holidays like. Instead of enjoying myself, I think of your father, my dad, Billy, and now we have . . ."

It's always men, Sissy thought. Women lamenting men. All the myths of fathers and sons were wrong. Sentimental slop. As close as Billy and Eddie had been, there were signs. When Eddie leaned on Billy for something—playing his phonograph too loudly, needing a haircut, coming home with beer on his breath— she watched the look on Billy's face. The look that said: my day will come and beware, be prepared to make room, you're ruling on borrowed time, old man.

Sissy had never looked at Mickey that way. Not even at the end. And Nellie had left a saint in County Wicklow.

No, the eternal theme was a fraud. It was pure propaganda: fathers and sons, sons and fathers. It had a proper ring to it, but it was phony. The heart of the universe was daughters and fathers, mothers and sons. It wasn't the cross that was the time- less symbol, but what took place beneath it. Eternal variations on the Pietà, woman cradling the male. Where was Joseph that day? Logic reinforced Sissy's theory. There wasn't a mother who had ever lived who would sacrifice her son for an abstract such as mankind.

"I guess that's the price of age," Nellie said. "All your big days seem to have sadness attached to them."

Sissy tried to placate her. "Well, maybe they're all looking down on us, Mom." She didn't believe a word of it.

"God willing," Nellie said. "But knowing your father, he'd rather have a ringside seat. Good Lord, can you imagine him get- ting a crack at the Mayor?"

Nellie laughed and Sissy couldn't help joining in. Each had immediately conjured zany visions of Mickey cavorting with the Mayor.

"If the Mayor thought the Republicans were a handful . . ." Sissy didn't need to finish the sentence to produce more laughter from Nellie. She still laughed like a girl when any mention of Mickey's nuttiness surfaced. She still could laugh like that in spite of everything. God, how she must have loved him. Her hus- band. Sissy felt as if she were less than her mother.

"Oh, he would have shined," Nellie said. "Especially for Eddie. It says something for Eddie that he won him over. Mickey ended up mad about him. It wasn't always that way, you know. There was a time your father didn't think anyone was good enough for you."

Sissy reddened, but Nellie didn't notice. She was enjoying herself. Even in memory, Mickey was her spark. "Oh, he would be dressed to the nines today. The rent money would be on his back. I never saw a man like him about clothes."

Sissy remembered how he had dressed her. None of those dowdy pinafores but dresses, dresses that like himself were full of embellishments. The most elaborate ones for Father and Daughter Night at the Knights of Columbus, where she parroted her scrapbook sirens sipping a Shirley Temple. She also went on the bar's annual bus trips to Bear Mountain and Rye Beach and Monmouth Park. He even included her in his racetrack trips. His losses and winnings (especially his winnings) were between him and her. On good days he slipped her a little grease, on banner days a five, with a wink and a warning that it was hush-hush from her mother. The bribe was unnecessary. His love gagged her.

She remembered their magical three-day excursions to Saratoga. The year he bought her an entire wardrobe and packed it in a small "Saratoga trunk," just like the one Ingrid Bergman had in the movie. And best of all, Nellie never joined them. She hated his gambling. So Nellie only complained about the trips ("It's no place for children"), while Mickey archly countered that all the best people's children, here and "on the Continent," were introduced early to the Sport of Kings. "Don't be such a goddamn immigrant," he'd say. "This is America." That always did it. The horn of green was the weapon to wound Nellie.

With Nellie, the practical expenses had to be met. The restaurants, the tickets for various outings, the outlandish dresses that had no practical use, the gifts delivered on whims or Mickey's gambling fortunes robbed Nellie of "house money." How Sissy had hated that phrase of drudgery! Mickey would sluff off Nellie cavalierly. "The way you worry about Con Edison, you'd think you had stock in the company." A big laugh, that one. The two of them scorning the frump.

When had Sissy learned that "house money" meant the rent and utilities paid and meat on the table without begging the butcher for extended credit? Was it only when Mickey died and left Nellie destitute and having to clean up the mess he left piled behind? Bar tabs, loansharks, useless insurance policies barren from borrowing against them, charge accounts used to obtain hockable items, and even two months' arrears in the rent for the same rent-controlled dump he had moved into with Nellie when they were married.

Poor Nellie, nearly a half century in the country only to have to return to the domestic work that had greeted her on landing. Emotionally, Sissy was Mickey's partner in all this. Not really his daughter, and certainly not Nellie's. In these capers she was more his . . . She had blurted it out once to that doctor when he kept badgering, "Well, just how did your father treat you?" That smug young prick, puffing his pipe and trying to look like a rock of wisdom. "Come, Theresa. Say it. If it wasn't father and child, how did you perceive it?" Puff, puff. "Delve, Theresa. Go deeper. Everything is confidential here."

"All right, all right," she had screamed under the pedantic grilling, "like a lover! That's what you wanted to hear, wasn't it, you snotnose?" (It was her father's favorite insult.)

"No," he said in chimney mediation, "that's what you had to say."

After she came through her bad spell, she did not return to him or any other doctor. Mickey had won even that one.

There was no doubt about it, Mickey McKenna was some piece of work. "A piece of work." That was the proclamation he bestowed on himself in his glass-stained mahogany realm. A cutup, a character of note, a charmer, a spellbinder (a polite term for bullshit artist), a knight errant in the nighttime world he and his cronies lived in. The Irish wife's lament. Nellie could have charged a neon sign with alienation of affection.

Yes, Mickey had all the moves, a dapper to his dying day. An early exit. You name it, he had it. Blood pressure, an erratic heart beat, a liver the size of the Goodyear blimp, damaged kidneys and pancreas, and lungs that had been tar traps for who knows how many cigarettes. But always imported, mind you, English Ovals. It was the little things that distinguished Mickey McKenna from the vulgar herd. Things that "didn't matter," Nellie said in polite company, or that didn't amount to "a mound of manure" when only family ears were perked. That was Nellie's justifiable bitterness. They did matter to her, as they did to Sissy. Mickey's pretensions were Nellie's passage from pig slops and a servant girl's kitchen.

"With his carrying on," Nellie reminisced, "he could mortify a saint. Nothing could shame him. Still and all, it's awful quiet without him."

The folderol *was* missed. Something went out for both of them when he died. He was the window decorator of their lives. Even in his last year and a half, when he knew he was dying, he faked it for the crowd. Sissy and Nellie kept pushing the realization away. "Ah, he has the constitution of a mule. If only he'd get some good food into him," Nellie would say.

But Mickey was a tightrope walker working on memory. If all the pipes inside had had it, he still kept the exterior as spruced as a carousel calliope. English blazers, turtlenecks, a cravat for special occasions. (Need one say St. Patrick's Day?) He even had the gall to affect patent leather pumps. Pumps in an Irish slop joint!

Summers in the Rockaways at The Emerald Isle and winters in Bay Ridge at Stephen D. The latter was a watered-down generational joint with a crowd from St. John's and St. Francis colleges. No Tin Pan Alley Irish on the jukebox there, but the Clancy Brothers, the Irish Rovers, the Chieftains, and for the lit majors, Siobhan McKenna reading from *Finnegans Wake*. That plus the literate touch in neon hanging outside the place erased the stigma, the genetic curse, and hinted at upward mobility. Heaven forbid that so much tuition would be pissed away in the likes of a Blarney Rose.

It was a crock, his whole damn life was a crock, but Mickey knew how to skim a crock. At both places he was the host (maitre d' would be social speeding). As the joke had it, a host is the guy you don't trust behind the stick. But he was worth his keep, half on the books and half under the table. If you couldn't charm the IRS, you screwed them. Same thing in the Irish lexicon.

In Rockaway he wooed the old biddies, those hats and veils who drank Manhattans and crooned along with Ruthie Morrissey on the way home to Mayo or with Bing Crosby as he watched the moon rise over Galway Bay. And with their husbands' permission, he whirled them around the floor, never getting too close (at the lower levels anyway). Mickey was no dummy, he knew the rules. Some stanchions should remain unconnected, a bridge too far. In those circles no adequate penance had yet been devised for adultery.

For the men, there was the blather. As Sissy grew older and began to notice things, she suspected they hated him. Occasionally they would make a minor nasty scene, an insinuation, more a burp, about his paying too much attention to one of their "colleens." But this was rare, since he kept the women active, thus removing their third-degree eyes from the men's elbow-bending. One could drop two quick ones in the course of a waltz or a Stack of Barley. Besides, the momentary insinuation never went beyond that. The women would counter with an invite for their mates to get up and dance. That meant abandoning their clandestine input, plus the embarrassing comparison of their tromping through the furrows with Mickey's glide.

Sissy suspected Mickey's real problem with the other men was that he couldn't join in their talk about work. In their eyes, he didn't have a real job. She could empathize with him on that count. When Eddie invited other cops and their wives or dates over for an evening, the women were cast into limbo. She hated the snobbery of it, as if the women were unemployed. What the hell did they think running a house and raising kids was? Worse, she hated the cops' attitude toward "civilians," as if those not blessed with a badge knew nothing about "the real world." Cops were like priests and doctors. They always talked down to you. Pander to the naive nerds.

Mickey got around it by continually talking of "the old country." Not that he was born there. Indeed, his bay was not Galway but Sheepshead in Brooklyn, St. Anselm's Parish. Truth having it, he was far removed, third generation. Many of the pimply faced students who adored him at Stephen D's were a generation closer to the holy land than he. But this was a well-kept secret, and when he was called on it, he claimed he had been born in a small farming town in Ulster, in the north (always scheming, records were tough to check in an eternal battlefield), when his parents went back on vacation. The fairy tale was so farfetched it had charm. Mickey a lost prince with a strawberry birthmark on his bottom.

It was here that Nellie was indispensable. She was authentic. The bog was upon her, so she lowly legitimized him while he perfumed her. Like every other bed pact in life, each partner got a pound.

But Mickey wasn't foolish enough to let his birthright rest on such fragile ground. He made more pilgrimages back to the old country than a bishop on the tit. He organized annual chartered tours from each of his places of employment (Mickey was a two and three job man all his life, pursuit of the good life didn't come cheap). He was designated as the pied piper of these tours, so his freight was somehow always incorporated into the group price. Charm travels light.

The general consensus was that he was worth it. He did his homework: history, lore, myth (Brian Boru could swab out a cannon with his prick), literature, theater, and an encyclopedic knowledge of Yeats to be dropped to fit the occasion. Poor Yeats. Did he know he had become fodder for countless frauds.

Mickey didn't neglect the economic side either. He knew where to get bargains at hotels, carousing spots, castles in the air, and lakes so clear you could shave in them. That a little finder's fee came his way from the proprietors was all in the bargain. His horseshit was always well-greased.

It wasn't that Mickey was money-hungry—quite the opposite. Tapping him was as soft as flouncing a pillow. It was just that he had learned as a boy that it was valuable in Sheepshead Bay (thus, he presumed, the world) to be Irish. The Irish got all the plums—cushy jobs in the Police and Fire Departments or as glorified flunkies on Wall Street, the officers' positions at the Knights of Columbus and the American Legion, hooks into Con Ed and Ma Bell, the best bartending jobs, and the role of head usher at eleven o'clock high mass on Sundays.

The Swedes in the neighborhood, those white aberrations, were tolerated only because they passed pigment. Then there were the Italians, who were even more clannish than the Irish. But Mickey's bag wasn't crime, not major crime anyway. Mickey's muscle was in his mouth. And what else did they have, the Sanitation Department? Emperors of Ice Cream Wrappers, Mickey called them.

The one thing Mickey wouldn't do was repeat the mistakes of his father, except one—shadowing his father's path to the grave. His father had been a dour, solitary-drinking house painter. Mickey blamed his father's gloom on the inherited drab blood of Northern Ireland, just as he blamed his father's drinking on his profession. Mickey had come across an article citing the tie-in of heavy drinking and certain professions. Painters loomed large in the statistics and this satisfied him. "Goddamn chemicals in the paint." Alcoholism was a word that never entered his vocabulary. The clinical sound of it terrified him. Boozer, heavy hitter, juicer, yes; but never alcoholic. That was sick, not only sick but probably hereditary. No, as with all other things in his life, logic was cast aside in favor of the conspiring stars. It made no difference whether it was money, booze, or a photo finish. The cosmos was rigged.

Hadn't he read the article in the *New York Times?* Not that shanty rag, the *Daily News*. Mickey put great stock in the *Times*. He scanned it daily for tidbits, tidbits he could drop on the tabloid readers who surrounded him. An economic prognosis, a breakthrough in health, an insight into an arcane Third World country, a perusal of a play or book review. Nothing in depth, no punishing work. Just enough to add to his verbal footwork. It was part of his wardrobe, the grooming of a cosmopolite.

His father had put him in painter's overalls early, and until his dying day he ran from the memory of it. The godawful stink of paint and turpentine that a sea of Lourdes water couldn't wash off. In his self-pitying moods, he used to say that he would like to pluck his nose hair out, because he was sure it was permanently infected by the stench. He wouldn't be caught dead in a house with an open paint can. When the railroad flat was due to be painted every three years, he left on vacation to go fishing on the Jersey shore, which also meant sanctioned afternoon drinking.

Besides, a six-inch brush wasn't made for Mickey's hands. He prided himself, fairly, on his hands. They were thin, tapered, and elegant, more like plumes. He worked on them continually, daily applying cocoa butter. Day in and day out, he pared his nails and shaped them. When a foreign speck appeared under a nail, he mused that it probably was a residue of paint. An absurd notion since, from what Sissy could determine, he had worked only about six months as an apprentice with his father. Nonetheless, decades later he would complain that particles of paint were still embedded under his nails, tiny craters marring the perfect half moons of his cuticles.

He often told Sissy she had his hands. "Patrician," he pronounced them. This delighted her, and she, too, became obsessed with hands. Mickey was right. Most of the Irish had mitts, laborers' hands; even Nellie qualified. There wasn't an ounce of kindness in them. Square white blocks with an ugly relief of blue, bulging veins. Not hands that idled time. Signposts that said: no frivolity allowed. Not Mickey. He made holding his ever-present glass look sacramental.

As a teenager, she often gave him manicures. It was their physical communion, the fondling, the warm soapy water, the prolonged and heated hand-holding, like lovers in a movie balcony.

Eddie had lovely hands, too. That was a big attraction. What did the shrink say? "Theresa, subconsciously many girls marry their fathers. It's not as dire as it sounds." Not as dire as it sounds! Bless me, Father, for I have sinned: I wanted to sleep with my father. Who needed to be told that kind of stuff?

What Mickey really hated about house painting was the solitude. He often said, "Why would a man want to spend his time cooped up in a room with himself and four bare walls? It's beyond me. Jesus himself loved conviviality. Don't laugh, Sissy. It's in the Bible. The man loved to eat and have his glass, and he always had his disciples around him. Twelve of them." It was Mickey's genius that he could reduce Matthew, Mark, Luke, and John to carousing cronies.

The four bare walls were never for Mickey. Even at home, he wouldn't stay in a room alone without a radio or the television set going. The program wasn't important, the sound was. Any schmuck babbling was a pardon from the purgatory of silence or the hell of being alone with himself. That was his father's curse, that and drinking alone. If his father had drunk in company, he would have been good for another fifteen years. The talk slowed down the pace. But of course he didn't have a chance, inhaling those goddamn chemicals.

But Sissy didn't hold court on Mickey. She was hardly in a position. If it weren't for the bond of blood, she and Nellie might never have passed a civil word. And what had happened between her and Mickey was a canker that would never heal. The same thing with Eddie, and to some extent with Billy. What was it? Was she a genius at beginnings? A promising play with no second or third acts? A case could be made for that. Lay off yourself, woman. Damn, she'd pardon a rapist because she'd excited him.

The shrink had told her she made a case for everyone. "The road to health, Theresa, is to look out for yourself first. If you're down on yourself, nothing good can happen. Clear water can't run from a contaminated fountain. Learn to appreciate and love yourself." At twenty-five dollars a half hour, she needed a cheerleader telling her she was number one?

She had screwed up. She was not sure how, but deep down she knew it. What did the dear doctor say? "Guilt can be as seductive as it is corrosive, Theresa. You seem to need it. I would ponder that, if I were you." She had, but it didn't change things. The doctor didn't even understand his own game. Her guilt was a manifestation of her ego. She had been good enough once to make things work. She always had a sense of herself. She was Sissy Sullivan, and that was something special. (After all, she had paraded with a duck, hadn't she?)

"God rest him, but he could wear you out with his shenanigans," Nellie said.

"That he could," Sissy replied, remembering.

"Ah, but sure he meant no harm. He'd just get off on things, and he didn't know where to stop. Like that business with you," Nellie added tentatively.

Sissy didn't answer. She didn't know what to say. Obviously, Nellie wanted to air it. Sissy understood. It was the nature of the day.

"It was just that he had trouble changing," Nellie continued. "I think he thought you were going to be a little girl all his life. You shouldn't have put any stock in it. I never did, I knew him better. He'd be broken-hearted for weeks after he had a row with you. He knew he made an ass out of himself, but he was too thick to admit it. You know, with the drink on him. I always hoped you didn't hold a grudge. He was his own worst enemy, God help him."

She was begging. Sissy couldn't refuse her. It was a day for lying. "Of course not. I knew it was the drink that was talking."

"Good," said Nellie, relieved.

Sissy knew her mother couldn't bear the thought of hate worming into the grave. Failings were for this world.

"Good," Nellie repeated. "I always knew you saw through him when he was like that. After all, I warned you about him when he got strange. But it's nice to hear you say it."

Indeed, Nellie had warned her back then. Nellie suspected charm—honest laborers always do. Nellie had told her it had a double-edge. "Oh, you think your father is the cock of the walk, with all the airs he puts on. The great Irish playboy. Dancing with all the ladies and lathering them with blarney. Narrowback (Nellie loved the pejorative for Irish-Americans) blarney at that. He's a great street angel and a house devil. If I ever dolled up like all those old hussies he twirls around, I'd be dead in the morning. Do you think I don't wear lipstick because I like to walk around looking like a corpse? It's because he won't allow it. Years ago, when

I was going to your Aunt Maureen's wedding, I put on a little, and he ordered me, 'Get that crap off your mouth.' Does that sound like your gay blade? You've got a lot to learn, girl. Wait till the boys start coming around. You'll see how charming he is then."

She had underrated Nellie. Sissy had interpreted her attacks on Mickey as jealous bile. But her mother was as right as rain. When Mickey ceased to be the only male in her life, the trouble started. The demands to tone down her wardrobe (no sweaters, and nylons a must even on the hottest days of summer), the imposition of unreasonable curfews, and the constant grilling. The degree of nastiness depended on his alcohol intake, "Where were you? Does he have a car? I don't want you driving around with some snotnose with only one thing on his mind. I don't want you going to those bars with jazz bands. They're loaded with drugs, and they're only fancy fronts for whorehouses anyway." (Could he have been serious? Conrad Janis and "When the Saints Come Marching In"?)

When he deigned to "explain," it was, "Don't try to teach your father about life. I know what's out there, and most of it ain't good." Eddie would echo that theme years later. The two of them, pioneers trailblazing for the innocents. The Lewis and Clark of Tribulation Trail.

It had culminated the night she came home an hour and a half after her midnight curfew to find him mad drunk, throwing her clothes down the stairs and screaming that she had been out with the biggest whoremonger in town. Poor Tommy. Sissy occasionally dated him because he was so sad. A sensitive, beer-logged kid who was scared to death of his shadow, or more precisely, his breast-beating mother. Whoremonger, indeed!

It was Nellie who stood her ground that night. Sissy was frozen. She had never seen that side of her father before, but she would see it again and again as his drinking became more malignant. He broke Nellie's cardinal rule: he was putting on a show for the neighbors. She picked up the child's belongings and shepherded Sissy up the stairs. When Mickey raised his hand to strike Sissy as they reached the landing, Nellie dropped her armful and lunged at him, putting her formidable hands around his neck. "You won't ever hit a child of mine, do you hear?" she hissed, ever mindful of the audience crouching behind the doors. "Never!" she emphasized, banging Mickey's head off the wall until he turned white and went limp in her grasp. "You're getting to be the same brute your father was."

That took the last ounce of fight out of him. It was a psychological knockout. Sissy pitied her father. He was no match. She had never realized he was so slight physically. She hated her mother for the demonstration. Mickey muttered, "Then you talk to her. You see if you can do anything with her. I'm going out. If I stay here, God knows what I'll do. She's your daughter, you handle her. I wash my hands of her. I'm going out where I'm appreciated." He tried to muster his jaunt as he descended the stairs.

Nellie hissed, "You come back here," as Sissy prayed she would let him go. Mickey sheepishly ascended the stairs with his head pulled back, expecting a blow. Nellie pulled a change purse from her housedress and took out two tens. "Here, take a cab to and from. It's late."

Mickey made a mock show of rejection, but Nellie knew her man. The money was a goodnight kiss to a child who'd just been spanked. Mickey would be sober in the morning, and life would have to go on. In the future, Sissy never saw her mother try to capitalize on her midnight edge. Mickey, if somewhat tentatively, resumed his role as the lord of the manor. On reflection, it was an awesome performance. Nellie had been a diplomatic enforcer.

But the ugliness wasn't lost on Sissy. She went to school on Mickey. He was a primer on the men of the world. Perversely, it was Mickey who enabled her to land Eddie. What did Nellie say? "You've got to give the devil his due."

When Sissy was campaigning Eddie, she had subdued her sexuality. She didn't bury it, merely toned it down. Her makeup was moderate; her sweaters, if they didn't bag, didn't cling either. Her bathing suits were never gaudy advertisements, two-piece affairs. (God, what would Eddie have thought of his "little" Eileen's new bikini? Sissy wore one-piece Jantzens, her favorite being white, just like the one Ruth Roman wore in *Champion*. That, with her wall-to-wall tan, did the trick. If you had the equipment, you didn't have to gussy it up. Grecian columns didn't need gingerbread.

She walked the line between being feminine and a "good sport." She joked freely with all the boys, going along with a little double entendre, but she always removed herself when the talk began to skirt the vulgar. She occasionally bought a round of beers at a summer bar to set herself off from the cloying types, the Melanies of the world. She even joined in the touch football games on the beach, though like Mickey she wasn't physically adventurous (not in sports anyway). But she never, *never* allowed the boys to put her at center, bent over the ball. No, she invariably positioned herself at end. Not that she could catch well; more than one pass had brought her to the verge of tears when the force of the ball bent back her fingers. But at the solitary end position her long legs were highlighted, and with her stride, she could always shake loose from a girl assigned to cover her. "Crazy legs," the boys dubbed her.

She'd always seemed to be aware of what she was doing. Perhaps that was why the limited sessions with the shrink and her later foray into the women's movement didn't fully take. She couldn't quite buy that she was a poor, manipulated thing. In a way, she supposed, that would have been a blessing, but she didn't really think so. What solace was there in admitting you were a schlub?

At the very least, she was duplicitous. She could always read men. And why not? They were so damn easy. They wore their hearts (or their hard-ons) on their sleeves. Even her father, the consummate actor, couldn't mask his emotions. Sitting around in the summer in her white short shorts, she would catch him staring at her as he got progressively drunker. Her father was a self-pronounced leg man. His one overt gesture of sexuality toward Nellie was to reach over in boozy reflex and rub the back of her calf. He insisted Nellie wear heels around the house. When she frumped around in flats, he would grouse, "What are you—entered in a track meet?"

Mickey was at his best when Sissy's girlfriends had curves. He would give them status. No offers of ginger ale, but a clandestine Tom Collins with impeccably sliced fruit rimming the frosted glass, and banter that would make their heads spin.

But it was she (and occasionally Nellie) who caught Mickey's heat. What he admired in others was verboten to her and her mother. Nellie was doomed to paintless lips, and Sissy (especially when she caught him staring) got, "You're not going to go out parading in those shorts, are you? Don't you have a nice pair of glen plaid Bermudas in the drawer?

"Goddamn, women are always complaining about getting no

respect. Small wonder there aren't more attacks going on, if all of you insist on walking the streets with everything you own hanging out. Jesus Christ, those sweaters! Doesn't anyone wear blouses anymore? What the hell are the nuns teaching nowadays?"

Then the preamble of every aging sexual revisionist: "In my day . . ."

Nellie handled it better. She had a saying for every one of life's calamities, a teaspoon of tonic: "There's no fool like an old fool."

Nellie sighed and rose from the rocker. She picked up Sissy's empty teacup along with her own. "I'll give these a rinse before we get on the road."

"You don't have to do those now," Sissy protested. "You're all dressed."

"Sure, isn't there an apron in the house? Besides, the Sullivans are sitting down there alone. They might think we're being clannish. You know, it don't look right on a day like this."

Sissy laughed. "I always thought it was only the IRA who cooked up plots. I'm beginning to think it's a national disease."

"Well, you know what I mean." Nellie smiled.

"Okay, I'll wrap it up here."

"I enjoyed my cup of tea," Nellie offered, "and our talk."

"So did I," said Sissy.

"It made me feel better," Nellie said, her eyes down. "Your father always loved you. Like my father loved me. It's best to forget the mistakes and remember the good. There was plenty of that. Concentrate on the good." She rushed out before Sissy could reply.

Nellie didn't know how right she was. Mickey had been invaluable research. He was as indispensable as Cro-Magnon man. Too bad the penis wasn't bone like the skull. The unearthing of prehistoric pricks would be a lot more valuable to women than craniums. Then we might be able to divine where it all went wrong, Sissy thought. Get to the cock of the matter.

To land Eddie, Mickey was primer enough. They shared similarities, social graces made life too easy for both of them. Not when it counted, but charm was enough for decades of reprieve.

She knew she had a shot the night Eddie left for Korea after basic training at Parris Island. That night he had chosen to drive her home after his farewell party at Kennedy's in Breezy Point. Somewhere around one o'clock (Mickey had lost the curfew war forever on the stair landing) Eddie became somber. The beer turned on the sad music in him, and for the first time he seemed to realize what he was facing. The gung-ho John Wayne jokes of his buddies no longer seemed funny. He took the mock Congressional Medal of Honor the guys had made for him out of tinfoil and ribbon and dropped it on the beer-greased floor, then sat next to her.

The amusement was gone from all the "gook" gags. "When they come over the hill, Eddie, shout a takeout order" and "If you kill one, Eddie, you get bloodthirsty again a half-hour later." This wasn't fucking around anymore, someone would be shooting at him in a few weeks. And it wasn't going to be some barroom fight with all the rules enforced—no hitting when a guy was down, no kicking, a drink afterwards with the winner or the loser, so that no permanent damage was done. These guys weren't Irish—anything would go.

Eddie excused himself and went to the bathroom. She knew he had gotten sick, because when he returned to her table, his face was freshly washed and his hair combed with water. He simply asked if he could drop her at home. As she walked out with him, she had never felt more alive. He had sometimes driven her home before, but that was casual. This was a special night! There was no other way to put it—she had been anointed. What a flush of power she felt when his buddies begged him, to no avail, to stay on; and those lost simps who had hoped to be chosen batted come-ons at him with their eyes. How hopeless those girls looked, in distress, flashing unanswered semaphores. Little dinghies sinking in their teary coyness. Sissy exited with Eddie, delighted that the departing sight of her was her black sheath, cut low in the back (exposing cleavage wasn't the only way to get a man), and her legs. It was as good as any movie. She couldn't resist a slight, insouciant wiggle as they left.

They sat for hours on her stoop. She had heard the second-story window open and was grateful for it. Nellie would convince Mickey it was all right ("For God's sake, the boy is going off to war tomorrow!") and Mickey was the last one to spoil a patriot's parade. There would be no scenes.

Eddie talked about how, when he was discharged, he would use his G.I. bill to go to Delehanty's to study for the cops. Plus, he said, veterans got moved up points on the test list. And there was his uncle who worked inside at Centre Street. He had a lot of pull. Who knew, he might be a sergeant in five or six years. He felt he had screwed around long enough with pickup jobs to keep afloat. He was getting too old for the beach scene. The kids he used to hop in the ass for being wise guys on the block were now bellying up to the bar. He wasn't going to end up in his thirties like some clown, standing around summer joints with a baseball cap decorated with cute charms, beer can trinkets, on it. The Marine Corps was the first step in breaking away. He wanted a future, and he didn't have to tell Sissy a future meant a wife and kids.

But she didn't push. She listened. All her groundwork was beginning to pay off. He asked *if* he could write, not the cocksure "I'll write." They kissed goodbye for about fifteen minutes inside her hallway. It was more sexual than it had ever been before, but his hands didn't roam. Their bodies squirmed some, and she could feel the hardness inside his pants. She was dying to touch it, she had never held a man's naked prick in her hand. Occasionally, she had allowed a date to push her hand down to his lap and momentarily brush his hard member, but that was done more out of curiosity than passion. She had to learn someday. Someday, she would have to animate those statues she stared at in the Brooklyn Museum.

But this was different. She wanted to open his pants and explore his penis. She had only ventured that far in her masturbatory musings. But she felt he was nearly hers now, and by claiming his penis with kisses, she would seal her possession. But that, that one moment of dumb gratification, could undo everything she had worked for.

She dislodged herself from the steam that was melding them and said, "Eddie, it's your last night. I'm sure your parents are waiting up for you." It was the perfect conciliatory touch. Not priggish but responsible. A man plotting a future would understand it. As she walked up the stairs to her apartment, she was magically shrouded in well-being.

If she played a cagey hand when he was present, her conduct during his three-year absence was closer to the proverbial vest. She viewed all the smiling girls in her crowd as saccharine spies. One mistake on her part and she could imagine the letter Eddie would receive, written in an ever-so-friendly fashion, "On my

way to church the other evening to make a novena to the Virgin
Mary for the preservation of my hymen, I happened to see Sissy,
who looked wonderful in a low-cut dress, getting into a convertible with a guy I didn't know." They weren't conning Sissy;
she knew lots of them thought she had merely lucked out on
Eddie's last night home, and they hadn't abandoned hope. And
his male friends would be worse. Eddie was their leader, and many
of them were lost without him. His memory became a shrine
to be tended in the neighborhood with the litany, "When Eddie
gets back . . ."

So Sissy became the untouchable, idyllic girl back home. It
wasn't so tough. She had seen Teresa Wright do it in scads of
movies. She didn't become totally inaccessible; she occasionally
made the weekend scene at the bars and, of course, the formal
events such as weddings and christenings; but she socialized in
groups and was always driven home by a crowd. She didn't dance
with anyone who might be considered sexually attractive. She
shepherded the lost souls around the floor. And she never danced
with the Italian guys, though they were more dangerously attractive to her than the Irish. Cold tactics ruled foolish passion.

Those years of waiting for Eddie were well spent. For once, one
of Mickey's countless connections delivered. The linen supply
man for Stephen D's had a brother-in-law who worked in the
personnel department of a Fifth Avenue hotel, and he secured
Sissy a job as a receptionist. A Gal Friday, they called it back
then; now the title would be enough to cause the feminists and
the blacks to raze the hotel.

Light typing, answering the phone, greeting salesmen and clients (the best part), and rarely ever having to pull out a steno
pad to chicken-scratch. Sissy fit in well. She had the looks and
Mickey's blarney to banter with office visitors. The Irish were in
vogue for those jobs then. Now they'd be too bland. With the
advent of the Age of Aquarius, exotica was in demand for re-
ception desks. Imported English girls and minority women who,
in hairstyle and dress, accentuated their roots. The hippest companies parlayed roots and kink—and hired black homosexuals.

Sissy's job was better than being a mole filing in the basement
of an insurance agency or one of "the gals" at the phone company,
squirreling your pension for the day that would never come.

The bonus was that the job was in Manhattan, the isle of

Sissy's celluloid dreams. She knew it was the place to be. None of her heroines had ever left Smalltown U.S.A. to set Brooklyn on its ear. Holly Golightly breakfasting in Bensonhurst just didn't make it.

Sissy had always suspected Brooklyn was second-rate. Perhaps it was that long-held feeling, more than grievous ruptures, that drove a wedge between her and Eddie. Eddie adored the borough. He liked working and partying in Manhattan for the action, but live there—never! Sissy wondered if he was frightened by the city, wondered if he knew the kudos bestowed on him by his neighbors wouldn't be so easily granted across the river. By implication (though she tried mightily to suppress the thought), she suspected Eddie might be running scared.

He campaigned against the city like an upstate politician trying to make points with his rube constituency. By God, we may be boring, but we're moral. The subway led only to Sodom.

Sissy understood Eddie's fears. As hard as she'd tried to achieve a Manhattan look, she still felt she couldn't disguise her parochialism. The borough was heartier than her adopted veneer. She never felt more exposed than when she went to the theater, the step up she'd longed for. The legitimate stage represented class. Its audience was select, not like the egalitarian movie crowd. Much as she loved the movies, she knew them to be too accessible. The "nabes." That said it all. Entertainment for the proles. They didn't have dish nights on Broadway. But in her heart of hearts, she knew she'd rather win a vulgar Oscar than a stuffy Tony.

The women at the theater intimidated her. Arriving in fashions Sissy could neither afford nor carry, with men who were beyond her, or solo with parcels from stores that were prohibitively expensive for Sissy. These women looked as if they'd never worked a day in their lives. At least not at the jobs Sissy knew. She imagined they spent their days in oily, sudsy, step-down tubs, lunched lightly, and shopped in stores where a saleswoman was always available and acquiescent. Their skin looked pampered. Not like her own, which she imagined was pocked with subway grime. Their nails never seemed to have hammered down on a stubborn shift key. Sissy imagined they made love in a leisurely, untaxed way. Humping and strain was for the popcorn munchers.

At times she hated them. She imagined they stared at her and read her as cheap goods. Her Brooklyn bile rose. It was like

Eddie's. They were aloof, uncaring snobs. Eddie had said it better: "In Manhattan, if your ass was on fire, they wouldn't piss on it to put it out."

But nothing could have spoiled those special years. She had the time to read voraciously, and despite her reservations, she attacked the theater. Her taste was eclectic, musicals or drama— it didn't matter. She could cry equally at *Carousel* or *Cat on a Hot Tin Roof*. It was all new, magic. Miller, Inge, Williams, Rodgers & Hammerstein. Only O'Neill disturbed her. She attended out of ethnic loyalty, not desire. He hit too close to home. He was as melancholy as the plastic holy water fonts on the walls in her apartment, as the smear from the night before left by Mickey's beer glass on the Formica kitchen table.

Sissy cheated only a little. She dated guys from the office who lived in other boroughs, and she never gave them her home phone number. The assignations were set in the office. Besides, they were good dates in that most of them, like her, were new to Manhattan, and they insisted on putting on the dog: theater tickets or dinner and sometimes both. Mail boys and sales trainees who had to brown-bag it for a week after such an evening. But besides the nights on the town, she needed a male (other than those aging altar/mommy's boys she danced with) to be next to. Her sexuality had become a force. With the more attractive ones, she went in for heavy petting (only below the waist was off-limits). When she came home from one of these evenings, she invariably masturbated. But before the act, she douched the memory of her date by reading a handful of Eddie's letters.

The most interesting come-ons were from the married men in the office. They were such cagey bastards. The propositions were offered cavalierly enough to be interpreted as jokes if she took umbrage. The original disciples of fail safe. She would have taken a few of them up on the offers of a date, if she had thought she could handle them. But these guys, she knew, weren't mail boys who became ecstatic with some tongue and a feel for their night out on the town. Also, she didn't trust herself if someone dominant cornered her. She was too heated up lately to chance it. And dominant they would be. You didn't risk blowing the 5:10 to Crabgrassville and missing dinner with the ball-and-chain and the kiddies to get rhapsodic with a teenager in a theater, holding hands to the strains of "I'm a Stranger in Paradise." Then there was the knowledge that they were the most attractive men in the office. Which said something about her species. They skimmed the top, nothing interesting escaped their nets.

But she did find an outlet to burn off her mounting physical energy. For a lark, she tried playing tennis, and to her surprise she not only liked it but was good at it. She plunged into lessons. Every weekend she was on the courts at Riis Park. The absence of harshness made the game attractive to her. It was something a girl could do with grace without all that grunting that went on in touch football. Not to say that the white uniform, the constant sun, and what the game did for her legs wasn't a bonus. Her legs, if that were possible, got better than ever.

Then there was the letter-writing. Three times a week religiously. Full of gossip of the neighborhood and chocked with humor and the right amount of warmth. Never gushy. She wouldn't make that presumption. She waited for Eddie to get flowery (which he eventually did as the war grew worse), while she signed her letters simply "Love," a general term of affection that wouldn't embarrass a brother or a friend. Not for a long time "All my love"—he ventured that first. He was light and funny in his letters, easing her fears by punctuating the pages with cigarette-burn holes and explaining, "Wow, that one was close." What had happened? On the force years later he couldn't bring himself to smile at his tough guy role.

The depth of his affection came to her first through his close friends. They began to introduce her as "Eddie's girl," and she knew Eddie had written them with this designation. Confirming that all this time in limbo was going to be worth it. She had passed the test, the lonely warrior's woman, Caesar's wife. "Eddie's girl." It was set for the ages.

When he came home, neither of them had a chance to back out if they had wanted to. You can't disappoint a neighborhood. Turf survives on legend, the citizens get mean when myths are mucked with. It seemed as if they had always been understudies for the little figures on the wedding cake. No one questioned it. That they had never formally dated before Eddie's departure was washed away in the bathos of neighborhood lore. To one and all, they were (and presumably always would be) "Eddie and Sissy."

Stinking memory. History. The new generation was right: "It fucks you over."

* * *

Sissy's face was set again, retooled, as good as new. Yet it was there. History. Mickey dying in a drug daze, begging someone to remove the paint from under his nails, pathetically staring at his hands like an infant in a crib.

And Eddie's engagement ring. The one he had slipped into the pretzel basket at the Hotel Taft bar before offering it. She remembered picking up the pretzel with the ring on it. She had even saved that pretzel. Where was it now, the pretzel?

Her face threatened to go again. She picked up the ring and placed it in her mouth. She sucked deliberately, watching herself unblinkingly in the mirror. She spit out the ring on to her vanity, and it rattled loudly as it wobbled there. It sounded like metal. Her composed face told her she had succeeded by force of will. The residue in her mouth wasn't alkaline but mineral.

WHEN EDDIE returned from Korea, Sissy was ambivalent about the ways in which he had changed. He was more attractive in that he seemed light years more mature than his stay-at-home friends. There was a leanness to him, an edginess she associated with maturity and an eagerness to move on with his life. He seemed only to tolerate his happy-go-lucky buddies, he no longer meshed with them. He was a man on the brink of embracing responsibility. He had seen a larger world.

Though these things distinguished him, Sissy now and then wished he would lapse into the old Eddie, the softer Eddie who could goof a night away in nonsense. She knew he was finer but wasn't sure he was as lovable. He reminded her of Prince Hal in Shakespeare's *Henry IV*, which she had seen in two parts Off Broadway. She knew she was expected to applaud Hal's ascendance, but when the Prince banished Falstaff, the chronicle was ruined for Sissy. It didn't help that she saw her father as Falstaff.

After a while, she interpreted Eddie's impatience as nerves. When they went out, he couldn't sit on a bar stool and chat as he once loved to do. He would stand shuffling his feet, an act disturbingly reminiscent of the tribal footwork of the tough corner boys who were in Brooklyn gangs. But their prancing was punk peacockian, a strut confined to their corner cage. You had the feeling Eddie was going to bolt.

That was before Sissy knew about his wound. Only his parents had known, and he'd admonished them by letter to keep it secret. He had told her of it in sparse terms just before they were married, presumably to spare her shock when she saw his scar. His friends eventually heard about it from him in a breezy fashion that rebuked inquiry, "I got nicked in a fire fight." To her, the explanation was more cavalier, "I got shot in the ass charging."

It wasn't until she gave birth to Billy that she got the true story, and then it came from Eddie's father. Christy presented her with two boxes, one containing the Purple Heart and the other the Silver Star. "This is between you and me," he'd said. "They're supposed to be forgotten. But I think the proper place for these medals is with the son of the man who won them." Christy told Sissy how Eddie's company had been overrun by the Chinese, and Eddie had stayed behind and emptied every weapon within reach while his company evacuated the hill they were holding. When Eddie finally pulled out, he was shot from the rear, running down the hill. Shot in the ass charging, indeed. Eddie's silent beau geste moved him right into the pantheon of her movie heroes. But it had more substance than that. Sissy had grown up observing Mickey, who milked every physical discomfort for drama. She had picked up the *Camille* syndrome from her old man. Only when the final chips were down did Mickey break a lifetime pattern of begging for sympathy. Nonetheless, Sissy knew she could never have smothered such gaudy material as a wound. So her Eddie had silent grace under pressure. Sissy would have opted for a parade and bunting, even though she knew her choice, high drama, was distinctly low taste.

When Eddie told her about the wound before their marriage, she was both curiously fascinated and repelled. The idea of a wounded warrior intrigued her, but the idea of Eddie maimed was unjust. That her symmetrical summer boy was marred was a sacrilege. The idea of looking at him for the first time on her honeymoon night, that shimmering ceremony, and seeing him scarred angry red was heart-breaking. Besides, Sissy hated betrayals of the flesh. She preferred visits to funeral parlors over hospitals. The sick were mocked with tubes and agony, the dead had cosmeticians and peace.

But her honeymoon night wasn't diminished, only enhanced. They booked the bridal suite at the Hotel Bossert in Brooklyn Heights overnight before they left the next morning for the

Poconos. When she came out of the bathroom wearing a lavender negligee (to set off her hair and eyes), Eddie was standing naked by the bed sipping champagne and smoking a cigarette. Her eyes frisked his body for its mutilation, but he was only silhouetted in a dim light. As she lay on the bed, he turned on the light to put down his glass and extinguish his cigarette in an ashtray on the night table, and she saw a small crescent carved out of his left buttock. It was perfectly formed and not red at all. Skin must have been grafted over the wound, because it looked whiter than the rest of his body. Opaque, like rice paper. As he bent down to undo her negligee, she reached up and stroked the gap. It was as smooth as marble. Her fingers fit into the curvature perfectly, as if it had been carved for her touch. She had been afraid she might panic on this night, that her vagina might contract in fear. She had heard the horror stories from other girls— the pain, the need for messy vaseline. But touching him, she felt a flow of liquid between her legs and was shocked by her own smell. Hovering above her, perfectly chinked, he looked like those statues in the museums. It was a glorious girlhood fantasy come true, and she pulled him down to her with her right hand locked in the niche in his left buttock. It was better than she could have conceived. It was beyond mere flesh. It was as if she was consorting with the exalted ages as she lowered this precious antiquity, her husband, between her legs.

In those days everything seemed open to Eddie. Even Manhattan. Maybe it was just a gesture to her notions, but before they got married, they discussed finding an apartment in the city. Now, the magnanimity of that gesture seemed to come from a different man.

One Saturday, with the newspaper opened to apartment rentals, they even went apartment hunting. Perhaps it was a game, but it was a sweet child's game—a game of pretend.

It was also fun. After some lunch and a few Irish coffees to bolster them, Eddie insisted they check rentals far beyond their means. At first Sissy was frightened to do it, but Eddie insisted. "I always wanted to turn down something I couldn't afford in the first place."

It was also Eddie who had all the cool and daring when he dealt with the person who was showing the apartment. He would nonchalantly survey the layout and find various faults. "It's nice, but the floor space is so limited." "I was hoping there would be room for a study." And catching the Village mood, "I just don't think the light is right for my work." Sissy was impressed that Eddie knew about artist's light. What a delight it was to realize she had underestimated her husband.

The search was so much fun that by the time they started to look at apartments within their financial reach Sissy believed Eddie had gotten serious. Maybe she read it wrong, but she thought not. To Eddie, the search became competitive, and Sissy began to believe he wanted to win. Winning was never a small thing to Eddie.

The problem was that when they called the listed numbers for these affordable apartments, they were no longer available (Sissy started to doubt they'd existed in the first place) or they were cubicles in fine buildings. It was heart-rending to walk into a wonderful building with your expectations soaring and to be shown the equivalent of a dumbwaiter. What most offended them both about these cubbyholes were the minuscule kitchens. Not really kitchens at all, but places to store dollhouse refrigerators and stoves. Compared to the kitchens they knew, the stoves looked like hot plates and the refrigerators like beach coolers. Sissy wondered what kind of people could tolerate such rooms. In the Irish galaxy the kitchen was the sun.

Eddie was equally astonished. "Maybe they eat standing up. I didn't want to check the bedrooms. Maybe you have to do everything standing up." That was as coarse as the young Eddie got. "I think I have it," he said. "They eat spaghetti standing up, one strand at a time." He stood shimmying as if to slide a strand of spaghetti down his throat. Sissy laughingly joined in. She sucked in her cheeks until she looked consumptive. "And drink wine from the bottle with a straw," she added. They were standing in the street and Eddie took a clean, white, folded handkerchief from his pocket, opened it, and draped it over his face. "And one napkin to a customer," he said through the cotton.

He bent his covered face to Sissy's and moved the handkerchief back and forth across her mouth. Though she laughed, the oddity of it excited her, and she pushed her tongue into the cotton to find Eddie's waiting on the other side. During their marriage she would expand on this veil technique. Sometimes in bed she wouldn't let him take his shorts off, and she would grind against the cotton. When she was ready, she would take his penis out through the fly and have him make love to her as she slipped her hands inside the elastic in the back of his shorts. At these times she granted herself a life removed. She was the small-town cheerleader in the back seat of a car being fucked by the football hero. Odd how something as gamey as that made her feel so All-American.

That day, there were no rah-rahs, but a shout from a bearded guy pedaling by on a bicycle, "Weird, baby, weird." Eddie pulled his covered face away from hers, and Sissy could see his forehead was flushed with embarrassment. He recovered deftly. He pulled the handkerchief down until it was covering only his nose and mouth like a surgical mask and shouted at the cyclist, "What's wrong, didn't you ever play doctor?" The cyclist laughed warmly and shouted back, "I'm not knocking it, baby." Eddie was having such a wonderful day.

They both were, until they made the last stop. A one-bedroom apartment on West Street was listed for $75. Neither of them knew the location of the street, and the phone number wasn't answering. They asked for directions to the street and were told to keep walking west. Neither of them was good at compass directions. When Eddie had been asked where the enemy was in Korea, he wished he could have given it in blocks of time, "About twenty minutes away." It was a Brooklynite's curse.

As they continued to walk west, the neighborhood grew seamier. The buildings were older, derelicts lurched on the sidewalks, and menacing homosexual bars began to appear. Both would have liked to call it off, but neither would admit to being intimidated. Another Brooklyn legacy.

The West Side Highway loomed before them, and Eddie tried a weak joke. "Maybe the apartment is in the passing lane." Sissy couldn't muster even that. This wasn't Manhattan, not *her* Manhattan. Her Emerald City didn't smell of urine.

They learned a geographical lesson. West Street ran under the West Side Highway. How were they to know? Their access to Manhattan was by subway. In fact, how would anyone but a truck driver know? Sissy saw a dead cat crushed on the cobblestones, and the whipped cream from her Irish Coffee curdled. By following the numerical declination on the buildings, they finally found the address at 11th Street. A narrow door next to a sleazy saloon.

After the third ring, a blowsy woman opened the door. Sissy noticed only her disastrously dyed hair. She looked like the neighborhood. Christ, this wasn't Manhattan, it was a set for *Anna Christie*. The woman was truculent from the start. When Eddie said conversationally that they had tried to call before coming, she countered, "I was tired of being bugged by that phone all morning. They expect you to paint a picture of the apartment over the phone. I stopped answering it. I figured if they were serious, they'd come around."

The apartment was a fourth-floor walkup. The landing floors were a filthy cracked pattern of small marble hexagons yellowed by the years and, Sissy suspected, by a shower of drunks. The walls were painted pea-soup green with grease smudges permanently embedded in them. Someone should have skimmed the soup, Sissy thought.

"No elevator, huh?" asked Eddie.

The woman gave him a disgusted look, "The elevators and the doormen are over on Park Avenue."

When they reached the proper landing, the woman went to a door halfway down the hall and pulled it open. Inside was a commode and a tub. "No shower. But you have a nice size tub. You share this with the tenant at the other end of the hall. There's only one. An older man."

Sissy and Eddie stared at the woman in disbelief. "You mean there's no bathroom in the apartment?"

The woman inhaled, sizing them up. "No. You know what the rent is here?"

"Yes," Eddie answered, "$75."

"And you're asking about elevators and private baths?"

"Well, I don't think my wife would be comfortable, and if kids come . . ."

"Kids!" the woman snorted incredulously. "Where are you from?"

Eddie was slow to answer. The woman waved her hand at him. "Never mind. You're not interested, right?"

Eddie nodded his head. He was being battered down.

"Jesus, I should have spotted you two at the door before climbing these damn stairs. Elevators. Baths. Kids. This is New York City, mister. I don't know what you expected to find for seventy-five bucks, but it ain't here. Out in the boroughs, maybe. I don't know what they're offering out there, but not here."

Sissy and Eddie skulked down the stairs with the muttering woman behind them. Sissy was afraid all the way down that the woman might kick her. But what truly hurt, after such a magical day, was to have this old slut view them as hicks. In the nicer places they had looked at, everyone had been mannerly. Now, to be exposed by this tinted tramp!

When they got to the street, Sissy took Eddie's arm. She hated herself for being no help with the woman. God, she wished she had guts. If she were a man, she would have slapped the woman. "Do you want to go for a drink, Eddie, or catch the subway?"

Eddie looked hollow. "Let's get a cab, Sissy. I want to go home."

Sissy should have realized that "home" had the ring of permanence.

If Brooklyn was to make their relationship moribund, the Police Department would entomb it. But how was Sissy to know that? To be a cop was a neighborhood plum. She had grown up hearing the glories of Civil Service. Security, benefits, pension. The Irish economic Holy Trinity.

Besides, she never mused what else might have suited Eddie. There was no role model for him to bounce off. Cops, firemen, sanitationmen, Con Ed, the phone company, construction, the longshore, or some flunky white collar job where the salary would barely cover dry cleaning bills. She and her contemporaries had horizons that were equally defined, horizons so low they could be landscaped. Shooting for the moon was for the aliens who lived outside the orbit of their turf.

Who went to college? Sissy tried to remember. A boy or two. No girl in her memory. It wasn't much better now. Especially on the female side. The boys now went farther. It had nothing to do with the love of knowledge but with money. More minorities got high school diplomas now, and there was social pressure to hire them. Higher education was something to beat off the hungry dogs nipping at your heels. Hold the mongrels at bay.

But in Eddie's day there was no such pressure. The one or two boys who had gone to college went at night, after work, to take courses in business administration. Night courses at Brooklyn College. What had Mickey labeled that place? "It's a dumping ground for dumb Jews and dull Christians. Worse yet, the Jews, as slow as they are, are still the ones who graduate with the honors. Don't tell me about that place. In twenty years it will be abandoned to the black lads and whoever comes after them. That should tell you something. Notre Dame, Harvard, Yale— they're colleges. Brooklyn is a bargain basement for small brains with small budgets." That was Mickey. If you couldn't go first class, it was better to be left on the dock.

So Sissy and Eddie never did discuss "career alternatives," as the saying now went. The notion didn't even cross their minds. Eddie went to Delahanty's, as planned, passed the test for the department, and graduated from the academy. It wasn't all that bad for the first two years.

For that tour Eddie and his buddy Sal, whom he'd met at the academy, worked out of a precinct house. They were like kids on a new adventure. If the adventure was a little tawdry—breaking up domestic brawls, rousting neighborhood punks, shagging local numbers runners—it was cottage industry. Small rotten potatoes. And they seemed to get a kick out of being able to hold a neighborhood in check. The people they dealt with sounded more like colorful characters than real criminals. Two bit pipe dreamers who were brought back to reality by a good hassling. It was the big time that got Eddie. Manhattan. Sissy's beloved Manhattan. Eddie had good reason to be intimidated by it.

His uncle Mike had arranged Eddie's advancement through his connections at Centre Street. How that man could be Christy's brother had always confounded Sissy. He was a mutant seed. Sissy hated his hail fellow, flushed, plum pudding face. He couldn't pick sincerity out of a lineup. He reminded Sissy of a Dickens character—an aging, charming defiler of youth. It was he who had Eddie chosen for a special plainclothes task force being formed to combat organized crime in lower Manhattan.

Eddie was an ideal candidate. Besides his uncle's hook, he was a decorated Irish combat hero, with two years on the job. When Sissy learned police mores, she found out time was a prerequisite for such a special unit. The corrosive department logic was that if someone had been on the force for more than a few years, he was already corrupt. So they chose cherries, virgins. She often wondered why. So the department could debase them by their own peculiar, perverted lights? It was like a man bragging about how he broke an innocent woman: "When I met her, she wouldn't put her hand on it, never mind suck it. Now she's like a vacuum cleaner."

Eddie's tutor was his uncle. Mike taught him the way of the world. What nice, all-encompassing phrases the shoddy in life use to twist the innocent: "Grow up," "That's the way life is," "Do you think life is a fairy tale?" His uncle Mike—a fat, grim storyteller.

Sissy could pinpoint Eddie's turning point. It was the evening his uncle showed up at their house. Eddie had been working on the task force less than four months. When he came home that evening, he had seemed upset. When Eddie reached for a can of beer before his shower, it was a signal to Sissy that it hadn't been a smooth day. But he would never talk about the meaner things that went down on the streets. It was as if that were an extension of Korea.

The phone rang, and it was his uncle. Eddie did the listening. When he hung up, he said glumly, "Mike is stopping by. Some small business."

When Mike arrived, Sissy was spared his normal glut of bull-shit. She received a perfunctory "ravishing colleen" before the men retired with beer behind closed doors in the living room. Sissy knew it was trouble. She was spared eavesdropping by the volume of their voices through the closed door.

She gathered that Eddie had made a pinch that day. A book-maker. A bookie who informed Eddie that he had better call his superior before taking him in. Eddie not only took the bookie in, but obviously wasn't too gentle about it. She heard Eddie shout, "What the fuck did you expect me to do? The guy had so many scraps of paper on him he looked like a tickertape parade. I had him dead with his work on him."

"Why didn't you call in like he asked?" his uncle asked dispassionately.

"Why should I?" countered Eddie.

"Well, with that amount of work on him, did you think he was operating out of a candy store?"

"What does that have to do with it? He was dirty, wasn't he?"

"For chrissakes, son, don't give me that Jack Armstrong bit. The amount of work told you he was someone."

"Yeah. A thief."

"And you thought you, a wet-behind-the-ears rookie, discovered him all on your own? A regular Junior G-man, ain'tcha? Do you think anyone could be doing that volume without some-body knowing it?"

"Who?"

"That's none of your damn business. What are you—bucking for Commissioner? Just keep your nose out of Department business and do as you're told."

"By some shit-heeling punk?"

"Your partner wanted to dial in."

"Fuck my partner. He runs scared. He wouldn't take a coffee break on his own."

"He'll go a lot further than you, bucko, with that attitude."

"Being a gofer for punks? Look, I was in Korea with real . . ."

"Oh-h, that's it, is it? A war hero. Well, this isn't Korea, it's Manhattan South. We don't hand out ribbons. If you wanted ribbons, you should have stayed in the Marines or bought them in crackerjack boxes."

"Don't you make fun of the men I fought with. This punk . . ."

Sissy thought she could hear an exasperated exhaling. She heard Mike begin more softly. "Sure, and that's what he is. But that's the point, ain't it? I'm not telling you to turn your back on some murderer or some dope dealer. But this guy handles a lot of big clients. The Wall Street crowd likes their action. And is there any harm in it? Are they ruining the world with a couple of thousand on a baseball game or a football game? Don't we all love a little wager? You're not telling me you never dropped down a few bucks in a bar?"

"That's different."

"Only the denominations are different, Eddie. Christ, all you'll do with this bust is embarrass a lot of solid citizens, not to mention their families, if some reporter gets ahold of his client list."

"It's different, I tell you."

"Look, son, I've pissed around with you long enough on this. I have a supper waiting. There're only two ways to go. Either be gung-ho, a prima donna, a loner—or be a team player and make something of yourself on this job."

"That's the rules?"

"That's the rules."

"Maybe I don't want to play?"

"Then be a martyr, son. Christ, I seen enough of them. They usually end up drunks crying in their glass, pissing and moaning about the department. And be sure, your purity will be rewarded. You'll have a nice post on Staten Island where the mosquitoes from the marshlands will eat you in the summer and in the winter, when you take a piss on post, it'll come out like a frozen clothesline. Is that what you want? Some dismal limbo for twenty years?"

"I don't want to cater to scum either."

"Jesus, Eddie, is everything life or death? All you were asked to do was drop a fucking dime, not your pants. Nobody is trying to make a whore out of you. Damn, son, you're a family man now. You're not some fucking cowboy. Soon you'll be wanting kids and a house of your own. You can do all that with somebody looking out for you. Jesus, boy, I'm your uncle. I wouldn't ask you to do something terrible. This is catshit. Forget the punk. It's his clients we're worried about. Lots of them are friends of the department. They're influential men, Eddie. They do good by the job. We don't have many friends out there, son. What do you say?"

Sissy wanted to burst through the door and scream to Eddie to tell this corrupter to stuff it. Was it Staten Island, or a railroad flat like her mother's for life that stopped her?

"What do you say, son?"

"I just don't know."

"Come on now. The Sullivans are not idiots. Your Dad has tough compromises to make with that crew he works with. It's part of getting on in the real world. Don't piss an unlimited career away by acting like a thick Mick."

"I just didn't expect this."

"Eddie, I went out on a limb for you. What did you expect? I'm not asking for the world, son."

"What are you asking for?"

"Just to drop a dime when you're in doubt."

There was silence.

"Say you will, son."

"How about if I let my partner drop the dime?"

"It's a world of compromises, Eddie. That will do just fine. Hell, I'll smooth this little rhubarb over. I'll just tell them you're green. You needed a little schooling."

"Can we drop it?"

"If it's settled once and for all?"

"It's settled."

"Then let's both get to our dinners. You won't regret it, son.

If your old Uncle Mike lives long enough, I'll be salutin' you yet. With your brains, your appearance, and that great war record, you'll have half the department standing at attention."

"All for a dime."

"It's a bargain when you consider the alternative, son. Now let me get home to my table before the better half scalps me."

They left the living room with Eddie firmly in Mike's grip. He was squeezing, leading Eddie by compressing his shoulders. Sissy thought of the Baltimore Catechism with the pictures of the smiling Satan leading little boys off into darkness.

S ISSY OFTEN WONDERED if Eddie's corrosive idea of Manhattan was shaped by the twin disasters of his uncle's dictum of life in the big town and Eddie's demeaning encounter with the hag on West Street. It was entirely possible, like a childhood trauma with water or sex. His feelings about the city were so sharply pronounced they certainly couldn't be considered rational or adult.

To him, there was nothing venial about Manhattan, it was a mecca of mortal conflict. Even its pleasures were warped by wickedness. When he partied in town with members of the task force, Sissy thought of him as a misguided Pinocchio on Pleasure Island, succumbing to a rowdy romp with an eye for the escape route to beatific Brooklyn. Too long a stay on the island could transform him into a braying animal.

Sissy often heard his lectures on the shortcomings of the city. His discourse was so steeped in good and evil fables that Sissy had no response. It was like arguing with a child or a priest. Sissy didn't distinguish between the two.

Only on special occasions, their anniversary or Sissy's birthday, did he relent and take her out for a night on the town. And he set so many conditions that after a while Sissy didn't feel these evenings were worthwhile. He hated the restaurants she chose. They were phony, fancied up so that they could "hump you on the price." His standard line was that they could have had the same meal in Brooklyn for half the price, and the waiters didn't look down their noses at you. Eddie saw a fifteen-minute seating wait as an assault on the borough of his birth. It wasn't Walter O'Malley who moved the Dodgers to Los Angeles, but a conspiracy of Manhattan maître d's. The skyscrapers of the city were a collection of hard-ons zeroing in on Brooklyn.

He also dictated what shows they would see. No drama (Sissy's favorites) but fluffy comedies or musicals. This wasn't borough-bred but his newly adopted cop credo. The more Eddie got involved in the job, the more he shunted aside serious consideration of anything. His views became cop-capsulized. One- or two-line putdowns on every question of foreign or domestic complexity. Everything was reduced to motives and schemes. The globe could be deciphered from the precinct blotter. The world wasn't round but composed of angles. Sissy wondered if this pithy wisdom was updated at daily roll call. The precinct captain as Chairman Mao.

"I see enough drama every day. Enough tragedy and enough shit. I saw it in Korea, too. I don't have to plunk down twenty bucks to see it in my off-hours. Besides, I have my share of heroes. I don't need made-up ones. Some pretty boy actor pretending. I watch guys every day do things that take more balls than you can imagine, and nobody gives them standing ovations. Christ, the city doesn't even notice.

"That's why I feel sorry for people on the outside, Sissy. Especially women. I don't mean that as a putdown, but women just don't get a chance to experience anything. Well, I don't mean *anything*—I think having a kid is terrific. But all the other things. That's why women love books and plays and movies. They live off someone else's hook. I've watched guys put their lives on the line for their partners, guys crawling into burning tenements to pull kids out—mostly black and Puerto Rican kids —a fact the liberal horseshitters never seem to notice. Every day, guys with families crawling out on building ledges or bridge beams to pull in some fuckin' fruitcake who thinks the world hates him because he can't get laid or he's three payments behind on a Castro convertible.

"For me to take make-believe seriously, to pay bucks for it, would be to mock the men I know. I'd be a Judas."

Sissy stopped arguing. She preferred to sit through the most hackneyed musical to enduring Eddie's litany. No score could be as tinny as the policeman's dirge.

But underneath all the bilge, Eddie had a wellspring of faith that Sissy envied. She had never been completely committed to anything in life, with the exception of her father when she was young. In truth, Eddie never touched the depths of the original, he was only balm for an irretrievable loss. She was like a fallen-away Catholic adopting some other theology. It was safer and more comforting, but the aura of magic wasn't there.

Eddie always had a steadfast belief in his neighborhood. He was a part of the congregation, a prominent part at that. Sissy, like Mickey, longed to stand out from the throng.

Christ, it might be pride, but Sissy hated the predictability of it all. The very idea that everyone knew who was going to be at every function, and the endless inside soft barbs about each other's peccadilloes and foibles. "Watch Jimmy, he's switching from beer to gin." Or who lacked hitting prowess or speed in the softball games, or who danced a little wildly with half a load on. And those gagging, saccharine comments on the wife's cooking specialties. How many times did she have to hear the swoons over Loretta's potato salad with the dill or Janet's honey-and-pineapple glazed ham? You would think they were on a Michelin tour of France. Mindless chants, neighborhood *Kyrie Eleisons*. Sissy would be damned if she would spend a lifetime automatically filled in at a set position on the social scorecard.

Yet there was envy when Eddie spoke, not as a surly child, but in innocence. "You know, honey, I don't know why you won't socialize more with the crowd. I know you like to go to Manhattan. Sure, I admit it can be fun, but it's like a champagne buzz. It's a hoot once in a while, but it's not where we belong. And it means something to belong. It isn't a trap, you know. To belong might be dull sometimes, but it's warm underneath because people care about you. You can't expect your friends to be exciting all the time. We're used to each other. Relaxing isn't necessarily boring.

"It's easy to be on all the time around people you don't give a shit about. Everybody just works on one-liners. I see plenty of that in the city. Guys and broads at the bar playing leap frog. It doesn't have anything to do with sex. It's like watching smart-asses in a spelling bee.

"Hell, I sit there with the guys looking for some commitment, some feeling between people. You're in the wrong pew, baby. That city is the only place where Attila the Hun could be gang-banging the neighborhood, and some clown wants a citation because he yells out the window, 'What's going on down there?'

"Brooklyn's different. Well, our part of it anyway. I suspect other parts are the same. Anyway, I know our part's special. People look out for the oldtimers on the stoops and keep an eye on the neighborhood kids on the street. And if you're jammed up with bread or sickness, or you need a favor, people are there. You name it—a paint job, a job for someone's kid, an apartment, a hand in moving. You don't have to go begging.

"You know me, I'm not much on church and stuff. Once in a while, in the winter when I go surf-fishing in Breezy Point alone when the beach is empty and clean and all the sudsheads are tucked away till the next summer, and I look at all that empty beach and ocean, I figure maybe somebody might be up there. A main man. But I ain't sure.

"And I sure as hell don't picture some heaven with choirboys squealing like alleycats. But sometimes when I see the neighborhood with everyone chipping in and looking out, I think maybe heaven is like that, only more so. A place where the old and the kids and the women are safe on the streets, and there isn't a door chain in the joint. It's jerky, I know, but that's how I feel sometimes."

Sissy was aware that he also spent quite a bit of time in his anointed hell voluntarily. Getting home to dinner in Brooklyn every night wasn't one of Eddie's honored rituals. Then again, she had to doubt, to question. It was in her genes. It was an unalterable chemistry. God, it was despicable to be without any faith.

Sissy wished she had something to uplift her on this day. But that wish was tinged with sacrilege, since her enterprise was far from lofty. In fact, it was downright low. So low she shouldn't have been indulging in any moral bookkeeping on Eddie, or anyone else for that matter.

What she was attempting to pull off against the Police Department was an out-and-out scam. It was as corrosive a scheme as any cop could devise. Indeed, she reasoned it would be beyond Eddie. Eddie had departmental loyalty. Old Semper Fidelis. He had it for the neighborhood, the corps, and the force. Sissy was working a solo. It was something her husband wouldn't have the guts to float. That excited her. She felt deliciously on edge.

But she wished she hadn't brought up Eddie's promotion to Eileen. She had broken her promise to herself to play it close to the vest to the end. It was a breach of conduct. By divulging it to someone, she hoped to *make* it happen. It was something Mickey would have done. Try to pray a scheme home. More inherited, cowardly crap.

Now, if it didn't happen, she would look like an ass in front of the child. The kid had looked at her like she was out to lunch when she brought it up. Well, that was a fall-back position. Mommy in her sorrow was having consoling delusions. She'd probably play that card, too, if need be. Where would she stop?

She had hung too much on this promotion. Was it public vindication? That was too mild. Exoneration? Of what? A career, a life, Eddie's life, hers and Eddie's life together. Canonization was more what she seemed to be looking for. What a fool she was to gamble so much. She wasn't being cool and calculating, not, as she wanted to believe, manly. She was acting like a sappy woman. A dumb broad. Pussy, the boys would say.

If the bottom fell out, she'd be liable to crack for real this time. Not a minor emotional flurry like the last time. A short season with the jumps. And it could crumble. When she'd seen her engagement ring earlier, she'd thought how today also hung on a piece of jewelry. Circular symbolism. Like a woman's movie with Bette Davis. Warner Brothers intellectualism. More pussy. Freud was right. You couldn't escape what you are.

She promised herself she wouldn't bend. She had the ceremony invitation, and though it wasn't specific, she'd sit chilly. She'd bluff the pants off the New York City Police Force.

Breaking her code of silence a second time, she reached for the princess phone in the bedroom. The name of the instrument didn't escape her. More of the same.

The secretary to the Commissioner of Public Relations answered. The Commissioner wasn't in his office, she was told. He was coordinating plans for the day in a staff meeting down the hall. Sissy begged the woman to interrupt the meeting. Sisterly sympathy wasn't enough.

That was impossible. The Commissioner just couldn't come to the phone.

Sissy found her voice quavering. This time womanly solace and concern came back. "Perhaps I can interrupt for a moment with a message, Mrs. Sullivan, if it's that important."

Sissy pounced on the offer. "Yes, a message. Will you ask the Commissioner if everything is set?"

"Is everything set?"

"Yes, is everything set? Tell him Mrs. Sullivan wants to know. The Commissioner will understand."

"Nothing else?" asked the secretary, as if she was being sent on a fool's errand.

"Nothing else. I assure you he'll understand."

The secretary put down the phone with a sigh of resignation. Sissy waited. And waited. She heard a noise approaching the open phone line. "Mrs. Sullivan?"

"Yes, I'm here."

"Well, the Commissioner was a bit perplexed. He said the invitation was self-explanatory. He didn't seem to understand."

"Is that all?" Sissy pleaded.

"I'm afraid it is. And I'm afraid I can't interrupt again. Look again at the invitation, Mrs. Sullivan. I'm sure it will answer what's bothering you." She courteously said goodbye and hung up.

Look at the invitation! Sissy didn't need to do that. It didn't answer the big question. The damn thing was so general. Sissy was sure it was a plot. They were going to expose her, humiliate her in public. She was going to be a public lesson for anyone who dared to take on the department. A battered test case that would live in department annals. A reference point, a legal precedent for all those who tried to put a chink in the blue wall. It took all the courage she could summon to descend the stairs, abandoning the cocoon of her beckoning bed.

*P*HILLY BARBIERI was waiting with the Cadillac. Sissy had arranged for the neighborhood car service, a cab was out of the question. Brooklyn cabs were like Brooklyn residents—they had a trauma about crossing the bridge. Sissy didn't want to go through that song-and-dance when she gave the driver the destination—Manhattan. "Gee, I'd love to, but I was just heading back to the garage." The garage was their umbilical cord to the great belly of Brooklyn.

And if an available cab was secured, that would be only the beginning of the problem. What would follow would be a sociological roundelet by the cab driver, Nellie, and Catherine on the decline of the fair borough. Catchall phrases would be clucked in cadence with the mindless click of the meter. "It's a shame, it used to be a grand neighborhood." "Well, there's a lot of new faces." "Nothing is the same anymore." "Look at the kids." "Poor is poor, but soap and water isn't expensive." "It's so sad to see the streets this way." "Do you remember the way it used to be?" "God, it would break your heart."

The higher price for the car service was well worth it. Philly's chatter would be a buffer between her and the family. He was slightly dizzy, but he was a harmless kid.

Sissy had to laugh. Another neighborhood trap. Kid. Philly had been at her and Eddie's wedding. He was a teenager then, his mother's escort, a stand-in for her dead husband. Twenty years later, he was still understudying the same part. Whenever and wherever Carmela Barbieri appeared in public, her boy, her kid Philly, would be in tow. A balding kid, fading in the worst place—up front. Philly compensated as most bald men do. Whenever it was possible, he opened the top buttons of his shirt, revealing scrolls of black hair. Sissy missed the logic in this. The house is still in great shape, the tenants merely moved downstairs?

Sissy made mental studies of things such as open shirts. She concluded the Jews and Italians went in for them most. The Irish rarely were unbuttoned, but that was dictated physically. Propriety had nothing to do with it. The Irish rarely had chest hair. When they were attractive, they bordered on a soft prettiness. There was a nice sexual ambivalence about them. You could mentally sample the forbidden fruit without making the journey into unknown country.

The Italians and the Jews generally were too hairy for identity fantasies, though they liked to gussy up more than the Irish—rings, chains, medallions, and a kneebending reverence for swank tailoring. At first Sissy thought they were prone to be gay, but after deeper scrutiny she abandoned that notion. She decided the desire for custom-made was philosophical. Unlike the Irish, they couldn't bear the drabness of life.

That was the Celtic strength—sloughing through blandness, those bowls of mashed potatoes were character-builders. The Jews and Italians were wedded in their love for show biz. Ideally, life should be a class lounge act. Philly Barbieri, with his maroon Caddy and silk shantung suit, was living testament to that.

Sissy had it all planned. After the ceremony, she and Eileen would head for Columbia, while Philly conveniently delivered Nellie, Catherine, and Christy back to Brooklyn. It would have to be done immediately, a calculated move. Any pause would bring disaster. Not even the nicety of a cup of coffee was possible.

Something as simple as that—a momentary gathering—could drive Sissy over the edge. First, there would be the grilling about Eddie's posthumous promotion (was she counting her chickens?), and that was ground Sissy didn't want to dwell on. Her story was flimsy enough for one telling, any in-depth examination would stretch it beyond belief. Hero cop, undercover drug case, heart attack in the selfless line of duty. Even Kojak passed on scripts like that.

Besides, Sissy just wanted to get the day behind her. The day, Eddie's death, the marriage, her goddamn unrelenting memory. She hoped getting Eileen started might prove cathartic, though in truth she didn't see Eileen's entrance into college as a springboard for herself. Right now she was too weary and brittle to be captivated by what was euphemistically labeled "a new life." That was for Eileen, who was young enough for assaults on new terrain. Sissy was seeking only an interlude, a breather, which seemed, she thought, within reason.

But the desire to unload them quickly today was even more basic. She just didn't feel like socializing. Not with them anyway, which was nothing new. Aside from holidays and birthdays, she had managed to keep her distance from her family and Eddie's over the years. Now and then, when Sissy's guilt caught up with her, or when either Nellie or Catherine sounded on the verge of putting her head in the oven, there was the exception of a bonus dinner. At those times Sissy invited them together, along with Christy and Mickey when he was alive. It was her logic that if she had to face the music occasionally, it was better to get the blare of the whole orchestra at once and be done with it. And usually the encounter was so traumatic for all concerned that nobody had the heart (or stomach) for a reprise until the calendar softened the memory of the day. The format could be billed as Armageddon etiquette.

Yes, they were a regular Hallmark family. The family that prays together stays together and, if truth be known, eventually slays together. But this flip attitude didn't soothe Sissy. All right, nobody expected Currier & Ives—"Over the woods to Grandma's house"—but there should be more to family than what she had. If it weren't for the command of blood, she doubted she would ever see them. Maybe Christy, but Christy was inseparable from Catherine, so he would be jettisoned in the package deal.

Her litmus test was that if she were feeling on top of her game, truly super, with a bankroll to squander, would she call any of them to join her on a spree? The Mickey of her girlhood, that dandy of ducks and Saratoga trunks, to be sure, if she could isolate his ghost. But never the latter-day Mickey, he least of all. And under no circumstances when she was flying high would she ring her mother or Catherine. And that was the test—flying high. Bottomed out, she would talk to anyone, but that didn't count. When she was at her lowest, after Billy was killed in Vietnam, she was shameless. She had seized ears—Nellie's, Catherine's, discarded friends from high school days, strangers, her doctor until he trespassed, and even the priests. The good, old, reliable Church, it was her pronounced business practice to welcome back the wayward. That must be a tough guarantee to hang your shingle on. Sissy often wondered what she—the Church—thought of being a refuge for the walking wounded. Sissy was sure Christ, looking down from His cross on the altar, would like to see someone in better shape than Himself occasionally come through the door. That was it, contact when you're wired, flushed with life, and it saddened and sickened her more than she would admit that her own family never entered her thoughts when she was cresting.

And now she was scheming to deny them a simple cup of coffee after what would surely be a trying day. But it wouldn't be that simple, she argued to herself. Menus would be scanned, and Nellie and Catherine would go through a litany of what food was "dangerous to eat out." Pork could kill you; meatloaf, they could put anything into; soups sat on the stove too long; hamburgers were loaded with grease, and even the milk for the coffee had been "sitting on the counter all day." And there would be those mortifying conspiratorial conferences with the waitress. "What do you recommend, dear? I have a weak stomach, and if I eat something that doesn't agree with me, it keeps me up half the night. The gas bends me in two. Everyone tells me cottage cheese is wonderful for you, but I can't get a spoon of it past my lips. It tastes like chalk, a bit like Milk of Magnesia."

"You know what I would love, if I was able, of course—I loved them when I was younger—a Western omelette. But it has onion and peppers in it, don't it, dear? God, a green pepper would be the death of me. What would you have, dear, if you were ordering?"

No way Sissy would go through that scene today. She had squirmed through it hundreds of times. The infantilism of it! As if the waitress, standing on legs with cable size varicose veins, wanted to hear about some old bag's bodily dysfunction. Was that what growing old meant? Reverting to crapping all over yourself in public, mewling to be taken care of. If so, Sissy hoped she died before reaching that stage. She knew she had better, since she was superstitious enough to believe God would grant her company as sympathetic to her as she was to Nellie and Catherine.

But today, for a while, Nellie and Catherine would be catered to. Carmela Barbieri's absence didn't free Philly from his anointed role. Today, Nellie and Catherine would serve as surrogates—not a burden, but a bigger audience. Eddie used to talk about cons who couldn't handle freedom. No matter how many times they served time and were released, they couldn't be sprung mentally. Free, they longed to return to the happiness of confinement, where their existence was defined.

"You put those fuckers on the street," he would say, "and in forty-eight hours, they'll be back in action at their old stand. Never trying anything new, repeating the same old gig even if it was catnapping, smearing their M.O. and finger prints all over the place like an infant merrily smearing his shit all over his crib. The pathetic suckers. If they had the bread, they'd hire the Goodyear blimp to fly over Centre Street with their addresses flashing on the side."

Sissy translated Eddie's criminal catechism to civilian life: There were some who could never be sprung. In the larger world, like Manhattan, they were harder to discern. The disguises were better; there were masks, no matter how transparent, of sophistication. Even the most vulnerable were bestowed the shield of cosmopolite geography. But in the neighborhood it was different. Everyone was naked.

But that made it sound like an exposé, which it wasn't. Nobody in the neighborhood tried to hide or disguise their roles, they exulted in them. After all, these identities weren't shabby cloaks found discarded in a heap, but repertorial gifts handed down from generation to generation. Every quadrant of Brooklyn had its allocation of dutiful sons whose role it was to squire mothers to wakes, weddings, and christenings, and whose duty it was to keep the car polished and gassed, shimmering in anticipation, awaiting a Sunday summons from headquarters.

Then there were the vestigial daughters, those ageless children who looked as if they dressed in perennial Easter outfits, never without hats and gloves, all trussed up like the cake boxes they carried on their mothers' social calls. The boxes that, like their own, shunned the exotic for sensible, bland pound cake or proper ladyfingers.

All the neighborhood roles weren't so subservient. The repertory had room for flourishes. Gamblers, drinkers, and ladies' men were recreated with fidelity. If a departed plunger had the reputation of sometimes hiring a limousine laden with champagne to go to the track, an ingenue at chance would repeat his legend, right down to the make of the limo. First-class shuffleboard players had their styles mimicked to the nuance by other adults, in much the same way children in the neighborhood copied the batting stances of major league ballplayers. The only adoration the local legends were denied was bubble-gum cards.

On it went. If someone achieved the reputation of success with the ladies, his composite style was studied—hair comb, choice of jewelry, taste in clothes, make of car, brand of scotch (scotch for lovers, rye for drunks), the conquest of the cha-cha (a must), and even his speech patterns.

But all these roles were mere spear-carriers to that of the legendary "class" drinker. Sissy had watched this syndrome most of her life. Hell, she had seen the best. If there were an investiture for that sort of thing, Mickey would have been knighted for the way he carried it off. The D'Artagnan of drunks, a swashbuckling souse. He had all the sweeps, bows, and flourishes. The bankroll peeled inward, the benedictory wave of the hand that meant refilling the glasses of everyone within the range of his blessing, a hundred greetings, all meaningless yet sounding so individual and personal. The alchemy of turning the real terror of his hangovers into mock agony for a laughing audience. To the old women, who sensed a safeness in drinkers, he would be a charming, raffish boy whose hand had been caught in a grown-up cookie jar; and when they scolded him for overindulgence, he played it for what it was worth, short of tugging his forelock.

To the boys—of all ages—he was legend. Telling endless stories of other "legendary" neighborhood characters or rehashing "classic" evenings, he could weave a spell for hours. Mickey's power was such, and his self-delusion so formidable, that as he grew older and retold the tales countless times, he had personally been present at each "classic," regardless of the improbabilities of the calendar. And when he indulged in ranking out someone, the grace of his insult (only the "in" were abused) came from between his teeth, which were clenched on his cigarette. That touch, the business with the butt, became an instant stage gesture in the local repertory.

Her father wasn't dead. Nobody died in this fucking neighborhood. All she had to do was order Philly to pull over to the curb and walk into any bar. Not only would she find a Mickey, but a carbon of anyone who had ever died in the neighborhood. World without end . . . It was so safe, so attractive, yet so smothering. She reached for the car door, fumbling with various buttons until Philly spotted her distress in the mirror.

Ever solicitous, Philly turned and asked, "Is the air conditioning too much?" Sissy, embarrassed by her shortness of breath, gratefully accepted his prognosis. "Yes, it is too much. I hate to be a bother, Philly, but if you could please open the window for a minute?"

"No bother, none whatsoever. It's my pleasure." Just roll it down, Sissy thought, and stop the "It's my pleasure" bit.

She heard a whirr, and the rear window on her side of the limo inched down. "Enough?" Philly inquired. "Or would you like a little more?"

The obsequious sonnuvabitch was rationing out fresh air, the air Sissy needed desperately in her constricting lungs. She wasn't being rational, but she couldn't help it. Her voice whipped at the back of his neck. "More, will you?"

Philly bolted. Christ, she was going to puke on his upholstery, his gray velour. With a whoosh, her window disappeared into the door panel. Sissy sucked the hot air from the street in steady beats. The summer heat worked as a humidifier, her breathing began to fall into regular rhythms.

"It was only an hour ago you were complaining about the heat," Catherine said, annoyed by her daughter-in-law's inconsistency.

"Air conditioning is dangerous when you first step into it," Nellie proclaimed, jumping to her daughter's defense. Nellie would be damned if she'd let her rights of prior abuse be co-opted.

"I never heard of that," Catherine balked.

"Well, I read it in the *Times*," Nellie offered, then advanced deeper, "At the beginning of the summer, an article on summer colds."

"The *Times*?" Catherine asked dubiously.

Nellie arched imperiously, "Yes, the *Times*. You should pick it up. I find less and less to read in the *News* lately." Sissy marked her mother. Maybe she hadn't gone through her marriage with her eyes closed.

Sissy knew she had to cut this short now, or for the remainder of the car trip there wouldn't be any need for air conditioning. Nellie's raised hackles and Catherine's silent sullenness would put the whole day on ice. "Oh, what's the fuss," she cheerily offered, "it's just my allergies. I was roasting back at the house, but the first blast of air conditioning set my allergies off."

Catherine seemed relieved at Sissy's confession to earlier discomfort in the heat. A *Daily News* reader was vindicated.

Nellie wasn't all that pleased with her daughter's diplomacy. "And when did you get allergies, may I ask?"

Sissy saw where this was heading. She slipped into an Irish singsong, "And sure, what's surprising when age slips up on you? Thank God, it's only allergies." It worked. Nellie and Catherine, two obedient acolytes to age, nodded their assent at shared suffering. Christy, in diplomatic self-exile, sat silent vigil at the other rear window, trying to will his shirt to stay dry, while Philly, taking in the scene in his rearview mirror, rolled his eyes in despair over the Irishers' lack of class.

Clearly, Philly had to do something about this, this business going on in the back seat, or these crazy Micks would turn his limo into a zoo. He began to wish they had called a cab. That's what they deserved anyway. Some shit heap with broken springs and the seats a tic-tac-toe game of masking tape, and some *mulignan* up front with a radio the size of a fuckin' radar screen.

He hated these family gigs. Especially when death was involved. Though come to think of it, weddings weren't much better when you were dealing with the Irish. Wakes or weddings, there was always someone with a hard-on from the year one for some other member of the family. They were worse than Sicilians for vendettas.

He'd rather handle the airport, the theater, an occasional prom (the kids were shy, not nutsy yet), and the racetrack crowd. Class clientele, *they* knew how to move. Right now, he could be doping the double instead of hauling these stiffs into Manhattan. They looked like something out of the Addams family on TV.

But he didn't have a choice in the matter. His mother made him accept all the neighborhood family stuff. She wouldn't even let him sluff it off on any of his drivers, and he had three, besides himself, now. He still had to do it personally. That's the price you pay when you're bankrolled in business. The limos were in her name, but it wasn't only that. She made him do it because it made her a big deal at mass and at bingo. The neighbors raving to her about the grand outing they had in her son's limousine and of how she should be proud of such a boy. She ate it with a spoon, standing in the middle of an adoring circle. Philly could dig it, he had seen Old Blue Eyes in concert.

He could handle the day, though, as long as that broad didn't puke on his upholstery. That had only happened once—his cousin's kid stuffed with cannoli and, Philly suspected, some red wine after a family wedding. What a mess! A fuckin' disaster. For weeks he could smell the kid's heave, regardless of what he did, including sprinkling the car daily with cologne. The ritual made him feel like an ass in front of the neighbors, looking like some bishop blessing a ship. And the cologne wasn't cheap shit either, it was class—Chanel N° 5. He had a hook with a guy who worked the PX in Fort Dix, and he got a buy. That was also the source of his cartons of cigarettes, which made him a few bucks on the side on resale to a steady list of customers. Good, solid regulars, no free-lancing. Nothing big, but it covered a night at Yonkers, and that wasn't to be pissed on. But man, did that smell hang tough. Kid's puke must be like kid's shit—unbelievably nasty.

But at least that was family, though he still felt like breaking the little bastard's legs every time he saw him. To this broad, he didn't owe nothing, and she looked like she was ready to let go at any minute.

He had to admit she had had her troubles. Her son getting it in Vietnam, and now her old man. Hell, she could be proud of both of them. But was she? Maybe that was part of her trouble. The whole neighborhood had it that she wigged a little after the kid. The official line was that she was in the hospital with "woman's trouble"—change of life, ovaries, or something, some plumbing job. The family floated that one, and nobody openly questioned it. That's the way it should be (Philly understood family business), but he heard otherwise.

The word he got was that her nerves went south. She certainly looked a little spacey to him, but he reasoned she had a hairy day in front of her, so who could tell for sure? A ceremony honoring her old man, there was a whole story about it in this week's *Tablet*, and Father Hogue even announced it at Sunday eleven o'clock high mass from the pulpit.

No doubt about it, Eddie was *somebody* in the neighborhood. He was regular, everyone liked him, even Philly's people who did business had only the best to say, which was rare enough for an Irisher, never mind a cop. Eddie gave people air, he wasn't a hard-on, a tin saint. That wasn't meant to say he'd look the other way if some jungle bunny in sneakers was bouncing your sister. No way. He had *culloons*. He didn't go for the needle trade either—shit, that's how he went out, shagging some spic pusher.

Philly, in a way, understood spades. They were animals, pure and simple. But the Puerto Ricans were beyond his comprehension since they were Catholics. It didn't jibe that they'd end up that way with such a beautiful Church. At least the spades had an excuse. What did they have going but a bunch of hopheads rolling around a storefront with tambourines in front of a crucifix made from the slats of an orange crate. Jesus, but the PRs went through life as bad or worse. God knows who taught them their religion, but Philly was sure it wasn't a white man.

He thought it was the Latin blood. When he was in the army in California at Fort Ord, he and his buddies took the prerequisite trip to Tijuana. He was in basic training, eight weeks without leave. He was so horny, if he had tripped, he'd polevault. He was never much for jerking off, dropping a load in the cold marble bathroom or on the sheets you had to sleep in—what kind of class was that? Besides, he hated to look down and see his big hairy fist wrapped around his cock. It startled him and made him queasy.

But he had heard enough about Mexican cunt to frighten him off getting laid. Clap was the least he was told you could expect, you'd be lucky if your thing didn't fall off like a ripe banana two weeks later. The only way he'd put it up one of those holes was if a Roto-Rooter went ahead of him. No, he planned for a thorough pipe-cleaning, a dynamite, leisurely blow job, regardless of what it cost.

It proved easy enough, finding a hooker was a piece of cake. She was young, too, perhaps too young, but it was that or ending up with some skag who had serviced more GIs than a quartermaster. She started off by giving Philly some snow job about a tubercular baby brother and a dead mother and a father who'd abandoned the family, but Philly shut her up immediately with an offer that was twice the going rate. He didn't want any talk, especially talk about disease. He was wary enough about clap, crabs, and syph without hearing about TB, especially when he was tracking a blow job.

He didn't even want her name, he settled on calling her "Chiquita." He was pleasantly surprised by the neatness of the room she took him to. The bed linens looked clean, and the few pieces of furniture in the room were in good repair. And he didn't spot anything crawling anywhere. You bet your ass he checked.

When he spotted a small sink in the corner of the room, he slipped her another five. He'd read somewhere where French whores bathed your dong and balls in warm, soapy water. It had been eight weeks since he'd even seen a broad, since he didn't count those mutts who worked in the snack bar. They were the human equivalent of the saltpeter that laced his mashed potatoes. So an extra fin for some luxurious foreplay was well worth it.

She was so terrific at the sink, he figured she wasn't new at it, or else he had drawn the rookie of the year. He had to fight not to pop his nuts right then and there. This would prove to be the high point. Later on, Philly wished he had let go in the sink.

What happened was the dumb trick didn't get his drift. She undressed all the way, like Philly was going to lay her. He had liked her better in clothes; naked, she was too young, too thin. He got the same queasy feeling he had when he looked at his male hand on his joint. Her bush was all right, though it looked a bit scraggly, like those beards kids try to grow that never develop. Besides, he didn't want her drawers off. He wasn't sure that disease couldn't leak. For sure, he knew crabs were mobile. But worse, she had no ass and no tits. Guys in the barracks had more shape to their butts, and her tits only differed from his in nipple size. Her nipples reminded him of a bathtub stopper.

He had to explain to her again that all he wanted was head. She looked crushed, the insult seemed too much for her to bear —at least till he added another ten. He was being taken, and it pissed him off. For prices like this, you could get Harry James on the horn. But he was prepped, soaped, rinsed, and patted dry, what could he do—walk out? It would be like dressing a Thanksgiving turkey and then throwing the fuckin' thing out the window. He sprang for another ten, bringing the fee to fifty-five. Vegas showgirl prices for a Mexican mongrel.

She had told him to lie down on the bed, which he did while she drew the drapes and darkened the room. Behind the headboard, she lit a candle. He saw its flicker on the ceiling. The half a yard plus hurt less now. Chiquita seemed to move her tongue with the sputtering rhythm of the candlelight. Hell, the kid had a class act going. He watched the ceiling and thought about lying in a Brooklyn lot watching fireflies. He remembered the empty mayonnaise jars he used to catch them in, with lids perforated for air. He also remembered some neighborhood jive that you could make rings out of the captured flies by mounting them in hollowed-out chestnut shells, and if you knew the trick, the light, although the fly was dead, would remain luminous. Philly always suspected it was bullshit, but it never stopped him from catching the flies or hoping to meet the local wizard who knew the secret of the ring.

But eventually this, the ceiling, bored him. To tell the truth, he wasn't much of a blowjob man—poontang was his thing. He could never get deep enough in the mouth, and besides, he had no room to maneuver, to stroke, or strut his stuff. To Philly, blowjobs were like putting a bronc buster on a merry-go-round.

The best he could do was to roll Chiquita over and straddle her, so he could hump her mouth. At least his ass would be moving, and he could watch. As he muscled her into that position, he saw that the candle in the niche behind the bed was encased in rose glass. It served as a flashlight for the statue of Our Lady of Guadalupe to look down. Our Lord's Mother, the Blessed Virgin, focusing on his salami stuck in this pagan's throat. His prick shrank instantly, diminished as profoundly as any belief that Spanish-speaking people would ever be granted the ear of God.

But it wasn't only Latins, all broads were a little weird. Not mothers, of course, but then again, mothers weren't broads. Take this one in the back seat, the one who was about to change the color scheme of the upholstery. Philly could never understand why Eddie married her. She was a first-rate-looking piece and all that, but Eddie wasn't exactly prowling the streets begging for nookie. So why did he need her? Philly had never been able to figure it out. Eddie was a guy who moved easily, he made you feel at ease, nice, regardless who—the guys on the corner, the old ladies on the stoops, the old men in the social clubs. You name it, everybody dug him, even the smart guys, the neighborhood wise guys who were connected. Though you knew he was Irish, you never thought of him that way.

Eddie didn't go in for that bullshit. When he sat eating a dozen on the half shell with hot sauce, he acted like one of your own. He even sipped some wine and seemed to enjoy it. That alone was astonishing. Eight-to-five, if you meet a Mick who digs wine, he'll be trying to smear your windshield with a dirty snot rag. No, Eddie knew how to travel. He also knew a tailor did more than let out and take in waistlines. He was all right people.

Philly could never dig her—Sissy. "Sissy?" What kind of fuckin' name was that anyway? Especially for a young broad. It would be all right to peg on a nun in your family, but that was about it. Nobody even called faggots sissies anymore. But she always was a little weird, even as a kid. Philly remembered the duck.

Now what kind of act was that—a duck parading around a city street after a kid? Christ, she used to think she was hot shit. He remembered she didn't even talk to him or his friends, because she was a couple of years older. At least he hoped her snobbery had to do with age and wasn't because she had a duck. That really would be sick. He would rather have walked a rat from the cellar of Bellone's butcher shop than a dumb duck. At least, a rat could kill. All that thing could do was sound like someone with adenoids and drop shit pellets in the street. Man, that would be really far out if she snubbed him because of the duck.

"Miss Yankee Doodle," the kids used to call her, after the Drake's cupcake that had a duck on the wrapper. Miss Fruitcake would have been more like it. But it was easy to see where she got her ideas. Her old man was a prime nut, a real juicehead. Philly never liked him. He always made you feel he was laughing at you, looking down on you, the way he talked to you with all those flowery greetings: "Ah, Mrs. Barbieri, doesn't the sun hitting the shimmering water on the street make you think you're looking at a canal in Venice?" What shit. Venice! The sanitation truck had just sprayed the street. Philly's mother just laughed at him, she thought he was funny and nice, just a little crazy from the booze. Philly knew better. He vowed as a kid if Mickey McKenna talked to him like that when he was a man, he'd break his sarcastic Irish mouth. He'd splatter his ass all over the shimmering canal.

Sissy had the same superior way, and why not—she was always with him. That was weird to Philly, too. He had seen plenty of inseparable fathers and sons, but never a father and daughter who palled around together. He remembered she didn't have many friends either. Not close ones, like Eddie did. She hung out all right, but whenever she was with just one other person, it was her father or the "Iceberg." What was her name—Margaret? Margaret something or other. Prim Margaret, the school whiz. She was such a brain every class in the school knew about her. The nuns always cited her as a perfect example to the dumbbells of the school like Philly.

Yeh. Philly was so dumb he had his own business, he had a fleet of limos (well, him and his mother), while he bet a bunch of those goody-goody ass-kissers couldn't move around town without a token. That was Sissy's only buddy, the Iceberg. The older guys used to say if you put your prick into her, it would turn into a popsicle. Two snobs, they used to walk through the streets as if they were special. Always going to or coming from the library with arms full of books and their noses up in the air. What a life she had led—ducks, books, the Iceberg, and her whacked-out old man. No wonder she was strange.

But it was more than being a little odd. Philly could have handled that. After all, some of his own relatives were so *pazzo* in the head you could get a price for them. For that matter, how swift was his own father? But that was religion, a lot of the old-time ginzos were like that. Dominick was an embarrassment, but there was no spite in him. Besides, some neighbors thought he was saintly, with his talking to the statues in the church and drinking the holy water from his cupped hands. He could be lived with, though, and the old lady could always handle him when he went too far. Well, most of the time anyway.

Palm Sunday was another story. Philly hated it. If his mother didn't force him to go to mass, he wouldn't leave the house. To this day his insides puckered whenever he remembered the sight of his old man coming back from mass, literally staggering under the weight of all the palm branches he collected by pestering the ushers and begging from other parishioners. The Irish heaped them on him, too. Dominick reinforced those bastards' notion that Italians only came to church when something was being given away: palm, Easter water, dispensations, blessings of the throat, and of course, ashes. How many jokes had Philly had to listen to about Italians and ashes? Ginny broads wore their ashes like mascara—too much and smeared. Or they said carrying your ashes for three days was the first part of the sanitationman's exam. But that he could handle; given a chance to make noise, the donkeys acted like donkeys.

It was Palm Sunday that killed him. To see his old man coming through the streets with the stalks of palm sprouting from every pocket, a sheaf of it in his arms obscuring his face and tangling in his hair 'til the stuff looked like it was growing out of his body. Year after year, that was how he came home from early Palm Sunday mass, and year after year, Philly watched him from behind incisioned curtains, knowing he had to walk through those same streets later on his way to the children's mass. Through the same streets this fuckin' Carmen Miranda of a father had just traveled.

Oh, he was a bother all right, but most of it could be endured. Even the ice house. Philly finessed that one on the streets. Imagine calling a business the Galilee Ice House. It was Dominick's notion that Jesus had transformed the Sea of Galilee into a sheet of ice so he could walk on it. So what could be more natural for a pious man than to christen his ice business after that ancient miracle. Philly's mother (God bless her, what a woman) couldn't talk him out of it, but she put her foot down about painting the side of the trucks with a likeness of Jesus cakewalking a frozen pond. Sacrilegious, she screamed, commerce and Jesus! She told Dominick he would have the same fate as the moneylenders in the temple. That was enough to back him down, though he got his way with the plastic statues of Jesus standing on a clear, magnetized cube for the dashboards of the delivery trucks. But that was acceptable, since only Dominick saw the clear cube as a block of ice. The drivers saw it as just another dashboard gizmo to go along with toting St. Christopher, the giggling hula dancer, and the dunking dodo bird.

As for the name, Galilee, his mom figured that one out. She said it was an abbreviated combination of the names of the two villages where Dominick's parents were born. Nobody even questioned it. She was dynamite in a pinch.

Dominick was just a little off the wall where religion was concerned, otherwise he was regular people—neighborhood. Not like this broad, McKenna. His strongest impression of her was still that of a stuck-up schoolgirl. Philly didn't forget, he had a mental list of those who had dumped shit on him. And he didn't think she'd changed over the years. She still had that superior way about her. What really burned Philly's ass was she thought she was better than the neighborhood.

Hey, this neighborhood produced some great people. Hadn't Susan Hayward and Barbra Streisand gone to Erasmus Hall? And besides them, what about the regular legends? Shit, her husband ranked as one of those. But she never appreciated that. Philly had seen them out on occasion in neighborhood joints, and she always acted like she was slumming. Like she was visiting the neighborhood on a pass. She didn't even appreciate the job her old man was doing.

How could she go down to Washington to hear Martin Luther King? Man, how could *she*, a cop's wife, go parading for rights for *mulignans*? What did they want—the right to carry tommyguns? They did everything else in this city. And a Catholic broad traveling to hear a black minister preach, a commie at that! On top of it all, he didn't even sound sane, ranting and raving about a promised land and mountaintops. I mean, Philly thought, here was a broad who heard Dominicans and Jesuits give sermons during retreat week, listening to that loon praising God like he was a hot watch that wouldn't ever stop ticking. Nobody could tell Philly she was playing with a full deck.

No wonder Eddie did pussy on the side. Nobody needed a putdown artist for an old lady. Besides, she wasn't above suspicion herself. Chicks like her who got weird liked to try things. Philly wouldn't put it past her to have tried a spade at one of those rallies.

Philly didn't think he was being unfair to Sissy. How could anyone be unfair to her after what she did when her kid got killed. That shit was unforgivable, forget the rest: the duck, the nose up in the air, the niggers. That was catshit to what she did to that kid's memory and his father.

Anyone else, anyone decent, would have joined the Gold Star Mothers and hung a little flag in her window. Man, it was an honor to have a son die for his country in the service, and not just the service yet—the Marines. That's what he meant about her not being neighborhood. She knew nothing about tradition. Billy's name would be put on the plaques outside the American Legion and Veterans of Foreign Wars posts. With Eddie's clout in the neighborhood, they might even have named a new chapter after the kid. After all, he was the first Marine in the neighborhood to get it in Vietnam. Didn't she realize that? There could be a William Sullivan Post of the VFW!

She was plain ignorant. Those posts didn't disappear, they were there forever, part of the neighborhood, part of its legend, part of the stories that would be passed down. Didn't Philly know about the neighborhood guys who bought it in World War II? He knew what citations they received and when and where they died. He didn't even remember those guys existing, but now he knew about them, everybody who was neighborhood did. Those guys were sacred, they ranked higher than the great boozers, gamblers, and stickball players. Hell, if she knew anything, she'd know those guys, Billy included, would live as long as the memory of her beloved Martin Luther King. For that matter, a lot fuckin' longer in this neighborhood.

But she didn't know shit. If she did, she wouldn't have joined those mothers against the war. What a disgrace! Why didn't she just spit on the kid's grave? She certainly spit in her husband's face, though it was Eddie's style to ignore it—in public anyway. Philly believed that's where the outside pussy came in. The serious stuff, he meant, not the one-nighters. Every married guy takes his share of that. But who could blame Eddie? How could you make love to a broad who was going around saying your son died for shit? Philly couldn't, not if she was the last lay on earth. He'd rather whack off, and for him, that was saying something.

Philly wasn't a holy roller, down genuflecting every morning. But he gave respect upstairs, and that's why he believed God punished her. A just God wouldn't tolerate an insult to a hero, and that's why she ended up with head trouble. And she deserved it. Woman's problems, my ass. Nobody bought that. They were trying to get that poison out of her head. But publicly, Philly went along with the "woman's problem" story because Carmela decreed it, even though she knew better. His mother always made Philly feel embarrassed. She was such a class Catholic.

In Philly's mind, McKenna wasn't exclusive in her shortcomings, she was just worse than most. He had watched the progress of his friends' and relatives' marriages and concluded that all wives were pains in the ass. Not that he had anything against broads, mind you, you could ask anyone, he had more than his share on his arm. But that was different, that was romantic—a night out at the 802 Club, or a good Broadway musical, or dinner at the Cloud Casino at Yonkers Raceway. Broads were always on their best behavior for such occasions. Charming, gay, and dressed like Sophia Loren. That was the way to do it.

And when you wanted a little action, you checked into a class hotel in the city for the night, or better yet, you took them off on a singles weekend to the Catskills or the Poconos, where you woke up in a circular bed and rang the desk to send up breakfast and the morning papers. Not to mention the bath together in one of those sunken jobs, where Philly could try to hit her battleship with his soapy torpedo. That was class. Not like his first cousin Allie, who had to look at his wife every morning in that damn quilted housecoat from A&S's. It was like waking up with the Vietcong.

Worse, Allie told Philly that sometimes she came into the john when he was shaving and squatted on the bowl. Philly didn't care even if it was just to piss (he was too horrified to ask), how could you ever feel romantic about a woman again after seeing that? Philly had a lock on his bathroom door at home, though it wasn't needed, because Carmela always knocked. Three or four times. Philly even had his own face cloth and towels laid out fresh every day. His own, not some doormat for wives and scroungy kids and maybe the dog to wipe themselves on.

Broads and kids were the kiss of death. You could forget it once the first kid was born. Philly had seen it too often. It never failed, the old man might as well take a hike. Philly liked kids as far as they went, but he couldn't stand the way women gushed over them. You would think they were Christ in the manger. Meanwhile, all they did was wreck your pad. They were cute all right (when they were dressed up), but they didn't know how to act. They had no class moves. You could sum up their action in two words: ripping and shitting. But if you believed their mothers, they were shellacking the floor with Breyer's Chocolate.

Philly also couldn't stand the way women let themselves go after kids. Sagging tits, pot bellies, veiny legs, and fat all over. The worst of it was, they didn't have to. But broads were born actresses, ever since they were kids, they were on. Miss Yankee Doodle in the back was a perfect case. Philly had seen all the roles: ass-kissers in school, hard to get when they got older, the married-lady bit when they entertained the poor, unfortunate unmarrieds in their new houses, and mommy. In their heads, mothers should look like mommys, so most of these dipshits let themselves fall apart. And everything was for the new kid. No more romantic aura, the old man might as well bronze his dick along with the baby shoes. It used to nauseate Philly to be in a friend's house and watch his wife absentmindedly finish the food left over on her kid's plate. Man, the chick you wined and dined ended up a brat's garbage disposal.

That would never happen in Philly's house. Carmela set an immaculate table. Philly had both wine and Pellegrino water, plus his special dishes. He had a delicate stomach, not like the old wops who could swallow napalm and call it sauce. Carmela—for him exclusively—cooked Northern Italian, continental, the classiest of cooking. You name it, he had it: an air conditioner in his bedroom for summer and an electric blanket for the winter. He even had the color Sony in his room. Carmela said it hurt her eyes, and she liked the black and white, but Philly knew better. His dry cleaning went out weekly on Tuesday and was back for the weekend, and Carmela did his shirts by hand. None of that commercial laundry shit, or the Chinaman who put so much starch in your collar you felt like you were wearing a piss hard-on around your neck.

Philly had the best of everything, and he knew it. But to each his own. He had a secret, and he kept it to himself. There was nothing unnatural about living with a woman unless you were fucking her.

CUTTING OFF the side streets into Ocean Parkway, Philly found his solution. He would take them on a tour through Prospect Park enroute to the bridge. This way, the broad would get some fresh air, and the old ladies would get a chance to see some greenery. The only color they had was on their forearms, from leaning out their living room windows.

Philly couldn't fault them for staying indoors, though. With the way things were now, you should get combat pay for entering a park or going to the beach. Maybe it was still possible on Long Island, but not in Brooklyn. The park was a hairy trip these days, with these spade kids roaming like dog packs. Every one of them outfitted in high-top sneakers—where the Christ did they still find them? Not only could they do a number on you, they could do it in a matter of seconds. Fuck the college track stars. They should have these little bastards sprinting against the Russians in the Olympics. Every pawnshop in Bed-Stuy would look like a trophy room.

Philly would give them a treat. He knew the old ladies would dig it—Carmela loved a Sunday tool around the park. And it might settle Sissy down. Besides, Philly was getting more concerned about Eddie's father who was looking like a used condom in the back seat.

As the limo reached Park Circle at the entrance to the park,

Philly made his announcement. He could have booked the reaction. In unison, the bags cooed, "Ah, that would be grand."

Nellie added, "You're a wonderful boy. I hope your mother knows she's blessed."

The others were noncommittal, but Philly didn't give a shit. Carmela would get the report from those who mattered, and that was the bottom line. She'd lap it up for all it was worth. But knowing his mom, he knew it wouldn't be a one-way street. Over the weekend he could expect a special side dish of polenta or fried baby eggplant. Carmela understood a class move.

The lack of reaction from the kid upset Philly, though. It might not be a trip to Coney Island—that was no bargain anymore, either, unless you wanted to wade through chicken bones and dried corn cobs and get your eardrums busted by those radios, not to mention Riis Park with those oiled-up fags parading around with their schlongs hanging out—but it *was* a trip through the park on a summer day in a Caddy. Probably if he'd put some loud shit on the radio and offered her some pot instead, she'd have flipped. She was a nice enough looking kid, but he suspected she was a space cadet, like her mother.

It all came too easy to kids today, broads especially. If you didn't have to bust your ass for a buck occasionally, everything ended up boring you. And they were yelling about equal rights! It was like Rockefeller campaigning for unemployment insurance. Philly would love to give broads equal rights. He'd die to see their asses drafted into the army. Not for combat—everyone knew that was ridiculous—he would just like to see them go through basic training.

Besides the slop you had to eat, he'd give his left nut to see those queens sitting on thrones without doors in a company crapper in the morning, with collective grunts and groans sounding like Godzilla trying to digest Tokyo. One month of that and they'd start a hope chest of Betty Crocker recipes.

But the last thing in the world Philly was was a tightass. Growing up, he'd been taught to go out of his way for people, so he decided to give it a shot. He worked up his enthusiasm, displaying the full keyboard in his mouth as he turned his head. "Hey, Eileen, on a day like this I bet the bears will be outside feeding. I'll slow it up when we come to the zoo. What say?"

Eileen couldn't believe her ears. The zoo? Bears? Didn't this goop have eyes? Next, he'd probably offer her a lollipop. She glared at Philly till she felt the insistent pressure of her mother's foot on hers. It gagged her, but she got it out, "That would be very nice, Mr. Barbieri."

Philly ignored the glare and seized on the formality of "Mr.," beaming, "You know, Sissy, you did a great job with her. Most kids today don't know from 'Mr.' and 'Mrs.' Even when they're trying to bum money off you on a street corner. Some fifteen year old said to me the other day, 'Hey, Jim, do you have some change?' Jim! Where do they get that stuff—television? Man, I don't even look like a Jim. But you got no worry with that little one. Anyone can see she's a real little lady."

For Eileen's sake and her own, Sissy wished he'd run out of air. "I've always been proud of her," she said, hoping to end it. But it was hopeless. His mouth was an open hydrant.

"I know her dad was proud of her (you creep, thought Sissy), the same way the whole neighborhood was proud of Eddie. But look, Eileen, we're all the same people, neighborhood, and you can forget the 'Mr.' stuff, though I appreciate it. Look," he added, reaching his hand back futilely, trying to touch the girl, "you can talk to me like you did to your dad."

Like a band leader checking the sections, Sissy's head scanned her family for reactions. Eileen's was perfect, the girl looked like she wanted to spit. Christy was too busy trying to keep his head above his own sea of sweat to notice anyone else's dilemma. It was Nellie who nauseated her. Nellie was dabbing a handkerchief to her eyes, while Catherine patted her hand in mawkish accompaniment. How did Sissy stand a chance coming out of that womb?

Eileen was seething at the tyranny of adolescence. She wondered why everyone made such a fuss out of staying young. All it meant was that you had to mind your manners in the company of older fools like the balding clown in the front seat. Her mother always complained that the old Irish thought children should be seen and not heard. What did she think she was doing to Eileen with her menacing foot?

She could have tolerated Philly's Captain Kangaroo crap about the zoo, but the idea of Barbieri trying to supplant her dead father was way out of bounds. If he tried that again, foot or no foot, he'd hear from her.

Her father wouldn't give a jerk like him the time of day. Sure, he had been a bit too protective of her—that was because of his job—but he'd always treated her as if she had a brain. He understood kids, he never embarrassed them. He'd always acted young. Really young, inside, not like Barbieri who put a swinging finish on a rusty gate. God, he was tacky, like those aging show biz types who tried to act "with it" on Johnny Carson.

It wasn't only her who thought her father was special. Every one of her girlfriends said he was their favorite parent in the neighborhood. Lots of them hinted, and some of them said openly, that they wished they had him for a father. And she knew it was even a little more than that. But she didn't mind. It was kind of fun to have a father your friends had a crush on.

It was easy to understand. Unlike most parents, he never made you ashamed. He knew what kids liked, and he not only went along with it, he seemed to get a kick out of their pleasures, too. She remembered how he used to bring her and her friends shopping in the Village and get them discounts on records, jeans, T-shirts, and sandals. The store owners all knew him and loved him. It was like shopping with a famous rock star.

He even used to bring them into the bars for a hamburger and a drink. Never alcohol—Eileen was allowed a glass of wine at home only on special occasions—but he never embarrassed the girls by ordering sodas or milk. He knew they liked to pretend, so he always ordered them Virgin Marys or a tall orange juice decorated with fruit. Besides, as he explained, the bar owners were his people, and he would never put their licenses in jeopardy. The girls understood that, and besides, who else knew their tomato or orange juices didn't have vodka in them? Boy, those were special days!

And could he ever take a joke! She knew for sure the day her friend Karen got them all to chip in for a T-shirt for him, Porky Pig wearing a cop's uniform. Eileen hadn't been so sure of the choice, because he took his job so seriously, but she went along so she wouldn't look square. She couldn't believe it when they handed him the bag in the store and he took off the shirt he was wearing to put on their gift, then gave each of them a sloppy kiss on the cheek, punctuated by a snort. She was never more proud of him. But that wasn't the best of it. The gift so delighted him that he took the girls to—would you believe!—Trude Heller's to dance. It wigged them all out. Everybody there, including the band, knew him, and it seemed like everyone who was anyone asked them to dance. Nice like. Nobody was fresh. They just wanted to make a fuss about Eddie, Eddie's kid, and her two friends.

When they got home, her mother had complained that they were only kids, and the other girls' parents might not like it. Eileen felt her mother was the one who didn't like it. She was pretty possessive about her father, but Eileen didn't really blame her, because women usually fell all over him. He dismissed Sissy by saying, "What do you expect kids to do? Wear a mile and a half of crinolines and go to Rockaway and sing, 'The Irish Soldier Boy'? Life has changed, Sissy." The last part really seemed to hurt. Her mother excused herself, and later on Eileen noticed her eyes were raw. Eileen, though she was bursting, played the evening down.

If her mother ever knew she had danced with the black drummer, there might be hell to pay. Not that she was prejudiced —she was always telling her father how liberal she was—but Eileen suspected her mother liked people for what she wanted them to be, instead of what they were. Her father was always more natural around different types. He had cracked up the girls when they went inside and he twisted momentarily with the gay maitre d', who adored it. And when Eileen was out dancing with the black drummer, he'd shouted, "If you come on to that kid, you'll end up like Sammy Davis, Jr.," broadly closing one eye. Then when Eric, the drummer, shot back, "Man, I don't dig white chicks. I ain't Jewish," both he and her father broke up.

He was always easy around black cops who came to the house, too. He often criticized her mother for trying to get them to talk social issues. She had heard them arguing in their bedroom one night after such a gathering. "Look," her father had said, "I throw parties, not goddamn CORE meetings. These guys face enough shit on the job without going out for an evening to hear more of it."

"I don't think you're in any position to instruct me," her mother had replied. "It's you who comes home bitching about the niggers. Don't you feel full of shit having them in your home?"

"I don't have niggers in my home. I have Negroes, colored people, or is it blacks, as you hip liberals call them. What you don't understand is 'nigger' is a state of mind. It's how you live.

If you wallow in shit, regardless of your race, you qualify. Especially if you pull down a family with you. Do you get my point?"

"No, I don't. There are social conditions at work. Every black can't be a cop."

"Tough shit. He doesn't have to be a nigger either. But I told you, race doesn't matter. The world is full of qualifiers. Your father could have graduated with honors."

Eileen was terrified when she heard her mother's moan, followed by choking sobs. It seemed to go on forever, and there was no solace coming from her father. She heard the bedroom door open and slam, then the sound of the car starting up on the street. Much later, when the sounds from her parents' room ceased, she peeked in to find her mother sleeping alone. She learned that her father, his charm aside, was a dangerous man to cross. During a subsequent gathering at the house, she heard a visiting cop friend say, "Eddie's a good cop because he lords it over the gutter. I'd rather face a junkie with a knife in a dark alley than Eddie barehanded in Macy's window at high noon when he believes he's right." Instead of bridling, Eileen recalled the evening in the bedroom and filed the information.

It disturbed her to find her father had a dark, menacing side. Her mother's problem was her clinging and prodding. But that could also turn menacing when Eileen rebelled. Often, her mother mistook assertiveness for betrayal.

Eileen wasn't sure college was the answer either. About escaping adults, growing up. Maybe somewhere else, but Columbia was too close. She wouldn't mind bugging out to school—California would be groovy. But that was impossible because of her mother. Eileen was sure she wasn't a hundred percent, and she worried about her. She had the feeling Columbia, any college really, was more for her mother than for her.

It was a mean idea, but she couldn't shake it. She was sure she was right. All her life she had listened to her mother complain about the fact that she'd never gone to college. Eileen felt her mother thought that was the downturning point in her life. Like things turned out badly because of it. Eileen thought her mother had been lucky, ending up with her father. A lot of her mother's friends thought that, too, if the way they played up to him was any indication. Eileen thought her grandfather was the real cause of the problem. Her mother had picked up her nervousness, her speedball speech, even her chain-smoking from him. The leaning on people was his, too. Though she never dared to say it, Eileen thought her mother's father was a chop-buster.

It wasn't that he disciplined you and things like that, but his two cents was into everything. "If you're any indication, Sissy, your kids will fall away soon enough. At least give them the benefits of a Catholic education, then let them make up their own minds." Make up their own minds! Boy, coming from him, that was some crack.

He tried to take over everything. Not the big things—her father wouldn't have tolerated that. But everything else. Family dinners, family picnics, communions, confirmations, graduations, weddings, wakes, even TV shows. He thought he was a pied piper or something. Eileen found him an embarrassment. Her mother had some of that in her, too, especially when she got sick. But that didn't count.

He made such a clown of himself. On her First Holy Communion he had bought Eileen a bouquet so big you'd have thought it was for a pizza parlor opening. She could have died! On picnics he had to chef with his special barbecue sauce "from the gourmet column of the *New York Times*." Sticky, sweet gunk.

And the games. Everyone had to play softball or horseshoes. Worse yet, by his jerky rules. And always the beer and the sun would get to him, and he would be mortifying. Floating in stupid, sky-high pitches (what had he called them—his ephus ball?), and it was worse when he got on base. There was no stealing, but he would dance off the bases, bluffing the pitcher with what he thought was an imitation of a black ballplayer. "That's the way Jackie used to do it," he would say. Grinning like Alfalfa in the "Our Gang" television show. Eileen didn't know why some of the blacks watching on the sidelines didn't kill him. But they laughed. A lot of people laughed at him, including her mother. Eileen thought he was a drunken fool.

He was the same way at home. Oh, how she hated to go there for dinner. Carving the bird like the old-fashioned fathers in Christmas shows. He bossed everything. Especially the TV shows. You couldn't even watch a Mets game in peace. There had to be nickel bets on every batter, who would get a hit, walk, or strike out. Even that wasn't enough. An extra nickel on *how* a batter would make out. There was never a horse race on without a pool picked from that corny derby he'd gotten in Ireland. Election results were the same. Her father once said that if Christ had died during Mickey's lifetime, he'd have had a pool on which day he'd rise from the dead.

The dead. That was when he was really at his worst. You wouldn't have minded the way he carried on if the corpse was someone close to him instead of some distant relative he had seen twice in twenty years, or some guy who stopped in his bar. He made collections for mass cards with gross crucifixion scenes that looked like gory horror movies. Then the sentimental crap came out of his mouth: "It may be God's will, but he surely works in mysterious ways," or "As long as this neighborhood exists, it will never be the same without Jimmy." That was the kind of gibberish her mother grew up hearing.

She'd heard Sal, her father's friend, say to him at one of those wakes, "We have to arrange more of these, so Mickey can get more nights out." They had both laughed, then fell into silent embarrassment when they realized Eileen had heard. But she'd looked at them and said, "Only in the summer, Dad. He hates dark winter suits." Both howled, then took her with them across the street to a bar for a tall iced orange juice. God, she missed her father. For lots of reasons.

That was another thing about the college business—her father. He wasn't caught up in it the way her mother was. He said it was a Jewish ballpark—they owned it. It was all right, he used to say, if you wanted to be a doctor (but *they* had that locked up) or a lawyer, all of whom he generally hated. "Little rich creeps explaining how every mugger, junkie, and rapist had a traumatic childhood. It's all right to rape an old lady if you never went to Yankee Stadium as a kid, or never got a set of Lionels for Christmas. They have no respect for law. They use it like a three-card monte dealer. To watch them work, you'd think the cops are the enemy. 'Did you read him his Miranda?' 'Did you have a warrant?' 'Did you use entrapment?' " She had heard it so often it stuck in her mind like the lyrics of one of the Top Forty.

Her father didn't believe college was the route for neighborhood people. Whoever went that way ended up a flunky. Batboys on Wall Street and in the giant insurance companies, working for peanuts so they could leave their houses in the morning wearing suits and ties, carrying their attaché cases. "If you opened those cases," he would say, "you'd find a Swiss cheese sandwich and an apple. All those cases are is fifty-dollar brown bags."

The way to make a buck if you came out of the parishes was to have a "hook." A rabbi, a contract, and he liked to point out that he had a network of them. "One hand washes the other" was his theory.

When she went to the city with him, she found no reason to doubt it. If she had wanted to be an airline stewardess, he was connected with a guy at American who ran the office football pool. At the big hotels he was tight with the managers. "We keep the scum from loitering." There would always be a receptionist's job there. He had often told her she didn't have to worry, he'd land her in a good spot.

She just wasn't sure which way to jump. She didn't want to insult his memory, but on the other hand, her mother was just as gung-ho about her going to college. That's what she meant about adults. It was always what your parents wanted.

It was easier for Billy. At least she thought that way once. He was his father's son. The Marines, then on to the cops where he would be looked after. Eileen couldn't accept yet that he was dead. She kept waiting to hear that he had been found in a prisoner of war camp, a mixup of dog tags or something. After all, the coffin had been closed, a landmine, they said.

Nothing had prepared her for Billy. At all the funerals she'd gone to, the dead had gnarled, liver-stained hands wrapped in rosaries. Kids you knew didn't die. In books, movies, or on television, sure; but not kids you played and fought with, and certainly not your brother. She was glad the coffin had been closed. Who knew, someday a happy telegram might arrive, erasing the first one?

But even if it did, it would be too late. The news of Billy had destroyed her mother. That's when she got strange. None of them could get through to her. Her father, Eileen herself, her grandmother, the priest, old friends. Only going to the hospital worked. But she still wasn't like her old self. She was okay, but not like her real old self.

The embarrassment her mother caused during her sickness brought Eileen and her closer. At first Eileen thought it was a girl thing, girl helping girl, talking about it, crying about it. After all, men never seemed to be any help at a time like that—not in Eileen's memory anyway. Even when she or Billy got sick as children, it was her mother who got them through it. Her father always acted angry. Not at her or her brother, but at something he couldn't touch. Eileen had the feeling he would have liked to shoot the disease. You could feel the mixture of his fear and temper in the sickroom, even when he sat coloring books with you.

Then there was his escape into whiskey. Eileen had grown up with that. Her two grandfathers, scores of relatives, and, it seemed, every man in the neighborhood who went to a wake. She wasn't a prude, but it bothered her, like they took drinking to be their due.

Her father did it when Billy died. But he did do it differently. He didn't get sloppy, though sometimes she wished he had. That would have been understandable, he had reason. Billy was his favorite, though he took pains to hide it. After all, they had more to share—sports, the Marines, the cops, and all that rough-housing. The sparring, the arm wrestling, the headlocks. She got hugs. But he tried with her. Better than her friends' fathers. She understood, but it hurt all the same. Men just liked other men better. It was the truth. Maybe that's why they were so touchy about queers.

Eileen couldn't believe the amount of whiskey her father took to drinking. He always seemed to have a water tumbler of it in his hand. And he began to stay out more nights, though he did that quite a bit before Billy died. She didn't know what that was about. Her mother, in her sickness, said things, but Eileen couldn't believe them. Her mom's strangeness made her feel unloved. She got hung up on the sex thing. She even grilled Eileen about boys. That was as silly as the stuff about her father. Her father was a terrific family man.

But God, he was scary to watch after Billy. Never a beer anymore, always whiskey. A quarter of what he drank was enough to make either of her grandfathers drunk, and they were no slouches. But he hardly showed it. It was just a steady intake that never seemed to faze him. Like glucose dripping into a sick person. She'd even seen him put it into his morning coffee. He had never done that before. Once in a while he had a cold beer on Saturday morning after a particularly rough Friday night, but that was always after breakfast. And his eyes never changed. Looking off at nothing, just staring. He would occasionally get like that when something especially awful happened on the job,

something unspeakable. In her way, strange or not, her mother
was easier to handle.

Besides, they had their kinship. Not just the girl thing, but
rearranging the life they had had with Billy. There was a lot to
do. It wasn't a disaster—Billy and them—but when he died, they
wished it had been something more. There was plenty of love—
how could you not love your own family? That only happened
with weirdos. Eileen had even cried genuine tears when her
grandfather died, and she thought he was, well, at best a nuisance.

No, it was all right with Billy, no big thing. It just should have
been nicer. Maybe people should say every morning when they
wake up, somebody I love might die today, and I'm going to
treat everybody like they've got twenty-four hours to live. Eileen
laughed inwardly at the thought and involuntarily reached over
and squeezed Sissy's hand. She sounded as strange as her mother
used to be.

It wasn't that Billy was nasty. He just misunderstood so many
things. His problem was that he had his father's looks, and he
thought that was enough. He didn't realize his father added
other things, charm, and a sense of fun. Billy couldn't tell the
difference between good-natured teasing (the kind her father
did) and an insult.

When her father teased her and her mother about reading so
much, he would add that he got bogged down halfway through
a summons. Sure, it was a twit, but by putting himself down, he
took the meanness out of it. She knew her father was touchy
about her mom's interests and about her mother influencing her,
but he was pretty good about it. He wasn't crazy about her
mother's sketches, but at least he'd say, "I'm no expert, but
they're better than Corbellini's at the precinct. But then he
learned to paint by the numbers: Ramirez, Victor, 1082473,
armed robbery, possession . . ."

Billy took everything outside his interests as an insult. "Punk,"
he labeled it. Reading was a drag, drawing was a waste unless
you got paid for it, ballet was for fags who couldn't move under
a fly ball, Greenwich Village didn't have a "real sports store,"
just stuff for (lisping) "joggers, skiers, and body builders." And
college was out of the question. "I wouldn't fit in. I don't hate
America. Besides, I learned to scribble dirty words on walls when
I was twelve. What could they possibly teach me?"

He didn't really mean it. He was just acting. He thought it pleased his father. He had all that body, so he made sounds he thought were manly.

So Eileen and Sissy spent nights at the kitchen table, after the telegram came, remembering and inventing brother and son. How he used to leave peanut butter sandwiches for Santa Claus on Christmas Eve with the crusts cut off, because he was sure Santa liked his bread the same way he did. How, when the cat had a litter, he tried to nurse the kittens who weren't aggressive enough to suckle with Eileen's doll's bottle. How he beat up his best friend for ducking Eileen at Coney Island and never palled around with the boy again. And how, when he had his first job, delivering the Catholic weekly, *The Tablet*, he bought Sissy a birthday present and insisted she model the outrageously flimsy pair of baby dolls in kelly green. "Fancy Irish pajamas," he had called them.

Never mentioned was the surliness, the putdowns, the dismissals, the doors slammed, and the curses when he didn't get his way. Nor was the smartass swagger when he departed for Vietnam ever brought up. A perfunctory kiss on the head for Sissy and a playful clip on the jaw for Eileen. None of the stabbing shards, only the shimmering tinsel. But what they saw had at least been there sometimes, Eileen reasoned. What her father saw in his glass or on the flat walls was unfathomable, and scary.

It was a heavy load to be toting around. A dead brother, a dead father, and a fragile mother who campaigned for college as if her life depended on Eileen's going. It was so muddled that Eileen couldn't get near her own feelings on the subject. A happy compromise would be to go to some jock college where she could major in sports. Something for Mom and for Pop.

If her mother would only give her a little time to think. To go to work for a year at something, at anything (when had it become a crime to make money?), and then let her make up her mind. But when Eileen broached this, you would have thought she had declared she was going off to become a topless dancer. "God, Eileen, don't you know what a trap work is? Do you think you're the first girl who ever said she was going to work for a year or so and then go back to school? Office buildings and maternity wards are filled with them.

"Sweetheart, it sucks you in. You begin to like the idea of the extra money, the blouse or the pair of shoes you're able to pick up on Friday, the weekends off with the girls, the shared vacation house in the summer, and all the office hotshots pressing you for dates.

"That's when you'll feel the pressure. The engagement parties, the weddings, the baby showers of your girlfriends, until you feel like a leper unless you jump on the bridal trolley. Listen to me, Eileen. I've watched legions of them, a whole generation. The only thing work expanded was their waistlines. No way, daughter, no way."

Eileen couldn't handle it. Who could? She was going to make up for a whole generation of pregnant housewives. What did her mother think college was—easy? Four years of cramming your head full of facts nobody gave a hoot about anyway. Did you need romance languages to speak into a switchboard?

She knew damn well what her mother thought college was about. She thought it was like those halls-of-ivy movies she watched on late night TV. All the girls in those hokey glen plaid or dikey tweed skirts with penny loafers and sweat socks, sitting around the fireplace in the dorm, while the sun fell outside the casement windows, and talking about how they were going to conquer the dizzy challenges of Life, as they drank eggnog.

But her mother's head was stuck back there in those old movies. When she was strange after Billy, she was the worst. Dressing up in all those square old clothes and calling her girlfriends—Jesus, they were mothers now—to go for drinks in Rockaway or Breezy Point. Eileen could have understood if she had wanted to go out and drink to kill the pain, that's what the men did. But in those places! She wondered how her father stood it. Those were the places where Billy hung out before he went away!

Her mother just couldn't shake that stuff out of her head. It would never happen. She'd end up in a nursing home wearing bunny slippers.

She was the same way about her own father. Watching *A Tree Grows in Brooklyn* on television and crying over that conniving old drunk of a father in the movie. God, she thought he was "too sensitive for life." When Eileen made the mistake of telling her she thought the movie was a "clunky tear-jerker," her mother wasn't civil for two weeks. Lean, lean, lean. That's what parents do to you, all of them. God forgive her, but the way families acted, it's a wonder you didn't wish they were all dead.

*A*s THE CAR wound its way around Prospect Park Lake toward the intersection of Flatbush Avenue and Empire Boulevard, Christy was suddenly energized. 'Ah-h, Ebbets Field. It's hard to believe it's not still there. Look at that. A lousy project where a cow pasture of dreams once stood."

"Yeh," piped in Philly, "where the Dook used to hit them out, and the old Reading Rifle, Carl Furillo, pegged them on a clothesline from right field."

Christy's gaunt features softened. "I know old Phil Wrigley's dictum that baseball is a game to be played under God's sunshine, but whenever I travel this way, I look at the sky to see the glow of the arc lights. I think half the pleasure of going to a night game was walking through the park with what seemed like half of Brooklyn along with you, all looking skyward for the first shimmer of the lights. When my boys spotted that bright rim on the horizon, they'd run ahead of me like mad. All the other kids had the same impulse. Even the adults picked up their pace. For some damn reason, at that moment 'Casey Would Waltz With the Strawberry Blonde' always piped into my head."

Sissy remembered similar treks with Mickey. She used to pretend that the glow in the sky was the northern lights she'd read about in her science book.

"Now it's all gone," Philly lamented. "It's a shame."

"Things change, son," said Christy softly. "The blessings of progress. Generations ago, the farmers probably cursed the coming of the park. They lost good, fertile planting land."

"Yeh, it's a shame. The new crowd chased the Dodgers away, though."

Christy's voice turned prosecutorial. "The new crowd?"

"You know what I mean, Mr. Sullivan, it got pretty rough there with the drinking and the language. The family clientele stopped going."

"And to think I mistakenly thought all these years it was Walter O'Malley," Christy said in that muted, deadly derringer tone that accompanies bad hangovers. *Family clientele!* How Christy hated this breed with their fancy-mouthed clichés. It was this kind that made retirement inevitable. They were all the rage now in city unions, these mutants of immigrants. Flashy know-it-alls in their leisure suits and gold chains, who thought a shirt and tie at a public meeting was a show of weakness. A tie made you "old guard," "establishment," "a sellout." Christy could do without the brave new world where the main force at the bargaining table was Barney's Mod Shop.

"Well," Philly offered, "I don't know if the man had a choice. It isn't only Ebbets Field. This is getting to be a tough city for family living. You know that better than me, Mr. Sullivan. Your own son Peter moved to Canada. Don't get me wrong. God bless him, and I hope he's happy."

"Peter's in Rochester," Christy corrected evenly.

"Whatever. Lots of snow up there. You know what I mean? Same thing."

God, even national boundaries didn't make any difference to this know-nothing. But what really seared Christy was the "You know what I mean." The presumption that everyone wallowed in his bathetic sewer.

Didn't the young have any sense of history, roots? They perfumed everything with their own prejudices. The blacks chased the Dodgers, indeed. The green, the love of it, chased them. That lace curtain banker O'Malley, with the flypaper fingers that couldn't keep off the thighs of the girl of the golden west. Why the hell was he agitating himself with this ass? His own son probably would call O'Malley's move "prophetic" or "trailblazing a new market."

He often wondered how and when Peter had discovered the comforts of smart money. Not at his knee, that was for sure.

Maybe it was rebellion against the constant talk of unionism in the house, or marching in the Labor Day Parade with Christy when he was a boy. But he had seemed to enjoy that, especially helping to carry a banner when he got a little older. Maybe it was just generational rebellion. After all, he had grown up on his own father's farm in Ireland, and he couldn't look at a horse unless it had a jockey on its back, nor could he get a glass of milk by his lips. He could still see and smell that warm stream coming out of the cow's udder like ghost piss. He guessed Peter's choice was understandable. But did it have to be Eastman Kodak?

Labor nearly had to blow up that scab outfit to organize it. Maybe Christy should have seen it coming. You don't apply for management trainee to plot the overthrow of capitalism. What was Peter's title up there anyway—labor analyst? More perfume to work over the troops. Those efficiency measures in time and motion. Financial diddling. How to make the rich richer by employing less labor. He was wound up now and couldn't get off it.

"Philly, did you ever go to Hawaii?" he offered.

"No, I didn't, Mr. Sullivan, but I always wanted to. Pretty nice, huh?"

"Nah, Philly, a waste of time. Go to Memphis instead, same temperature. Same thing, you know what I mean?"

Philly was baffled but as called for with elders, polite. "Yeh, sure thing, Mr. Sullivan. Memphis, huh? Thanks for the tip. I'll give it some thought."

"You do that, Philly."

"Cheaper, too, I bet."

"Infinitely. And the best thing, no natives."

"Hawaiians not so good, huh? I wouldn't know. The only one I know is Don Ho. Not personally, but I saw him sing on television. He's a little . . ." Philly jiggled his wrist effeminately, "for my taste."

"Good man, Philly. The island is rampant with it. You wouldn't want to bring your wife and kids there. You know what I mean, with *that* (Christy mimicked Philly's wrist motion) and the language and everything."

"You mean foul language? Wow! I never heard that before. Not that I'm doubting you, Mr. Sullivan, since you've traveled a lot more than me with your union work and visiting your kids and everything. Real bad tongues, huh? Wow! That's something."

Christy was now enjoying it. In lieu of a drink, it would suffice.

So was Sissy, and she was delighted Eileen had picked up on it, too. The girl was choking back laughter. Nellie and Catherine looked as baffled as Philly, but Sissy reasoned that they had spent their lives genuflecting to one male voice or another. If the octave was low enough, any opinion from how to run a home to the horrors of Hades from the pulpit to Hawaiian culture wasn't challenged.

But in this instance, Sissy was being a mite too historical. Catherine's silence was due to mortified decorum. Realizing that her husband had never made the acquaintance of Hawaii, except on television, she surmised Christy's intake of the previous night was being percolated by the heat. She wished to God he'd fall asleep, so that he would be all right for the ceremony.

Nellie was merely nonplussed. She had spent a lifetime listening to fanciful talk coming out of Mickey's mouth. Now this one with Hawaii. God, it was depressing. As rough as she'd had it, there wasn't one day in her life she was sorry she was born a woman. And as she got older and watched men, that went double.

"Yes, terrible tongues, Philly. And worse yet, they say it in Hawaiian. You don't even know what they're calling you. You'll never have that problem in Memphis, son."

Eileen took a handkerchief from her purse and honked furiously into it to cover up her laughter, while Sissy once again pressed her foot. It wasn't an individual admonishment as before. If the girl kept it up, Sissy was sure to join in, and she doubted if she could afford Philly the courtesy of cover. Christy knew he had an audience and batted them a discreet wink. He loved these two girls; moreover, he was proud of them. Like Eddie, they knew about life, they had a sense of roots.

"That's something, Mr. Sullivan," Philly said. "Thanks a lot. Man, where can you go these days? Bad enough Ebbets Field is gone, but now Hawaii. Boy, that's something." He shook his head in dismay at the colored contagion he saw creeping across continents.

Christy had had enough of the fool. In the last years on the job, he seemed to have had a permanent seat next to the Phillys of the world. A generation of know-nothings who forgot where they came from. If they had ever seen the shenanigans of the old Irish and Italians on the way up, they would think the blacks and Hispanics were devoted adherents to Roberts' Rules of Order. In those days, it was worth your life to try and forge something. None of these genteel picket signs with fancy lettering from a printer. Christ, the scrawled anger of the signs on display when Christy was starting out was enough to frighten you. And there wasn't all this baked-up rhetoric for TV. Baseball bats, fists, and boots in the balls did most of the talking. Television had cleaned up both sides. Now it was all billing and cooing and compliments, while you tried to figure out how far you could shove it and get away with it. Now when settlements were reached, labor and management were so solicitous of each other, it made you gag. The bedroom had come to the bargaining table: "I hope I didn't hurt you, darling."

To Christy's way of thinking, the worst was this new breed who only really hated the ones under them. "The dissidents," they tarred them. Christy had been one of those and proud of it, but in his day the word wasn't perfumed. It was "rebels," those among them who would put their jobs *and* their bodies on the line.

Now it had turned into a whispering campaign. "The dissidents want everything." Christy knew who that meant. And why not, Christy reasoned, their time had come. Christy knew what it meant to be a guppy in the labor pool until the County Kerrymen like Mike Quill and he made their move. When you're on the outside, you don't go in for niceties. If Christy ever related what really went on in the great glorious labor movement in those earlier days, his own family would have turned their backs on him in horror.

Now the sons of men he had worked with and dealt with in the city unions—men off a boat from someplace or other—scraped to management while they savaged the lower ends of their own ranks. The only time they brought up their history was to lie about it, perfume it. How Christy loathed that. To hear some whelp who'd gone through life on his old man's back stand up in a union meeting proclaiming how "we" founded this union, and "you're" trying to rip it apart. *They* founded a union! God, talk about revisionism. They couldn't find their privates if they weren't attached.

The boy in the driver's seat was so typical. Christy had heard it all, over and over again. Foul language, forced busing, welfare cheats, unruly kids, drunks, dopeheads, screwing around on their wives. The "dissidents" always do that, he thought, the "haves" never. They keep their business in their pants, except for domestic unveilings, sip their whiskey at a snail's pace, and speak only the King's English.

Christy had heard it on his way up, and now he was hearing it on his way down. Peter, his own son, was no better. In fact, he was a prime example. Poor Peter just couldn't quite make up his mind. On one hand, the poor stole the system blind and were living in mansions; on the other, he had their children using the living room floor for a potty. Dichotomies never entered dull brains.

You needed a lot of blind luck with kids. His daughters were no better. As he got older, he didn't remember which one lived in Minneapolis and which in Columbus. Did it matter? They and their husbands had gone there to get away from the busing, the language, the welfare, etcetera. Those were the civic delights they gave you when you visited. And their kids were worse. They pointed to blacks on the streets as if they were some species off a spaceship.

Christy didn't exactly love blacks (he wasn't head over heels about Italians either), but he understood what they were up against. He had to admit he got a kick out of them with all that African culture gab. It reminded him of how he had helped organize not only the Irish as a whole, but also the various county men: Kerry, Galway, Tipperary. Pitching local color and pride till they were stuffed with it, even though everyone knew they had gotten their asses off that forlorn bog on the first boat that had breathing room. What the hell was it but tribal mumbo jumbo he had been selling back then?

He liked that in the smart, young, tough blacks. He saw his young self. No more would one of them jump on a boat back to Africa than Christy would return to the Emerald Isle. For what? To look at poverty and kids without dreams? He left that to Catherine. To lord it over her land-poor relatives, or make her county-by-county tour of the churches and castles. A country corrupted by fairy tales.

His kids were big on Ireland, too. Them and their narrow-minded brats with their Celtic names. All of them had come back from visits blathering about the "romance" and the "enchantment." Why not? It's grand to find a country where everyone is willing to wipe your boots and curtsy for a shilling in the palm. Ireland was not for Christy. He'd go back when they started to torch the churches instead of each other and began to organize working men instead of sodalities. Any place that had to peddle its quaintness to the world to survive was not for him. To Christy, Ireland's only mortal sin was its perpetuation of poverty. If he had his way, he'd turn those castles into foundries.

No MATTER how often she encountered it, Sissy remained astonished by the ongoing metamorphosis of the neighborhood. Polite, unobtrusive kids like Philly transformed by constant exposure to the streets into opinionated bores. Every one of them became editorial writers without portfolio.

It certainly wasn't a trek down a knowledgeable path that brought them to this destination. This idiot's sense of geography proved that. Canada! To Philly's mind, any place that got over ten inches of snow a year probably had a citizenry who went around shouting "Mush." Mush, like him. Mushmouths. The notion delighted her. What a marvelous connection—it stretched across countries. She'd better slow down. The Valium was beginning to play tic-tac-toe in her head.

Philly wasn't in the dock alone on this count. Mickey and Eddie (if she wasn't sentimentalizing them) were, once upon a time, fair, open-minded men. They once seemed to consider nuance, though maybe that was a bit high-falutin. But they did consider the other side of questions and people once. God, did that change! In his downhill slide, Mickey had the goods on everyone and everything. He said he had studied the human race as he studied horses. He clocked everyone.

What a notion. He was baffled by what he found in the mirror every morning. But to hear him tell it, he had the cure-all for the nation's ills. Given a chance to remedy things, Mickey McKenna would have made Franklin Roosevelt's initial days in office look like an exercise in sloth.

Eddie, of course, thought his opinions were based on definitive logic. After all, he was a cop, and they were the landlords of logic. Every one of them thought they could give seminars on society. Hadn't they studied it through the telescopic bung hole, their magical "looking ass"?

Philly, Mickey, Eddie, their claims to credentials aside, were one and the same to Sissy. Their minds were molded by their faint hearts. A diverse opinion or an odd notion might mean ostracism from the neighborhood chorus. Another wonderful connection! Like the hippies they slandered, they were wedded to the love ethic.

How Sissy hated the confinement of the neighborhood, of Brooklyn as a whole. As the car wound through the park, the promise of the Brooklyn Bridge excited her. Even a dicey occasion such as this was acceptable, because it would deliver her to Manhattan.

She could have been happy there. She should have pursued one of those office Lotharios when Eddie was in the Marines. Who knew what they were doing now? One or two of those striving clerks might at this moment be living in an East Side townhouse or in a duplex in the Village. Just to walk out into that rarefied air every morning would have made a difference. Not to mention the night life. Not the real glamorous stuff, but Off Broadway theater, an occasional trip to Lincoln Center, and the evenings in the restaurants and bars.

Real restaurants. Not "Let's eat at the Chink's tonight," or "Let's go for a pie." Worse, when the invitation was tendered, you knew exactly what "Chink's" or what pizzeria was being offered. There wasn't even speculation about your limitations.

To sit in a bar where the talk was as diverse as the drinks served. Where a different idea wasn't considered as threatening as a stranger walking into a neighborhood pub. Sissy remembered all too well the evenings out when her "odd" opinions were greeted with a monolith of hostility. It was like being drowned out by the Mormon Tabernacle Choir.

She would like to believe her wild love for Eddie made her take the safe route. That had played a part in it. But in truth, she didn't exactly pine away for him while he was in the Marines. She had had alternatives, but no guts. Like her father, Philly, and her husband, the neighborhood got to her early. All her protestations aside, she was as hooked as the rest. There were few Columbuses in the borough. Like the rest, she believed the world outside Brooklyn was menacing and flat. Parochialism was the pusher that wouldn't let go.

What bound her, and everybody, were those sentimental Arthurian legends. She wondered if anyone outside realized that Brooklyn was a concrete Camelot. Philly had just been working one of the borough's cherished motifs, the fading of the boys of summer, the demise of the Dodgers.

Sissy didn't remember the refrain as that sweet. She remembered the vile talk when Jackie Robinson was called up from Montreal, the violation of the white man's game. The religious timbre given to that phrase, "a white man's game." Yet Robinson was now sanctified.

To die was the trick to owning Brooklyn. Expiration guaranteed you the key to the borough. Coney Island was now discussed as if it had been the expatriates' Riviera. "Do you remember Coney when . . . when Luna Park lit up the night and the Steeplechase's smile stretched across the boardwalk?" Forgotten were the vomiting trash cans, the strewn beach that looked like a dormitory floor on a weekend, and the ocean floating with used condoms. Little yellow submarines.

Also forgotten were those piggish boys with their acned faces who tried to rip the towels from around the girls who were changing. Those dashing swains who stretched out on your blanket on one premise or another so that they could cop a feel of skin. It didn't matter where. A brush of the leg, or even a clandestine toe burrowing up through the sand. Or those snatch peepers who telescoped their eyes through the cracks under the boardwalk, hoping to see a woman walking above without underpants.

The mean truth never mattered. Only legend upon legend. It all stuck to you like pigeon shit on a statue.

Philly checked his watch and decided on a prudent move. There was plenty of time. Even if the traffic built up on the bridge, which was unlikely at this hour, he could navigate it. He'd always thought that if it wasn't for his mother and the church, he could have been a wheel man for the mob. As long as he had the right machine under him, he was unstoppable. City Hall would be a cakewalk. Hell, he could deliver this collection of crazy Harps uptown in twenty minutes through the St. Patrick's Day parade without hitting one of their drunken relatives, if he had to.

He started to nose the Caddy over toward the curb near the zoo. No sweat. He had an NYPD sticker tucked up under the visor, a gift from the local precinct. He had dropped many a freebie on the guys on the job, an on-the-cuff trip to the city on an anniversary or a birthday. No sweat. They knew one hand washed the other. The violation side of his chauffeur's license was as clean as a showgirl's shaven cunt.

Besides, the stop would get these *giboneys* off his upholstery for a while. That broad could go barf somewhere else if she had to, and the old man could sweat on the pavement instead of his back seat. He'd buy the old ladies an orangeade. Carmela would like that. Best of all, the kid could look at the animals for a bit. What the hell, she didn't have a father to take her around any-more. So he would go out of his way a little. Eddie had been a class guy.

He didn't make a big deal out of it. The Caddy snaked to the curb, and he flipped down the visor. The old ladies didn't respond in kind.

Catherine panicked, "Oh, my God, is it overheated?"

Nellie immediately bought Catherine's assessment. "We're go-ing to miss it. The whole ceremony. Is there a phone nearby? So we can call the Mayor?"

Philly gave them his cool cockpit laugh: "Hey, whoa, ladies. This Caddy could drive through the Amazon without getting overheated."

"Not to mention Memphis," Christy muttered.

"Yeah," said Philly, tentatively. Wow, he hoped this old dud wasn't taking a stroke. He sure was acting strange. "Look," he continued, "we have plenty of time, and I just thought we might stretch our legs and get a cool drink. I'm buying."

"That's a lovely thought," said Catherine, "but won't we be late?"

"We have to get to Manhattan, you know," cautioned Nellie.

Christ, how Philly hated these rube jobs. They made Manhat-tan sound like the end of the earth. "Ladies, I know the city. I take our councilman, Pete McEvoy, over to 'the Hall' a couple of times a month." He was sure "the Hall" would assuage them.

He then switched to his Saturday afternoon cartoon show host voice and lobbed an elaborate wink into the back seat. "Besides, Eileen can get a look at the animals and maybe a box of cracker-jacks to hold her. This is going to be a long, tough, tiring day on her. With everything going on, I mean." He encored the wink.

The ladies beamed at his fatherly concern and decided to set their fear aside. If worse came to worst, the Mayor probably would wait for them. He seemed like a nice man, especially for a Protestant.

Eileen wasn't so bending. Sissy held her arm till she could see discoloration, red bursting from the white center of her grip. It was like holding a live wire. Sissy believed she was about to attack Philly. She had her mother's intemperate mouth. Why was the worst always passed on? You begin to dislike your children when you see yourself in them.

"That's a fine idea, Philly. I could do with something cold." She hissed in Eileen's ear, "Easy, we'll talk about it outside." The girl's arm reluctantly relaxed, the tense muscles easing. "Christy, you're game for a cold drink, aren't you?" Sissy needed an ally.

The old man picked up the playful gleam in his daughter-in-law's eyes. "Oh, how you read my thoughts, girl, how you read my thoughts."

Sissy returned a dazzling, flirtatious smile. Christy would be happy to settle for a sweet soft drink to avoid enduring any more of this monkey's conversation.

When they got out of the limo, Philly, playing impresario, ran for the drinks. Sissy took the opportunity to caution Eileen. "Look, I know he's acting like a fool, but he means well."

"Oh, Mama, that's a lot of shit, and you know it."

Sissy bristled. "Save the barracks language for your friends. You're not on your own yet. It's your mother you're talking to."

The girl was unrepentant. "I didn't pick it up from the wind."

She had Sissy there. She had to do something about her language. She had allowed it to get out of hand a long time ago, but she reasoned you didn't command a cop's attention with Hallmark sayings. "Okay, you have a point," she soothed. "I'll work on my tongue, and you curb yours. Okay?" She fondled her daughter's hair.

"And please, Mom, don't throw up that 'I'm not on my own yet' stuff. You sound like your mother."

Sissy exploded, an involuntary "Christ!"

Eileen gave her a wide-eyed look of horror, and the two women broke up laughing. "I didn't mean I would reform immediately," said Sissy. "I'll swear off tomorrow." She had her daughter laughing now.

"He's just such a goop, Mom."

"I know. But I don't want any scenes today, not with everyone here. Especially not today." Sissy showed too much vulnerability, and Eileen's merry face crumbled into concern.

"You're going to be all right, aren't you, Mom? I promise I won't start anything. I'll even go and goo-goo over the bears."

Sissy was touched but also angered by Eileen's concern. She couldn't stand to have people looking at her as if she were going to go over the brink at the slightest provocation. But the child's look of love and worry stifled her temper. She wondered how bad she appeared to be back then. To her, it was just a rest, a hiatus, like Scarlett going back to Tara. "Look, I'm fine. I just don't want a scene. Your grandmothers wouldn't understand. They think Philly's the cat's pajamas."

"More the horse's . . ."

"Hey, now, we've got a bargain. Besides, you won't have to see him again."

"I only wish, Mom. But he's always hanging around the neighborhood. You can't help falling over him."

"I promise you won't see him again," Sissy reassured.

"Mom, I don't know how you can say that."

"Because," Sissy said, in a throaty parody of a blues singer, "he's a-goin' to Memphis." They had to bury their laughter as Philly came into view, awkwardly cradling six soft drinks.

"Here we go," boomed Philly. "A quick pick-me-up. And if you ladies would reach into my jacket pocket, there are straws. Two each for the ladies, so you don't mess up your lovely frocks."

No wonder Italians own the catering and undertaking trade, thought Sissy, they don't miss a flourish. Still in all, the stop and the sodas were nice gestures. Nellie and Catherine seemed delighted. She supposed one of the cushions of old age was that it didn't take much to turn your clock. That was something to look forward to. Whooping it up for the table scraps.

"Hey, Eileen, how about checking out those bears?" Philly invited. Sissy waited for the explosion. Instead, Eileen turned on her full beams.

"Sure, why not, Mr. . . . Philly."

Grinning at her mother, she reached over and took the astonished Philly's hand. His face became a solar explosion of embarrassment and delight. That daughter of hers would be all right. If you couldn't beat the chowderheads outright, stir them up.

Philly turned back as they started to walk away and asked without much conviction, "Does anyone else want to join us?" Sissy and Christy waved them on their way, while Nellie and Catherine nested on the pastoral scene.

"You two go off now and enjoy yourselves. You don't need the likes of us tagging along," pshawed Nellie.

Philly, enjoying his role with the girl completely for the first time all day, dropped his maitre d' seductiveness and didn't try to woo the women along. Nellie was flushed with the scene. Sissy wondered what sanitized wet dream was going on in her mother's head. Philly as a stand-in father? Perhaps as St. Joseph who didn't demand sexual rights as a husband, and Carmela overlooking the holy family? What a power that would make—Carmela and Nellie. Godmothers at bingo and church, regally dispensing their respective hands to be kissed by the grovelers. The Don-ess and her Irish *consiglieri*.

Catherine, though smitten, had business at hand. "Don't be too long, we have to get all the way to Manhattan. We'll keep an eye on the car," she added.

The orange drink didn't seem to be doing the trick for Christy. Sissy knew it was more than the hangover. Eddie was very special to his father. He saw Eddie as his sole genetic link, he felt the rest of his children had spit on his way of life.

That was what had made Sissy's life with Eddie so difficult— the way others perceived him. It was such a contradiction to her own perceptions, those she'd formed in their later years together anyway. But she could use Christy's eyes.

In truth, it wasn't only the outside vision that confused Sissy. Eddie was so inconsistent he baffled her. His work as a delegate inside the PBA was a perfect example. How often had she heard him and Christy talk schemes and tactics into the night? Tactics that ultimately would prove offensive to the entrenched Irish Mafia who ran the union and beneficial to the black and Hispanic cops. It wasn't the way to career-climb. His uncle Mike had warned Eddie he was bruising friendly toes that could eventually kick him upstairs. But that was too big an orbit for Eddie, his only concern was for the rank-and-file, those who put their asses on the line (one of his and Christy's pet phrases). Jesus, when he had campaigned for (and won) the right for black cops to wear Afros, Sissy could have made love to him till he was weak.

What was even more baffling to Sissy was that at every party they threw, there was a complement of black and Puerto Rican cops, and they seemed to adore Eddie. Maybe all cops were perverse. Their racial and ethnic humor slashed like a stiletto. They reveled in gore.

That was not Sissy's idea of fun or party conversation. She swore there was hidden malice behind it. Sadistic cats pawing a mouse to hide their real intentions. But Eddie never bought that.

"What you don't understand is that horsing around takes the heat out of what we see on the streets. In your enlightened head, did you ever think how a black or PR cop feels when eighty percent of the arrests we, meaning them, too, make are of their own people? Like hell you did.

"We try to make believe we don't notice. So we say scum is scum. It's a lot easier. What would you do? Make a pronouncement in the stationhouse: 'Don't feel bad, fellows, your people are only wall-to-wall in the slammer because they were born black or Puerto Rican in a racist society?' Is that what you'd do?

"What would you tell them? They lucked out, they were chosen for the job on a quota system? Don't panic, fellows. You're the same as some ding-dong who slapped his salami in some old yenta's hand on the Canarsie line.

"It might surprise you, but if it wasn't for the white guys on the job, more busted blacks and PRs would be having what we call 'accidents' at the hands of their own. Do you think that's weird? Well, it isn't. When I bust an Irish punk, I lean so hard on the sonnuvabitch he wishes he was bagged in Harlem where he could get his Miranda on a platter, instead of my Irish foot up his shanty ass.

"It works the other way, too. You know Tommy, who we call 'Gentle Ben,' because he's such a big, lovable bear of a guy? Yeh, you know him. Black and gentle, with four daughters who are a credit to him. You could play handball off their dresses, they're so starched. Well (Sissy didn't want to hear, he was moving in for the kill with his menacing finger), he busted a father of a nine-month-old black girl last week. You know what for? Do you?" he screamed. "For fingering the kid in the crib. Think of a big black finger going up a nine-month-old vagina! You got the picture?"

Sissy wanted to throw up.

"Well, Tommy took his nightstick and broke every one of the guy's fuckin' fingers. He smashed his hands so bad they're up for retirement. And he was just warming up when we stopped him. He could have lost his job because of that scum, the livelihood for his wife and beautiful kids."

Sissy wanted to offer that the father was sick, but she didn't dare. Eddie was too close to treating her like an Irish punk.

"But he won't. You know why? Because the Captain, the white, Irish, and, in your book, nigger-hating Captain, saved Tommy's ass. He put the pervert out on the fire escape, outside the window in the interrogation room, put his hands on the sill and cut the window sash. That's how the ambulance doctor found him. His hands pinned and crushed under the window. And you know why the Captain did it? Because Tommy was one of his own, not a nigger!"

So much of it went like that. Eddie believed anyone who didn't work the streets knew nothing about life. Intellectuals and politicians were "hump-de-humps who pull their yo-yos in ivory towers." Liberals were "frauds who isolate themselves with their money, while they tell some working stiff to put his kid on a school bus." Priests were not even to be considered. "You think I'm going to listen to some guy who never had to make a buck in life, never had to put bread on the table, and never sired a son?"

Yet Eddie had a lot going for him in ingots. He was generous to a fault. Not just with her and the kids, but with everyone. When it came to the neighborhood or his friends, he had an old-fashioned barn-raising mentality. She couldn't count how many apartments he had painted for newly married friends, how many times he had moved furniture in rented U-hauls or engineered "buys" for people on a whole range of items. He was always organizing things—picnics, bus outings, baseball leagues for the neighborhood kids, trooping legions of them off to Coney Island and never losing one of their socks, never mind one of them. It was easy to see why he had been a good Marine.

Good Jesus, he had even played Santa Claus every year at the American Legion post. And not only to the kids. It was Eddie who collected funds for presents for the old-timers in the neighborhood. Wobbly widows' and widowers' eyes glistened with tears as he dispensed turkeys, sweaters, scarves, and booze for those who still cut up occasionally. The gleam in their eyes was only distinguished from the kids' by its wetness. She never knew how heartfelt it was, but did it matter? The recipients of his kindness never questioned Eddie.

Only Sissy. She began to be wary of his little touches. Sissy wanted his flashes to be stoked by an inner fire. Maybe that was their undoing? In their respective emotional fields, they were both absolutists. Warring gods struggling over the future mold of the world.

It was a nice, comforting, cosmic notion: failure in the firmament. No. It was not heavenly, it was smug arrogance. "Unbending," unable to accept the good with the bad. Only one will could prevail. A refusal to adjust. Buy my philosophy, or I'm emotionally packing. Not gods shaping a world really, but obdurate children refusing to recognize any merit in each other's mound of Play-Do.

What Sissy could not dismiss even now was the intensity, more, the quality (that wasn't too fine a word for it) of their lovemaking. She couldn't buy all those tales that were tossed around at her feminist meetings. It couldn't be possible that so many women were unhappy in bed. They made lovemaking sound as arduous as cleaning the oven before the invention of Easy-Off. She wrote it off to anger, getting even.

That was where men were most vulnerable. The barest suggestion that their pricks weren't as magical as Jack's beanstalk drove them to despair. It had to be that. If it wasn't striking back, if all of them were telling the truth, her loss was unfathomable.

Eddie had given her such an erotic legacy. She couldn't shake his presence. He was like a remnant of a cherished teaching she had put aside but couldn't completely abandon.

But it wasn't truly pleasure she was seeking the one time she strayed, it was revenge. Revenge for the things he said and did with other women. Especially the things she imagined he said to them in bed. If he had fucked them mutely, coldly, out of a yen for strangeness, she might not have retaliated. But that was not Eddie's style. She knew her man. He was a wooer, a devotee of details. She knew the women were projects to become immersed in, like . . . like playing Santa Claus. Flourishes had to be added. The Eddie touch.

What tortured her was that she was convinced he had made

love to other women during that special time. It drove her to avenging despair. She wanted to think that was reserved for her; to be made love to during her time of shame and terror, her period.

It was Sissy's time of shame anyway. She panicked when her menstrual cycle started and she found her underpants full of blood. She had suffered from a kidney ailment as a child, and blood in the urine had been one of the symptoms. She thought she would bleed to death when her first period came.

During the first months of their marriage she had kept Eddie at arm's length in bed while she was bleeding. But he persisted, with gentle fondling and kissing. She was astonished that she could be so aroused in such a distasteful state, but she was. He catered the entire thing, putting one of his old khaki towels from the service under her to protect the bedding.

She was mortified not only by the blood, but the flagrant smells of strange discharge spiced by her excitement. The love-making proved more exciting than when she came fresh from her bath because her transformation was so much greater. She never felt more like a woman, more wanted. What she had painfully felt all those years was false. Eddie revealed that there was no need for shame. Indeed, her cunt was magical during this inter-lude, a scented, spell-weaving cauldron.

He even got her over her embarrassment when they had fin-ished. Instead of slinking off to the bathroom to wash off the evidence, he would stand naked and blood-spattered in the room, holding up his red-stained penis and testicles and affecting a southern accent as he staggered about: "Ma'am, it was the Yankees at Chickamauga. A cannonball right in the balls. But General Lee was proud of me." He not only laughed her embar-rassment away, she subsequently became proud of how much he was decorated by her. He was her canvas, hers, to spatter pas-sionately and lie back and admire.

She could have forgiven the rest, but playing out their private tableau with some cheap cop groupie was something she couldn't bear. It was ironic, she thought, that it was his incredible tender-ness with her that moved her to stab him with another man.

She thought about offering Christy one of the Valium from her purse. But as understanding as Christy was, that would be stretching the generation gap. Christy's Irish worried about mortality, Sissy's about madness. A twentieth-century limited advance.

She sidled up to him. "How are you holding, Pop?"

"If that ass were struck dumb, I'd feel a lot better. If he was any dumber, he'd be considered presidential timber." Eddie was his son all right. The humorous swagger was the same.

"It won't be long now. Maybe when we get to City Hall, they'll offer us some refreshments."

"You mean our progressive Mayor? I wouldn't bank on it, Theresa darling. If he does, you can bet it will be white wine. What do they call those watered-down abominations?"

"Spritzers."

"Ah yes, spritzers. It sounds like how he runs the city—airy bubbles. I wonder if some future historian will chart the decline of the great cities from the time when the politicians switched from scotch to spritzers.

"You know, Quill once said he was a union man, not a labor leader. He said the difference was a union man ate too much roast beef and drank too much scotch at political dinners. A lot of know-nothings thought he was a Kerry clown, but he was one astute sonnuvabitch."

"Who knows, Pop? There may be an old bottle of scotch left around from Bill O'Dwyer's time."

"Well, if there is, that would be the only thing he didn't cart off to Mexico with him. At least, we can be thankful for one thing—it isn't Wednesday."

Sissy was perplexed. "Wednesday?"

"Yes, we can be grateful Hizzoner will be at home, not soft-shoeing at some musical matinee."

Sissy laughed. "Oh, come on, he isn't that bad."

"That's the problem, Theresa. None of them are *that* bad. They're just pretty and bland. They're like the television they use so well. Perfumed narcotics. Not really bad. You watch them long enough and you doze off peacefully. The sadness is that by the time the people snap out of it, everything that once meant something has been trivialized. Public relations has replaced political philosophy."

Christy wasn't as harsh as his son, but all the same it was there. God, how he must miss Eddie!

"If you keep that up, Pop, I'll hop a cab and abandon you to Philly."

He realized he might have taken the soft slide into self-pity and checked it. "Jesus, don't," he mockingly begged, "he might cart me off to Memphis."

Sissy squeezed his arm. "That's more like it."

"Sorry, sweetheart, to be sounding like the end of the world. Last night's fire went out, and I belabored my point."

"Which was?"

"Hire an actor for Mayor, and you get a musical comedy administration."

"Do you really think he's all that bad?"

He gave her a broad grin that relieved her. "Not really, honey. He just needed two more years out of town to get the kinks out."

Catherine and Nellie, slightly out of earshot of their conversation, suspiciously started to inch toward them. Spotting their reconnoiter, Sissy offered, "Do you want to go for a walk, Pop?"

"No, I better not. I'll stand vigil with them over the car. Besides, if I saunter off, Catherine will swear I'll be swigging a shot of the balloon man's helium. You go get a breather for yourself."

Though she hated to desert him, Sissy didn't need any further urging when she saw them closing in. She walked toward the circular pond where the seals were cavorting. It looked so cool, with an occasional misty spray from the fountain blowing teasingly near the onlookers surrounding the low, wrought-iron fence. She loved seals, she had signed petitions for their protection. They looked so elegant diving, like the girl in the Jantzen swimsuit ad.

She could see Philly and Eileen off to her right, eating peanuts by the bear enclosure. She could hear the lions groaning in the distance, the sound owing more to stomach disorders than majesty. She didn't care for lions, their kingship was lost on her. She hated their foul breath, it was male-heightened. She imagined that being devoured by a lion was similar to being mounted by a man after an evening of dining, drinking, and smoking. Not sexuality, but suffocation by another carnivore.

It had been a long time since she had been at the zoo. She couldn't remember when. She had never visited much as a girl. Mickey's idea of tigers, bears, and lions were creatures with numbers on their uniforms that you bet on. The closest Mickey came to the bucolic life was the racetrack at Saratoga, where there was action under the elms. He thought civilization ended with the pavement and the disappearance of late-night newsstands. Sissy agreed. The summer home Eddie bought terrified her on the nights he stayed out late or didn't return from work at all. She had mastered the malicious gossip of the ticking clock in the city, but the tattooing of the crickets was impossible.

When she was allowed freedom as a teenager, she didn't come to the park much either. The park was the cruising ground for those bubble-headed, gum-snapping sluts from commercial high schools who were pursued by toughs with vaseline-lubricated heads. Greased phalluses in pegged pants.

She was once such a nice girl.

She had doubts about her niceness now. Eileen was right about her language. It was shameless. She would never have thought of using such language as a girl. Being around Eddie and his friends had coarsened her. Coarse. That was a word that once meant something to her. Maybe experience just toughens your tongue. Or was it that "going to bed with a boy" just didn't apply anymore? "Getting fucked" was more like it.

But the last thing she wanted was to be considered coarse, especially by her own daughter. As she reached for her cigarettes, she knew that was another thing she had to work on. She once had tennis lungs, as white as her shorts. Now the color of both, her lungs and her talk, was that of shit.

So much to work on.

She wondered if she had the energy. If she did, who would notice? More precisely, who did she care to notice? Maybe it was a waste, like cleaning the graffiti off a subway car. The spirit of the scrawls would remain.

No. Eileen would notice. Dammit, she herself would notice.

Sissy looked back over her shoulder at Christy, leaning against the car, and her eyes got wet. Maybe it wasn't Brooklyn you couldn't escape from, but the roast beef and the scotch. The notion didn't displease her.

Standing by the guard rail to the seal pond, Sissy started to register the parent and child pairings. It reinforced what she already knew. Without exception, infants in strollers and toddlers were accompanied by women, while children who were gracefully mobile and verbally graduated beyond goo-goos were with their fathers. It was typical of them. Men. They were like the UN Security Council. They didn't recognize half-formed states.

Once again a connection pleased her. Maybe it wasn't the

Valium. Her mind might just be peaking, matching the import of the day. That excited her. She might pull off the whole day without a hitch. As they said on TV, she was up for the game.

Certainly, the thought wasn't spurious. Eddie was that way. Not with Billy, but with Eileen. It was as if Eileen was redundant —he had done it before.

Eddie was attentive and charming during the prideful flush of Eileen's infancy, and, of course, years later when she developed social graces. The dog days, the sandbox period, were delegated to Sissy.

Much later, when she began to dissect their time together, she realized the advent of Eileen was when Eddie started to play around. Back then, she'd thought the staying out late or not coming home at all ("I shacked out on Sal's couch") had to do with his disenchantment with the job. He was still on a solo then, not playing by departmental rules. He raged at what he saw— the after-hours bars that couldn't be touched, the bookmakers and the policymakers whose work miraculously disappeared after the busts, and the strange testimony of the arresting officers that allowed a legal loophole for a shyster to spring his dirty client. He still had the guts then to turn his back in anger on an envelope when it was offered by the precinct bagman. My sweet, sweet God, she thought, he had even raged against the disparity in treatment of black and white prisoners. No wonder she never thought of other women. She loved him blindly for the purity of his anger.

If you could hold on to them during that period, as Sissy had, they could become good fathers. Eddie had. Even those who strayed, eventually came back to their paternal duty with relish. Their phrase was "when the kids became people." The male elitist tone of that scalded Sissy. "When the kids became people!" Just what did fathers think they were before? Vises that stretched daddy's pleasure box?

But it was true. She knew that as she watched the fathers in the zoo. "Gee, the kids are company now," Eddie used to say, meaning not pains in the ass. Charming, literate, witty reflections of himself. Mommy was the governess who brought them through the mewling stage to present them to daddy later as a "chip off the old block" or "Daddy's little girl."

Sissy suspected men knew what they had done. All the lavish activity with the kids later was testimony to that. She looked around her at the father-squired children festooned with balloons and pennants, groaning under the ingestion of pop, crackerjacks, and ice cream. The world always worked the same for men. Everyone could be bought for a price. Grease was their form of love, and maybe they were right. Ask any kid to remember who walked the floor with him, or who took him to the circus and the ballpark. Sissy knew memories of kickbacks would ace those of colic anytime.

Sissy also knew men's passion for cameras was part of their guilt. The photos of happy times would always be evidence, no matter how bogus, that daddy was bountiful. The men in the zoo carried cameras (Eddie had, too), while the mothers were equipped with bottles of formula. What would the mothers pull out ten years hence—a stained bib? No, daddies were oriental in their belief that images reflected true history.

"They're something to watch, aren't they?"

Until she turned and saw the man smiling at her, Sissy wasn't sure whom the comment was meant for.

To erase her doubt, he qualified: "The seals, I mean."

She hadn't really been watching them, but she turned toward the pool as though commanded. "Yes, they're very nice," she said mechanically.

"Yes, they are," he replied, moving closer to her, "so much more natural than people. Don't you agree?"

Something scary in her stirred, and she tried to check it. He was imposing, looking down at her. He had to be close to six feet, six.

"Don't you agree?" he asked again.

Sissy felt she was being badgered. She mustn't panic. He looked as if he could be a nature lover with his full pepper-and-salt beard. She decided to be innocuous.

"I suppose so. They sure seem to be having a lot of fun in this heat."

"I think it must be their lack of inhibitions." He moved even closer, it seemed as if he were going to smother her with his beard. She tried to back up, but the guard rail checked her. What kind of casual talk was this? "Natural." "Inhibitions." She realized he was wearing a bush jacket open at the neck, exposing a cloud of white chest hair. Yes, he just might be a nature lover. He certainly didn't talk or look Brooklyn to Sissy. But that was faulty, old-fashioned. Cops and hardhats were so hairy these days they looked like rock stars. Don't panic, she cautioned herself, that business is over.

He placed his hand on the rail, closing one avenue of escape. She felt her breath cut off involuntarily. Her legs clamped shut like a dry cleaner's press. Hot vapors started to fill her lungs. It was like after Billy died all over again, when everything spooked her. No, it wasn't. Get hold. She unsealed her compressed lips. "Whatever. They sure know how to beat the heat."

"You don't really believe it's that casual, do you?"

She swore he was trying for a seductive tone, as he negotiated the few inches left between them.

After Billy's death, she began to view men as a menacing breed. She became wary of the whole species. She gave them room whenever possible. But there were the subways, with the cramming in of bodies. It wasn't the bodies per se but the isolated member she thought she could feel seeking her out. That's when her breath began to cut off.

She felt like a little girl with just enough knowledge to be frightened. At that age when the admonitions not to take candy from strangers became vaguely understandable.

But she thought she had beaten all that. Until now.

The tall man brought the panic back. She wanted to run, to clear her constricting lungs. But she didn't. She hadn't willed her way back onto the subway to go haywire in an open park.

It was the pressure of the day. It was the heat and the Valium. It was everything but the subway again.

"You don't, do you?" he prodded again.

"Don't what?" she croaked.

"Believe they're so casual."

"Please. I'm hot and confused. Whatever you say. I don't feel like talking."

"Talk is never essential," he went on in a hypnotic monotone, "at the best moments, the most natural moments in life."

She felt herself shrinking, eroding defenselessly into anklets and Mary Janes. Her eyes darted for her mother. Her mother would sense her dilemma, even at a distance. But Nellie was engrossed in conversation with Catherine, while Christy walked a nervous sentry around them.

"Look how free they are." He started to motion with his middle finger, the finger that . . . "The way they're so slippery and shiny, going in and out, in and out of the water."

She wanted to beg. *Please, mister, leave me alone, or I'll call my mother* was surfacing to her lips.

Then she saw Eileen and Philly, heading back toward her, toward the car.

"In and out, in and out," he repeated. "It's so natural." His finger was coming closer to her face. Oh, my God, her . . .

Eileen and Philly walked past, not looking at her, headed directly to the car. She wanted to scream, but she didn't want to frighten the child. Eileen had been so worried.

But why didn't that other ass look her way just once? Maybe, just maybe, she could bring herself to signal.

The man took the back of Sissy's neck. Ever so firmly but without pain, he turned her head back toward the pool.

"That one over there is the one that fascinates me. Look at the way he dives into the holes in his house. He has a great primordial instinct."

Her eyes welled up. She forced her head away and saw Eileen walking alone toward the car. She retraced her daughter's steps. Philly was standing alone, watching her, looking baffled. Could he see the tears in her eyes?

Apparently not. He joined the others at the car, then disappeared around the back of the vehicle. She was lost. In a moment, she was going to scream.

The man had her hemmed in now with both arms. His arms were so long it would appear to an onlooker Sissy had room to maneuver. A taller person bending over a shorter one for a better view of the pool.

He was now whispering in her hair. "I like the way that one makes noises, don't you? The sound has a ring of ecstasy to it. Not only him. Listen to the sounds around you. Wonderful release and freedom."

Against her will, Sissy's ears responded to the cacophony of animal climaxes. She felt filthy, as if she were wiretapping an orgy.

"Wonderful, isn't it? So liberating. We're all capable—you, me, everyone—of making such sounds if we all let ourselves go."

Sissy was about to add to the primal screams, when she heard the unmistakable, nasal, urban stiletto of Philly's voice insinuate itself.

"Are you ready, Mrs. Sullivan? We'd better leave if we're going to make Manhattan."

Without unlocking Sissy, the man turned toward Philly with disdain. He towered over him.

"Whatya say, Mrs. Sullivan? The traffic will be building up."

Sissy thought she managed a nod. The man stared at Philly.

"Maybe the lady likes it here."

"No, she don't," replied Philly, bouncing on the balls of his feet, with his hands folded behind his back.

"Really?" said the man, mocking him. "Who are you to say?"

"Who the fuck are you?" countered Philly.

The man dropped his hands from the railing and pulled himself up to full size, facing Philly.

Philly's jaunty motion was slowed by intimidation.

The man affected a street accent. "Who the fuck are you? Who writes your lines, buddy, the Fonz?"

Looking at Philly's face, Sissy suddenly felt the man had won her.

Philly paused, then slowly took his hands from behind his back, displaying a tire iron. He rhythmically tapped it into the palm of his open hand. "I got your Fonzie swingin' in about two seconds, motherfucker."

Sissy felt the man's hand on her back, pushing her toward Philly. She reached out for him, and he pulled her into him with his free hand.

"Hey, fella," the man began, comradely, "I was just talking to the lady."

Philly menacingly hefted his equalizer. "Hey, stick it, you hear? You have two seconds to join your buddies, the monkeys, in a jerk-off contest. Two seconds while you still got something to pull."

Philly moved the tire iron backward as the man, feigning dignity, fled along the perimeter of the rail. Sissy started to cry in silent relief, but Philly checked her with his pocket handkerchief.

"Come on, tighten up. You don't want the kid to see you like this."

It worked. She stemmed the flow. His smile and nod told her her eye makeup was still intact.

"I don't know how to thank you," she began.

But he would have no more. With a chivalric wave of his arm, spiced by a grin and a wink, he dismissed her effort. "For what? You're neighborhood, ain't ya?"

*B*ACK IN THE CAR, Nellie realized something was wrong with her daughter. Sissy had that look, as if she were yearning to be somewhere far away, like a child who believes physical transference is a solution to a problem. Nellie knew the look all too well and it frightened her.

It was the same look Sissy affected when she wouldn't come out of her room after Billy's death, when she was on those pills. Nellie had been against those drugs from the beginning. She wanted a daughter, not a zombie. What was the sense of having come to the New World if that was the best they had to offer? Nellie loved America's gadgetry—her toaster, her electric percolator, her self-defrosting refrigerator. Surely, the country had something better to offer than numbing pills. It was terrible to be ignorant in such matters: mental illness. Especially your daughter's.

But what could *she* do? She was ill-prepared for it. Damn ignorance! And everyone had been against her. The doctor, Eddie, Catherine. Christy was, of course, noncommittal. She didn't expect more from him. It wasn't Christy's fault. That's just the way men were. At least, he hadn't made a nuisance of himself. All he offered was simple self-absolution: "I'm not good at such things. The rest of you decide." Nellie swore that if Pontius Pilate had been a woman, Christ would have been saved.

If Mickey had been alive, it would have been worse. He would have filled everyone's head with his high-flown, fancy, silly opinions. Barroom diagnoses would have run rampant: "Jimmy Cosgrove has a sister who had the same . . ." His cronies would have given him cures just as they gave him those worthless tips on the horses. And in the end he would have gone off and gotten drunk until it was all over. Sissy would have been treated like an apartment that needed painting. And that would have crushed her.

In such times no one is much help, she thought. Everyone you talked to had a similar case somewhere in their families, and they all held out home-tested recipes. It was "change of life" or "the death of her father and her son so close together." Those were the most sensible ones. The others ranged from "She would be fine as rain with a hysterectomy" to "a chiropractor could loosen her tense nerves." A chiropractor!

Nellie knew her daughter too well to go for such nonsense. Her daughter had been on the verge of something before Mickey's and Billy's deaths. They certainly didn't help, but Nellie had spotted the trouble long before. Something was sour in that house. You could smell it, like boiled cabbage.

Nellie knew it had to do with the marriage. Sissy (Nellie couldn't help loving her for it) expected so much from life. Her father had convinced her early that she was special. It wasn't such a bad thing, she was so exciting to watch as a child. Even though she often sided with Mickey against Nellie. There was no denying it, she wasn't run-of-the-mill. The nuns, the neighbors, everyone noticed it. It excited Nellie that she had sprung from her.

Sissy's charm and specialness reflected back on Nellie through small compliments. Nellie wasn't used to pats on the head, even once removed. She had no delusions about herself. Her strength was rock-hard sense, and that never brightened a room. She kept her family and the ledger in some semblance of order even under the most trying circumstances. She was proud of that. Mickey and Sissy were fond of flashing full sail to the neighbors, but it was Nellie who launched them. Good, solid, secure, dull Nellie. Her self-estimate wasn't tinged with pity. It's hard to think of oneself as merry and charming when the most frequent compliment bestowed is "God bless her, she can work like a horse."

But her constitution couldn't help her daughter. She'd even tried the church for advice. Fat help they were. "I'll offer up my mass for her this morning, Mrs. McKenna." "I'll keep her in my prayers." "Let's all make a novena for her speedy recovery." The only thing they didn't pull out was the Lourdes water. Nellie had no truck with miracle workers. They sounded like a holy version of Mickey's silly schemes. Miracles were all right for the kids in catechism class. They made nice bygone stories. But Nellie hadn't seen any miracles come down the pike in her day. God knows, she could have used a minor one or so.

She should have stuck to her guns. But they all were against her, and they frightened her with the alternative. Heavy medication to get Sissy back on her feet or a long stay in a hospital. After all, there were the neighbors.

The threat of gossip muted her. Not for herself. But the family would be brought into it. Her family's lives scattered like crumbs for all those sniping birds to peck. That would never do. She kept a tight fist around her family. For more years than she could remember she had covered Mickey's bum checks with a minimum of fuss and propped him up so that at least he was a fairly presentable alcoholic, not a fall-down drunk. She'd be damned if she would let them at her only child.

But it was a mistake. She should have toughed it out. The medication did get Sissy going again, but Nellie was sure it never reached the thing or things that made her sick. It was like not moving the refrigerator when you cleaned the kitchen floor.

Catherine had a heyday with Nellie during the illness. She was such an "expert." After all, she'd say, wasn't her father a pharmacist, the rare Irish professional man? "Dr. Tierney," as she was fond of calling him.

Sure, didn't Nellie and everyone who had the sense know his Jew assistant was the one who ran the drugstore. God forgive her, but with all his airs "Dr. Tierney" couldn't put a patch on a real doctor's ass. Mickey said his only claim to genius was that he had found an educated Jew without money.

But to hear Catherine tell it, she was the fount of knowledge about medicine, with her talk of Valium and such, and she was all for the drugs. "The child's system is just out of whack. It happens to women of her age, even those who have gone through a lot less than she has. What else could it be, with the beautiful home she's got? It's a common cure. I heard the doctor speak of it often."

Nellie wasn't so sure of all that—the stuff about the beautiful home life. No denying Eddie gave Sissy a castle, and Nellie didn't make light of that. After shaking out Mickey's pockets to scrimp together enough for occasional odds and ends for her own house, she respected a good provider. But she didn't know if everything else was all sweetness and light. Eddie was always a bit of a ladies' man. He had the looks for it. And from phone calls to Sissy, she knew there were nights—too many nights, if you asked Nellie—that he didn't find his way home. That was all right if you were married to a Mickey. You knew he would be asleep alone in a booth in some bar. That's one thing you didn't have to worry about with Mickey. Maybe the only thing. If it came down to Marilyn Monroe or another round with the boys, Marilyn would be paying her own cab fare home. Come to think of it (Nellie allowed herself an inward chuckle), if Mickey left with her, Marilyn would still have to pick up the cab fare.

But Mickey was the exception, not the rule. Nellie knew men strayed, and as they got older, it got worse. The old fools. They thought the bulge in their pants would keep the coffin lid from closing. Nellie thought she saw some of that in Eddie with his fancy wardrobe and jewelry. Not that Sissy complained. Indeed, the only reason she ever said he was not at home was when Nellie pressed a dinner invitation on them or called to say she was thinking of dropping by.

Then Sissy always tacked on an excuse. A cops' golf outing or bowling tournament or a poker game. "You know how they are when they get together, Mom. They're probably so paralyzed they all flopped in one of the guys' houses. To tell you the truth, I like it better that way. I hate Eddie to drive in that condition, especially being on the job."

Nellie knew the sound of sad, brave tunes all too well. She had spent a lifetime whistling pardons for Mickey.

She wished she and Sissy were able to talk more openly. Maybe she could have told her daughter not to expect too much of husbands. The trick was to make it endurable and then you could survive. You just had to stick in there till they calmed down or were laid down, like Mickey. To outlast their madness, that was the ticket. And in most cases you did outlast them. Nellie could count. She didn't see many widowers tending graves with flowers.

But how could she approach Sissy on the sex thing? Maybe Sissy could do that with Eileen, maybe the new generation. But her to Sissy—never. It wasn't only the fault of the old-timers, as everyone thought. She knew how Sissy looked at her. That was the problem with know-it-all kids, they thought they invented it. They were so smug they thought the only reason you ever opened your legs was to have them. Well, Nellie could give her daughter some news. She and Mickey had had their day. She wondered what her daughter would think of her mother making love in the woods on a camping trip, jaybird naked in broad daylight. And did she know her father adored Nellie's legs? They were a sight better than most of the ones Nellie saw parading today. And where did her daughter think she got her own? From the wind?

But kids never think their parents were ever young. Just someone to put the food on the table and the clothes on their backs. Like they were so special God gave them a maid and butler at birth.

Well, Mickey didn't always have a glass to his mouth, and Nellie didn't always need support stockings. The food on the table and the clothes on the back had done that. She and her husband had their times. And after a while Nellie wasn't shy about it. Mickey made such a fuss over her legs she kept a pair of high heels next to the bed, so that after they made love, she could slip into them, instead of slopping about in slippers. Naked, she'd parade in her heels while he watched her every move, and she loved his tracking eyes. "Christ, you could dance in the Copa line," he used to say. Kids didn't want to hear you were once young. Mothers came from heaven equipped with varicose veins.

She wished she had an open channel to her daughter. She thought she could have helped her with her marriage. The idea was not to resurrect the honeymoon but to adapt. As long as the men didn't stray in their own backyards, you could pretend it wasn't happening. Embarrassing you in the neighborhood was another matter, but she was sure Eddie didn't do that or she would have heard of it. Oh, would she ever! Some "well-meaning" friend would have dropped it on her on the way home from church. Not for gossip, mind you, but "for the sake of the kids" or some such. God would have to die *every* Friday of the year to cleanse the human race.

Besides, Nellie didn't think it was the worst thing in the world when a marriage got a little dull. Who would want to spend a lifetime madly in love? It was foolish. Like the way you thought of God when you received your First Communion. Nobody could go through life like that without being committed. No, she didn't mean that. It just popped into her head. She looked over at her strained daughter and squeezed her hand, by way of apology.

But she knew the slip was darkly accurate. Her daughter was like Mickey. Nothing was ever enough. How hard it was to live with such people. There was never peace. Every day had to be greeted as if it was a telegram bearing good news. Everything had to be touched up, fussed with, embroidered. Nellie knew she knew more about life than either of them, but they would never admit it. Life. Nellie had the sense not to curry-comb a mutt every day.

That's why Mickey's drinking, for the most part, was tolerable. It dissipated his lunacy and energy—away from Nellie. When he went out at night, Nellie's day began. She could feel her body relax, as when dinner guests whom you're pledged to please depart. It was then Nellie could get into her robe and scan the papers for sales ads and watch her television shows.

Sissy always criticized her for watching so much television. "It's all so phony," she'd say. "It has nothing to do with real life."

Nellie knew that well. That's why it was such a blessing. The one thing Nellie didn't need after her day was more reality. Like a dose of epsom salts when you had diarrhea.

The nice thing about her shows was that they had endings, conclusions—not like life. People were either reunited or divorced, rescued or murdered. One way or another, it was over. As neat as a good spring cleaning. Nobody in the shows went to bed setting the alarm, knowing the same misery would begin again with the whistle of the morning kettle.

But you couldn't tell that to Sissy. When Sissy watched television, it was Channel 13. Public television. She tried to get Nellie into that. The ballets were nice (they reminded her of Sissy's childhood dance classes), but for the rest, you could keep it. Who in her right mind (that slip again) would watch shows about people starving, people with cancer, children retarded or on drugs, or politicians lying about how they had answers to everything? Worse yet, the channel was always asking you to send them money. For what? Rubbing your nose into God's failures? They would never get a dime of Nellie's.

Sissy just never knew how to put her feet up and relax. Everything had to be such a to-do. Just like her father. That was all right if you kept it to yourself. But both of them insisted everyone else should be on the same wacky wave length. They were like camp counselors who thought everybody else was a bored child.

Sissy nearly drove her crazy when she and Eddie first got married. Nellie didn't have a Sunday to herself. If it wasn't dinner, it was a drive to Coney Island or Sheepshead Bay. And when the children came along, it was worse. God knows, Nellie loved her grandchildren, but she didn't want to monitor their every crawl, toddle, step, and tooth. It wasn't as if she hadn't seen it before. So gone were her Sundays. Her best day, really. Mass and some good talk outside the church and on the walk home. Plus the best breakfast of the week. She didn't have to watch Mickey push his parched scrambled eggs around the plate like a bullied child. If they ran a bit, it was an excuse for a beer to settle his stomach. "Those goddamn things are raw. Dammit, you did it again. You turned my stomach." The compromise was a can of beer and a slice of dry toast. The urinelike smell of the open beer always ruined Nellie's breakfast.

But Sundays were different. Mickey's Saturday night hangover dictated that he be at the Knights of Columbus chapter early. It was their biggest day. Flushed-faced men lining the bar like rows of radishes. Great patriots, all. Nellie often wondered how many loyal knights there would be if there were no privileged drinking on Sundays before the bars opened. It seemed to her that that's what pledged their allegiance. It didn't matter though. It got Mickey out of the house, and Sundays stretched before her as calm and as peaceful as an open field.

It was the one day she pampered herself. Two sunnyside eggs, a couple of strips of bacon, fresh seeded rolls, and a slice of calves' liver. The liver was extravagant and dented her budget, but it was worth every golden ounce for what it did for her spirits. When she was a greenhorn and lived out in a doctor's house, the doctor had his slice of liver with eggs every Sunday. To Nellie it was the most lavish thing she had ever seen, the epitome of being a well-to-do Yank. She vowed that one day she would have such a Sunday breakfast. After all, if you had to leave your home and your father, there should be some compensation in the new land. Her Sunday morning liver made her feel more American than her citizenship papers.

But that had gone out the window when Sissy and Eddie got married. Sundays became another day, like all the others, to be on the go. No more leisurely breakfasts and no more stretches in bed with the Sunday paper, the very best day for sales ads. The kids didn't mean any harm. They probably thought they were going out of their way to please her. They probably were sacrificing their own Sundays. Nellie was newly married once. She knew what Sunday afternoons meant then. It was nice to do it, well, when you weren't supposed to. So everyone was losing something.

No one ever took time to try to figure out other people's lives. It amazed her that the young thought growing older meant you were bored all the time, that your life needed cluttering. She never knew where they picked that up. Probably public television.

There was no correcting the strange notions people got into their heads. The problem, as Nellie saw it, was that people were always presuming their feelings were held by everybody else. It was pretty nose-in-the-air stuff: as they went, so went the world. Since Sissy loved to celerabte her own birthday, she thought Nellie couldn't wait to blow out candles either. Nellie could wait. She didn't think life was any holiday, and it was foolish to pretend it was. Nellie had gone through life on her knees—not thanking God, but scrubbing.

She couldn't blame the girl though. Her father jammed her head with most of his wild notions. That man could shame a stone. If you had the parish priest for dinner, he'd start a football pool. And when Mickey had the thirst on him, it meant everyone within earshot was equally parched. "I bet everyone would love a drink." How many times had Nellie heard that line, and in how many places? It was the cure-all to escape traffic jams, launch occasions from birth to death, and all that fell between. It was the eye-opener that got you going in the morning, or the nightcap that got you down to sleep. It opened constricted stomachs and dammed rampaging bowels (blackberry brandy for diarrhea).

Even the dog wasn't immune. When Kelly (a bitch, Mickey had named her after the temporary job agency, the Kelly Girls) was off her feed, a veterinarian was never considered. Mickey's cure was to soak white bread in red wine and put it in her bowl. "That will bring her around." Of course, it was really what would bring Mickey around, and he knew in his heart that if Kelly could speak instead of bark, she'd say, "I bet everyone would like a drink." Even the mongrel wasn't immune to takeover.

It was senseless to try to change people. Nellie knew that. Besides, it wasn't her job anyway. If doctors and priests, with all their warnings and admonishments, had failed, what chance did Nellie have? Them with their fine education, clothes, cars, offices, and pulpits couldn't dent an ear. What could Nellie with her brogue and housedress expect? If she had said to Sissy, "Listen, because I'm your mother," it would have been worse. "Mother," to a headstrong child, was a dare. It was her daughter's loss. Nellie knew a thing or two about living with a high-flying man.

Yes, even the sex thing. If Eddie was hanging his hat where he shouldn't be, it wasn't the end of the world. There were still the kids and the lovely home to consider. But you couldn't tell Sissy about that—narrowbacks thought property was their due. They acted like the gentry in Ireland.

Though she sometimes longed for better, Nellie would rather be in her own railroad flat than a guest in a palace. That's where she wanted to be laid out, not in some fancy funeral parlor where a mourning neighbor couldn't even get a cup of tea. And why not? It was her home and full of memories. Love once lived there, a child grew there, and the curtains and slipcovers came from her hand, not from a department store where you pick your home from a pattern book.

And did those rooms know laughter! Gales of it when she was young. She would never let an upholsterer near her chairs or sofa. As battered as they were, they were shaped by the people who had made up her life. A spread arm on a living room chair wasn't an eyesore but a memory of Mickey's lively young leg slung over it, jiggling away as he told hilarious stories. The cigarette burns on the dining room table brought back parties when they were young and irresponsible and without a child. Every scrape on the floor brought back the shuffle of dancing feet and the strains of the accordion and the fiddle and her heart pangs for Ireland and her father. That's what her home was to her—a life. To Sissy, Nellie's home was a dump, and maybe that was part of the problem.

Nellie even had her original bed (she had changed the mattress and boxspring off and on through the years), her marriage bed. A grand, big, sturdy, sensible, mahogany affair with a headboard a person could put her back against. You could read all night in that bed and never have a crick in your neck in the morning. You could feed a boarding house on that headboard. And there were plenty of memories *in* that bed—enough for Nellie in later years, more than enough. In fact, a sight better than the real thing.

That was what she would have liked to tell Sissy about men. Whatever they would do later on to spoil it, and by God they would, they couldn't rob your memories. You could exist on memories, they were better than God, because you once touched them and always owned them. Didn't her daughter know that?

Didn't she know, even if nothing went wrong, if men were perfect husbands, age would ruin it. Nellie hated making love as she got older, except sometimes after a big affair, a dance or a wedding, where the pretty clothes, the drinks, the dancing, the joy of the occasion played silly with the calendar. But only then. Other times it was a mockery of what you once were. Stomachs in the way, Mickey's shortness of breath, her Copacabana legs too thickened and pained to remain aloft. It was insult to memory —like some smart-alecky American actors who took off on the Irish on the screen. Her bright-as-a-button daughter wasn't as smart as she thought.

Still in all, Nellie was full of guilt. Guilt for not trying to broach touchy subjects at least, and heartsick for not standing firm on those drugs. It was gutless to back down because of her fear of the neighbors' tongues. A lifetime in the country, and she still reacted like a dumb greenhorn. The neighbors, indeed! The look on her daughter's face now indicated the price for Nellie's propriety.

Out of contrition and instinct, she picked up her daughter's hand and cradled it between her own, rocking Sissy's hand back and forth in a miniature to maternal memory. Sissy responded by moving closer to her mother on the seat. She was content to surrender her hand to this feminine gesture and proud of her mother for sensing her anguish. The hand was full of animal comfort, like her childhood books where the frightened four-legged young were nuzzled into security.

As much as the show of warmth gratified Nellie, she knew she had to break Sissy's mood. The day hadn't really begun yet— the most trying part was still to come—and already her daughter was rocky. Nellie settled on Eileen for an ally. "So, young lady, I hear you're in for a bonus today."

Eileen, never quite sure what her grandmother was after (always gossip, she presumed), looked back in cagey silence.

"Well, what about it?" Nellie nudged. Sissy, sensing a break, a hint of danger, dislodged her hand. Her daughter looked threatened.

"A bonus?" the child questioned back.

"Well, I would call having a scholar in the family a bonus, wouldn't you?" Nellie boomed, too jollily.

Now Eileen was truly confused. Someone had changed the ground rules. She didn't think her grandmother knew about Columbia.

Sissy saw the child's panic. When did her mother find out? Then Sissy remembered dropping it casually to Nellie weeks back, a small opening salvo into Nellie's plans after City Hall, if she had any. The wise old pigeon never missed a crumb. Sissy filled the breach. "Oh, that. Don't go out and buy any dress for graduation day yet. We're just going up to Columbia to check out some courses today."

"Today?" Catherine sniffed.

Nellie immediately picked up Catherine's hostile tone. "And why *not* today, if I might ask?" challenged Nellie.

Catherine seized the high moral ground. "Well, I mean, today of all days. I would have thought it could wait." She stiffened empirically in her sense of things.

"It seems logical to me," Christy said in his best negotiator's voice. "After all, we are in the city. It will save another trip."

"Exactly," said Sissy. "It's such a long trip, so why not kill two birds with one stone." She knew it was a disastrous metaphor even before Catherine struck a horrified look.

"You know what I mean," she tried lamely.

"Of course, we do," said Christy. "The sensible thing to do. With the subways being what they are and the cost of a cab. Perfectly sensible."

Sissy looked at him admiringly. He must have been wonderful at the bargaining table. Fear and money—an irrefutable argument. Catherine would be defeated by the image of rampaging blacks or of a runaway meter.

"Well, I just thought . . ." Catherine stammered.

"Perfectly sensible, perfectly sensible," Christy intoned, like a priest calming a multitude with a blessing.

Sissy could feel the dissension dissolving when Philly piped up from the front seat.

"Hey, if I knew the kid was planning college, Sissy, I would have run her up there next week. Half fare. What am I saying? For my Eileen back there, no charge." He hoped the Christ Carmela never heard of his offer. Discounts she'd go along with, but freebies even relatives didn't get. Besides, Carmela, like Philly, believed girls going to college was a lot of shit.

"See," Catherine said triumphantly, "it could have waited for a more proper time."

A more proper time! Sissy had to clutch the seat. She wanted to hit the silly old bitch. What did she think this day was—a reprise of Eddie's death? Instead of attacking, Sissy took a page from Christy. "That's very sweet of Philly, but I'm sure he has a full schedule of paying fares without taking a free one. With the time it takes to see the campus, he could miss three or four calls. And after all, like the rest of us, he has a family to support. I'm sure he and Mrs. Barbieri have their bills to meet, too." Let Catherine argue with that immigrant logic, thought Sissy. She didn't.

Everyone, looking to dispatch the problem to the future, praised Philly's generosity. Except Catherine. Not to be deterred, Catherine said, "Well, I for one don't know what the rush is all about."

"What rush?" said Christy evenly. "I'm sure the girl has to check out the courses. We might not think it with this heat, but the fall is right around the corner, and the fall means school."

"I don't mean that," Catherine snapped.

"Well, I'm sorry, dear. I'm confused. What am I missing?" How could he call that mean-spirited drone "dear," wondered Sissy.

"I mean rushing the whole thing. College, I mean. We're all called on to make sacrifices at a time like this."

"I'm afraid I'm still not with you, dear," said Christy, with malevolent condescension.

"Is there something wrong with the way I speak? Are you so used to hearing those union types screaming obscenities at the top of their lungs you don't understand the English language anymore?" Catherine charged.

She had crossed Christy's Rubicon. He'd accept singular abuse for the sake of tranquility, but never an attack on his membership. His response was reflexive. It wasn't his wife he heard, but a bureaucrat across a table, trying to club him with Yankee class. "I doubt if you know how a union man speaks. After all, you rarely heard one, since your father only dealt with scab labor."

Philly couldn't believe his ears. He allowed the Caddy to swerve but recovered quickly. "Sorry, folks," he said, flashing a sickly grin, "these roads haven't been repaired in years."

"I think we should all cool down on a day like this," said Nellie, figuring a new voice might break the deadly duet she saw forming between Christy and Catherine. Nellie had been there before. Many nights when she and Mickey were jawing, she was grateful to have the dog interrupt with a bark.

"Well, I thought you'd never speak up," said Catherine. "You know what I'm talking about, or did I learn to speak French without knowing it?"

Marron! Philly couldn't figure out where this was leading, but he knew it was no good. These people were unbelievable, they never let up. It was like watching the television news and seeing those nutty Jews talking a mile a minute to that wall of theirs.

"I'm sure," said Nellie, "nobody in this car thinks you're speaking anything but perfect English, dear. With the day it is, and the heat, our heads are probably addled."

"Well, I'm glad to hear it," said Catherine. "I was beginning to think I should commit myself as a raving lunatic."

The car fell dead quiet. Everyone tried to avoid looking at Sissy. Eileen's eyes filled with angry tears. Philly checked the scene in the mirror. Jesus, what a thing to say in front of the kid. And when he looked at Sissy's face, he couldn't help but feel sorry for her. Forget all the other stuff. So what, she was a bit of a flake. She had it rough with Billy and Eddie, plus that jomoke in the zoo just now. She didn't need this shit, too.

Catherine started to sniffle. "Are you all happy now? Is this what you wanted—to see me make a fool out of myself? To say something that sounds horrible when I didn't mean a thing by it. Just an innocent figure of speech. Are you all happy now that I'm mortified?"

She turned toward Sissy. "Surely, child, you know there was no wrong meant in what I said."

Christy took his wife's hand, but she yanked it away. "Don't you come around now. It was you who got me in this state." She turned back to Sissy. "You know I took to you like you were my own daughter."

Eileen was now on edge. She hoped her mother would tell her off. Her own daughter! What mush.

Nellie knew for sure there was going to be a scene, and she was helpless to intervene. This was why she dreaded family get-togethers of any sort. Instead of bringing up happy times, families acted like pigs in the old country, wallowing in their slops.

Sissy, her face set in smug superiority, looked at her mother-in-law. Nellie knew the look well. That was how she used to look at her father when they argued. Her calm, controlled deadliness used to drive Mickey crazy, especially when they discussed the colored. Nellie could see Mickey's face on fire, screaming at Sissy, "Don't you lecture me like a goddamn snot-nosed social worker."

Sissy reached across toward Catherine, and Nellie's heart jumped. But the girl was smiling. "Come on, Mom," she said to Catherine, "dry your eyes. I know you didn't mean anything by that remark. Don't be silly. Next thing you know this family will be afraid to bake a fruitcake because they think I'll be offended. Come on, Mom, let's not let the Mayor see a lot of red-nosed Micks or he'll think we've been drinking."

Eileen was the first to laugh. Then Catherine started through her sniffles. Nellie wanted to, but she was too impressed with her daughter's performance, and touched, too. It had all the earmarks of the old master, Mickey. Sissy hadn't called either Nellie or Catherine "mom" since the early days of her marriage, and here she was using it twice! And making herself the butt of the joke!

If Nellie was impressed, Philly was awed. He had underestimated this broad—that was a class move if he had ever seen one. Tears actually came to his eyes, they always did when he encountered real class. Like Old Blue Eyes sitting alone on a stage under a blue spot singing, "One for My Baby, and One More for the Road," hitting the high notes while he sipped booze and exhaled Chesterfields. Philly was a sucker for class.

CATHERINE WAS NOW calmer but not placated. Sissy's graciousness left the door open for her to refine her theme. She had no intention of being soothed by her daughter-in-law's good humor. All that would do was absolve her from an innocent slip of the tongue. Nobody had considered the righteousness of her argument. Now that their ears were open again, she intended to justify it.

"Well, I always said to Eddie, that girl you married was a rock of sense. I knew you were listening to what I said, Sissy. All I was asking, simply, was why did Eileen have to start college right away? It's well known that, like the doctor, I'm a great believer in knowledge. Books were never scarce in my house, but Eddie had his mind on other things."

Catherine caught herself on that one quickly. "The cops, I mean, dear, and he did himself proud there. The Mayor today is living testimony to that. I mean, I grew up in a house where education was highly regarded. You couldn't look at the doctor without seeing him with a book in his hands. The doctor always said the Jews knew the ticket. The books were the way up. Put your back straight in the chair with a book, and you'll never bend over laboring. In all his life he said he never treated a Jew with back problems. That's how much he regarded education."

Sissy hated these Irish arias. She had heard these dirges all her life. She wondered if it was exclusively Irish, or just another symptom of growing old. She was sure they weren't rendered for the consumption of others, since they were unintelligible. There was never an effort to make verbal binges lucid, to edit out the nonsense. It was spieled for the deliverer's ears, a monologue of self-satisfaction, like a cricket rubbing its legs together, or a child reciting the catechism to reinforce himself: Who made the world? God made the world. Who made God? God made me in His image and likeness. If the latter were true, thought Sissy, there was an insult in there somewhere.

Catherine was still running on. "So far be it from me ever to discourage education, even if it is for a girl. What I mean is, a girl has other things going for her. In today's world a boy is lost without an education. I just thought Eileen might put it off for a while. An extra paycheck would come in handy at a time like this, and Eileen could pick up school later, if she had a mind to. That is, unless something better comes along. She's quite a looker—like her mother, I might add."

Christ, Christy hated these pretentious fairy tales. The "doctor" and the intimation that Eddie had married beneath himself. It was such an insult to his career in labor. Mickey had probably squandered more money on booze and horses than he'd ever made. Only the Irish hand down their ignorance like an heirloom, he thought.

Catherine's mouth looked like a rectum to Sissy. She thought of how she used to give Eileen and Billy enemas when they were children, and how they sometimes failed to make it to the bowl. The liquefied shit just exploded out of them, splattering everything within sight.

"What other things do girls have going for them, Catherine?" Sissy asked.

"Well, you know, child. With all Eileen's got going for her, she won't be running around free for long, if anyone wants my opinion. I bet the marriage proposals will be dropping at her feet."

"That's not the be-all," Sissy said, never changing the cadence of her response.

Catherine didn't know how to handle that. What was this snip saying—her son wasn't good enough for her? He took her out of that dump of a railroad flat and away from that crazed, drunken father and a slattern of a mother who would answer the door in a housecoat, regardless of what time of day you rang the bell.

Catherine wouldn't have been caught dead in those flower-print rags.

"Well, I don't think you did too badly by it. Marriage, I mean," she said, taking up the cudgel of her fallen son.

"I didn't say I did," Sissy responded, never deflecting from her monotone. "But times have changed. Girls don't go around playing with bride dolls anymore, or haven't you noticed?" Eerily, Sissy heard Eddie's quiet malevolence and tactical grilling in her rebuke. The underplayed menace pleased her. She was sorry she had come to it so late.

"Well, first I'm accused of not being able to speak. Now I find I can't see either." Sissy picked up on Catherine's tone. The spear was piercing Catherine's side.

Christy intervened, "The girl just means things are not the same as when we were young. It's commonplace for girls to go to college today."

"You're a fine one to talk about education. You didn't take advantage of it when the doctor offered it to you on a silver platter."

"I went for a while," Christy said, "and enjoyed it."

"A lot of good it did you. You could have gotten a law degree like the doctor wanted you to, but you scrapped that soon enough to chase your union business."

"The two years of law came in very handy in my business. Besides, working during the day and going to school at night is not the ideal way to do it."

Catherine had hold of one of her favorite bones and she wasn't about to let up. "Now don't look for sympathy in front of strangers. You know well you didn't have to work. The doctor offered to send you to school full-time, and you refused. Didn't you? Go ahead. Deny it."

"Indeed, he did," Christy confirmed. "It wasn't my way."

"My way!" Catherine snorted. "Your way was to take what little education you got and use it to run that band of hooligans."

"Countrymen, Catherine, countrymen. Some people might think a good transit system is as important as a bottle of calamine lotion."

"What are you inferring?"

"History, my dear. Historical perspective. They teach that in college."

Catherine was baffled by that kind of talk. She sniffed haughtily. "I don't think there is any greater gift than the gift of healing. I mean, along with a religious calling, of course."

Healing. What an ignorant woman I married, Christy thought. Ignorant and lace curtain. A deadly combination. Even the doctor wouldn't have a cure for that on his shelf. A poor poseur like her father. That pathetic shell of a man. If you took epsom salts and milk of magnesia away from him, he wouldn't know what to recommend to the poor dumb souls with their nickels and dimes whom he lorded it over. He was a doctor because his customers couldn't afford a real one. But Christy couldn't deny he had used him, rather like the doctor had used his patients. Christy never had any intention of getting a law degree. Just enough of the books to make his move in the union. The "doctor's" connections also didn't hurt. Plenty of fat pastors to be photographed with at social functions.

The doctor's daughter was no liability either. She had enough airs about her when she was young to impress Christy's co-workers, who thought that anyone who won her was a comer. A future leader. She cut quite a figure on a dais with him. Her clothes alone made the other wives coo over her as if she were Eleanor Roosevelt.

Like the doctor, Christy knew he wasn't above using snake oil on the poor to get ahead. But Christy thought that what he was after justified his actions. So he lied to the doctor and his wife about his intentions to get a law degree. Damn, there was a social movement that had to be forged. The doctor didn't miss the partial tuition he paid for him. The pittance gave him bragging rights about his son-in-law.

Christy connived to put money in other men's pockets, not his own. But he had his guilt. After all, the doctor had only lied to his customers, and Catherine had only deceived herself. Christy's subterfuge was in his marriage bed. That knowledge made his longing for a drink intensify.

"Well, I'm sure Eileen understands I'm just looking out for everyone's good," Catherine pandered. "Don't you, honey?"

The child didn't know how to answer. Her grandmother was rekindling her doubts about college. Maybe she was right, college did sound like a selfish thing at this moment. Money had to be tight, and Eileen wasn't sure about that story her mother told her this morning. A lieutenant's pension? It didn't seem logical. The

highest her father reached was plainclothes. She never even remembered a lieutenant or any officer visiting their house. She was
terrified that her mother was still sick and this was one of her
wild stories, like the one about Billy dying trying to save a
Vietnamese village of women and children, instead of at the front.
She came up with one wild story a week when she was bad.

Eileen hoped this wasn't another one, and that she wouldn't wig
out at the ceremony when the Mayor didn't announce her father's
promotion. God, she wished her father was here to deal with all
this. Couldn't he have been more careful? Couldn't Billy have
been more careful? Ever since she was a child, she couldn't understand why boys took such reckless chances. It was almost like
they hated life.

"I talked about all this with my mother, Grandma. Getting a
job and everything."

"See," said Catherine triumphantly, "the child has more sense
than the lot of you. I was sure the idea of a job didn't frighten
you, or you wouldn't be your father's girl."

"No," said the girl hesitantly, not wanting to betray her mother,
"I think I might even like it, but Mom . . ."

"And much to your mom's credit. She's generous to a fault. So
much so, it sometimes clouds her judgment. I'm sure that through
the school or the church, or through some of the doctor's old
friends or their sons—many of them are influential, you know—
we could land you a smashing job."

Eileen was on the ropes and Sissy knew it. Catherine was
undermining everything she had built up. Sissy knew what was
behind it. If the doctor kept his daughter in a porcelain vase, it
was good enough for every woman.

"There will be no job," Sissy said flatly. "She's going to school."

Eileen felt like a kid being buffeted between two bullies in a
school hallway. She didn't like the finality of her mother's state-
ment. Suddenly, she saw no difference between her mother and
her grandmother. She felt an instantaneous dislike for both of
them.

"Well, I thought this was a discussion," said Catherine. "I'm
sorry I opened my mouth. I'm used to a civilized answer, an
explanation, not to being told off."

"Do you want a civilized answer, Catherine? Well, I'll give
you one, if you're sure you want it."

Nellie winced at the use of "Catherine." She knew her daughter wouldn't give a performance this time.

"Well, I'm waiting," said Catherine.

"Simply, Eileen's going to school because most jobs are shit. And I don't want my daughter to spend her life wallowing in shit. Okay? Does that satisfy you?"

Christy smiled at Sissy. His daughter-in-law had good union blood in her.

"Well, I must say I'm not satisfied with your language. Nor your answer, I might add. A job was good enough for a lot of people, some very, very good people."

"It had to be good enough," Sissy answered. "We didn't have anything else. Eileen doesn't have to worry about putting bread on the table. That was yours and my generation."

"Well," huffed Catherine, "I guess that's what they call women's libber talk. I know where you get that from. (Channel 13, thought Nellie involuntarily.) But *I* personally don't see anything disgraceful about putting bread on the table. Many a good . . ."

"Relax, Catherine," Sissy interrupted. "I didn't say it was disgraceful. But why do it if there's something better?"

"Well, it was good enough for a lot of our people . . ."

"It was good enough for your mother to wash clothes in the River Shannon. That doesn't mean you shouldn't have a washing machine."

That was too much for Catherine to bear. "My mother never set her foot near the Shannon with clothes, I'll have you know. And furthermore . . ."

"It's only a figure of speech, dear," came Nellie to the rescue.

"Figure or no figure, I won't have my mother insulted as an Irish washerwoman."

"Catherine, I was making a point. Don't get in a dander. All I meant was that a lot has changed, and Eileen should take advantage of it."

Catherine sallied from another flank. "Well. I'm glad to hear money is not a problem. I guess this is my day to be kept in the dark."

Eileen checked her mother for a reaction. Was she going to tell the lieutenant story?

"Money is always a problem for most people, Catherine. But we'll get on. Comfortably."

It was the way her mother said it that gave Eileen pause. The soft, assured "comfortably." In her sick days she told her wild stories at a feverish pitch, but this was different. Her mother was so confident she seemed serene. So much so that Catherine, defeated, turned away from her. Sometimes she wished she had died with the doctor, who alone understood her.

THEY CONTINUED around the park to the Third Street exit and cut out into the side streets which, with some maneuvering, would lead them to the Brooklyn Bridge.

As the car turned into Atlantic Avenue, Sissy flushed with anticipation. Atlantic Avenue, with its smattering of restaurants, antique and curiosity shops, and boutiques, was a prelude to Manhattan. Her Manhattan.

It was a teaser. Like languid foreplay. The sophisticated visions that skipped across her eyes weren't unlike the kaleidoscope that danced on the ceiling for her when Eddie teased her to desire. The added thrill was that there was more, the best was yet to come.

When the limo swung into Boerum Place, the long stretch leading to the Brooklyn Bridge, she felt every inch of her rev up. At the end would be the bridge, not really steel and concrete at all, but a perilous, swinging, storybook bridge spanning a chasm with the mythical conquest at the other end. The danger was muted by the allure of the shimmering towers: come to the Emerald City.

Sissy refused to dampen her emotions with logic. She knew down deep that the bridge was an economic shuttle for workers schlepping to and fro for survival. But that was their bridge, not hers. To her, it was a spiritual span, the escape route from her parochial purgatory.

When the limo's tires bounced on the bridge grating, her spirits were jolted. She had never been an adventuress, she'd always been a tourist. The only part of the city she had ever possessed (she didn't count her girlhood job) was the portion Lynn had given her. She was Sissy's guide, and without Lynn, she was lost. She had used Lynn as a machete to clear the foliage of her fears.

She had met Lynn Lombardi at a feminist meeting when her marriage was in the doldrums. Billy was in Vietnam, Eileen was immersed in the exploration of teenage life, and Eddie, even when he was at home, was removed.

She didn't know exactly what prompted her decision to go to the meeting other than boredom and the excitement about the movement in the articles she read in *The Village Voice* and *Ms. Magazine.* A gathering exclusively of women had never been her cup of tea. She considered most of her girlhood friends, with the exception of Margaret, featherheads. But even Margaret was intelligent only in a rote sort of way. You would crib from her algebra paper, but never from her notions on life. Margaret knew all the dates and facts about major historical events, but the theoretical machinations behind them were either beyond her or held no interest for her. And now Margaret was married to an engineer and living in California. Her few annual letters to Sissy reflected Margaret perfectly—all data and no frills, like a list of chores pinned to a pegboard.

But the written accounts of the women's movement made it sound as if a new breed of women was on the landscape. The articles were chocked with theory, confession, historical grievance, real anger, and the reckoning of a new day—not with pathetic whining. Vengeance is mine, said these lordesses.

Of course, if Sissy had wanted to be true blue, she could have cast her lot with other cops' wives whom she met at departmental social functions or at house gatherings that Eddie hosted or attended. But these women were parrots of their husbands. They mimicked their spouses' every bitch about the job, right down to the endless amounts of time their poor dears had to spend in clogged night court with their collars.

Yet Sissy had no idea what she would do at a feminist meeting. Certainly, she wouldn't seize the floor and lay out a battle plan for womanhood, and she certainly couldn't see herself divulging Eddie's transgressions to a collection of strangers. She wouldn't even confide those to a priest in the confessional. It wasn't loyalty to the solemnity of the marriage contract that dictated this, but the mortification of equal time. She would die if she thought that Eddie ever buzzsawed her to the boys at the bar.

When it came right down to it, Sissy merely hoped to meet a new friend. A friend who would share her sublimated interests. Some talk over a cup of coffee about politics or a book, a night at a foreign film, going to a restaurant with a menu that listed appetizers and had a wine list, and maybe the extravagance of an evening at the theater—seeing a real play. Sissy embarrassedly realized her motives sounded more like *Mademoiselle* than *Ms.*, but loneliness dwarfed the motives.

Her major problem was locating a meeting to attend. Most of the gatherings listed were in Manhattan, and Sissy didn't have the spirit for that trek—she was a long way from eighteen. And she didn't know if there were any local meetings; certainly, they weren't heralded in the Brooklyn papers. She found it hard to believe that Flatbush or Flatlands would be the feminist equivalent of the Sierra Madres. Even if such meetings existed, Sissy pictured them populated with battered housewives. She wasn't looking to join a civilian defense unit.

The perfect compromise hit her—Brooklyn Heights, not quite Manhattan, but connected enough to be considered the big burg's bastard. But the compromise brought with it a sickening echo of her whole life. A flyer with a safety net underneath. Was the moon to which she longed to soar consistently crescent, symbolically half-assed?

Sissy chose a weekly Wednesday night meeting at St. Ann's Episcopal Church. In her mind the Episcopalian designation insured civility. Only High Anglican would have pleased her more. For the first four weeks she was a virtual lump on a log. She sat silent, absorbed. Of course, she went so far as to introduce herself, stating her role in life, and soon became familiar with some of the regulars. After the sessions, she lingered for coffee and some small talk, but she made no seismic connection. Her mythical buddy did not materialize. Yet Sissy gained a bit of reverse cachet. When the word spread that she was a cop's wife, some members' condescension was tinged with curiosity. The chapter had its mandatory black member *avec* Afro, now they also had the equivalent of an albino.

In her silent observation Sissy found one solace. Her language wasn't as bad as she had presumed. These women, who were far better off financially and scholastically than she, used graphic and technical language, mostly to the sexual detriment of men. Sissy was titillated. This was the first time she felt the strength and exhilaration of bonding. She now understood why men huddled at bars and sporting events.

But deep down she disliked the showoff vulgarity, since she suspected it was cast in privilege in a world where indulgences were tolerated. She wondered if Annette Scalzone from the neighborhood—with her pedal pushers, ballerina slippers, and scarf-shrouded, roller-filled hair—were to come marching into this gathering spouting the same words, would she be received as liberated or as a tacky slut? Fat chance. Revolution, like rich cream, had trouble filtering to the bottom.

Besides, Sissy had heard coarse language all her life—in the streets, in the bars, and in Eddie's cop circles where it reached its nadir. She was now a live carrier, dangerously in jeopardy of infecting her own daughter. The strain was so virulent it should have been codified: meningitis of the mouth.

She wondered why these women didn't realize such talk wasn't anything new. It was just the age-old lingo of aggression. Sissy had seen enough of that, too. Eddie against all-encompassing evil, now Billy against global creeping Communism. Sissy didn't want to cleanse the world with male muscle or mouth. If she could divine the way, she would dust the planet fair with a rose.

At her fifth meeting the chairperson asked Sissy whether she would care to add to the dialogue. Sissy would have been content to be designated the group's mute neutral observer. God, she didn't want to get up and speak! But it seemed all eyes turned to her, and she felt like such a schnook. It would have taken more courage to refuse. She rose.

What came out when she spoke were starts, stops, stammers, and dodges. Something along the lines of, of course, her home life wasn't really that bad, but with a son in the service and her husband on night shift (a lie), she was a little lonely. She felt the need for some company, she didn't feel anyone would mind. She jumped from one tack to another when she knew she wasn't getting a rise from the assembly. She felt like a desperate comic going in the toilet on the Carson show.

She began to feel that her Mickey Mouse monologue matched her clothes. It struck her that she was the worst-dressed woman in the room. What was considered chic at an Emerald Society dinner didn't cut it in this room. She was early A&S in a French foreign legion. She knew she had failed. She, who had the local rep of Turkish bazaar of opinions. She knew the verdict, she only had to hear it read.

It came, kindly, from the chair. "Theresa, it's always difficult in the beginning. To get started is the trick. Why don't we leave you to your own time schedule. When you're ready, and only then. Besides, it's getting late, and maybe someone else wants to say something before we adjourn."

Sissy was red with mortification, but grateful. Until she heard a low, anonymous crack from across the room, "And let's hope curtain fall is coherent and interesting."

Sissy turned toward the sound of the voice, but she couldn't find the offending face through her tears. The faces all blurred—smiling, even teeth, vogueish tombstones. She didn't know where her reply sprang from, but its vengeance had the sniff of the streets. "Your clothes might be more fucking interesting, but not your lives. Not your lives."

Emerging from the embarrassed silence, the most astonishing woman Sissy would ever meet put her arm around her and said, "Sister, I would love to buy you a drink. I'm Lynn Lombardi. Don't let these dames get you. After so many meetings, they would boo Scheherazade. If you hang around these sessions long enough, they turn into feminist versions of 'Can You Top This?' You struck out, this time, but you'll get the hang of it. I'll say one thing, though. Your exit line was boffo. Now how about that drink?"

*N*ow that she had been removed for a time, she wondered if Lynn was truly so astonishing. Her mother had always said she made too much of everything. The doctor at the hospital concurred, saying she granted people "mythic dimensions," and thus was crushed when they showed human vulnerability. What did that mean? That Mickey was never the cock of the walk? Eddie was never Dick Diver? Billy was a hotshot gung-ho kid, and Lynn was run-of-the-mill?

"Mythic dimensions." It was the glibness that came from talk-show couches and passed for wisdom. Sissy had memories, irrefutable, bankable memories. Mickey's booze didn't wash away the days of his specialness. Eddie, the hard-nosed cop-tomcatter, didn't snuff the loving, tender boy who launched her womanhood. Eddie, the newly minted cop who was as untarnished as his shield. Who railed against guys on the take, shysters who plea-bargained mayhem down to mischief, judges who sprinted through their calendars, and yes, even the foul treatment of prisoners. And Billy? The special child who drew and wrote children's books and brought them to her bed, the child who wept every time he saw the television version of "Rudolph, the Red-Nosed Reindeer" because Rudolf was ostracized; the child who screamed hysterically at the vet's, "Please, please, do it to me instead," when his first puppy had to be put to sleep with distemper. What to do with him? God, he had been so fragile Sissy harbored a secret dread that he was going to grow up gay.

And then Lynn. It was true Sissy had never put Lynn in perspective. From the first evening, she simply blitzed Sissy. To begin with, her looks bowled you over. The combination of a bronzed Italian father and a Jewish mother. She didn't fit any standard of conventional beauty. She seemed to be comprised of sharp Mediterranean planes and voluptuous Jewish circles. Her features would move Modigliani to brush. And you couldn't say she dressed —she costumed. To some articles of expensive, elegant clothing, she added outrageous accessories. Scarves dashingly tied around her throat or cinched around her waist in lieu of a belt, her arms a steeple of bracelets that jangled discreetly like Chinese wind chimes. To Sissy, her outfits seemed to be jointly secured from excursions to Bergdorf's and raids on Goodwill stores. She could carry anything off, much like the young Eddie in his razor-creased fatigues on those summer beaches. There was no doubt about it—Lynn won the opening inning.

When Lynn began to expose Sissy to her world and conversation, Sissy became helplessly enthralled. Lynn should have been accredited. In ensuing months she put Sissy through a crash education—art, antiques, experimental theater, and even sports. "Don't be one of those female snobs about males' adoration of sports. Willie Mays was every bit as beautiful to watch as Nureyev, and more impressive. Rudi's every move was choreographed, while Willie took his cue from the crack of a bat hundreds of feet away." And again. "I hope you don't think everything that happens on a football field is muscle and chance. When you sit up high in a stadium and look down, you realize runners don't *just* scamper free, and pass receivers don't *just* shake loose. See the blockers as sacrificial pawns. The game is as orchestrated as chess."

Sissy felt like the provincial Marjorie Morningstar held spellbound by a female Noel Airman.

In fairness to the Good Doktor, the time she spent with Lynn did seem mythic. The memories were so heightened Sissy couldn't be sure she viewed their patch of history together judicially. On top of everything else, Lynn was brimming with gall. She had the guts of a cat burglar. Indeed, her behavior often mortified Sissy.

In antique stores she would crawl on the floor to check the

workmanship and period of a piece of furniture and loudly proclaim, "My mother has plastic slipcovers on better drek than this." In galleries her boundless enthusiasm could be matched by her sarcasm, "He went Van Gogh a step better—he cut out his eyes."

In a jazz joint one night, when they were standing at the bar, Lynn pronounced the piano player "hollow." A black standing within earshot challenged her. "If you're so swift, sister, why don't you go up there and show the brother how it's done." Lynn didn't answer, but on a break between sets, she approached the leader of the quintet. When the band members returned, Lynn took her place at the piano and led the group in a rousing rendition of "St. James Infirmary" to the delight of the house. Was this really happening, or was Sissy fantasizing? Kay Kendall with a jag on, playing the trumpet in *Genevieve*.

That was the truly fascinating aspect of Lynn—she had so many "S" (surprising!) curves. She was unlike Brooklyn, where everyone had a slot: "a great wife," "a super cook," "a good provider," "a blessing to her (or his) mother." Valentine's Day card designations. Even Sissy's hope, her Eileen, was in danger of joining the team. Eileen often remarked how much daddy had sacrificed to give to the family. Little did the child know his sacrifice was his soul. His flag of surrender was the white envelopes he accepted. Eileen even reminded Sissy how fortunate they were to have a summer home. An ill-gained, sealed hothouse, Sissy thought, where she was consigned while Eddie plowed a pubic field.

But in the beloved team lingo, Sissy still had some late innings in her. She'd burn in hell before Eileen became a label, someone to be treasured a few times each year through the postal system.

And why should Sissy have questioned Lynn's magic? When she was with Lynn, she noticed she began to move better, the middle-aged housewife's resignation leaving her step. Also, she seemed lighter, swifter, although her bathroom scale didn't show a marked decrease. It was an inward grace, the feeling she once had after confession.

Nor did she question deeply the new people she met at meetings, jazz clubs, and gallery openings. Oh, she had nudges of conscience about some of them, but she dusted off these occasional nags. Christ, it was all new, wasn't it? Wasn't that the foundation of faith—indeed, her own faith? What the hell was heaven but a divine drawing room for only the most dignified people following a session in the spiritual slums?

Yet she was uncomfortable with the thought that she now missed Lynn most of all. More than Mickey, Eddie, and Billy. It was a terrible thing to feel, a lack of proper reverence for your own blood. Maybe that was because so much of it had been needlessly squandered. Even Eddie wouldn't argue with her on that. He'd told her the majority of the homicides committed within the city took place between spouses and blood relatives. "Loved ones," he phrased it. Was that supposed to be cop irony? You were safer in the Hades of the transit underground that snuggled next to the heart.

But Sissy had been raised another way and she couldn't escape it. She should have been able to save her family. The shrink had told her she was arrogant in that respect. "Who do you think you are, God?" Considering the state of the world, Sissy felt as if she were qualified to drop a resumé. She didn't relish the notion that she should have suffered more for them. Damn, she'd bled enough, but she knew she had played neutral Sweden when it mattered—no war on Mickey's booze, Eddie's unexplained booty, and Billy's exit for Asia. She'd played all that as if it had been beyond her. That white, deadly sin of omission.

It was a woman's remorse she was suffering. Men didn't suffer and whine about what was past. She was like the loyal baying dog at a grave site. Maybe that was why men called women dogs —it had nothing to do with their being unattractive. Men saw life as an alley. Cats on the prowl looking for action everywhere. Even their lovemaking was like that. After climax, Sissy could lie in bed for hours luxuriating in the bliss of her full domestic bowl. Eddie couldn't wait to withdraw when his objective was accomplished, to get on to the post mortem of a piss and a cigarette.

"Mythic dimensions," indeed. Only her blood would think she needed that idiot to counsel her. Outside his prescription pad— those magical pills that played "Fantasia" in her head—he was worthless. But when it came right down to it, the medication wasn't effective enough. It only altered when it should have scorched her brain. That's why she only used it on rare occasions, like today. What she wanted from a pill was a barren terrain.

Today, she wanted to be replanted. She wanted her childhood again. How lovely, a psychological "Sesame Street."

But there was no such remedy, her only hope was retribution for her sins of silence. Maybe the snip was right about dimensions. Hadn't she cut school to go to the New York Paramount to see the premiere of the first 3-D movie, *The House of Wax*? A nice, dissolving omen, that. Who was in it? Vincent Price and Phyllis Kirk. Sweet Mother of Jesus, Phyllis Kirk. Only Sissy, Phyllis's mother, and her agent knew of Phyllis's existence.

How could she pull off this day against the toughest in the city when she still had that vapid focus in her head?

She had the sinking feeling that it was all beyond her as the towers of Manhattan would always be beyond her. If there had been a bar on the bridge, she would have asked Philly to pull over and dragged Christy in for a stiff snort. Another parochial remedy. Maybe that was always the problem. Freud had fucked up. It was origins, not organs, you couldn't escape. A lesson, Dr. F., Sissy thought, geography dominates genes.

*I*T WASN'T ALL magic with Lynn, though. Lynn became a grounded angel when Sissy met members of her friend's family. Dear, dear "loved ones" in Eddie's phrase. It didn't surprise Sissy. She often thought the cold, thin blood of families was what formed the berg that sank the *Titanic*.

Sissy met Lynn's ex-husband Nick when he dropped by Lynn's apartment in Brooklyn Heights. Since it was Sissy's first visit to Lynn's home, she resented Nick's intrusion. All she knew of him was Lynn's flippant capsule description, "Nick is a gorgeous, worthless Italian, but I never got a bum table when I was on his arm." Sissy couldn't buy the *gorgeous*. In her salad days she wouldn't have put out bait for such a flounder.

Instead of a Don Juan, Sissy found Nick a bit of a drudge. A regular fussbudget. He spent his visit straightening the mess on Lynn's desk, putting her papers into plastic folders, and muttering in disbelief, "I don't know how anyone can live like this. How can you find anything in this mess? You put a lot of work into these projects, Lynn, and you've got them thrown around like kitty litter." Another lesson learned—you can divorce a husband, but you can't douche his conscience.

It was easy for Sissy to ignore him, since her attention was riveted to the walls from which an array of canvases hung. The paintings astonished Sissy. The use of color was so audacious it bordered on the outlandish. Most of the subjects were women in chic, urban settings—galleries, Greenwich Village streets, posh restaurants, dingy clubs, and in racetrack paddocks. Regardless of the setting, the woman was always dominant, like a flame that heightened and heated the painting. They all had Lynn's unmistakable flair.

There were two canvases out of sync with the others—their macabre meanness fascinated Sissy. In both canvases the subject was the same: a grossly fat, middle-aged, dyed blond woman in the foreground, with a silhouette of a svelte female figure menacing in the background.

One painting showed the fat woman in a bubble bath with her enormous breasts surfacing above the bubbles. Across her breasts was printed "Goodyear," while the shadowy figure held a long pointed object—a knife, an icepick, or an immense hatpin? The other canvas only depicted the fat woman's head. Her body was a chocolate bon-bon slit at the bottom to expose an oozing cherry red fluid. The silhouette had the word "Caution" evilly drifting from its mouth. The lines of both silhouettes traced Lynn's profile. But who was the Fat Lady?

Nick noticed Sissy's fascination with the paintings and tried some recruiting. "Theresa, can you imagine a woman who can paint like this blowing her time doing commercial layouts? Advertising posters! With a talent like that!"

Sissy couldn't, and enthusiastically asked Lynn if her work was ever shown. For the first time her friend turned glacial. "No. I paint for therapy. Well, it was once, and I was deemed 'competent.' That's like getting a pat on the head in the Special Olympics. Don't listen to Nick. The problem with Italians is that they think everyone who picks up a brush is a budding Michelangelo."

Nick switched ground. "Well then, the least you could do is finish your book. You know the publisher is dying for it."

"I wouldn't exactly call a $2,500 advance 'dying,'" Lynn snapped.

"Well, you can't expect the moon. A large part of it was already published in *Ms.*," Nick countered.

"*Ms.*?" Sissy blurted, and immediately regretted it.

"Yes, *Ms.*," Lynn said resignedly. "I published a five-part series on the history of women artists."

Sissy had to squelch a squeal of delight. She had read the articles and admired them, so she'd saved the issues. What censored her response was that she hadn't remembered the name of the writer. She was disgusted with herself. She knew that if John Canaday or Hilton Kramer had penned the series, she would have remembered. That brought it home. The level of her consciousness had stopped at the height of the oven door. "But a book . . ." she said meekly.

"If they want it, let them put their money where their mouth is. Let's drop this." Lynn wasn't asking, she was telling.

So Sissy found something to dislike in Lynn. Didn't she realize books saved lives as surely as penicillin? It was crushing to find that her ideal was scarred by a stupid streak.

Sissy was to find that Nick wasn't the only sandbag weighing down Lynn's high-flying ways. Lynn had parents. That shouldn't have come as a shock, except that Lynn so mesmerized Sissy she thought of her as a sprite, whizzing about the kingdom of Manhattan and creating enchantment and mischief. Her roots proved more basic than that. Ocean Parkway in Brooklyn.

Sissy met Lynn's father, Vincent, when Lynn invited her to lunch with them at his club. "Lutece it isn't, love. Are you ready for this—'Chez Chic'? It's on Avenue U. And it combines the best of both my cultures, so wear your sunglasses, because the fixtures will blind you."

Lutece or not, Sissy was excited. When she asked Lynn if her father had always been a restaurateur, Lynn laughed, "Are you kidding? He made his bundle in construction, but don't, for heaven's sake, bring that up. He'll probably tell you his ancestors founded the company in the old country and provided the marble for the statue of David."

Lynn's wisecracks aside, Sissy rather liked the club. It was overdone, to be sure, but Lynn provided overkill of her own. "The chandeliers used to be Zsa Zsa Gabor's earrings." The cherub spouting water from his mouth into the fountain in the center of the circular bar was "early Truman Capote." Still, Sissy preferred it by far to the Irish spittoons where Mickey had spent his time. And she found Vincent (as he insisted she call him) charming and touching. He appeared in riding jodhpurs and a suede jacket. He informed her he was going riding after lunch in Garrison Beach, where he stabled his own horse. His ensemble recalled Mickey's blazer and pumps, but Vincent's obvious robust health and monied taste kept it from being ludicrous.

The similarities didn't end there. As Mickey used to do with Sissy's girlfriends, Vincent showered his daughter's companion with charm. He gave Sissy a tour of the club, introduced her to the staff, including the chef, of whom he requested something "squisito" for his special guest. Sissy was even amused by his adopted Italian accent. It reminded her of the way Mickey used to lapse into a brogue to give the proper coloration to an occasion.

Where Lynn's conversation was peppered with artistic references, Vincent substituted show business names. The night so-and-so dropped into the club, the day spent fishing on a famous comedian's boat in Miami Beach, the luncheon at Hialeah with a pop singer. Sissy noticed that all the names were male. She wasn't sure if this was more male-bonding or if the names of females were excluded in deference to Lynn and, more pointedly, Lynn's absent mother. Sissy suspected the latter. Vincent was too attractive to play Mickey's game of perpetually cavorting with the boys. Besides, he only sipped two glasses of wine during lunch. Because of Mickey, Sissy made it a habit to check the alcoholic intake of men. Another happy legacy of an Irish Catholic girlhood.

During lunch Vincent left the table to place drink orders personally and to check whether "the stock has arrived." There was a little too much laughter with the barmaid for such routine business. The foreplay was hard to miss, since the barmaid dulled the chandelier. Sissy noticed that Lynn rigidly refused to look in the direction of the bar while her father was away from the table. That's the way it was, Sissy mused, either booze or broads. Nellie would tell you to count your blessings if you didn't hit the parlay.

When Vincent announced during lunch that Lynn's mother, Lily, was going to Miami for two weeks, Lynn allowed herself a peek at the bar. She seemed devastated. "Two weeks alone?"

"She needs a rest," Vincent said. "And my head is so preoccupied with business I'd be no company. Besides, you know how she loves to shop. I hope they have a plastic detector at the airport and confiscate her credit cards," he added with a lame laugh.

Sissy thought she saw a snarl starting to form on Lynn's lips, but what came out was a plea. "Why don't you go with her? She'd love it."

"Oh, daughter, if only I could. But this is a tough economy.

I'd love to escape to the sun, but . . ." Vincent threw up his hands in a martyred gesture. Sissy wondered if there was a touch of Catherine in everyone.

"Just this once?" Lynn asked, like a child.

Now Sissy turned her gaze away. Lynn's eyes started to moisten. Sissy didn't want to watch. Good God, was this an inevitable tableau between fathers and daughters?

"If only I could," said Vincent self-pityingly, before delivering the lollipop to Lynn, "but next time for sure, sugar. I promise. Even if we're in the midst of a depression."

When lunch broke, Vincent told Sissy she must join him and Lynn in the near future for an afternoon of horseback riding. When she protested, he said, "Don't be silly. You'll be marvelous at it. Besides, you'll have plenty of instruction. Lynn is an extraordinary horsewoman."

What else is new? thought Sissy. Only ballooning was left.

"And Lynn, darling," he added, "I want you to do me a favor." He took a white envelope from the inside pocket of his jacket.

Lynn waved a protesting hand. "Now, come on, none of that. I'm not twelve anymore."

"Don't be silly," he said. "It's just that we got a little information on a trotter tonight and it would be a shame to pass it up. His name is inside the envelope."

"Daddy, don't embarrass me. Take it back."

What embarrassed Sissy was not the scene but Lynn lapsing into "daddy" (she had called her father Vincent all through lunch) when he pressured her.

Vincent looked extravagantly pained. "Can't a father make a small wager for his daughter and her new friend? Theresa is included, of course. If he wins, buy yourselves each a pretty hat. Ah-h, what an old fool I am! Do young women even bother with hats anymore? Theresa, I'm so hopelessly out of date." He kissed each of them warmly on the cheek and turned away, leaving Lynn holding the envelope.

Like hell you are, thought Sissy.

"Well, what did you think of Cesar Romero?" Lynn asked.

Sissy resented the power play with the money, but she disguised it. Not so much out of propriety, but because she was inwardly excited to check out the contents of the envelope. She tried to keep it light. "He certainly doesn't need a semester of charm school."

"No, he can get to you, the old fraud," Lynn smiled.

"You're not really going to bet that money, are you?" Sissy asked.

"No," Lynn replied, "*we're* going to bet the money."

"But suppose the information is no good?"

"That rarely happens," Lynn said flatly.

The cop's wife, putting everything together, sniffed connections. She also had a make on the Fat Lady.

THE COMBO of Lynn and Vincent proved to be a boost for Sissy's sagging marriage. Eddie was aware that Sissy had a new friend and was attending feminist meetings with her. But unlike other ventures in Sissy's life, Eddie didn't find this threatening. Sissy reasoned why. Her spirits were better, her time out gave Eddie more latitude to maneuver, and the bonus was that her activities were being conducted outside the neighborhood. The latter, of course, was most important. For once, Sissy wasn't sullying the home team's ground rules.

Indeed, Eddie was Marquis of Queensbury about the whole thing, even to the point of feigning polite interest. That is, until after the luncheon with Vincent.

When Sissy returned home from the lunch, flushed with excitement and wine, she told Eddie about it and about the pending bet on the trotter. He looked at her wearily and said, "It sounds like your old man all over again. Where does this guy work?"

When Sissy informed him that Vincent owned the club, he was interested just enough to look up. "Where is this joint?"

"Avenue U. Chez Chic."

Eddie let out a low whistle between his teeth.

"What's the matter?" Sissy asked.

"Nothing. Not a thing. Just that some very important people twirl their linguine there. Do you know the name of the horse?"

"Sure."

Eddie's tone got softer. "Do you mind if I call the guys at the precinct so they can get a little down on it?"

How ironic, Sissy thought. After all these years of striving, she had casually mentioned a tenuous hook that landed in his world and she was being treated with deference. Sissy slipped into her Barbara Stanwyck cool and delivered the name. Vincent and Lynn might prove to be her Price-Waterhouse to fame: "The envelope, please!"

When the trotter won at odds of nine to two, Eddie received phone calls of thanks for a few days. Sissy surmised from his end of the conversations that he hadn't put anything down for himself. Sissy knew he had never liked to gamble. The reflected glory was payoff enough. But something else prompted his reticence—that was evident when he asked Sissy whether she thought she'd receive any more information. It was clear to her which apostle Eddie would have been. All the wounds would have to be probed before he made a commitment. Old Doubting T., in the twentieth century, would have been a detective first grade.

Three weeks later, when Vincent gave them another trotter that scored, Eddie asked how come she never invited her friend in for a drink when she picked Sissy up in her car. It was Sissy's turn to score. "I never thought you were interested in feminists."

His squirm was discernible. "Aw, come on. I was only talking about those loudmouths who show up on TV wearing peacoats and combat boots."

"It's only the lack of decorum that upsets you?"

"Yeah, something like that. I believe in people's gripes, but there's a way of going about it. You don't have to break everybody's eardrums."

"I see," Sissy said, "the same low-key, dignified approach the police used when the city tried to set up a Civilian Review Board."

He was stung. "Look, if you don't want to invite her in, don't. But I don't meet my friends by the curb, they come through the door."

Sissy doubted if that was all-inclusive, but the experiment— the clash of chemistries—intrigued her enough to ask Lynn in the next time she pulled up in her Volvo.

Lynn looked at Sissy dead-on. "How many shekels did he and the boys make on the tips?"

Sissy turned red. "Shouldn't I have told him?"

Lynn broke into a broad grin. "Your Irish guilty rouge is rising. Tone it down. I figured you'd pass on the info. I do the same for Nick. Besides, I admit I'm curious to see who was lucky enough to land you. Come on. But only for a minute, we're running late."

Eddie was not only solicitous but honest. He immediately thanked Lynn for the tips.

"They come in handy," Lynn responded, "but I'd rather do it on my own. Besides, I hate trotters. It's a sport for geriatrics— bingo on wheels. Give me the flats and the *Racing Form* any day."

Eddie looked confounded by this sacrilege to cop logic—self-satisfaction over a sure thing. "You can read the *Form?*" he asked incredulously.

"My numbers have been known to be valid," Lynn replied.

"Next thing, you'll tell me you work the football line."

Lynn lapsed into southern belle simp. "Well, sugar, my daddy taught me the red dog is not necessarily a hound of hell."

Eddie was awed. "Won't you sit down and have a drink?"

"Not this time. We're running late, we have to split. I'll take a raincheck." She shook his hand at the door.

"Next time," Eddie said, "come earlier."

Lynn winked an okay. When she reached the bottom of the steps, she turned, "Hey, Dick Tracy, Sunday take Detroit with the points."

When the women got into the car, Lynn turned to Sissy. "Lord, he's lovely to behold. With that punim, he could move Bella from the barricades to the bedroom."

Over the next few months it seemed to Sissy that Eddie stayed at home consistently on the evenings Sissy was planning to go out with Lynn. It would have been nice to think he was doing it for Eileen's sake, but that didn't wash. Eileen had been capable of fending for herself for some time; besides, she was at the sleepover-at-a-girlfriend's stage. Indeed, it was Sissy who had to bow to Eileen's social calendar before making any plans that would involve mother and daughter. No, it was the hope of meeting with Lynn that kept Eddie at home.

Eddie and Lynn? Sissy thought it was a ludicrous match, but she couldn't deny her jealousy. At first, she thought it was the betting information, but that trickled in only rarely. It was Lynn herself who was the attraction. Sissy watched the easy, delighted way that Eddie bantered with her about sports and the "in" joints in the Village and Brooklyn and the names connected with them. Sissy began to feel that Eddie might be thinking if he could con and charm Lynn out of her aberrant feminism, he would have his mate to face "the real world."

Unlikely as it seemed, downright ridiculous, Sissy felt ill at ease watching Lynn operate publicly. "I've got to go hondle," Lynn would say, and Sissy watched enviously as she enchanted stogie-puffing old Jewish jazz joint owners, gay gallery types, junior league mafiosi, spacey musicians, bookmakers, and black studs. The dudes, as Lynn called them, were a far cry from the blacks Sissy knew from the civil rights movement. An impassioned plea for passive resistance would be hooted down by these cats. Pulpit purrings were not for panthers. Watching Lynn work a room gave Sissy insights into Eddie's legend as a plainclothesman in Manhattan South. These smart-money, "edge" guys were in consort with cops. Together, they would be as smooth as a trapeze act. The only difference was that one group flew while the other caught. All of them would find a shortcut, cut a corner, to get to the mountaintop. Sissy, like Martin Luther King, was so much pussy in such company.

And Lynn had Vincent, a club owner with a pad in Miami who had access to gambling information. A connection. The cop's Spanish fly.

A connection could give substance to a blue boy's wet dream. A connection could grease you to squirrel enough away to get your own joint when you threw in your papers. The new centurion's nirvana, except for the straight-shooters. They were content to get a security gig in a department store where they rode herd on kids and bag ladies.

For her own peace of mind, Sissy decided Vincent was Eddie's amore.

*L*YNN PROVED to be an aphrodisiac more powerful than advice from "Dear Abby." Sissy discovered that when Lynn took her to the opening of a collection of women's paintings to raise funds for the ERA. Sissy was awed to see so many feminist legends in the flesh. My God, these were the women who were shaping her thoughts in print, and now she was in the same room with them. She had hardly recovered from that when she began to realize Lynn was on friendly terms with all of them.

"You never told me," Sissy whispered.

"I told you once," Lynn said, "I was no Johnny-come-lately to the movement. I met the rest, the unwrinkled kiddie corps, when I published my series on women artists."

Sissy was so ecstatic she acted a little dumb. She began, not too discreetly, to point to various feminists. "Do you know who that is?"

"Sure," Lynn replied. "Do you want to be introduced?"

"And her, too?" Sissy pointed at someone else.

"All of them," replied Lynn, laughing. "I believe you're impressed."

"I am," Sissy said. "I am. If only . . ."

"If only what?" Lynn asked.

"No, it's silly," Sissy said. "It's just plain dumb."

"Come on," urged Lynn.

"Well, promise you won't laugh?"

"I promise." Lynn grinned.

"Well," Sissy began, "I'm only here because I'm on your coat-tails (Lynn started to interrupt, but Sissy stopped her with a raised hand), and don't say I'm putting myself down, because I'm not. After I have a drink or two, I'll even have the guts to let you introduce me around. But the truth of the matter is, imagine how many other women would love to be here. Why do all the exciting things take place in Manhattan? Of all the places that don't need any more excitement.

"Now imagine if you could put this show out on the road with the artists and all these celebrities. A week in each borough, say, in a different neighborhood every night. The boroughs have a lot of big halls, and the people who need it, people like me without my luck, could come to see the paintings and talk to the artists and writers. People like the girls I graduated high school with, and even . . . even people like my mother. Is it that dumb? Why does it always have to be Manhattan?"

Lynn glowed at her. "No, it's not dumb. Even people like *my* mother. You know what I love about you, Theresa Sullivan? You've got a platinum shit-detector, and you're still goofy enough to believe. Besides, your Irish Tammany sense of how to get things done borders on simplistic genius." She impulsively kissed Sissy on the cheek. "Don't ever lose your specialness, Sullivan, or your sense of fair play."

This was a lot for Lynn, the abandonment of hipness, and Sissy realized it. Her eyes misted, and she thought Lynn's eyes were gleaming with more than pride in her protegé. Lynn, of course, was the first to recover. "Now, Sullivan, let's find the bar, get you lacquered, and sic you on these elitists."

Even flushed with the confidence of a few highballs, Sissy was tentative about setting forth her proposal. Dogmatically, all her life Sissy had been taught to know her place, and clearly these women were out of her league. Suppose they questioned her credentials? What would she show them—her stretch marks? Weren't these the same women who pronounced Sissy's life—homemaking—"shit work"? Besides the insult, Sissy hated the political ignorance of that phrase. How could they alienate the majority of their constituency? Their idea of "the domestic drudge" matched that of their sworn enemy, the male chauvinist pig.

But with Lynn running interference, she haltingly offered her plan. The reactions were polite, nothing more. "That is an original concept." "Do you really believe any of those people would show up?" "It would take quite a lot of planning and coordination." "I mean, with the subways and everything, you would think that if they were interested, they could find their way to Manhattan." "Perhaps if you did a proposal to the National Endowment for the Arts, and there was funding for the artists for their time and transportation? You should pursue it, and keep us advised. Yes, a grant might make it possible."

Lynn led a defeated Sissy back to the bar. "I know they're busy, but I thought maybe a few nights in each borough?" Sissy stammered. "Christ, one night would be a breakthrough. I wish I'd kept my big mouth shut. I made an ass out of myself."

"*Au contraire*," said Lynn. "I thought it was the other way around."

"No," said Sissy.

"Original thought is never easy to float, Theresa. Especially among the entrenched. Look, if the Academy had its way, they would have guillotined the Impressionists. Take solace, love, that you're ahead of your time."

"When are things going to be synchronized?" Sissy asked ruefully.

Lynn, with a flicker of disgust, said, "It had better be soon, soon. Because some of us are getting tired of talking to the same people all the time. Converting the converted is one big drag. I, for one, never blamed the missionaries for mining the Mau-Mau circuit."

"Is that what the boroughs are?"

"You presume right, Mr. Stanley. And not nearly so exotic. Your quaint little parishes don't have the allure. Now if we could get those women out of their housedresses and into dashikis, we might have a chance."

"Are you making fun of me?" Sissy challenged.

"Not at all. I was thinking of my mother and her friends. Don't be a proletarian snob. The Irish don't have a lock on suppression—or housedresses either. I grew up with an array of them. Plus the smell of soup pots and the clop of mules in the kitchen."

The Fat Lady, Sissy thought. "I'm sorry. I'm just pissed," she said.

"Well, you should be, bubbela. Pissed, I mean. You know my

fear of the hereafter? That is, if there is one, and I get there. That even there, there will be separate latrines for the officers and the enlisted. Come on, let's have a drink before the bartender finds out we're schleppers from Brooklyn."

Sissy was glad when a tape of some music began to play, and the dancing started. She would be spared anyone approaching her about her "intriguing" idea. She watched the couples on the floor. Lynn was right. Even to a novice like Sissy, it was becoming apparent that the faces were always the same. Not only the women, but the men.

The men were a traveling repertory company—husbands and escorts, artists, writers, and book critics sympathetic to the cause, young male politicians from swank Manhattan districts who had made the ERA, ecology, and gay rights their career stepping-stones. They were so earnest, Sissy found them ludicrous. When women talked to them, they bent forward with the intensity of the hard of hearing. Their heads bobbed up and down continuously, like those plastic goonybirds she used to see sitting on local back bars, repeatedly dipping their beaks into a glass of water. Sissy looked for a horizontal shake of the head, but it was rarely evident. When she'd observed it, Sissy presumed the female speaker had mentioned Phyllis Schafly. She wished one of the politicians would get high and make a blatant pass at someone. It never happened.

Sissy found no drama, no challenge in them. These men took pleasure in guilt. They haughtily assigned themselves to suffer for the sins of the rest of their sex. Sissy never could divine the charm of martyrs.

Besides, she found them condescending. They would have you believe they understood every iota of female degradation. It was just another male conceit. Eddie used to hit Sissy's similar attitude toward the blacks. "Don't play nigger," he'd say. "If the shit ever comes down, you and the rest of the liberals will be waving your white birth certificates. Isn't there enough pain in your own life without stealing somebody else's?" Maybe Eddie had been right.

Sissy also suspected these men were bored, their intensity programmed. Sissy had seen the same look on Eddie's face when he orchestrated the kids' birthday parties when they were young. The look that said, "I'm really into pin-the-tail-on-the-donkey and hot beans." In Eddie's favor, she had to admit it took a while for the look to develop. Maybe that was so with these men. That's as much as she could grant them.

"Uh-oh," said Lynn.

"What?" Sissy asked.

Lynn pointed across the room to a dazzlingly beautiful woman dressed in a tuxedo. Sissy the moviegoer recognized that the woman had affected Marlene Dietrich's decadent Berlin look to the letter. The woman looked as if she had the full arsenal of both sexes. It panicked Sissy.

"Janie Andrews," Lynn said. "The high priestess of radical lesbianism, and she's into her act."

Sissy knew the name from women's magazines. She was a celebrated lesbian writer whose main issue was that any woman who slept with a man was a traitor to her sex. True feminists, she argued, made love to other women, thus to themselves.

"What act?" Sissy asked.

"Watch her. She goes around the room at these parties asking women to dance. Usually leaders in the movement. And when they refuse, she labels them penis-oriented traitors in her column. It's her standard schtick. She gets it off embarrassing anyone who won't adhere to her party line."

Sissy was spellbound as she watched Andrews in action, going from group to group. The scene kept repeating itself. Andrews obviously asking for a dance, while her intended valiantly tried to smile and make light of the request. Charm is even the last defense of generals, thought Sissy.

After each refusal, there would be a red-faced woman straining to be nonchalant. Laughing too hard, lighting a cigarette too cavalierly. The bigger the name in the movement, the harder Andrews worked. There were shows of persistence, Andrews trying to drag her prey out onto the dance floor by the hand, or bending over and whispering something in her ear. Sissy pitied the women. If their faces were any indication, their bodies must look like thermometers running rampant. But as much as she pitied them, she wished one of them would accept. None did, and Andrews dismissed them with a throaty laugh.

She was coming perilously close to where Sissy was standing. Then she was there. Sissy saw the tuxedo and the red lips and nothing more. The balcony of her brain thought of holding up a crucifix.

"Why, hello, Lynn," Andrews said, octaves lower than any other woman Sissy had ever heard.

"Hello, Janie. I see you're spreading your normal good cheer. You'll never have writer's block as long as you've got your sisters for fodder."

"And you'll never have a civil word in your mouth, Lynn darling. That's your charm. You've perfected the best bitch act since *All About Eve.*"

"Second best, Janie," Lynn countered. "Second best."

"Well, dear, now that we have the ratings out of the way, how about a . . ." Andrews paused and turned to Sissy. "Well, well, what have we here? Where have you been hiding her, Lynn? A virgin face (she canvassed Sissy top to bottom), not to mention a virgin body on the barricade circuit. What's your name, little one? Small matter, we'll get acquainted on the dance floor."

She moved toward Sissy, and Sissy felt her will drain. She was engulfed by a swooning terror. The creature could have her way with her! Lynn intercepted Andrews, grabbing her outstretched hand. "Slow down, Janie. You asked me first. You don't want to get a reputation for being fickle."

Andrews was astonished. "Well, how protective, mother hen. But this is a first. After all these years, Lynn. I didn't know you cared."

"Madly, madly," said Lynn, as she ushered Andrews to the dance floor.

The whole room watched the action. As they made their way to the space reserved for dancing, the other couples relinquished them the center, retreating to the perimeter and falling into a walking two-step, ideal for watching. Andrews seized the initiative and pulled Lynn close to her. Lynn, far from resisting, cranked her bottom in parody and started to grind into Andrews in a humping motion. It was broad burlesque, and Andrews didn't know how to handle it. The women in the room clocked the action. There was vengeful laughter. The thunderstruck Sissy, once again awed by her friend, joined in with relief.

Not so the men. They watched every bump and grind with dead earnestness. Sissy saw their eyes become like coils in a hotplate. She noticed them fidget, the familiar sexual itch that sent tingles down to their feet. She had watched this all her life, their little Saint Vitus's mating dance. But the parody was so . . . so gross, as Eileen would say. She realized they were getting it off on the two women simulating lesbian love. Eddie had told her once that lesbian films were big in the male porn market. She couldn't understand it then, and certainly not now. Not in this setting. Was that what they believed women really wanted, that that was the bottom line? Archie Bunker wasn't confined to the other side of the Triborough Bridge after all.

When the charade on the dance floor ended, Andrews knew she had been made the fool. The maliciously grinning women were all the evidence she needed. She tried to recoup by rendering Lynn the sweeping bow of a gallant, but Lynn had a flourish of her own. She took Andrews's face between her hands and kissed her roundly on the lips, then left her standing in the middle of the floor.

When she reached Sissy, she turned and bellowed for the benefit of the room, "Hey, Janie, when the Gay Rights Bill comes up this year, don't hassle me. Tell them I gave at the orifice." She turned and winked conspiratorially at Sissy. "Grab your coat and let's go before someone auctions me and that dike off as a mobile."

That night, when Sissy returned late, she was surprised to see Eddie sitting up in bed doing his paperwork. Usually, if he was at home at this hour, he was already asleep. Either a tough day or a booze stop with the guys retired him early. It was Sissy who was the night owl perched before one of the television sets, watching an old movie that connected with her past.

"Is everything all right?" she asked, slightly wary. She hoped he wasn't steaming for a row.

He put down a sheaf of papers. "Fine, fine. Just catching up on some reports. What a job! They want you to play sheriff and secretary. Now that's what I call wearing two hats."

Sissy smiled.

"How did your night go?" he asked.

She tensed for no good reason. It was all innocence, but he had a way of making you feel guilty. What was it with cops? When they stopped you for running an amber light, every indiscretion ever committed came to mind, right down to letting an overage child crawl under a turnstile. "Okay. We went to a women's art exhibit."

"Yeah?"

"Pretty dull stuff. Those broads must have something against laughter."

She got the reaction she wanted. He grinned, but she hated herself—"broads" and the cliché of glumness. At least Judas got a payday. She had sold out for a smile. In her embarrassment she compounded the treachery. "God, I'm exhausted. I feel like I've done a night's work." She turned her back and got out of her clothes, quickly shimmying into a flannel nightgown. The flannel made her feel secure and warm, less vulnerable. All she needed was a glass of juice, her girlhood room, and a stack of comic books to close him out.

"Did you stay long?"

"No, we stopped for a while." She let it hang, while she made her way to the bathroom to wash her face and brush her teeth. She took her time, but she knew she couldn't outlast him. The bathroom became like a dentist's waiting room. It was better to get it over with. She returned and crawled into bed.

"Are you ready to turn out the lights?" she asked. "I'm beat."

"Yeah," he said, pitching the papers and his briefcase to the floor. "Next, they'll be asking me to make the captain coffee. I think I'll join you at some of those meetings."

She laughed in sync with the click of the lamp. When his voice, with forced casualness, came out of the darkness, she was expecting it. "Where did you stop?"

"Some disco in Soho. God, what a din," she snorted disparagingly. She would be a lousy prisoner of war, she thought. Her utterances stank of collaboration.

"Yeah, those joints knock your head off. Sometimes we stop in the precinct. The younger guys dig them. Plenty of fannies to watch."

"That's for sure," she said, her back turned to him. "They're not made for out-of-date Lindyers."

"For sure," he said. "But you're a good dancer. You should be able to handle it. I tried it a couple of times and looked like a March of Dimes poster."

She smelled the good cop routine. "I know what you mean. God, I'm exhausted. I think I'll tuck."

There was a pause. "Can you do it?"

"Not very well. Lynn is good at it, though."

"Usually only the blacks and Puerto Ricans look good on the dance floor. A couple of barmaids tried to give me lessons, but they said I was a hopeless honky."

He was offering too much information. "Did you ever dance with one?"

"With who?" she offered dumbly.

"You know. Someone who could really disco. A black."

So that was the bottom line. She'd be damned if she'd lie. She had humiliated herself enough. "Oh, once or twice. Musician friends of Lynn's." She laughed nervously. "I did as well as you. They never asked me again." She didn't tell him she had felt like Rhonda Fleming in a jungle movie, moving in the glow of a campfire, a burnished white goddess in the heart of darkness.

The silence was menacing. She lay there, hearing her irregular breathing, waiting for the worst. He said nothing. She froze when he put his hand on her hip. He hoisted her nightgown and moved in behind her in the fetal position. She felt his prick. It was immense. It felt like a hot tracing of her spine. His hand started to fondle her breast. She wanted to beg off, but her ass instinctively started to move into him. It had been so long since she had felt spontaneously excited. She could feel he truly wanted her, was not just paying his dues to the notion they were still "Eddie and Sissy." The heat emanating from him seemed to reach her shoulders. He rolled her over on her hands and knees and pulled her nightgown over her head, hooding her. Not so much as a kiss. The subjugation excited her.

She pulled a pillow under her forehead and arched her rump up to him. He was on his knees behind her. Her bottom was straining backward to locate him. She felt a clot of hot moisture drop into the crevice of her ass. She realized it was spit. It was something new, and she groaned. He rubbed the moisture down the crack to where his prick was poised at her vagina. He blended the juices and began slowly to slide, inch by inch, into her box, moving himself from side to side, and then arching the base of his stem to hit her upper wall while the head of his penis plumbed the bottom. She was traumatized with pleasure.

He went on, alternating between slow, probing strokes and jabs of fury, slowing down at the brink of climax. She squeezed and bit the pillow and joined him in vigorously making circles with her bottom, then shaking his prick back and forth horizontally—like a face being slapped by two hands.

She was so wet she had to be careful not to slide loose. She realized he wasn't making love to her, but performing for her, as if he was in a competition. That was it! That was fucking it, not reborn affection. He was excited by the fact that other men, black men, had asked her to dance, wanted her. She had gotten some hip seal of approval from other men, so once again she was desirable to him. It should have disgusted her, this male certification, but it was so base it only excited her more. The only adjustment she made was to control the ending. She reached back between her legs and grabbed his scrotum, dictating the tempo of his thrusts. She slammed him deeper into her, faster, faster, until she felt the panic in him that he wasn't in control. The baton had been passed. She was now conducting. She rose up on her free hand, arched her head back like a wild thing baying at the moon and drove down on him, sealing the space between them, forcing their mouths open in ejaculatory roars.

Not a word was said afterward, no tender kiss offered. Not even congratulatory pats, not the flicker of a match. They pulled up the blankets in total exhaustion and turned their separate ways. As the exhilaration subsided, Sissy felt a flush of disgust. He had used her with artificial stimulus. She should have terminated it when she realized that, withdrawn with dignity. Ejected, aborted him. She queasily knew she wouldn't have missed it for the world. But it wasn't her he had wanted, only the perceptions others had of her. God, it was so sick.

Then she remembered when Eddie was trying to quit cigarettes and had switched to a pipe. She remembered the first time they made love when his breath smelled so strange from the pipe. It wasn't a cop inside her that night but a tweedy, pipe-puffing, fantasy professor. A Rex Harrison dream. She remembered it had driven her wild. And that was when they were still close, in love. It would be worse than hell, she thought, if when we died we were made to divulge what we thought of every time we made love. Her solace was that God, as presented, would have no interest in such sleazy voyeurism. She took her passionate accessory, the pillow, and put it to another use, pulling it over her head to black out the sadness of human imperfection.

*A*s PERVERSE as that evening was, it was something. Contact of some sort that just might ignite the old flame. And there had been genuine excitement in the lovemaking, however engendered, not like the occasional dutiful thumps in the night Sissy had come to expect. On those nights Sissy felt she should have paid Eddie the minimum wage for performing distasteful labor.

In all honesty, Sissy wouldn't have minded a reprise. But Eddie dashed that hope when he overreached with Lynn. Eddie's charm, since he obtained his shield, had lost its cool. He pressed too much. The fault was part cop and a good deal Irish. He was a direct descendant of those fawning Democratic precinct captains you encountered at the polling booth. Too much research—dossiers going back to your dear departed Aunt Kate—to be genuine. The wrong tactic for Lynn, who floated on a riff.

The rupture occurred when Lynn came to meet Sissy for an evening of experimental theater in the Village. After the usual sports page banter, Eddie asked Lynn their destination and, when she told him, said, "My old stomping grounds. The Village is a great action place."

"Do you want to join us?" Lynn asked with a sly grin. "You might enjoy the plays. One is mime—you know, D&D, deaf-and-dumb."

The reference made Eddie uncomfortable. "Nah, I'm afraid

that's not my game. But some night maybe you'll let me show you both my haunts in the Village."

"That might be fun," Lynn replied noncommittally.

Eddie shuffled a bit. Sissy knew the nervous prelude too well. He was about to propose something. The foot pawing was his point patrol to a proposition. "And after that," he said, "maybe you two will let me join you at lunch with your dad. My treat, of course. Unless you practice reverse sexual discrimination on those occasions," he added with an elaborate grin.

Lynn turned stone cold. "Let's think about the Village first."

"Yeah, sure," Eddie replied greedily. "I know some out-of-the-way spots. I was in plainclothes there for a few years."

"Yes, I know," Lynn said.

"A special unit."

"Yes, that unit was well known."

Eddie didn't like the tone of that. "Yeah, the bureaucrats broke it up. We all went back in uniform. I'm in East Flatbush now. It's not the same ballpark. But I guess the powers that be figured we did our jobs or were going stale. You know bureaucracy."

"The Santa Claus Squad," Lynn said.

"The what?" Eddie queried.

"That's how it's remembered in the Village."

"I never heard that," Eddie declared.

"Well, they say everyone had a bag over his shoulder."

Eddie looked as if she'd spit on him. "That's just wise guy, asshole talk."

"Maybe, maybe so," said Lynn. "But the word is that the squad had creases from the bags in their shoulders. The creases, they say, were the unit's epaulets."

Sissy thought she could see the word "cunt" forming on Eddie's lips. His parochial manners were all that held him in check. He was so rigid and white he looked marbleized.

"But then again," Lynn added, "the Village is full of talk. Look, we have to breeze." Without so much as a goodbye, they left Eddie standing there like a desecrated statue.

When they got in her car, Lynn said, "I'm sorry for that. I don't mind being hustled for myself, but not for my father. That shit has been tried before. I just hope he doesn't come down hard on you. If I were a man . . ." She paused. "Now that's a female cliché for you. But if I was, I would have cleaned his clock."

Though Sissy would never tell her so, Lynn's prognosis was

on the money. Eddie started to land hard on her. A lapse of any kind—no clean laundry, an occasional dinner of warmed leftovers, a late return home—was greeted with surliness and the suggestion he and Eileen should "form our own movement."

Sissy's socializing became occasions for savagery. "That's my turf—my turf—do you hear? I'm known in practically every joint. I don't want my wife and some bimbo running around my old haunts. I built up a lot of respect there, and I still pay courtesy calls. Find someplace else to wet your whistle."

His arrogance astounded her. Did he think the only identity she had in life was her connection with him! That the drummer gave a roll whenever she walked into a place and announced that Eddie Sullivan's old lady was there without him. If it weren't for Lynn, she wouldn't even be noticed on "his turf," yet he thought her world revolved around the axis of his organ. His monogrammed organ, to boot.

Stonewalling him with silence didn't help. "Besides, that broad is using you," he'd say. Ah, the "good cop" gambit. He was looking out for Sissy's welfare. Where was this going to lead? "She's got 'recruiter' written all over her."

"What?" Sissy asked.

"Recruiter. I've seen it a million times on the job. She's tired, baby, nearly washed out. Notice the crows' feet around the eyes. She's no different than burned-out cases on the job. Former hotshots, rookies of the year, who have gone to bat too often. So they hustle newcomers to keep their ass in the spotlight. I watch these buzzards on the job, checking the bodies of promising rookies, trying to partner up with them so their collar rate won't drop. They're weary, and so is she. Too much time and grade on the front lines. They're ready for the bunker, the game is to send somebody else's ass over the top. And you're fresh meat, baby. Prime."

This jarred Sissy. His insidious scent recalled her conversation with Lynn, coming home in the car after the fund-raising art show, when Sissy asked Lynn if she'd champion Sissy's idea of getting the show out to the boroughs. After all, Sissy thought, Lynn's clout might carry it.

"That's your baby to carry, Theresa," Lynn had said. "I organized art collectives, fought for equal gallery space and prices for women. And believe it or not, out of guilt, because like so many of my sisters I employ one, I told them we should try to obtain social security and health benefits for domestics. That one went down the toilet when we campaigned for the right of hookers on Eighth Avenue, the Minnesota Strip, to solicit. How the media pulled their pudding over that one! No, my love, this one is yours. It's dues-paying time. Enough is enough. Sainthood was never my bag.

"Theresa, honey, I have this horrible fear. Lombardi as a relic of the movement. That's the danger of staying on the circuit too long. They waltz you out for every occasion, but you're so old hat that everybody's eyes cloud over when you open your mouth. Do you want me to name names? I respect style too much to become the Georgie Jessel of feminism."

Damn, Sissy thought. That hadn't been insidious, it was touching. Then Eddie played one card too many. "Besides, she's the vainest broad I ever met."

Without fear of consequence, Sissy moved her face within inches of his. "Vain! Eddie, you poor dear, though you might not have realized it, you have been running for the local drag chapter of Miss America all your life."

This tilting of his crown left him without an exit line.

After that, Sissy waited outside the house for Lynn. And though she never mentioned it, the significance of this was not lost on Lynn. Her way of acknowledging that dirty domestic linen was flapping was to invite Sissy to meet her mother. Quid pro quo. The Fat Lady was to be unveiled.

When they visited Lily at her Ocean Parkway apartment, Sissy understood Lynn's reluctance to showcase her mother. Lily was not the kind of mother the liberated Lynn would put on display. Not that Sissy didn't like Lily; in fact, the opposite was true. She was immediately at ease with her. Lily was a composite of all the married women Sissy had ever known.

Sissy understood Lynn's hesitation. After all, Lynn was a heralding angel of the new life, and her progenitor was an infidel with a seemingly contented deaf ear to her daughter's avenging trumpet. But Sissy had spent too much time in the domestic field to assume contentment. It could be numbing shell-shock. Lily showed tattletale signs. It was obvious the blond woman had been a looker; now she had gone to fat, though the fat didn't hide the sensuality that was once there. Once you had it, it could never be fully extinguished. The bloated Elizabeth Taylor in *Who's Afraid of Virginia Woolf* was proof of that. The banked fires were always evident to men. When Sissy occasionally gave way to heft, Eddie used to call it "sucky fat."

The burying of sexuality with shovels of calories wasn't all that Sissy noticed about Lily. There was the clutter with which she filled her life. The apartment with its bric-a-brac, throw pillows, and framed photos of the younger Lily and Vincent and Lynn were lifelines to the past. The overly effusive speech that said little and went nowhere, the constant apologies for "running on," the overripe makeup, the obsequious and frequent offers to cater to guests. The verbal orifice overflowing in compensation for the one that had been neglected. Sissy saw her mother, her friends, herself. The communion of kindness with this woman was easy.

Like most women Sissy knew, Lily was at her subservient worst on her own turf. She couldn't be still. Sissy was afraid to shift her eyes, knowing that the slightest movement would spur Lily to bolt from her chair: "What are you looking for, dear?" "What can I get for you, dear?" And, of course, nothing was adequate—the condition of the apartment, her appearance, the food, the temperature of the beverages in the cups. Afternoons of tea and obsequiousness.

But Sissy understood. She had spent a great deal of her own life bowing and scraping for her "inadequacies," as Nellie had before her. Sissy had vowed she would never do that, but escaping the yolk that had hatched you was no easy thing. And it got worse as one got older. Sissy not only echoed many of Nellie's apologies, she was startled to hear herself deliver them in her mother's cadence. But there was a slight difference. Sissy's self-deprecation was couched in nebbish humor. Modern woman's weapon, the tongue of fire that self-immolates.

When Lily was free of the responsibility of her home, her nervousness became attractive energy. That was another syndrome Sissy had noted in women—the emancipation from the caretaker role. Seeing Lily let loose on the town, Sissy could finally connect mother and daughter. Lily was an intrepid shopper, a spirited haggler, and, like her daughter, a guide to the arcane. There wasn't a flea market or charity bazaar in Brooklyn Lily didn't know about. She was completely ecumenical. Her quarry could be Jewish, Catholic, or Episcopalian—the connective thread being an undiscovered bargain. Watching Lily hunt out exotic swatches of material, saying, "I think I could do something with this on my machine," it was evident where Lynn got her flair for clothes. And indeed, sometime after the purchase, the piece of material was transformed into something startling—a skirt, a blouse, or scarves that were presented as gifts to Lynn and, occasionally, Sissy. "Just a little something," Lily would say.

Once Lynn realized the excursions were not a drag on Sissy, she dropped her arch pose of "Let's humor the old girl," and Lynn and Lily scoured counters as a fevered tandem. Watching this pleased Sissy almost more than anything else she learned about Lynn. She wasn't, after all, Wonder Woman on a visit from an isle of Amazonian feminists, but a daughter with a past and with connections. A daughter who had some of her flawed mother in her, as Sissy carried parts of Nellie. Seeing the two of them perform together with gusto, fighting for space at a counter, working over a saleslady on price (Christ, they could have been cops!), and exulting in getting what they wanted reminded Sissy of herself and Nellie preparing a holiday dinner back when there was still something to be festive about. Or she and Nellie getting up to dance an Irish set at a wedding, to "shake a leg," as Nellie put it, and feel the admiring eyes from around the room, hear the rhythmic clapping and the shouts of "Up Galway" and "Up Mayo." Sissy could remember the pride of mother and daughter defying age, theirs the liveliest and shapeliest legs on the dance floor. It was times like that, and when the holiday baked goods were coming out of the oven, that Sissy felt she and Nellie together, given the chance, could do anything. Not only do it, but do it better than anyone.

In a way Sissy felt more gratified to be included in Lynn's family orbit than in the more exotic swirl that so fascinated her. Though she didn't want to sacrifice one for the other. But this access gave Sissy cachet. She had never heard any of Lynn's other acquaintances even mention Lynn's parents. It was as if Sissy had passed some secret trial Lynn had set for her. Maybe it was the bond of Brooklyn.

The people they met in Manhattan seemed to have no past. The rare mention of family or the place where they were bred was savaged by insult. It was as though their parents were imposters, primitive custodians who had kidnapped these princes and princesses of the shimmering night from their rightful realm. Sissy could never understand that. For better or worse, like Dracula, she carried her turf with her.

And now it was clear that the mercurial Lynn did, too. Besides her parental visits with Sissy, it was obvious from Lily's and Vincent's conversation that their daughter kept in touch by phone. "Keeping your hand in," as Eddie used to call his network.

The need to connect also cleared up an ambiguity in Lynn's life that had baffled Sissy. She couldn't figure out why Lynn didn't live in Manhattan. No one was better groomed for it. Lynn always brushed aside Sissy's queries on this point by blaming sky-rocketing rents. "Even Jackie O has to moonlight to afford her pad." This never sat well with Sissy, since she knew Brooklyn Heights rentals were nearly on a par with Manhattan's. But now she knew. You couldn't drop in for a casual cup of coffee from the city or, more to the point, deliver a gasping parent to the emergency ward from the upper East Side. That was stretching the supply line, the umbilical cord, too thin.

So Sissy and Lynn now had a bond in timidity. Lynn, to be sure, was more daring. She had gotten to the Heights, the foot of the Brooklyn Bridge, a mortar lob away from the front lines; while Sissy still nestled a howitzer away safely in Flatbush. But it was a matter of degree.

This was a dizzying revelation to Sissy. Armed with this shard of equality, she felt freer to exert herself with Lynn, especially on their days with Lily. Like Sissy, Lily was a movie buff, so at Sissy's urging, the women spent sunny afternoons in the darkness of movie houses. Sissy had loved this ritual since she was a girl. It was one of the things that made her feel special—to be sequestered in a theater while the rest of the world scurried about its mundane business. But it had to be in the afternoon, better yet on a school day when she played hookey. You had the feeling you were beating the rat race. She had heard Mickey say once that the magical hours in a bar were in the morning, watching the frenzied world pass by the window. Forever her father's daughter.

Nighttime movie-going just didn't do it for her. When she was a child, it meant being dragged off by Nellie as a companion on dish night. In her teens it meant fending off groping boys. God, you would have thought her besieged breast was a jammed door knob. Such things never happened on her afternoon soirées.

Sissy introduced Lynn and Lily to the ways of afternoon nabes. Instead of eating lunch before the movie, Sissy would insist they go to a deli and order lunch to go. Hot dogs, pastrami sandwiches, knishes, cans of Dr. Brown's cream soda in smeared brown bags to be opened in the far reaches of the balcony. The initiated women loved the greasy feast, and Sissy was granted the status of a pathfinder. To play Pygmalion to Lynn elevated the brown bag to an elegant picnic basket and the Dr. Brown's to Bordeaux.

At first, Lily was tentative when the women discussed their choice of movies. "Oh, don't pay any attention to me. I like dumb romances and fluffy comedies. These foreign movies lose me. If I need depression, all I have to do is call my sister. When I see those decadent Italian movies, I think I miss the point. Afterward, I always want to call my travel agent and book Rome. Alone."

Sissy howled while Lynn said, "Mom, I think you've found your niche—movie reviewing. You make a hell of a lot more sense than those *auteur* theorists."

There was no need for Lily to hesitate. She had an ally in taste in Sissy. On television Sissy could accept "problem" shows, the television set was, after all, nothing but another carping family member in the living room. But movie houses weren't made for such niggling. Movie houses were meant to transport. Troubled movies were like going for a medical check. There was enough woe in life without seeking it out.

So Sissy and Lily, through their shared taste in movies, became easy, chatty companions. To them, movies were what baseball was to men. There was a history to explore. The two women bridged the natural gap of the difference in age by culling up past favorites—films and stars. Lynn was content to be an outsider in this, taking reflected glory in presenting such a friend to her mother. Besides, when she tried to join in, her choices were slightly off-center. "Greta Garbo in *Camille*," she offered.

"You're letting your higher education get in the way," Sissy boldly countered.

"That big Swedish horse," Lily added, "could cure consumption with two aspirin."

Sissy shrieked at her compatibility with Lily. "My God, do you remember the way she fluttered her fan as a coquette? She looked like she was swatting house flies."

Lily, sensing she had her daughter caught in a rare middle, came back, "Oh, yes! The size of her hands and that bone structure. In a dressing gown, Lynn, Garbo looked like the transvestites in that Jewel Box Revue your father took me to see at the Town & Country."

"I vant to drag alone," vamped Sissy.

"All right, all right," Lynn conceded good-naturedly. "No more arty pretensions from me. I'll leave the field to the two experts." There was no surliness in Lynn's remark, just a good-hearted retreat. Sissy liked that. Her friend didn't have to win them all.

So Lynn became a rapt listener as her mother and her friend shamelessly evoked the magic of bygone musicals with Betty Grable, Judy Garland, June Haver, Marge and Gower Champion, Dan Dailey, Betty Garrett, Ginger Rogers, Fred Astaire ("A shame they weren't in color"), Gene Kelly, and Cyd Charisse. When they got truly esoteric, Lynn expressed incredulity. "You have to be kidding. Gloria deHaven? That broad was a failed carhop."

"Unlike Garbo who could handle the Swedish meatballs," Sissy retorted.

"Okay, okay," said Lynn, throwing up her hands. Lily hugged her newfound partner.

Lily lamented that she couldn't "make it" with the modern musicals. "I don't know. Maybe it's the new music and the kids who sing it. I enjoy them on the radio. Not crazy about them, mind you, but still enjoyable. But in the movies something is missing. I just can't touch it."

"Maybe it's the new directors," Lynn offered.

"Directors, shmerectors," answered Lily, "what would I know from them?"

"It's the color," Sissy said.

"What color?" commented Lily. "All the movies I am talking about are in color."

"Not Technicolor," Sissy said reverentially.

"There's a difference?" asked Lily.

"Oh, yes," said Sissy. "There was never a color like Technicolor. Do you remember how the front porches looked? And the amusement parks? Especially Coney Island. I wish I had never gone to Coney Island in person. It crushed me. I expected to see everything cast in that magical glow, and it was just another tawdry beach filled with tacky people. They don't use the same process anymore in films. I read an article about it. Worse, many of the old prints are fading, since they didn't have a way to preserve the tint back then. It will be gone forever, and there will never be that kind of color again. It haloed everything it touched. As a girl, the closest I could come to imagining God's heaven was to think of a Technicolor kingdom where all our imperfections were tinted away. My heaven would look like the St. Louis World's Fair or Hollywood's turn-of-the-century version of Coney Island at night." Sissy smiled and said, "Dippy, huh?"

"Ah, sure, you have the touch of the poet in you, girl," Lynn said in a broad brogue, smiling protectively.

"Well, I guess we're all dippy," added Lily. "I mean, the things we like. I know it's pretty silly stuff, these movies and television shows I like. But I'm hooked. No wonder men get tired of us," she ended with resignation.

"Men, men," Sissy said angrily. "They'd have you believe they're never foolish. If you believed them, they would tell you they spend all their waking hours trying to find a cure for cancer or mulling over the international balance of payments. Why should movies, television, or going shopping be any more stupid than their preoccupation with sports, barhopping, or a million other stupid things?"

An astonished Lily said, "I never thought of it that way. Vincent will watch anything you can bet on. When we go to Vegas, I can't get him to go to bed all weekend. He sits shiva at the blackjack table."

"That's what I mean," Sissy said.

"To me, watching some dumb, starving dog chase a mechanical rabbit that he'd break his teeth on if he caught it is the worst." Lily shuddered at the memory of it.

The duo was now in full bloom. "Yeah," Sissy said, "and did you ever hear them moan about a favorite ballplayer who's been traded? We should be so mourned when we're gone."

"Enough said," Lily determined. "Let's find a delicious dumb movie to go to today."

Reciting male foibles became a ritual with Sissy and Lily every time they met. The challenge was to come up with a fresh one for each meeting. Lynn was so pleased to see her mother, for once, question male dominance that she was content to sit on the sidelines. The game became so spirited that Lily and Sissy, upon meeting, would shout out their new entries before exchanging greetings. "Sports cars." "Gold chains." "Brut cologne." "Hairpieces." "Season tickets." "Hair dryers" (a real howl). "Nights with the boys" (delivered mincingly by Sissy). And the final raise of the ante by Lily, "Vapid young broads." Lynn was exhilarated to see her mother cut so deep, finally draw blood, no matter it was her own.

At the end of one of these days, when Lynn drove Sissy home, she said, "Do you know, Theresa, from the first moment I heard you sound off at that meeting in the Heights, I said to myself, if we're ever going to the barricades, we're going to need her kind. Don't you ever get world-weary like the rest of us."

She reached over and kissed Sissy on the cheek and held her for a moment. "Thanks for Lily. Now get your ass out of this car before that cop of yours comes rushing out declaring that he knew this is what the movement was about all along."

Sissy exited from the car in a glow not unlike Technicolor.

H ow Sissy would long for those days. Not only for the wonderment with Lynn, but because of Eddie's interest and antagonism. Domestic brawling, she reasoned, was a slight quiver on the Richter scale of love. Then the word came: Billy had been killed in action. A body bag replaced her baby boy. A hero, a credit to his nation, they said. Sissy only wished she could believe it. Even an ornamented lie might help her get through.

Seemingly, Eddie couldn't find an anchor either. Previous patriotic talk was no match for the news from the War Department. Eddie retreated into sullen solitude, while Sissy took to frantic searching. To her, the key to her woes had to be in the past. A missed opportunity, the wrong path taken—be it God, her family, her girlhood. Perhaps the cosmic clue could be coaxed back. Somewhere she was sure she had erred gravely. She was positive about that. Why else was it that only she among all her friends had lost a child? The absolution was back there, in the past.

That notion spurred her bleak period. She sought contact with ignored friends (maybe they could tell her?) and made pilgrimages to her girlhood haunts. Eddie filled his void with steady alcohol maintenance, a drinking pattern that induced eerie trances. His disappearances from home for nights in a row weren't up for debate.

But it was Sissy who was the disgrace. Once again she was violating neighborhood mores. Eddie's quiet, deadly demeanor was within the turf's code of ethics. Sissy's frantic scrambling meant she'd gone public—the local notary seal of insanity. Her conduct didn't miss Eddie's zombie gaze. He even began to champion Lynn. He urged Sissy to call her friend and "get out for a night." Sissy knew what that meant. Get out of the neighborhood.

She didn't tell him Lynn had called repeatedly, offering solace and invitations. She had even wanted to attend Billy's funeral service. "My parents, too," she'd said. When misery hits, even wild mustangs paw like ponies. Sissy refused. Refused all invitations. She needed time to herself.

The reason for not seeing Lynn was more profound than a need for solitude. In examining her conscience Sissy started to make a connection between her woes and her association with Lynn. Before she had met Lynn, Billy was still alive and her marriage was still tolerable. As good as any, Nellie would say. But then she started to exert herself, to give voice to suppressed thoughts and opinions, to spend more time away from home. What if she had spent some of those evenings at home, writing to Billy to be cautious? Might he not still be alive? The letters they had exchanged now seemed unsatisfactory. Not the letters of a mother and son at all, but of two independent people posturing about their newfound worlds. God, she could have sent more food packages.

It wasn't that she blamed Lynn for any of it. Lynn simply symbolized the period. That period (there was no other word for it) of vanity. The nuns had warned her about that sin early, and she had passed them off as jealous dullards. But the signs were always there. Her duck, her wardrobe, her Shirley Temple cocktails. Later, her tan and her legs. God, she was often told, didn't take kindly to strutting. So Lynn had to be ignored as penance for that period. It couldn't continue. She still had Eileen, and the catechism had instructed that God's wrath was as bottomless as His love.

If nothing else, the hospital rest and medication reprogrammed her, while the doctor challenged a new vanity—she couldn't control the tides. That was nicer, much nicer, and easier to live with. The medical equivalent of the harpies' "Ah-h, it's beyond us. God works in mysterious ways." The false line of life was as circular and soothing as a tit.

She took up with Lynn again. Things were calmer. She had taken a breather, nothing more. Like when she was out of sorts as a child and stayed in her room for a week. She didn't even think the drugs were necessary. It was the pampering.

Mind, heart and soul were soothed by all those who had access to her. She had done all she could—a perfect wife, a good mother —the cosmos was beyond her control. The mirror became her accomplice, giving the lie to her siding with vanity. There was no distorted, supercilious sneer, only the gullies of lines and the hollow eyes of an accident victim. Besides, she needed Lynn again, now that Eddie seemed forever beyond her reach. When she tried to reach him, she only made it worse. One of her consistencies. He so needed help. Asking him to find someone to talk to was the wrong tack, though. Maybe it was male tough-it-out or ingrained cop. Probably cop. Telling on yourself was still squealing.

But she truly felt sorry for him. She, at least, had been able to ventilate her sadness. She had been so sick inside that she finally had to unload, regardless of who caught it. When she was bursting to puke, she didn't worry about the splatter. Did Eddie suppose it was manly to choke back the suffocating bile and lumps? If that was what the real world was about, they could stuff it.

She'd hear him, late, in the living room, dropping glasses and ice, and then he'd hit something violently. The temper was endurable, he'd always had that. The snorting crying that followed was what rocked her. She had tried a few times to come down from the bedroom to him, but he'd heard her, and by the time she had descended the stairs he was gone. The car starting outside rebuffed her intrusion. The clock told her the bars still had a few hours to run. Finally, when she found him gone while his shoes still remained by the chair, she decided never to come down the stairs again. The idea that he, with his sense of neighborhood propriety, would leave the house in his slippers was the true measure of his pain. Nothing he had ever done before so broke her heart.

Sissy came to realize that Billy's loss affected Eddie more profoundly than it had her. It didn't seem so on the surface, since Sissy was the one who was outwardly rattled. But that was no more than normal. Pining mothers were the world's staple.

And in the most horrible sense Billy's death vindicated Sissy. His body bag was irrefutable evidence of the war's wickedness. Eddie not only lost a son but a philosophy. His way of life had been scattered in the wind. And she, dammit, had to live with the smugness of her righteousness.

To Eddie, the war wasn't the glib machismo Sissy conveniently labeled it. It was a belief, as deep as his convictions about the force and the neighborhood. They were intertwined. All had to be supported, they weren't disparate spokes at all. If one broke, the protective umbrella of the decent life would collapse. As Eddie said, "You can't pick and choose. Either you fold or you're in for the pot."

After Billy had announced his intention to join the Marines, she and Eddie argued nightly. It was Sissy's contention that Billy had made his decision to please his father. Billy was going to fight his father's war. Eddie had poisoned the boy with his vision of life. Eddie didn't raise his voice during these arguments. His anger ran so deep it was frozen. "We've had our problems, Sissy, but I always thought it was part of a normal marriage. I never realized you thought I was first-class scum."

"I never said that."

"Then what's your definition of a father who would send his kid off to fight his battles? A father who would put his boy's ass on the line while he stood on the sidelines like a cheer-leader. Sorry, Sissy, the only word that comes to mind is scum."

"You have to admit you support this war, don't you?" she countered.

"Yeah, and I like short haircuts and fox trots, and I'm dead against grass. From what I gather, Billy hasn't followed those commandments too well."

"But you support the war?"

"And you oppose it. If the kid hightailed it to Canada, I'd have the sense to blame the kid, not you."

"You have the power to change his mind. He adores you."

"And you think that gives me a license to screw with the kid's head? I adore my father, but if he stopped me from going to Korea, I would have hated him."

"Why, in God's name? For trying to stop you from coming home wounded or dead?"

"No. Because I thought I belonged there."

"And you think Billy knows his own mind well enough that he

feels the same way about Vietnam? He's ignorant about the issues. What does he know about the South Vietnamese government?"

"About as much as I knew about the South Korean one, I guess."

"Which was?"

"Communism should be stopped."

"Oh, Jesus."

"You have a strange idea about kids, Sissy. You think they're just something to manipulate. As long as the manipulation works your way. Kids just aren't like that. They gotta stretch."

"Stretch in a war?"

"You can't choose the way they're going to make their mark."

"There are better ways."

"Like college?"

"Yes, like college. Don't you try to manipulate Eileen away from it."

"No more than you con her toward it. I just want Eileen to know she has other options. I bait her on the subject, sure. And I know at times I'm nasty about it. But if she wants it—not if *you* want it, Sissy—she'll tell me to stuff my objections and go. And I'll be one pround sonnuvabitch when she walks down the aisle. I just don't want her buying your party line that college is the be-all and end-all. I know plenty of nebbishes walking the streets with their liberal arts degrees."

"Don't tell me children shouldn't be encouraged."

"Do you encourage, or are you trying to rewrite your own history? You know, Sissy, after all these years I feel like I was a compromise for what you couldn't get."

Sissy's eyes flooded. "That's not true. I never loved anyone like you."

"Only one."

"That's so unfair and lousy."

"Lousy, yes; unfair, no. Because your father didn't fulfill your expectations, you lean all over the kids. He's your bogeyman, Sissy. You relate everything back to him. When I drink too much, I'm acting like your father. When I blow up at the kids, I'm acting crazy like your father. When I test Eileen about how much she, *she*, really wants college, I'm your father denying you your big chance at education."

"Stop it. How can you be so cruel?"

"And if I say something good about the country, I'm an

American Legion asshole like your father. You know, there's nothing more pathetic than someone over thirty who is still hung up on their parents. You'd never guess how many nights in bed I dreamed about blowing that motherfucker away."

"How can you say such things?" Sissy couldn't stop the tears.

"Because he made me feel like a piece of shit compromise."

"What do you know about compromise? You're a man. You always did what you damn pleased. You said so about Korea."

"Oh, I know about compromise," Eddie said, his voice defrosting.

"Name it. Damn it, name one time. You never gave up a thing."

"Me being your father again. Now he's all mankind. When are you going to build a shrine for him?"

"Never mind my father. We're talking about you."

"Not really. We never do."

"Don't run and hide. What did you ever compromise?"

Eddie fished out a cigarette, lit it, and exhaled deeply. "The job."

"What do you mean, the job?"

"Too much of that kind of information isn't good for you, Sissy. Grand juries have subpoena power."

"What's that supposed to mean?"

"Let's just say once upon a time I wasn't a team player. Once upon a happy time."

"So what happened?"

Eddie's eyes reddened. He waved his free hand in front of his face, and with the other squashed out his cigarette in the ashtray. "Bad enough this shit eats your lungs without scalding your eyes." He paused for a moment and then heaved with resignation. Sissy was reminded of how she took deep breaths in the confessional before offering a major sin. "Let's just say I got lonely. I was never good at being on the outside. That's one thing I always envied about you, Sissy. You take as much pleasure in being a loner as I take in being accepted. I always thought you got off on being shut out. You know, you always light up when you get into a pissing match. I think agreeable conversation bores you. I wish I had some of that."

"Couldn't you stick with it? If you were happy, I mean."

"I wasn't happy. Just right. I'm just not made that way. I couldn't stand the way the guys I worked with looked at me. Like I was a tourist."

She reached out to him. "Couldn't you come to me?"

"No. Because you wouldn't have seen the problem. You're a natural loner. You wouldn't understand what it meant. Naturals are never any help in life. And you're a natural. Sam Snead once said about his sweet golf swing that he just pulls the club back and lets go as hard as he can. The worst advice for a duffer. Naturals can never dig the problems of scratch players. You would have grown fat and content as a cop if the entire department gave you the silent treatment."

"But didn't you hate the people you had to deal with more?"

"It might come as a shock to you, but I do hate the wise guys, the sharpies, worse than the lowest street types. I never daydream about blowing away a spade or a PR. But the others—I have indictable fantasies."

"Then why?"

"Simple loneliness and not enough balls to stick it out. Besides, the high-toned scum are so nice to you. They try to make you feel like family. The street types see you as an oppressive cocksucker. As dirty as the wise guys are, they're closer to your world. You share a language. Maybe that's why some of us don't question the governments of Korea or Vietnam. Like the dagos, they're our kind of scumbags."

"And that's reason enough to send your son off to war?"

Eddie finally became heated. "Goddamn it, I'm not sending my kid off nowhere. He came to me and said he was joining up. He isn't the first. Quite a few of his buddies have already left. Did I send them? Or are all us fathers in cahoots? All us male chauvinist pigs."

"None of them stopped them from going. That's indictment enough."

"Sissy, did it ever occur to you in all your wisdom that these kids might believe in what they're doing? You know, not everyone, when they mention America, follows it with a putdown."

"You sound like you should have married Martha Raye."

"Don't be a smartass. Nobody is asking for a flag-raiser. But it would be nice for once if you said something about the food and medical help we give poor countries, or the technology we send around the world, before you launch into the war or the oppression of the minorities."

"I never say the United States is wrong all the time."

"Hooray for you. But you never say we do any good. Open

your ears, Sissy. Listen to the immigrants, the old-timers, what they say about this country."

"They're not from the Third World. That's what we're talking about."

"The Third World, my ass. I was in Korea, remember? I saw the Third World in action. A shitpile of ignorants who use kids—not Billy's age—real kids and women in combat. Malnutrition and corruption out the ass. Is that your wave of the future?"

"How does our bombing them cure ignorance and malnutrition? Those people, if you cared to find out, have a rich culture."

"Oh, Jesus, a rich culture. Where the hell are they hiding it? They'd give their left nut for what we got. The whole planet would. Go ask the people who came here from different places. Believe me, baby, the line to get into America is a lot longer than the one to get out. There's no Berlin walls on our piers, Atlantic or Pacific."

"You don't know what you're talking about. We're making a war on peasants. A giant stepping on a dwarf. If America is as great as you say, we should be ashamed of ourselves."

"Peasants! Another one of your notions. Pity the blacks and Puerto Ricans because they're poor. Give them carte blanche. Did you ever notice the poor always seem to have a nicotine fit the moment they get on a train or bus? As soon as their asses hit the seats, they light up and start blowing smoke in some old asthmatic's face. Do you believe that's a product of a poor upbringing? Being deprived?

"I'll tell you what it is—it's their way of sticking it straight in society's ear. A society they want to blow away. A society I'm out there to preserve.

"You have a million half-assed notions. That douche running a slammer in Cuba is a bearded Robin Hood. Don't you ever look at reality? You know, I'd be afraid to work the job with you. You'd snuff every spade and PR that didn't live up to your expectations."

That stung Sissy. She recalled her anger at watching Puerto Rican thugs on television while they were being led to arraignment, jive-assing it for the cameras. Or the dismal black teenage girls talking about their third pregnancy. "I'ze just can't helps it when I'ze gets excited." Sissy hated those ignorant sluts for disgracing their race. Maybe Eddie was more tolerant. All that plea-bargaining. Knocking down charges. Was it mercy, or like God's patience, a tolerance steeped in despair? Quietly she said, "I just like to believe people might turn out better if they came from different circumstances."

"I assure you communists aren't the answer."

"Is that what you told Billy?"

"No. Billy can read the newspapers. Do you think we're all mindless, flag-waving jerks? If we don't stop them, then who will?"

"Oh, Christ! Not the domino theory."

"Don't be cute. I don't think the communists are going to land at Coney Island. But baby, somebody has to say the shit stops here. We should have done it in Berlin and Hungary."

"The tough cop of the world, is that it?"

"You're close. The world is not much different than the streets. Everyone looks the other way out there, too, and neighborhoods fold like busted valises. People lock themselves up, and everything they own. Ghost towns, baby, that's what we're heading for. And everybody is saying, let someone else wear the white hat."

"And Billy believes that on his own?"

"Billy and a lot more like him. That's why it's his choice. I wish the world was different, but don't ask me to make a punk out of my boy by telling him he has to sit it out because mommy and daddy say so."

"Do you?"

"Do I what?"

"Wish it was different?"

"What does that mean?"

"I mean, how do you see the world? You know, good-bad. Fifty-fifty or what?"

"You make a generous line. More like eighty-twenty."

"Which way?"

"The shit has the loaded roster."

"Once upon a time that thought, if it was true, would have horrified you. You know, now I think it excites you. You remind me of certain writers who are so sick inside themselves they like to rub their readers' noses in their own shit."

"Is that so?"

"Is that all you have to say?"

"Nothing else. Except if you have to play this game, you might as well have the right scorecard."

"Brilliant, Eddie, really brilliant."

"And what do you have?"

"Have a laugh, Eddie. Hopes, dreams. Even if I thought it was eighty-twenty, which I don't, I'd hope at least to try to even it up."

"You're the regular Wizard of Oz."

"And you're the sultan of shit."

"Quite a combo."

"Once upon a time I thought we were."

"Sissy, I think you're too smart to be a fool. Maybe you're a latter-day saint."

"And maybe you died somewhere along the line."

"Then we're still quite a combo. Maybe we'll meet in a better world."

"I don't know if I'll still be interested."

He rose, signaling the end of the conversation. He was heading out to the streets that he found more comforting. "Well," he said, "maybe you can fit me in on your dance card—after your father and the Third World."

Another night Eddie made an unfathomable observation to her. He had come home after monitoring an antiwar protest at Brooklyn College. "You know," he said, "today, looking at those protesters and hearing those speeches with everybody kicking America's ass, I thought maybe we're on opposite sides of the war question. Like we should reverse sides."

Sissy looked at him, perplexed. She would offer no more than "How come?"

"Well, in the Third World, from what I hear, they're not so hot on protest. You know, everyone pulls for the common good. Everybody's a team player. It sounds like me, my kind of people.

"On the other hand, America gives a microphone and a TV camera to anyone who wants to dump on the country. In fact, the better the dump, the better the coverage. When I was watching this, I thought how we love loudmouths. Christ, we treat loudmouthing like a God-given right. Sissy, if I was you, I'd consider this. Think about it, Sissy. Think about becoming a patriot."

That was past history. But what she would give to erase it. Oddly, for his sake. She preferred Eddie's lively baiting to his morose silences. So Lynn once again became her conduit to all things adult. Eileen was the other half of her sphere. Eddie kept that half of his world open as well. With Eileen, it was hard to tell that he had ever changed from the generous, fun-loving boy

Sissy had once loved. That past tense would never be complete, perfect.

The only clue to his hurt in dealing with Eileen was his fierce protectiveness of the child. He wanted to know where she was at all times. Even his frequent nights away from home never passed without a phone conversation with Eileen or a check with Sissy on the child's whereabouts. His daughter was tracked with the diligence applied to a government witness. Sissy understood. After Billy, who knew where a contract was lurking.

Time brought them to a bearable junction. His drinking moderated, and when he was at home, he kept up the appearance of normalcy. He even included her in his joking with Eileen, and there were occasional family trips to a movie, to play miniature golf, to share pizza or a Chinese meal. All surface, but Sissy was pleased that he had regained his sense of form. When that went, everything was lost. Mickey had proved that.

The basics didn't change. They rarely made love, only when the abstinence became perverse. Their parochialism kept the final aberration at bay. Only weirdos and sickos would live together and never do it. But Sissy knew neither ever looked forward to it. It wasn't that they couldn't still excite each other. That would never be totally extinguished. But between them, they had given birth to their son by this act, and that forever darkened it. It was like reusing an apparatus that had produced a terrible accident.

All in all, life was manageable, a modest term but acceptable after the chaos. Eddie seemed better and better as time went on. Sissy presumed he had found something out there in his real world. For her, there was Eileen, and the magic of Lynn's world. If she was far from whole, she was equidistant from being nothing. Foolishly, she relaxed. Like her father, she refused to accept that impermanence was the course of the world.

She knew what had gone down as soon as she opened the door that early evening and saw Sal standing there with a captain. Captains didn't drop in at a line cop's house for coffee and danish. Sal's opening merely sealed it: "Sissy, this is Captain Tazewell from the precinct."

She heard enough of it to understand: a chase, a drug bust, five flights of stairs, heart attack. When Sal went into the family room and returned with a tumbler of scotch for her, she knew there was no intensive care unit to visit.

She thought she'd handled it pretty well. After all, it was a stock scene in her mental repertoire, every cop's wife had re-hearsed it. She had even been composed enough to ask questions. The responses were stock repertory, too: line of duty, always sacrificing himself, hero's death, inspector's funeral. The response to death was like playing chess with a computer, Sissy thought. Nothing wildly imaginative ever came back, just good, solid, programmed stuff.

She remembered that the captain had stayed more than a re-spectable interval while Sal worked the phone in the kitchen. Relatives had to be informed and summoned, Eileen had to be tracked down at a friend's home, funeral arrangements had to be made. Amazingly, Sal did most of this with a minimal assist from Sissy. She had forgotten how much and for how long he had been involved in every facet of Eddie's life. Even Eddie's hiatus in plainclothes hadn't altered that. It was fitting they had been re-united again in East Flatbush. Sal was part of them since the Police Academy days. Always a dim but constant reflection of Eddie's bright star. Always Eddie's gofer. In death nothing had changed. Sal was holding doors open for his partner's final exit.

Eileen was the major problem. She was near hysterical collapse. She was too young, much too young, to lose a brother and a father. Life shouldn't be brought home to you that early. The counterfeit of youth is the thing that gives people the courage to go on later. Sissy thought it grossly unfair to her daughter. At least, she would always have "back then." Mickey, for all his faults as a father, had demonstrated some staying power.

But Eddie's neighborhood didn't fail his daughter. Eileen's friends and their parents rallied to her. Nellie, too. Christy couldn't. He had all he could do to hold Catherine together. Eddie hadn't inherited his sense of style from his mother. Sissy hated her for betraying her son when it most counted.

But it was Eileen who mattered, and she held up. Her friends surrounded her, took her for lunch and sodas during the three-day wake, and at night brought her to their homes for dinner and let her sleep over.

Lynn, Lily, and Vincent were wonderful to Sissy. Like true family. They sent a magnificent wreath and attended the wake, where Vincent took Sissy aside and said, "Finances are a little pressing at times like this."

Sissy moved to hush him, but he raised his hand, "I just want you to know you're very special to our family."

She was so moved by the encircling kindness to both her and her daughter that she felt guilty she had ever said anything against Brooklyn. Eddie was being vindicated. This outpouring never would have happened in Manhattan.

The neighborhood's generosity held such allure that Sissy repaid in kind by following tradition. Each night after the wake she would bring mourners back to her house for food and beverages. Here Nellie was at her best. In the afternoons, before they returned to the funeral parlor for the evening hours, she would arrive at Sissy's bearing something—a ham, a turkey, a vast bowl of potato salad, and always a few fresh-baked Irish soda breads. She was the supply sergeant for the army of mourners who trooped in from other boroughs, the old who needed sustenance after their long ordeal at the wake, and the relatives who, until now, had been rumors.

Finally, this antiquated and barbaric tradition of marathon mourning made sense to Sissy. Not only was their socializing connected to it but logistics as well. Some of these people had even traveled from out of state, others were frail, and yet others you might not see again until it was their turn to be mourned. It was not a matter of generosity but of basic civility. What else could one have done with them? Especially those who had traveled. Shipped them off to a sterile all-night diner or a pizza parlor? Sissy was proud that when her turn came, with her mother's help she hadn't dropped the traditional torch.

Late at night after everyone had left (except Nellie who slept over and departed after she had made her daughter breakfast), Sissy would rummage through photo albums in her room. She tried to evoke the happiness of the young couple in the pictures in order to dredge up a monumental sense of loss. But the faces she saw in the pictures were so open, so unaware of life, that they seemed rather stupid to her. She almost felt contempt for the photographic images of herself and Eddie with their outdated clothes and hairstyles and the know-nothingness of their optimistic faces. What was Eddie's line? "You don't pity a willing mark." The albums proved that they had rube written all over them.

She took great pride in her own and her family's deportment at the requiem mass. All except Catherine, who had to be assisted for every genuflection and who wailed intermittently (Sissy thought they were timed), as if the sounds would sanctify her singular grief. For the rest of them, there were no breakdowns.

Their eyes glistened but never ran. The contained moisture heightened their appearance and gave them the Kennedys' shining look of eagles.

Sissy nearly caved in only once, and not at the expected time —the lowering of the coffin. It was when the Emerald Society band let out the lowly skirl of the bagpipes. The sound went through her, igniting all the memories of a life lived Irish. She could remember weddings, beer parties at Breezy Point, the March wind on her childish face as Mickey proudly swung her hand walking up Fifth Avenue. She watched her mother as she bit down on her lower lip until the blood left it. She knew Nellie was also trying to maintain her composure as the pipes set similar memories marching in her head. You could alter anything but your blood. Eileen was silently shaking beside her, too. Yet these generations didn't break. Sissy didn't know what that meant, but there was something to be said for it.

The aftermath wasn't so easy. Sissy began to realize surviving a death was like retiring to obscurity after a heady career. After all, she had held center stage intensely for days, and then there was nothing but the mundane business of survival. No, that was too dramatic a word. Continuing was more like it.

She felt like a great actress who had been abruptly shunted aside. She didn't find this allusion silly or pretentious. The wake had been her theater and the mourners her audience. Every night they came to her and told her how well she was conducting herself. Supplicants to the star. Kudos for Eddie were merely a reflection on her. Like praise for the props. It was strictly her show. She was the apex of the backstage receiving line.

The social gatherings each night at her house after the mourning also highlighted her. They were her after-theater suppers for "a few intimate friends." Though Nellie was prominent on these evenings, it was Sissy who truly shone. When they laid the substantial spread on the table, she was showered with admiration. "Ah-h, sure, just a cup of tea would have been fine." "Now, don't you have enough problems without going to such a fuss?" "Girl, you should be getting your rest instead of exhausting yourself with feasts." Sissy let them know, with a sad, sophisticated smile, that savoir-faire is never interred. What a valiant little trooper she was.

She couldn't believe she could go so quickly from the vortex to neglect. Of course, Nellie and Eileen were still attentive, but not in the way Sissy wished. They treated her as if she were a piece of property they had been assigned to protect. They never reached her inner needs but prowled her perimeter like watchdogs. They were ready to pounce at the first sign of an emotional mugging.

After the usual round of sympathy dinners, the everyday routine returned. Sissy understood that. After all, how long can you dine out on tales of woe? Not exactly the fare that had made the Algonquin Round Table spin. There should have been some kind of depressurizing period after the dizziness of the funeral. Sissy's spirit was suffering the bends from the abrupt resurfacing into life.

She wished she had the gall to wear widow's weeds. Elegant, basic black. She now knew the wisdom of that custom she used to scoff at haughtily. The grim garb was like a war wound, an invaluable limp that assured deference. Sissy didn't want to milk it like the immigrant widows who wouldn't let go and, as they aged, shriveled like charred paper. All she wanted was a decent interval of solicitousness. A period of pampering so that when she walked into a room the sea of people parted for her with a heartfelt sigh.

She couldn't believe she missed Eddie so. His death had only formalized what already was. But miss him she did. It was the female extension syndrome, as they called it in the movement. Identifying it didn't help. It was similar to the doctor analyzing her condition after Billy. Was that supposed to smother it some how? It can't be terrible if we can put a handle on it.

No, charting it didn't help. For better or worse, Eddie was a part of her, and now he was gone. One didn't love a dog less when it got old and surly or, for that matter, a piece of cherished furniture when it wore out. God, at least he was there. The filament in him still occasionally flickered for her. It didn't matter that he was indifferent. At least, that was an attitude, and it was directed toward *her*. There was an inert interaction at work. It was better than nothing, better than a void hermetically sealed. The recognition of this brought her some solace. She liked the emptiness of this intellectual exercise. It made her feel existential French, "Lament for Indifference."

The invitations for Sissy and Eileen to eat at Nellie's weren't acceptable either. That would only compound Sissy's misery. If Eddie were discussed, it would lead to Mickey, with Billy thrown in for good measure. A haunted house, a séance instead of supper.

Nor was Sissy eager to follow the most proffered road to recovery: "You have to get out of the house." That wasn't what she longed for. She wanted people to come to her, she did not want to have to search them out. There was no soothing in crowds. They wouldn't know what she was suffering. She would only feel more alone among a throng who were cavalierly ignorant of her suffering. In psychological palaver, she craved "a controlled situation." She wished she was outrageously rich and famous so that she could summon her own salon for sympathy.

She reverted to the philosophy of her roots: she plugged along, but it was getting to her. She turned down Lynn's numerous invitations for special reasons. She just couldn't bring herself to dull and burden Lynn's spirit with her wimpiness. Weeping on Lynn's shoulder would be like bleaching a peacock.

She finally relented one night when the circumstances seemed just right. For the first time since Eddie died, Eileen reluctantly said yes to an invitation to sleep at a girlfriend's house. Sissy urged her to accept. The last thing she wanted was one of those morose Irish daughters who served as a handmaiden to a mournful matriarch. Besides, the kid was getting on Sissy's nerves. Giving her the creeps, to be exact. If Sissy so much as blinked or spent what Eileen thought was an inordinate amount of time behind a closed door, a frightened voice would ask, "Are you all right, Mommy?"

Also, Lynn had structured something Sissy could handle. No night on the town, just the two of them for dinner at Lynn's place. "Plenty of wine and gossip," Lynn had promised. It sounded perfect. Now Sissy wished that of all the evenings in her life she could buy that one back.

Even though she had found Lynn's moussaka delicious, she had just picked. Nerves, too much wine, and too many cigarettes had closed off her stomach. Her speech was too quick, much too quick. Her words seemed to burst out with each exhalation of cigarette smoke. It seemed like parts of her congested sentences were exiting through her nose. Her talk lacked cohesion, remnants being flung from some emotional pile. It was a bad performance, and she knew it. The phrase "on my own" kept popping up in her speech. Lynn's assurances that Sissy was surrounded by people who loved her didn't help. "On my own" surfaced again and again. Sissy knew what it was about. Her deepest dread. A curse worse than cancer. She was destined to outlive her family. To carry through life the memories of her loved ones. And it would get worse. Realistically, how long did Nellie have? And if something happened to Eileen—Jesus, that was unthinkable. Why hadn't they all died together in a car accident when they were happy? Her whole unit assumed together into eternity, instead of this terrifying sniping. One by one, they were falling under God's crosshairs. Cross-cross hairs? She wanted desperately to get into a cab, pick up Eileen, bring her home, and barricade the house.

Lynn, sensing her panic, talked in slow, soothing terms. Through the veil of wine, Sissy thought Lynn sounded like a doctor. Lynn was plotting Sissy's future in measured tones. She would scout around to get Sissy some work. Lynn had connections.

Sissy recognized the sound of it all. It was convalescent talk. The world was a yawning oyster. She had heard it before. Her doctor, Mickey's doctor when he urged him to give up alcohol. What was it in people that they wouldn't let you curl up and die? It wasn't as if it weren't going to happen eventually, as if you were dealing in some unspeakable aberration. Who was to know better than you when you had had enough? Maybe it was misguided charity. Or maybe every broken-off link in the chain shortens the survivor's grip on reality. The malignant Irish appraisal of "misery loves company." She wished she was at home in her own bed with the television on. For all its shortcomings, it was the most sympathetic of night nurses.

Judging from the vomiting ashtray on the table in front of her, Sissy reckoned she had stayed a reasonable enough time. She wanted desperately to go home. When she rose from the table, she staggered slightly. "Damned heels," she muttered.

Lynn's alarmed face told her everything. "Are you all right?"

That question again. No, she wasn't all right. She was drunk. Drunk like her father. Irish drunk. Was Lynn being condescending to her? Her temper rose. She could feel a harangue coming on. One of Mickey's specials. Who was this snotnose who was looking askance at her? Sissy was searching for the ultimate riposte when she remembered a book of poems that Lynn had given her. By God, that would put Lynn in her place, hit her where she lived. "I happen to be," Sissy said with her father's hauteur, "as drunk as Delmore Schwartz."

Lynn looked momentarily puzzled, then she broke into laughter.

Sissy, holding the table for balance, realized the lunacy of her remark and capped Lynn's outburst with her own laughter.

"Delmore Schwartz," Lynn repeated, resuming her laughter.

Sissy was now convulsed. "Not to mention a skunk, a hoot owl, and Paddy's pig," Sissy added, laughing at each addition.

"Delmore Schwartz," Lynn said again. "I've heard of crocked pretensions, but that takes the cake."

"The kugel," Sissy corrected, driving Lynn to more laughter.

"I have to keep you out of the Village before you become insufferable."

"And Brooklyn Heights, too," Sissy said. "Oh, hell, I'd better get myself home while I can still navigate."

"Not tonight, Josephine, or is it Delmore?" Though she tried to make it sound airy, Sissy could hear the concern in Lynn's voice. "Your tush is not leaving this house."

"I have to. Eileen . . ."

"Eileen's at a friend's, and you're going to sleep that buzz off here."

"But . . ."

"But your butt. You're not going out in the street with visions of poetic grandeur."

"I don't want to . . ."

"Don't. Don't say 'impose,' or I'll slug you."

"But where . . ."

"You'll sleep in the bed, and I'll take the couch. I've flopped in worse places."

"But that's unfair."

"What is this degenerating into? Who gets the upper or lower at summer camp? Case closed. You're staying."

Sissy began to make a gesture of dismissal with the hand that held the table and nearly fell. Lynn grabbed her. "That's the last witness for the prosecution."

Sissy sagged back into the chair, surrendering meekly. "Okay, I guess you're right. I'm sorry for being such a mess."

Lynn smiled warmly. "Oh, shut up. We all sacrifice for great poets."

Sissy suddenly felt awful. The wine coupled with the exertion of laughter broke her into a clammy sweat. She was chilled to the bone. "My God, look at you," Lynn said.

The sickly, icy sweat made Sissy shiver. She was actually shaking.

"Get out of those clothes," Lynn ordered, "while I draw you a hot bath."

"No. Just let me lie down."

"Like hell I will. Off with those clothes."

"I'll be . . ."

"Off, goddamn it," Lynn snapped as she rushed to the bathroom.

When Lynn returned, Sissy hadn't moved.

Lynn pointed toward the bedroom. "Get going."

Sissy got up shakily and took small, hesitant steps.

"Come on. March," Lynn ordered again.

"Crawl would be more like it," Sissy offered, continuing her journey.

She sat on the side of Lynn's bed and began to undress. She could hear the water running into the tub. Undressing was a monumental chore. She just wanted to fall back across the bed. She was down to bra and panties when Lynn came to fetch her.

"Come on. Before you shake to death." Lynn took her arm and led her to the bathroom. The heat felt wonderful, and the bath looked sudsy and delicious.

"Thank you," she said. "I'm fine now." She tried to unhook her bra and tottered again.

"Here," Lynn said. "Let me do that before you break your neck." She unhooked Sissy's bra and pulled down her panties from the rear. "Hold on to my shoulder and step out."

Sissy obeyed, thinking how strange it was to be naked in front of another woman, never mind having her undress you. She remembered the gym classes at school, and how the girls, out of modesty, never showered but wore their sweaty gym suits home under their street clothes. Had the nuns ordered them to do so, or was it an unwritten commandment? Better to stink than to be an exposed hussy.

Lynn slung Sissy's arm over her shoulder. "Step up now. That's it. Now the other one."

"I feel like an infant."

"Okay, just sit down slowly." Sissy sank into the tub, and the contrast in temperature between the water and her body made her shudder violently. It stopped as quickly as it started. "Lord, does this feel good."

"Always listen to Jews when it comes to remedies."

"Thanks, Lynn. I hate being such a drag."

"Just hush and stew a while. When you're ready to get out, call me. It might be a good idea to try and upchuck that wine. Or was it my cooking? I have some Valium, but I don't want to give you any with all the booze you've had."

"I'll be fine. I feel toasty already."

"I still think it would be a good idea to get that stuff off your stomach."

Sissy made a joking face and shook her head. "Fingers down my throat, yuck."

"All right, brat, but call me when you're ready. I have a fresh toothbrush for you. And for chrissake, don't fall asleep and drown."

Sissy rolled her eyes upward, "Diabolique."

"You're a treasure trove of pretensions tonight. Try the fingers. The pretensions might come up with the wine."

Sissy stuck out her tongue.

"Just don't drown, okay?" Lynn left her, but left the door slightly ajar. Sissy heard the click of the turntable and Lynn say, "This should keep you alert." She sank down into the deep, oily, luxurious heat of the tub while Vivaldi's *Four Seasons* drifted through the opening of the door.

The hot water calmed Sissy's shivering, but not her nerves. She slid farther down into the tub until the water was at her neck. She felt the snugness of a sleeping bag. But as much as she was enjoying it, she couldn't maintain the position. She was too wired. She wanted to bolt. "I'm getting out," she shouted to Lynn in the living room.

"Out? You just got in."

"I've had enough."

"Did you try making yourself sick?"

"What? In the tub?"

"No, in the john next to the tub, idiot. I thought that was understood."

"God, no," Sissy answered. "I'm fine. I'm getting out."

"Hold on a second," Lynn called.

Sissy heard some foraging in the living room, and in a few minutes Lynn opened the bathroom door smoking a small pipe. "Here, try some of this and relax," she said.

"What is it?" asked a cautious Sissy.

"Condensed castor oil. You're worse than a child."

"Well, what *is* it?"

"Some first-rate grass. Hawaiian. It will calm you down."

"I don't really know if . . ."

Lynn handed her the pipe. "Just puff and relax. I'll come back and get you out in ten minutes."

Sissy looked skeptically from Lynn to the pipe. "Ten minutes?"

"Ten minutes. I promise."

"Promise?"

"That's when the statute of limitations runs out. I'll be back."

Sissy had tried grass before when she was out with Lynn, but only a puff or two. Not enough to take effect. She did it so that she wouldn't appear square. In truth, she found the whole ritual of passing a joint from one mouth to another disgusting. All that talk about the best part being the roach was even worse. "Don't drop the roach, man." Yuck!

But nonetheless she had puffed. Especially if the joint was passed around by a black musician. She was afraid he might think the refusal was racist. After all, she had grown up hearing her friends say, "Don't nigger-lip it," to sloppy cigarette smokers who asked for a drag. She couldn't let the pot-passing party think that was what had prompted her refusal. Ofay delicacy.

The pipe seemed more appetizing. She liked pipes. She associated them with intelligence. A baggy cardigan sweater, Sexy Rexy as Henry Higgins. Eddie had tried a pipe, but it didn't take. Wrong prop for his job, she figured. Cops were always butt guys.

She sucked in on the pipe and inhaled. What the hell, ten minutes. She waited for some dramatic effect, but none was forthcoming. She repeated the process a few times, then slid back into the water up to her neck, holding the pipe over the edge of the tub with her left hand. The sensation of panic had left her. She wondered if the stuff was working. It was truly a nauseating habit. She couldn't picture Myrna Loy in the Plaza bar turning to William Powell and saying, "Give me a hit."

But she had to admit she was feeling better. She was no longer cold, nauseous, or antsy. She inhaled some more. Instead of wanting to bolt, she began to drift pleasantly. Everything seemed to slow down and bob about gently. It was like being transported in a stately rattan chair. It was all very luxurious for a while.

Then she began to feel she was out of touch with things. It was like her childhood musings about how her soul would feel when it left her body. But then such spiritual aerations mingled with panic—the return to more base things—the body. That's what was happening now. Besides, she had had her fill of a lack of control.

She decided to check the floating before it got away from her. She called for Lynn, and when she didn't get an immediate response, she called again. Lynn appeared at the door holding an artist's smock similar to the one she was wearing. "Simmer down," she said. "So I cheated by five minutes. Here's your nightgown. Designer, it's not, but it's what I wear."

Sissy, halfway out of the tub, grabbed a towel off the rack. "It will be fine. I'll be out in a minute."

When Lynn left, Sissy quickly dried herself and pulled the smock over her head. She wanted to get out of the bathroom quickly. The small tiles on the floor were moving together and starting to run like lava. When she was hit by the cooler air in the living room, her fright subsided. God, she was tired. The emotional seesaw of the night had exhausted her.

"You look better," said Lynn. "Can I get you a cup of tea or something?"

All Sissy could think of was Lynn's turned-down bed. She pointed to the bedroom. "If you don't mind, I've had it."

Lynn smiled and pointed to an ashtray that held a pipe similar to the one she'd given Sissy. "I'm with you. I just have to use the john. You jump in. I'll put out the lights when I'm done."

Sissy didn't stand on manners. She crawled into the waiting bed. She could barely hear the water running in the bathroom. It seemed so distant. Like a voice before you went under anesthesia. She was valiantly trying to stay awake until Lynn came out. It was Lynn's voice that brought her back. "Goodnight, pal. Get a lot of Zs."

Sissy managed, "You, too," as the lights went out.

The dousing of the light broke her drowsiness. In the dark she became acutely aware of the strangeness of her surroundings. She thought she could hear Lynn breathing in the other room, but it didn't soothe her. All the little sounds, the sounds of one's own home, the sounds that matter were different. She could feel the dizziness coming back. The bed was no longer stationary, but a catapult that was going to propel her into space. It was like her first sickness from drinking beer. Nothing here was hers. There was nothing she could connect with. And Eileen was out there, somewhere, defenseless, while Sissy was marooned in this dark space unable to help.

The pillow was a failure, it didn't bring total darkness. She wanted to scream just to hear a familiar voice. She fought it back and began to cry instead.

She didn't hear Lynn come across the room. She only felt her lift her face out of the pillow and turn her over.

"Easy now, easy now," Lynn soothed, as she cradled Sissy in her arms. Sissy tried to apologize, but her words were choked grunts. "Easy now, just get it all out." Lynn rocked, while Sissy sobbed.

"Alone" was the one word she managed to repeat through the tears.

"You're not, you're not," Lynn soothed in beat with her rocking.

The tears made Sissy icy cold again. Between the chill and the sobbing, her body heaved in Lynn's arms. "It's all going to be all right," Lynn said, "all right." She wiped away Sissy's tears and gently kissed her eyes. It was like being a child again. The affection warmed her. Lynn dried every stained inch of Sissy's face with her lips, and the closeness of Lynn's body started to warm her.

She had never felt lips so healing and so tender. Nellie's soothing was rougher; with Eddie she could always feel beard stubble. Lynn's lips fell on her as soft as a bird landing.

She burrowed closer to her friend for warmth. Held her tight. The combination of softness and heat was strangely wonderful. No threatening male protuberances to ruin it. No menacing electric prod. Just a soft mound of heat, like an August beach, with contours that collapsed into hers. She felt Lynn's lips above hers whispering, "Shush, shush, everything will be all right."

It seemed like the most natural thing in the world to kiss those soothing lips. At first, Sissy merely brushed them. She found it so touching that they were wet with her tears. Lynn brushed back and continued to whisper. Sissy felt a jolt of excitement when she felt the opening in Lynn's mouth between her words. She flicked her tongue over Lynn's lips and tasted her own tears. She felt Lynn tense momentarily and say, "Sh-h, sh-h, it's okay." The "sh-h" shot a funnel of hot breath into Sissy's mouth. She felt her body tingle and squeezed Lynn closer to her. Sissy's nipples were hard and rubbed against Lynn's. The static ran through their smocks, their erect nipples acting as conductors.

Lynn was still talking. "Now, now," and the tips of their tongues touched. Each withdrew for an instant, but Sissy was committed. She used her weight to roll Lynn over on her back and placed her mouth full on Lynn's. She could feel Lynn stiffen under her in panic, and Sissy heard herself saying, "Sh-h, sh-h, it's all right." She put her tongue in Lynn's mouth. The difference in texture from a man's, so soft, like the fresh flowers she nibbled as a girl, charged her with an excitement she had never known. There was still something new on earth.

When Sissy awoke, Lynn was sitting on the window seat having coffee. "Finally—I was about to call a priest."

"My God, what time is it?" Sissy asked.

"A little after ten."

"Ten!" She swung out of bed. "Eileen will be in a panic."

"Wouldn't she have gone straight to school from her friend's?"

"Yes, but if she's called home, she won't know what to think."

"Easy, mother hen. She probably had such a good time she didn't even give you a thought."

Though the remark was meant to soothe, it rankled Sissy. It had the presumption of an outsider. "Can I shower?"

"It's all yours. I primped and powdered long ago."

As Sissy started across the floor to the shower, the skin on her upper thighs brushed and stuck for a moment until her stride pulled it clear. Oh, my God, she had forgotten. Did it really happen? She took off the smock in the bathroom, hoping against hope. Maybe it was just a pot-induced dream? When the steaming water hit her body, and she tentatively put her soapy hand to her privates, the evidence dissolved and flowed like glue. The whole scene came back to her with a sickly excitement. Why did the forbidden have such drawing power?

She remembered the time she had seen a man urinating under the boardwalk at the beach. Though everything in her had commanded her to look away, she couldn't. She finished her shower in a frenzy.

How in the hell was she going to get out of here? She wished Lynn would leave while she was dressing, but she seemed contented on the window seat with her cup of coffee and the *Times*.

"There's fresh coffee," she called. Sissy was longing for some, but it would mean prolonging her stay.

"No, thanks. My stomach is still a little off from the wine.

I'll just get dressed. I want to be home before Eileen breaks for lunch. She'll probably call."

Sissy fought self-consciousness as she dressed and feigned being casual. What does one say in the morning after spending the night with someone? Men did it all the time. She wondered if there was a set, all-purpose, male exit speech. Probably. They tossed their sperm around as casually as their socks. She wondered if she should say something by way of explanation. Too much wine, topped by pot, plus her distraught condition? She would like to have cleared the air, but it was so personal that was impossible. She realized that priests were in the world for something. They would listen to the smarmiest of plea-bargaining and pass it on up.

Instead, she tried to look chipper. "How are you going to spend your day?"

Lynn turned and smiled at her. "I think I'll bum around the city. You know, a little of this and a little of that. It looks like a perfect day for it. Why don't you come along?"

Sissy realized she was hurrying in putting on her clothes and made an effort to appear less frantic. "It sounds great, but I think mother hen had better make an appearance at home."

Lynn didn't answer. She went back to the *Times* as Sissy finished dressing. Then she gathered her cigarettes, lighter, and bag. Lynn was still immersed in the paper. "Well, I guess I'm off," she announced. Lynn looked up, bemused. Small wonder. Sissy felt her announcement sounded like a Girl Scout leaving for a camping trip.

"Are you sure you don't want to change your mind?" Lynn asked.

"I'd love to, but I really have to fly."

"Too bad." Lynn rose and followed Sissy to the door. Sissy turned to face her, "Well, thanks for everything." What a thing to say! If she was a diplomat, the world would be in cinders.

Lynn smiled, "For what—a meal that nearly killed you?"

"Oh, no, it was really . . ."

Lynn stopped her with another laugh. "You take care of yourself now. Do you hear?" Sissy nodded. "Hug that daughter for me, too."

Sissy nodded again, but added a smile. She knew Lynn was sincere. She and Eileen had hit it off famously.

"I'll call you in a few days, okay?"

Sissy nodded again.

"Next time we'll get you across the bridge. Your fan club in the city misses you."

Sissy blushed at the compliment, even though she didn't believe it for a minute. "I bet," she said.

"They do, you know." Lynn shook her head, "Always selling yourself short."

"I'll reform," Sissy said.

"Get going," Lynn retorted, leaning forward to kiss Sissy on the cheek. She had to fight the urge to bolt, but she couldn't control her rigidity as Lynn kissed her. "Let's talk soon," she said as she hastily made her way to the stairs.

On the street below she breathed easier and decided to walk to the subway. She wondered if she would ever be able to peck Lynn again without dread. She also wondered if she looked any different after last night. After their honeymoon, Eddie had told her, "You don't look like a little girl anymore. You move like a woman now." She didn't know if that was true. She had rather hoped it was. But she suspected it was really his cock crowing. If it wasn't, and there had been a transformation, could it be she was changed now after a lesb——. She couldn't even use that word.

She searched the faces of passersby to see if they were looking at her with a strange awareness. All she discerned were the normal prowling male looks. Maybe it was other women who had antennae for such things. She peered hard at the females she passed. They didn't seem to perceive her as odd. But then, maybe it worked the other way. Was she looking at the women any differently? What a thought! But she couldn't help herself. Her eyes began to fall automatically on women's legs, breasts, and crotches. Did she find them alluring? Oh, Christ, what was she doing to herself? She always could spot a sensual woman, what of it? Hell, yes, that one had great legs, and that one nice breasts. But did she want them? No, no, goddamn it! She wasn't going to let one interlude in a crazy state alter her thinking, her life. But that one without the bra did have huge nipples. She screamed. Luckily, what came out was "Taxi!"

The first couple of invitations from Lynn weren't difficult to turn down. Standing excuses: getting herself together, wanting to spend time with Eileen. But after four or five refusals, Lynn's voice turned testy over the phone. Finally, after another refusal,

Lynn brought it out in the open. "Is something bothering you, Theresa?"

"No, nothing. I'm just a little slow in putting it back together. I'm sorry to be such a drag."

"I think it's more than that."

Sissy tightened her grip on the phone. "No, no. I'll be all right soon."

"Look, Theresa, all we had that night was a little female tea and sympathy. A one-shot thing. Just forget it. It's not my or your bag."

Sissy was crimson on the other end of the line. She blurted, "I want to thank you and your family for everything you have done for me." She slammed the receiver down before a reply could be made. Thank you and your family? The obsequious tone shamed her. Had she been wrong all along? She wasn't her father's daughter, but her mother's.

That truly terrified her. She knew Lynn was right about it being a one-shot affair, about not being either of their bags. But what Lynn didn't know was that it was more than sympathy. She had wanted to possess Lynn and would have if she was emotionally able. In the same way she had wanted to possess Eddie, and Mickey before him. They were all so much more than she was. Through possession, they would festoon the lonely cell that was her inner life.

*P*HILLY EXITED from the bridge and hung a series of lefts, first on Chambers Street, then Broadway, and finally off Broadway and Murray into the City Hall parking lot, where he presented the cop on duty with a special pass Sissy had given him earlier. He nosed into a vacant spot, killed the engine, and ceremoniously looked at his watch, announcing, "ETA. Right on the button, folks. You have time to spare."

Nellie and Catherine looked at him in bewilderment, while Christy wondered if this asshole would now give them disembarkation instructions.

When Sissy stepped out of the limo, she saw an anxious Sal making his way toward them. She should have known Sal would be waiting. Since it was Eddie's day, it was his day. Sissy wondered if he, like an anxious kid, had camped outside City Hall all night in a sleeping bag.

His uniform gave the lie to that. He was resplendent in his pressed blues, decorated with various citations, with the fillip of white gloves. The white gloves, thought Sissy, were a bit much. He looked as if he were about to announce that the entire production would run three hours with one intermission and would be in Cinemascope.

"I was beginning to think you wouldn't get here," Sal said. Philly shot him one of those if-looks-could-kill glances.

"We have plenty of time," Sissy said.

"Yeah, but most of the other families are here already. Besides, the Mayor's guy who's in charge told me they want all the families inside. In the Blue Room. There's refreshments." He looked at Philly and added, "For the family. Well, maybe I can do . . ."

"Forget it," said Philly. "I'll get some coffee across the street."

"Well, I can try," offered Sal.

"Forget it," Philly said again. "Besides, I got some phone calls to make." He would be fucked if he had to depend on some cop's pull. Besides, he had never understood Italian cops. Italian and Jew cops you couldn't get a handle on. You never knew why they were into it. The Irish were simple. Where the hell else did they have to go?

"Well, if you say so," Sal concurred, grateful he didn't have to go to bat for an outsider. "This way, folks," he directed formally, offering Sissy his arm. He was a born usher, she thought. The analogy would go even further. He knew all the words, but never what the big picture was. Not now, not back when, not ever.

It astounded her that she could have had a thing with him. Perhaps she was ripe. Her Latin dalliance. She had known in her bones that Eddie was screwing around. The nights out and the absence of alcohol on his breath when he returned. The one too many phone calls she answered when there was silence on the other end of the line and then a click. More suspiciously, the calls came at offbeat times when Sissy might have been thought to be out of the house. That early morning she spied from the bed and watched him undress, and he wasn't wearing shorts. Where were they? Lying somewhere drenched with come? Or worse, stained with menstrual blood. To her, that was unacceptable. But the dog cinched it. The rest was circumstantial. The dog was concrete.

Eddie had never wanted a dog. "Shit machines," he called them. He didn't want any chaos in his home. He saw enough of that on the job. Chaos and shit. He lived with it eight hours a day. He didn't need it in his home. He only relented for the kids' sake, especially Billy. Eddie believed in things like a boy and his dog. Actually, Sissy wanted a puppy more than the kids did. She hadn't had a pet since her duck.

The purchase of the puppy came with strict ground rules. The kids and Sissy would care for it, walk it, exclusively. They greedily agreed. Then Eddie began to take an active interest in the dog. The evenings he was at home, he became the leash-holder when it was time for the dog's late-night walk. Hell, he'd virtually fight for the privilege. And Sissy noticed another thing. Before he walked the dog, he would always check his pockets for change. Dimes, she presumed, telephone dimes. She had been a cop's wife long enough to be into deductive cynicism.

But it was still iffy, not airtight, and that drove her to distraction. The speculation was maddening. She needed grounds more relative to catch her king of the roost. She decided to play off Sal.

It wasn't hard. He was primed for it. Sal's star was descending. When Eddie was plucked from the precinct for plainclothes, Sal had been left behind. That wasn't the way it was supposed to happen. Now Sal had to listen to Eddie's glamorous escapades in the big town, while his own material was restricted to breaking up drunken domestic brawls and hopping the asses of neighborhood rowdies. Strictly lounge act stuff.

And Sal was still stuck with the brass-buttoned blue coat and the clumsy service revolver, while Eddie dressed the dandy and packed a nifty, snub-nosed piece. The signs of discontent were there. Sal took to complaining that while the line cops were the nuts and bolts, the salt of the earth, they never got the ink. Ah-h, the salt of the earth. The grand neighborhood wail that the frivolous world was ignoring you.

Then there was the unmentionable blow. Sal D'Amato, center fielder extraordinaire of the neighborhood softball team, Sal D. (after his illustrious predecessor on the Yankees) threw out his back chasing punk vandals and could no longer prowl his hallowed ground with élan. Worse, Eddie, his friend, the team's manager, demoted him to right field, where the action was rare, against predominantly right-handed hitting lineups. Right field, the neighborhood destination for twerps, odd men out, men who got into the lineup on charity. A pussy position.

Oh, was Sal ever ready to be knocked over. Moreover, there was his feeling for Sissy. She knew that from the beginning he had had a crush on her. It was easy to figure out. If she was good enough for Eddie, a sultan would pay a ransom for her.

Besides, Sal was never a ladies' man. His dates, the ones she met anyway, wouldn't exactly light up a room. Solid, square, leftover local types on their last go-around to catch the ring. Sexual right fielders. Small wonder he looked at the vivacious Sissy with adoration.

But in all honesty it was just that, adoration, never lasciviousness. Sal was one of those men incapable of sustained passion. It wasn't as rare as one supposed. Sissy had known many men who found the rites of wooing, marrying, and fathering too Olympian. So they became barnacles who attached themselves to some family ship. Always a constant, but never integral. They enjoyed the designation "uncle." They never missed a friend's child's birthday, and because of their singular status, they could be counted on to be lavish on holidays and other high occasions. It was their presents under the tree that would be impeccably wrapped by department store professionals.

Men like Sal wanted a wife and children when the occasion fit. The commitment of lasting love, the messiness of children, the four o'clock feedings, the behinds to be wiped, and the horrible fear that responsibility brings were to be experienced only by osmosis. If a piece of ass fell into their laps, or a family could be decorously wrapped, they were in the market. Good-time Uncle Charlies, all.

Sal was at the front of the class. Not only did he view Sissy, Billy, and Eileen as his own, but better yet, Eddie was his stand-in, his surrogate, to deal with the day-to-day trench warfare of domestic life. Sal had a family and yet remained above the fray.

Not that he didn't care about their problems—he did. But there was always the buffer of being free of the blood knot. He would concern himself like an outside consultant to a business. He wanted them to succeed, but if the whole shebang went in the toilet, he would be the surviving chronicler whose sagacious, saving advice had been ignored. He would be the neighborhood bard who would weave the sad Sullivan fall into the barroom repertory.

Perhaps that was too harsh. After all, Sal was no different from any other suitor. He was true in his fashion. That's why Sissy was able to manipulate him so easily. That, combined with the slights of being displaced on both squads, the precinct and the diamond. Sissy knew she could extract the evidence confirming her suspicions from him. In his pathos, he would be a sucker for a flashy ploy.

So one day when Eddie called and said he had gotten hung up in an all-night poker game and was going straight to work, Sissy phoned Sal under the pretext that she needed him to drive her to the shopping mall at the end of Flatbush Avenue. She knew he was on the night trick and would be both available and willing.

So willing, she swore she could hear him fumbling for the car keys over the phone.

With Sal, subtlety was lost. In the car Sissy simply bluffed him out of his socks. "Of course, you know about the trouble Eddie and I are having." She watched his face fall apart. It was so unfair. He had come to serve, to chatter warmly, and to be thanked by Eddie for being a friend his wife could count on in a pinch. Now he was in depths he didn't understand.

"What trouble?" he croaked.

"I can't tolerate him screwing around with other women. I'm leaving him."

"Leaving him!"

"Divorcing him. I won't be treated like a piece of shit."

"But it's only one broad," Sal defended. "Plenty of married guys fall into that trap. These broads leech around cops. It's nothing, I swear to you. He'll get over it."

Normally, she would have pondered his reaction. His panic at his surrogate world crumbling around him. But his phrase, "he'll get over it," turned her to introspection. She never figured on an "it" to get over. She presumed her competition was the field, faceless one-night stands. Sal made it sound like an affair. She lost all her guile. "Who is she?" she demanded.

"It's not important. Believe me," he implored. "She's a nobody. A cop groupie."

"What's the nobody's name?"

"I can't tell you that."

"Yes, you can," she screamed.

"I'll take care of it," he said soothingly. "She won't be around anymore."

His promise excited her. What did he mean by it? Would he tell the woman to stop seeing Eddie? She thought of the male arrogance of that. "I've just cancelled your affair, baby. Your fucking days are over." Or did he mean more? "She won't be around anymore." Was this cop talk for a contract? God, would he kill for her? The idea electrified her. The slut, the homebreaker deserved it. What a testimony of his love that would be. It made her feel a prized lady of the court with Sal as her knight. Robert Taylor in *Ivanhoe*.

"How?" she begged tearily.

"Never mind how. It will be taken care of. Now dry your tears."

Suddenly he seemed so firm. "But . . ."

"But nothing. Dry those tears, and let's get your errands done."

"I don't feel like shopping now," she said. "Can't you tell me who she is?"

"No, I can't. That's impossible." His tone told her she had learned enough. Don't push him too far. She was trying to turn him into a fink. He was a cop, and Eddie was his brother officer and friend. Even she couldn't transcend that. "It will be taken care of," he said with finality.

"I want to go home," she pouted.

"No, you don't. You don't want to sit home and dwell on this." She didn't. "I don't want to go shopping."

"Well, since we've driven this far, why don't we drive over the bridge and take a walk along the beach. It's a great day."

Her silence told him she was considering it. He pulled the car over to the curb and parked. "You wait here," he said. He got out and went into a deli. After an aggravating delay, he came back with two large bags, which he put into the back seat. "Some heros and beer. I hope you're hungry."

"I'm not," she protested, incredulous that he would think she could think of food at a time like this.

"You will be," he said, "when that ocean air hits you."

The remark infuriated her nearly as much as the fact that he hadn't asked her what kind of hero she would like.

They drove to a secluded spot on the bay side of the ocean. Though Sissy welcomed the solitude, she didn't care for it. The smoothness of the sand was broken by patches of wild weeds that looked as offensive as underarm hair with a strapless formal. The placid bay had no undulations or drama to it. Norman Maine would never choose this spot for his last walk.

"I come fishing here a lot," Sal explained. "My father first brought me here when I was a boy. Not many people know about it. I kinda think of it as my own." Sissy was touched by the revelation. She thought of the young Nick at the Big Two-Hearted River.

Sal opened the trunk of the car and removed an army blanket to spread it on the sand. The contents of the trunk fascinated Sissy. Besides the obligatory mechanical accessories—a jack, a big wrench, the spare, various cans of oil, and highway flares—there was a softball glove, two old softballs, a cluster of bats, a football, a bag of golf clubs, and a full complement of fishing equipment. The toy chest had never really been jettisoned, only transferred to a mobile hiding place.

Sal took the two six-packs and submerged them in the shallow water to keep cold, then folded one corner of the blanket over the sandwich bag to protect the food from the sun. "Let's work up an appetite," he said. "A nice walk along the water's edge and then some lunch and a cool one." He began taking off his shoes and socks. Sissy kicked off her sandals in resignation. She could hardly tell him, after her prior protestations, that she was now famished and would be content with a hero and a can of beer. Also, she was bursting with curiosity about what he had bought her. Sal was one of those self-proclaimed gourmets who thought groaning plates and seas of red sauce constituted a good restaurant. Northern Italian would be lost on him. Sissy doubted if she was going to be pleased with the contents of the bag.

The day was growing hotter, and the bay breeze wasn't vigorous enough for Sissy. It was only mid-June, too early for swimming, but Sissy wished she were wearing a swimsuit. Even though the bay tide with its docile lapping at the shore like a dog at its water bowl was too timid for her. For that matter, Sissy didn't care for bay scallops either. Fey poseurs for their robust sea brothers.

But considering the alternative, the confines of her house and her bleak thoughts, the bay was a small blessing. Sal, sensing that Sissy was sufficiently appreciative of his private province, tried to whip up her enthusiasm with a running commentary on the joys of the spot. The various kinds of fish that could be caught there, the lack of an undertow that enhanced swimming, and the rare birds who found habitat in the surrounding marshlands.

Sissy didn't want to be an ungrateful drag, so she made an effort to match his mood. She ventured ankle deep into the water and was shocked by its coldness. The water stimulated her circulation, and she waded in a little deeper. She could feel her body being roused alert in ascending degrees. She imagined her cool, tingling blood racing as if it were on horseback. She remembered the opening lines of "The Midnight Ride of Paul Revere." How old was she when she had learned that in school? Many battles ago.

She was feeling better. She started to appreciate the surroundings: the sun, the water, the beach, the birds overhead, and the man walking next to her. She must have watched this scene in a thousand movies, yet she couldn't pinpoint a single example. She dug deeper into the celluloid library in her head, but still she couldn't place it.

Back on the blanket, Sissy was pleasantly surprised. Instead of having the deli owner prepare one sandwich for each of them, Sal had had him cut the loaves in quarters with different combinations of meats and cheese. A seaside smörgasbord. Sissy was impressed. She hungrily sampled most of the combos and finished two of the four cans of beer Sal had taken from the water. She asked him to fetch another to accompany her post-meal cigarette.

Sal attempted to make a brief for Eddie while Sissy smoked, but she wasn't in the mood for it. She was too content and lulled for nastiness. She laid back on one elbow while she finished her smoke so that the sun would have access to more of her body. She tuned Sal out.

She didn't know when she fell asleep, but when she woke up, she felt terrible. Sal had put a baseball cap over her forehead so that its sloping bill would protect her eyes and nose, but it hadn't helped. She had an excruciating headache, and her mouth tasted like larvae were growing there. Beer always did that to her. Plus there was the panic on awakening.

She pointedly avoided afternoon naps. She found that the few times she relented she had awakened feeling miserable, with unreasonable fears. It never happened after a night's sleep, only daytime naps. It was as if she let her guard down and was vulnerable to the terrible machinations of others. On awakening, she always had to run an inventory on her well-being before the panic subsided. Her sense of panic increased when she couldn't find Sal. Or anyone. She was sure he had brought her here.

How else had she been marooned on this barren beach? She couldn't focus well in the glare. Everything was too bright, suffused in light. It was like the unsympathetic harshness of a doctor's examining room. She commissioned an inner calm, slowly letting her eyes traverse the terrain like a turret. She hit upon a figure standing in the shallow water in swim trunks. That confused her. But it must be Sal.

She rose from the blanket and walked toward the water's edge. She was still too unsure of the presence to call his name. She picked a piece of wood from the sand and scraped it noisily across a crushed, wire-mesh trash basket. The act reminded her of how, as a girl, she used to rock her boat against the sides of the wall in the Tunnel of Love at Coney Island when she was terrified of the dark and the eerie lapping of the water. Sal turned. He was holding a fishing rod.

"Hi. Did you have a good sleep?"

"Between the beer and the sun, my head is about to burst."

"Really?" He looked crushed. "I put my hat over your head. I thought you would be fine. I wouldn't have let you sleep if . . ."

Sissy felt as if she had booed the Good Shepherd. "Oh, the hat was fine. I'm just not used to beer in the afternoon." She felt she had just shattered one of her father's beloved commandments. Crueler than a serpent's bite, or some such.

"God, that water looks great," she continued. "I wish I'd brought my suit."

Sal's face collapsed again. She wondered what the hell she had said now. He started to fidget, moving the reel on the rod in front of him. He held the rod low at waist level. "I'm sorry," he mumbled, "I planned to be through by the time you woke up. I'm sorry."

When she realized the reason for his contrition, she had to smother her laughter. He was wading in his shorts, worse, they were jockey shorts. If only he was standing up straight instead of cowering like a drag version of *September Morn*, it wouldn't have been so ridiculous. But with his hairy black legs and his balls ensconced in a white cotton slingshot, he looked like a tableau in a camp revue in the Village. Suppressing her laughter must have made her face look stern.

"I swear to God I didn't mean anything by it," he said. "I mean, you're my best friend's wife. God forbid it should even cross my mind. I should be struck dead right here in the water if I meant anything by it."

Sissy was about to break out laughing in his face. Poor sad Sal, that would be unconscionably cruel. Following a gracious impulse, she turned and shimmied out of her sundress. She rolled the dress like a newspaper and placed it on top of some castaway wood to keep it free of sand. Then, without looking at him, she turned and ran toward the water, breaking the surface with a flat racer's dive as the cool, refreshing water soaked her bra and panties.

When she surfaced, she let out a whoop as she shook out her

hair. Her enthusiasm released him from his embarrassment. He tossed the pole and disappeared under the water. When he resurfaced, he mimicked her cry. "Wow, that's great," he enthused. She agreed by plunging under again.

When she came up, he motioned to her with a tug of his head, "Come on." They started to swim in tandem, horizontal to the horizon. Sissy had always preferred swimming in that direction rather than straight out into the deeper water. It was less scary, and one had the peaceful illusion of circumnavigating the globe with the great ships and the dolphins.

Sal was a much stronger swimmer than she. As she tossed her head unrhythmically, she watched his smooth, neat strokes. He was one of those men who improved in motion. In a social situation he always appeared slow and gauche, but set free in athletic endeavor he exuded grace. Even his looks improved under strain. Sissy noticed that his hair gleamed in the water, and his normally docile eyes took on a sheen. He looked dashingly Latin, very much like Fernando Lamas.

Sissy liked the image of him she advanced in her mind, since she was in consort with it. She lengthened her choppy stroke to Esther Williams' proportions to keep abreast. The bay alternately became a backlot lagoon reserved for a *pas de deux*. She fell into rhythm with Sal as she tried to cull up the strains of the Jose Iturbi orchestra. After fifty yards of extending herself, all she heard was the kazoo of her lungs. Lousy cigarettes.

She stopped stroking, but before she could declare she had had it, Sal said, "Okay, back to the starting point." She'd be damned if she would beg off like an out-of-shape housewife.

"Gotcha," she gasped, took a deep breath, and began. She just couldn't quit, but the tide moving in and out seemed to confine her progress to lateral jostling. She could see Sal's fishing rod in the sand where he had tossed it, and it didn't seem possible they had swum that far. She would never make it.

Her chest hurt so much she didn't know if it was her lungs or an incipient heart attack. "Are you all right?" he called, his breath as even as his stroke. She hated people who asked you a question during exercise, especially when you were sucking wind. The in-shape's covert putdown. She was infuriated. She grunted back her well-being. Her anger steeled her resolve.

She started to swim with her face in the water to muster more speed. It also muffled the sound of her gasps and allowed her to blind herself to the trauma of her goal. With her face submerged, she was set free to fantasize. In her mind she didn't lie about her fatigue but justified it. After all, she was completing her Channel swim. It wasn't Sal next to her, but a rowboat with her handlers urging her on. On the shore there was not a cluster of inanimate objects—fishing pole and dress—but the cheering citizens of Calais. She churned to the cheers, going full out until she could take no more. She quit, pulling her mouth out of the water and sucking in the air.

Sal was standing beside her, running his fingers through his hair. "Hey, tiger, you gave me a run for my money. You're in some shape."

Sissy turned and looked at the shore. She couldn't spot their belongings until she turned her head to the rear. She had passed the starting point by ten yards. "Ah-h, that used to be a warm-up before those damn cigarettes screwed up my wind."

Sal shook his head in admiration for her cavalier dismissal of her feat. He walked toward the shore, saying, "Well, I wouldn't want to tangle with you when you were good." Sissy was glad he couldn't see her following in his wake, staggering like a slave on a shank.

Sal collapsed on his back on the sand. "Whew! You're a tough workout, kid."

Sissy noticed that he had more than overcome his embarrassment. He lay with his legs wide open, letting the water slosh around his thighs. His shorts, and her bra and panties, were now transparent. He seemed larger than Eddie. For sure, he was hairier. Size wasn't one of Sissy's hangups, that was a male thing. They couldn't even watch a basketball game on television without making crude speculative jokes about the black players. She couldn't figure out why it was such a preoccupation. Was it that a big stake guaranteed the permanence of the victim's impalement?

Sal saw her looking, and she picked up his stare in return. Her pubic hair stained her panties. He rolled over in the shore mud and asked, "How are you at sand castles?"

She was touched, not by his discretion, but the question-invitation. She had loved to make elaborate sand castles as a girl. She was tireless. Molding intricate curlicues with the wet sand and then quickly sprinkling her creations with handfuls of hot dry sand that she trotted from farther in-shore to firm the design. The finished products always reminded her of chocolate fairy kingdoms frosted with mocha.

She could never impart this enthusiasm to her family. Oh, to Eileen for a while when she was little, but once she began to worry about the sleek condition of her swimsuit, she refused to join in. Eddie and Billy thought sandcastles were "silly." They always harassed her projects. Under the guise of good grab-ass fun, of course. While Sissy worked on her castle (before she stopped for good), Eddie and Billy would ignore her. Then when the castle was complete, they'd swoop out of the water, hurling handfuls of mud at her fragile edifice, yelling, "Bomb the enemy fortress," until Sissy's dream dissipated into the sea. She didn't know what hurt more. The destruction of her castle, or their label for it. "Enemy fortress"—perhaps that should have told her something. How could they see things of beauty as menacing?

Sal was scooping armfuls of mud to firmer land. "Are you game?" he shouted.

"You betcha," she said, and she fell to her knees.

As Sal supplied, Sissy shaped. Turrets started to rise, and a moat to fend off the bay was hurriedly scraped out.

"Hey, you're out of my league," Sal said. "What should I do?"

"How about some dry sand?" Sissy asked without looking up.

"Aye, aye, sir," he replied, saluting and scurrying up the beach. Each time he came back with handfuls of sand, Sissy had added another embellishment. "Keep going," he said, "it's beautiful. Do something else."

Sissy was flushed by his enthusiasm. She had never had such a partner, so she stretched herself to please him by dribbling little dots, like chocolate kisses, along the castle walls. When his enthusiasm wasn't satiated, she deserted her building and sought out popsicle sticks in the sand to make a drawbridge. Using matches and shards of colored paper, she placed flags in the battlements. The last was the crowning touch. They both sat back, beaming at their accomplishment.

Sal grinned at her. "You're something else. Really super. I always say that to people." When she looked at him, he blushed. "You know, I always say how lucky Eddie is."

"Thank you. That's sweet."

He sensed he might have revealed too much. "I ought to go get a shovel and dig a real moat around this. It will be a shame when the tide gets it."

"Let's not think about that. Let's just sit here and watch our castle for a while."

"Yeah, the sun setting on it makes it even prettier."

It was the first time, his mentioning the sunset, that Sissy took cognizance of the hour. "I didn't realize it was getting so late," she said ruefully.

"Don't worry, it won't take long to get you home."

"Well, there's dinner."

"Come on, that refrigerator of yours always has enough in it to feed an army."

She laughed. Then real concern struck her. "Oh, my God, we'll never dry out in time."

"Don't worry. I have towels in the trunk."

"I mean our . . ." She couldn't say underwear. She was a married woman. What the hell was she doing sitting in her underwear, transparent underwear, with her husband's best friend? Building sandcastles? Run that one by the boys in the squadroom and you would be laughed off the block.

Sal read her panic. "You can change in the back of the car. I have plastic bags I keep for fish in the trunk. You can put your stuff in one of them and wash it out when you get home. Just put the stuff in your purse."

"Stuff?" He knew it wasn't right either. But his solution was fine. She looked back at her castle. They were silent for a time until she heard him say, "Hello? What do we have here?"

She watched him get up, walk a few feet and reach down. He held up a sand crab. "We have a visitor. An intruder at our castle." He held the crab up in the air and started to wag it in his hand. "And what should I do with you, Mr. Wise Guy? Huh? I got the solution for you, Mr. Buttinski."

Sissy sickened. He was going to ruin everything. He was going to do something cruel to the crab. Not kill it, or anything like that. That wasn't their way. She had watched Eddie and Billy with animals. They couldn't leave them alone either. Some game or test had to be devised for them. Some humiliating ritual—jump this, crawl through that, climb up this. Sal was about to put the crab through one of those numbers. She was too nauseated to stop him. She just watched, repelled.

Sal scooped out a hole inside the perimeter of the castle moat with his free hand. Then he picked up an empty beer can and walked to the bay to fill it. Sissy couldn't take her eyes off him. She knew now why people went to watch executions.

He returned with the can and filled the hole with water. "There, my friend," he said, kneeling and placing the crab in the hole. "Your private bath. You're our guest tonight in our castle. Our caretaker, too. It's your job to keep the water out of our castle. That's the price of a night's lodging. Keep the castle safe till we return."

Sissy looked at him as the crab merrily scurried about in the hole. "Is that it?" she asked.

"Well, there is a little bread left over. Do you think we should leave him breakfast? Are you going to earn your grub, Mr. Crab?"

Sissy's smile knighted Sal as she watched the crab. She thought of *The Wind in the Willows* and *Toad Hall*. She pushed herself up on one knee and walked over to Sal. "You're a sweet, sweet man and a great landlord."

He reddened as he looked at her. It was all so incredibly touching she bent over and kissed him on the mouth. He drew her down to him. In his clumsiness they rolled over, and she could feel the weight of his body. It didn't feel menacing at all. Just sweet. She opened her mouth, and he kissed her so tenderly it belied the bulge she felt between her legs.

She could feel the wet sand on her legs and feet and thought for a moment of Deborah Kerr and Burt Lancaster in *From Here to Eternity*. But she didn't feel at all sluttish like Kerr's Karen Holmes, she felt like a sweet kid on a Brooklyn beach.

She wanted the sweetness to continue. She arched her rump and slid down her panties, while Sal tremblingly unhooked her bra. It was so nice to feel unsure hands instead of the arrogant grip of possession. Sal pulled down his jockey shorts. He was huge, bigger than Eddie.

"Oh, darling," he said, "I always loved . . ."

She hushed him with one hand on his mouth, and with the other she started to guide him into her. When the tip of his prick touched her wet entrance, he went limp in her hand. She was stunned. She tried to bring him back to life by massaging him gently, but in his panic he tried to ram into her, futilely. "Calm down," she said, "it will come back."

But he wouldn't hear any of it. His limpness was like a child's fist, banging hopelessly at a door. "Easy," she said. But the more she cajoled, the more frenzied he became. The sweetness of his body smell soured to clammy sweat.

"Help me, help me," he pleaded, as he took her hand and wrapped it around his balls. "Put me in," he implored.

Dutifully, Sissy tried. There was no more pleasure. The innocence was gone. Now it was down to mechanics. She had gone through this with Eddie when he was drunk. An impossible task. Like trying to stuff a bean bag in your cunt.

Sal rolled off her and started to cry. "I'm sorry, I'm sorry," he kept repeating. "It must be the damp and the cold water."

"Sure it is," she said. She wanted to dress and get the hell away. "It's always awkward the first time between people," she reassured.

Tears were running down his face. "You know, I never had a lot of women, like Eddie."

Christ, how tactful, she thought. She wondered if he was a virgin. Could that be possible at his age? A bona fide cherry?

"It doesn't matter," she said. "It was a wonderful day."

He put his arm across his eyes to hide his tears. "Till now," he said. "This ruined it. And with you, of all people . . ." He couldn't finish through the sobs.

"It happens all the time," she said.

"Not to me," he said defensively.

"Well, it does. Don't carry on about it. I had a great day."

"You won't tell anyone about this?" he snorted.

Jesus, he was dumber than she'd thought. Just who would she tell? "Of course not," she replied, without chiding his illogic.

"Well, I don't want anyone to start talking," he said truculently.

"Talking?"

"You know what the wise guys would say about this," he explained, his arm still covering his eyes.

"Wise guys?"

"The guys in the precinct. I take enough kidding."

Was he mad? The guys in the precinct! What was he thinking! "Nobody will hear a word. It's between us, and it's forgotten already."

"I hope so. I can't handle their shit anymore."

"What do they say?" She was intrigued.

"You know the jokes those assholes make."

"No, I don't."

"You know, about partners. Well, we used to be partners, and we're still close. Eddie and me, I mean."

"What do they say, Sal?"

"You know. If you hang out with a guy a lot, they start calling you his wife."

"Do they call you Eddie's wife?"

He started crying loudly. "Yeah, and if they do it again, I'll break their fucking heads. We're best friends, and that's that. Those assholes can't understand that. So what if I do a lot of favors for him? That kind of talk is out of bounds. I ain't no fucking . . . Well, you know what."

Oh, my God, that was it. He was afraid he had developed a thing for Eddie. So Eddie was claiming two victims. His crying was heartbreaking. But she knew the answer to cure him. It never failed when Eddie was having performance trouble. She reached over and held his prick. "Come on, you must be kidding. With the size of this thing, you must have had half of the women in the precinct after you." She felt it stir in her hand. "And the other half probably stay away because they're terrified."

He jumped alive in her hand. She just couldn't abandon him like that. He had been so sweet. Why should he suffer because of Eddie, too? She pulled him over on top of her. She went into her domestic-tested litany. "Oh, let me have some of that, all of that," she crooned in mock ecstasy. As he got close to her, she felt a slight sag. "Put that enormous prick into me. Oh, yes, let me feel it up my stomach. Pin me to the ground with it."

He was stiff again, and she inserted him. "Oh, my God, it's huge. Easy, easy, no, fuck me, hurt me with that huge dick."

She wasn't surprised that he ejaculated within seconds. She had learned that all you had to do was talk filthy to God's most noble creatures. Appealing to their sadism didn't hurt either. The combination could turn a noodle into a flagpole. They were all alike on the libidinal line. What a wonder man was. Her ass!

"Was it good for you?" he begged.

"Absolutely wonderful," she declared. She couldn't tell him it was as arduous as doing a load of wash.

Sal returned to his fawning ways with Eddie and Sissy. The interlude was never mentioned. It never happened again.

But Sissy knew what she had done for him from the way he jabbered and whistled on the way home in the car. She was a cop's wife, and she held a marker on him. She banked it until the day it would come in handy.

SAL WAS in his officious glory as he led Sissy and her clan around the rows of folding chairs toward the steps of City Hall. Sissy had recognized early how cops loved to flaunt their edge over the average citizenry. Eddie used to mortify her when they were caught in a traffic jam and he left their car to saunter up the highway, like John Wayne heading to an assignation with the sunset. "I'll check it out," he'd say.

Worse, the jam invariably broke before Eddie reached the culprit, and Sissy was left sitting in the passenger seat while angry drivers cursed and honked at their stationary car.

Then there were his intrusions into arguments when they were socializing. One loud, angry word from a boozed-up husband to his wife was enough to bring Eddie to the rescue. "Look, I'm on the job," it always began, followed by the solicitous soft sell. If the couple behaved themselves afterward, there was a drink sent to their table, Eddie beaming on them like Dr. Rose Franzblau.

But it was the sartorial cop touch that Sissy found truly un-endurable—the ever-present piece on the hip. The stated excuse was, of course, that cops are on duty twenty-four hours a day. What a fanciful farce that was. If you bought that line, you'd believe they spent their waking hours checking the skies of Gotham for the Bat Signal.

What concerned Sissy most was that Eddie and the others car-ried their guns at functions where there was heavy alcohol intake. She had often heard stories of various cops relegated to the "bow & arrow" squad for ventilating some saloon's ceiling. What a fall that must be, gunless cops. No more piece to pack. No longer a *piece* on the hip?

Sissy hated how, in the course of the evening, the suit or sports jacket would invariably be opened and slipped backward to give a tantalizing glimpse of their holstered asset. It was so damn coy. It reminded her of those simpy broads at Breezy Point who used to loosen their bathing suit tops and lie face down on a towel, allowing a crescent of breast to peek out.

She just had to pull this day off. She'd exile the cop culture from her life forever. As strange as the term sounded, it was accurate. Why not "culture"? They had more tribal incantations and customs than the Aztecs. How refreshing it would be, how cleansing, to look at people as human beings again, not as potential rap sheets. To see a human body without believing "scam" was an integral organ. Jesus, she couldn't believe how crude and vile her vision had become.

Everything she saw was filtered through suspicion. It was depressing to realize she must have had a foundation for Eddie to build on.

Her daughter would see differently. Sissy swore that by the force of her will she would flush the stigma of looking for the crass from Eileen's eyes. She had allowed Billy's vision to be sullied. She had known it was happening. She had watched him ape his father and his father's friends, much to their delight. Eddie was fond of saying, "That kid really knows where it's at."

Sure. A black kid in hightop sneakers was never on his way to a playground but "in his second-story togs." She wondered if Billy also viewed romance as his father had. She hoped he had been spared that. That smarmy nudge and wink that passed between Eddie and his friends whenever they saw a couple kissing. It was never love but "hide the bologna time." They'd find a gimmick in the crucified Christ—a new way to boost lumber?

Sal was now leading her into a cluster of cops. She knew all their faces. They had worked with Eddie, been guests in her home. She wondered how many of them knew what really went down the day he died. That seemed moot. Sal had known; so must the others. Human compromise was what held New York's finest together. Mutual decay was their cement.

Sissy looked at their faces mustered into solemnity. They were wearing their public faces. There would be television cameras here today. Television liked staged Greek chorus tragedies. Their wives were also decked out in their demure best. Not a skirt too short, and white gloves and clutch bags to boot. Sissy didn't blame them. Impeccability, it came with the territory. She had played the same part often herself. Portia to a sidewalk Caesar.

She walked stoically through the group as hands touched and patted her. The voices were indistinguishable as they embraced her. "He was a real prince." "They won't replace his kind." "It's not only a bad day for the force but for the world." "It's the city, Sissy, the city has become unlivable." Sissy allowed herself a small, resigned smile and nodded as though their words were strewn palm. Stately, she moved among them.

Her composure was tilted when she reached the steps and saw the Halligans waiting for her. She couldn't understand her neighbors' presence. James was an investment banker, not a cop. He stood there with his wife Kathy and their teenage daughter Deirdre. They looked so lovely. They were one of the few neighborhood families Sissy admired. They were a cut above the rest. They went to the theater, summered on the tip of Long Island, and when you met James or Kathy on the street, they engaged you in real conversation—politics, restaurants, books. Sissy often fantasized that she and Eddie could have had such a marriage. She imagined the Halligans' breakfast table with flowers, cloth napkins, silver, two copies of the *New York Times*, and concerned conversation. Not glazed doughnuts, instant coffee, and the *Daily News* opened to the sports pages.

James approached and took Sissy's hand. "I hope you don't mind our being here. I know it's a family gathering, but we . . . well, we just wanted to be here."

"Of course, of course," said Sissy, deeply touched but not understanding.

"He just meant so much to our family. We wanted to be here."

Kathy added, "I hope it's not an intrusion, but we wouldn't have felt right if we didn't come. And of course, Deirdre wanted to be here so badly."

The gangly, oversized child smiled at Sissy and handed her a small bouquet. "For you," she said, "for you and the coach."

Sissy's eyes flooded. That was it. The coach. Now it was clear. Deirdre the tomboy. Eddie had befriended her after her girlfriend was killed by a car when she was roller-skating with

Deirdre. The child had witnessed the death and had become terrified of the streets. Her parents had to drive her to and from school, and after school she wouldn't stray from the front porch. Sissy remembered the terrible gossip about the child's screaming nightmares and the psychiatric visits. It was so long ago, but now Sissy remembered.

When Eddie learned of the accident, he called home from work every day to check on Billy and Eileen. Drunk one night, he had said, "This life is dirty enough. At least kids ought to be immune. Everything else has rules of fairness, except fucking life."

When Sissy told him what she'd heard, he couldn't bear it. "That kid was a better athlete than most of the boys on the block. To end up sitting on a porch scared to move! No child should need a shrink. It's sick. I mean, a kid. That's ludicrous."

Of course, she remembered. Why hadn't Eddie's action loomed large to her back then? It took the Halligans to remind her. Eddie had wooed the child off the porch to become his assistant coach in the Little League. After he built her confidence, he inserted her into the lineup—as a pitcher, no less! When the other kids and some of the parents complained that a girl pitcher would compromise the team's chances, Eddie came down on them like a ton of bricks. Not at first, though. At first, he patiently explained the situation, but that didn't placate the dissenters. Eddie told Sissy that he had threatened to disband the team if he heard one more complaint. He also let it be known that he would "lose his shoe up some parent's ass." That did it. Deirdre moved into the regular rotation and held her own with the boys. Sissy remembered Eddie crowing over her every win. "Nothing like a six-hitter to silence critics," he laughed. When and why had Sissy axed all this from memory?

She looked at the girl who was now burgeoning into womanhood. "Thank you, Deirdre, I'm very touched. And Ed—, the coach would be touched too. I'll bring them to the cemet—." She began to cry at that finality, and James gripped her hands and put his lips to her ear.

"He did what no one else was able to do. He was a very special man. My family will always be in your debt and would be honored if you call on us should you need anything. Our hearts go out to you." He kissed Sissy on her wet cheek and gently passed her to Sal.

As they moved up the steps, it weighed on her. Her husband, her Eddie, had done that for that child. That was before Sissy had given a thought to feminism. Once he did so much. It was true. She turned on the top step and looked back. She had to choke the urge to scream at the gathered cops, those defiled altar boys, "You stole my Eddie!"

Sal pulled her behind a pillar and began patting her face with a handkerchief, waving something under her nose that snapped her head back. Sissy pushed his hand away from her face, "What the hell are you doing?"

"Just some smelling salts. I thought they might come in handy. Now be still so your makeup doesn't smear," he added, as he continued patting her in furious little circles and tending to her hair. Sissy felt as if she were in a car wash.

"Don't put that damn stuff under my nose again, you hear?"

"Believe me, I know what I'm doing. I've had training in all this."

Sissy felt like belting him. He was finally getting a chance to put his hostage training into play.

"Don't worry, Pauline will survive," she said.

"What?"

"Oh, skip it. Let me have a look." She took a hand mirror and a handkerchief from her bag. The damage was quickly repaired.

Off to the side, her family was watching them. Eileen's face was in panic, and Christy looked pained. Nellie and Catherine were another matter as they looked on serenely. They nodded in affirmation, as though Sissy had successfully recited her sodality pledge. Their eyes were misted with beatification. That was enough to pull Sissy together. She knew what they were thinking. If they got the green light from Sissy, they would turn the day into a banshee bawl. Sissy walked toward them, putting on her glacial bitch, Joan Crawford look. "I'm sorry," she said, "the child upset me. Eddie meant so much to her. It was stupid of me."

Catherine put out a consoling hand. "It's all right, dear, we understand."

"You understand nothing," Sissy snapped. "It won't happen again. From any of us." She stared them all down. "Now let's go inside."

Inside, they were greeted by a young couple. "And you are, please?" the male half inquired.

"The family of Eddie Sullivan," Sal answered. "He's being honored today," he added with emphasis, to make sure the guy got the drift. Introductions were made all around, but Sissy missed the greeters' names. Aides to the Mayor, she heard, but that was all. They looked like the Mayor to her. Bloomingdale's shoppers.

"If you'll follow us to the Blue Room, you'll find some refreshments," the young woman said.

Sissy flashed a broad wink at Christy, and he comically rolled his eyes heavenward as they followed.

Inside the room a male aide pointed at a table set against the wall. "You'll find coffee, croissants, and danish on that table." Then, as if he were speaking for their ears only, he added, "The Mayor isn't here yet, but he'll be in to greet you before the ceremony. He's on campaign schedule, you know." Another chaser of the Bat Signal, Sissy thought.

They walked to the table and nodded to the members of other families milling about. Sissy looked at the spread and turned to Christy. "I'm sorry, Pop. You gonna be all right?"

Christy picked up a croissant and hefted it. "A little game of horseshoes should calm my nerves."

"Don't you dare," said Sissy, laughing.

"Well, maybe one ringer around the Mayor's clanky head when he arrives."

"You wouldn't want to muss his razor cut, would you?"

"Heavens no," said Christy, "far be it from me to expose that he has nothing underneath."

"Will a coffee do?" she asked.

"It will have to. Nice and . . ."

"I know, I know, sweet."

"Ah, I forget that you've administered to the needy before."

"I've got time and grade."

"Indeed, indeed."

Sissy pulled the tap on the automatic coffeemaker and filled two hard white plastic cups. She could hear Eddie: The china never comes out for cops. She heaped sugar in Christy's cup and handed it to him.

He sipped slowly. "Ah, to a turn. Where are the others?"

They turned and saw them down at the other end of the table with Sal who was pointing at various platters and talking, obviously giving a dissertation on the varied array of pastries. Catherine and Nellie probably wanted to know how long they had been baked, Sissy thought. As they walked toward her, Catherine flagged down the young girl who had greeted them. Sissy quickened her step, and Christy joined her pace. When she got within earshot, she knew it was too late. "I hate to be a bother, dear, but do you have any tea?" Catherine asked.

That mealymouthed phrase drove Sissy wild. Her mind automatically kicked into parody, as it always did. *I hate to be a bother, but I'm having a miscarriage on your municipal floor.*

She heard the girl reply, "I have some herbal tea in my desk drawer. Is that all right?"

"Herbal?" asked Nellie.

"Yes, Celestial Seasonings."

Oh, Lord! Sissy thought. They'll think it's a soap opera.

"It sounds like a flower," Catherine said.

"Yes, it does, I suppose," the girl replied.

"Well, maybe you have a drop of hot water?" Nellie came back.

"Hot water? I assure you, it's a nice tea. Why don't you try it?"

"No, the water would be dandy," Nellie said.

The girl looked perplexed. Sissy saw her bewilderment and moved to intervene, but Christy held her arm. He was smiling maniacally.

Nellie obviously spotted the girl's dumbfounded look. She took a small plastic case out of her handbag and opened it, removing a tea bag and wagging it before the girl's astonished eyes. "I always carry my own. The stomach, you know," she said confidentially.

The girl nodded in rhythm with the swaying tea bag. Catherine was delighted and gave Nellie a comradely shove. "Sure, I should have remembered you wouldn't be found dead without your tea."

"And lucky for you," Nellie countered defensively, "wasn't it you who asked for it in the first place?"

Sissy wanted to sink, but she heard Christy laughing. "Come on," he said, pointing to the portraits around the room, "let's explore the rogue's gallery."

"Don't laugh. I could die."

"Think of it this way," Christy said, steering Sissy toward a wall. "The Mayor just got hip to the Puerto Ricans with beer in paper bags. Now he will find a new ethnic peculiarity. Come on, child, smile. He'll probably find the whole thing very nitty-gritty." In spite of herself, hearing "nitty-gritty" delivered in a put-on Barry Fitzgerald accent made Sissy laugh.

Christy held her arm as they moved around the perimeter of the room, looking at the portraits of politicians. The rich, subdued oils in baroque frames gave the subjects the aura of statesmen. Considering the quality of their performances when they were in office, Sissy had second thoughts about art being the illuminator of truth.

Christy was on the same track. "It shows what a little varnish can do. A bunch of bandits look Jeffersonian."

"Were they really that bad? Bandits, I mean?"

"Well, I had a bit of affection for old Bob Wagner up there. On the face of it, he seemed milquetoast, but he had a bit of a flair. He looked like he was always just walking through the part, but on New Year's Eve he rose to grand heights. In this town he was nearly as big as Guy Lombardo."

"You're losing me," Sissy said.

"Well, if you remember, the transit workers' contract always came up at the end of the year, and by design Wagner would never settle it till the last moment."

"Yes, but wasn't that dangerous?" Sissy asked.

"Not at all. All the major components were in place weeks before. He'd hold out on some pissant issue until Father Time was on his deathbed, then he'd grant the final demand and some small bonus so we wouldn't get feisty at the last minute."

"But why?"

"Why, my girl? Don't you have the Irish nose for politics? The whole city was off acting madcap in their high heels and patent pumps without a thought in their heads except how to get their drunken carcasses home, and there was the Mayor with his shirtsleeves rolled up at the bargaining table. Now, I admit, it didn't look bad for our side either. Dedicated, tenacious union men fighting the clock. And as the ball was about to fall in Times Square, and Guy was cranking up his baton at the Roosevelt, out we would all come from the room like the College of Cardinals saving the city from chaos. Grand stuff. It was better than anything you could find on Broadway."

"All that production for one night?"

"You're missing the point, my dear. It had a residual effect, like the citizens' hangovers. Imagine waking up hungover the next day and wondering how the hell you're going to get to work after the holiday. Disastrous. A foul mood would have been on the city. But there were your buses and your trains at the ready in the morning, and nobody gave a damn what the settlement cost. For a week you had everybody saying, 'Thank God they settled.' And with the horns still ringing in their heads, they weren't in the mood to read angry editorials about crisis management and deficit financing. It was a great coup, and come next election, Bob could recount how he had wrestled intractable labor to the floor while the rest of the city was out dancing. If there was any justice, they'd change New Year's Eve into his saint's day."

Sissy had never heard Christy sound so cynical about his work before. "Didn't all that phony hoopla disgust you?" she asked, hoping for an affirmative answer.

"Only in theory," he said in a flatter tone.

"I'm not sure I understand."

"Well, theory is the way things ideally should be done. You learn along the way that if you're going to be effective, theory takes a furlough."

"You mean, sell . . ."

"Uh-oh, the red flag of the young. Sell out."

"I'm sorry, Pop," she said, touching his arm. "I had no right to say that."

"No big thing, darling," he smiled. "I've heard it before. You see, you know certain things cannot be peddled. You compromise on other things that you naively deemed untouchable at first. Cities are not built on cornerstones but on compromises and cutting corners. Cities aren't much different from life, are they?"

"I guess not," she replied, sheepishly, "but *some* things can't be put up for grabs."

"Right you are," he said wearily, "but less than you think, less than you think."

"But some things, huh?" She was pleading.

"There is always something you can't live with. Some things have to remain steadfast, or you sicken the soul."

"You mean they're a sin."

"Don't turn Catholic on me," he snapped. "I was using the word instead of conscience and dignity." Suddenly, he was sorry that he'd been harsh, and both realized where this skirmish was heading. "At least old Bob Wagner would offer a man more than coffee and a spongy horseshoe," he added lightly.

She couldn't let go. "But there are things you hold on to?"

He looked at her eyes. He knew there was no avoiding it. "Yes, there are. Some things are never worth the compromise. And the sad thing is that those who compromise those things learn that. Too late, to be sure. That only makes their lives sadder. I have nothing but sympathy for those who misunderstand."

It was out before she could stop it. "Then they shouldn't do it," she said. Even to her, it sounded so unrelenting, so Catholic, so much like a nun's dictum.

He didn't even blink. "True, they shouldn't. But then again, some people are tempted more. They lose their way. They forget what is important." He put more emphasis in his voice. "And sometimes the people who love them neglect to remind them. Often, they confuse them more."

She felt her face go red, and tears well up in her eyes. Christy smiled, took her arm, and moved her on to the next picture. "Ah, Governor Martin Van Buren. Look at the chin whiskers on him, will you? What was he noted for? The ferry boat, the steam engine, or was it the pop-up toaster?" Sissy smiled. She was being dealt with, negotiated with, by a pro.

"For me, it was easy," he explained. "My job was pretty matter-of-fact. Nothing fancy. Trains were only interesting in the Old West when people robbed them. It was hard to stray in my job, even if you were looking to." He paused. She knew he was on the brink. "But take building inspectors, or these guys here," waving at some of the gathered cops. "That's a different case altogether. I wouldn't want their job if it was handed to me on a silver platter. Too much temptation, too much confusion."

"I'm sure you would have acted the same way you did."

"Oh, don't be so sure. You never know till you've been there. Now take cops, for instance." Sissy knew it wasn't just any "instance."

"Most of them I've met were lovely lads at first, and many remained that way. At the beginning they were worse than poets with the way they talked about saving the human race. Lots of dreams, too much parochial school training. You know, the world divided into saints and sinners. Though I'm not belittling the Church for not preparing one for life. Not a damn thing does.

Your parents, teachers, anyone. We keep things from kids. That's not a sin either, since the reason we do it is to keep them kids. But there's no damn middle ground. Tell them a little, and they want to know it all."

He grinned at her. "The last thing we want is a bunch of world-weary kids out there. But we don't prepare them enough. Not for the streets. A jackal could get lost out there."

"You didn't," she said.

He sighed, knowing he had to see this through. "No, I didn't, but I had it easy."

"But you come from . . ."

He held up his hand and waved her off. "From a bog, from nothing. And I was better off for it. What in the hell did I want and need? Kids like you and Eddie thought you needed so much to make you happy. I, who had nothing, thought success meant a job where I wore a tie. Till this day, in spite of all those fancy business meals, I've still never got beyond a good slab of roast beef. Asparagus is still a punishment. And if the truth be known, I'd rather a good shot of Fleischmann's with a beer back than all the expensive hooch in the world. Now, I'm not trying to sound like Abe Lincoln for you, but it's the truth."

She knew how difficult this was for him, but she had to share her life and Eddie's with someone. She gave him a loving look and said, "Well, nearly the truth."

He looked at her like a suitor engaging in flirtatious byplay. "And that, my young lady, is the closest we all get."

"Is that philosophy or blarney?"

"Same thing really, only the Irish put the right label on it. But let the old man catch his point by the tail again. You take a young cop full of dreams, and he probably has a wife who shares them. (Sissy reddened again.) American dreams. Nothing wrong with them, but the Yanks have the most expensive dreams in the world. Now he gets out on the street, and he sees so much poverty and crime, and he begins to think the poor are enemies of those nice, neat, well-scrubbed dreams. And why shouldn't he? He's not a social worker. After all, the people who hired him see the poor the same way, not to mention the populace. It's easy to get confused. The smart money guys come along, and they're always dressed so neat. It would be so easy if all cops had to deal with were murderers, rapists, and dope sellers. Cops wouldn't have problems with that.

"But the landlords, businessmen, and gamblers looking for an edge, now there's the problem. Hell, they've all got what you're dreaming about. And Lord, they're so polite. The poor always have the disadvantage of being dirty and ill-mannered. If you try, it's not so hard to see how it happens."

"Then why are they so bitter about it? Bitter about everything and everyone. Why don't they just lie down in their beds?"

"Because somewhere deep down inside, they know it's all wrong. And if you make the whole world wrong with you, the bed is at least tolerable. Is that so hard to understand, Theresa? It's really rather tragic, you know."

"Isn't that a bit much?" she challenged. "Tragic?"

He toughened his voice. "Don't be an absolutist, daughter. They're people with a one-way mirror. It could be your failing. You were the same way about the war. You know, I didn't want Billy to go to that damn disgrace either, and I thought Eddie was bull-headed about it. But I would have been disgraced if Billy ran off to Canada or Sweden.

"That wouldn't have bothered you, would it? To me, he made a choice. A sad one, to be sure. I would have preferred him in jail. I would have been proud of him. But that would have horrified you. You see, when you go against the grain, you have to pay for it."

"Who's being Catholic now?"

"Don't be dumb, child. It has nothing to do with that. If you don't pay, the world doesn't notice. You end up looking as shifty as the ones you're fighting against. I hate moral glibness. Sometimes our pain is the only pride we have to show."

She started to cry, but he didn't relent.

"Life isn't the fall of saints, just the tarnishing of people. We all help to coarsen other people. Nobody's innocent. To live, you have to understand that." He handed her his handkerchief. "Are you all right?"

"Finish it, dammit," she sobbed.

"Do you think we really outgrow things?" he asked. "Let me ask you something. Do you enjoy books as much as you did when you were a girl?"

She didn't know what he was driving at, but it struck a chord. She shook her head negatively.

"And don't we find God has become a bit of a bore, too?"

She nodded.

"So we begin to think God and the writers are unrelenting moral windbags. But doesn't it make more sense that we've made so many compromises we can't stand to have them—writers or God—chide us anymore?"

She smiled. "That's perverse."

"True," he grinned, "but right. Look, I've compromised too many people to remember. Or to be accurate, I don't want to remember. And on the other hand, I've been disappointed in people. People I loved. My wife, my son, even you. But I look at people in the same way as the contracts I helped negotiate. I never was perfectly happy with any one of them. Nor do I have a perfect wife, nor did I have a perfect son."

"Or a perfect daughter-in-law."

He smiled. "Well, that's the closest I got. But my wife has done things for me that are special and private that outweigh her foolishness. And my son (she wanted to tell him 'enough,' it was despicable—she had pushed him too far), he let himself down at times and that's what hurts. He was far better than that. These people here today for him are no accident. And if the day was publicized, you know the room couldn't hold his friends. Regardless of what you think of the people who loved him, he had the gift to touch lives. That he could be cruel occasionally and sometimes mistook who he should have sided with doesn't alter that. Nor does the fact that he should have kept his hand in his pocket.

"You didn't think I knew that? Where the hell did you think I thought you two got the money you spent? Overtime?

"But I remember all of him. I don't forget his mistakes, nor should you. But he was more than his mistakes. He was a loving, loyal son to me. I can forgive on memories alone. And he loved you and the kids, Theresa. Very much. Christ yes, he was flawed, Theresa, but he was a contract I could sign."

She clutched him to halt the tears that were coming. "Thank you, thank you, Pop. I hope you can say that about me someday."

"Ah-h, will you hush, will ya?"

"You know something?" she said. "You're a very wise man. I'll get it right yet. I'll break that damned one-way mirror."

"Always be disappointed, Theresa. Always be angry, but remember, we're all part of each other's failures."

She kissed him. "I love you very much. I could still read a book you wrote."

He took out his handkerchief and patted his eyes, then dabbed at hers. "And why do you think we're sending that daughter of yours to college but to write my memoirs?"

All the tension was gone. "Motives, eh?" she said.

"Never," he said, "never try to outmaneuver an old union man."

Sissy hoped Nellie and Catherine hadn't spotted the scene between them. The tears would require an explanation, and Sissy would have to fabricate some golden memory of Eddie they shared. She didn't want to get into that. But when she looked their way, she was spared. Nellie and Catherine were talking with a group of women. Mothers, wives, daughters of other cops to be honored, Sissy presumed. Another compensation for old age—you become as guileless as children, you talk with anyone. The wonderful naive presumption that all ears are your repository. Sissy could guess at the conversation all the way around. Sons being sainted, cops being canonized. Tales so tall they were Alpine.

Sissy was getting antsy. She wished the Mayor would show. Sporadically, his aides would make their rounds of the room, reverently reassuring, "He's on his way."

Sissy began to think tongues of fire would herald his entrance.

Christy nudged her. "Do you think we should join the others? We'll be getting accused of clannishness."

"Why don't you, Pop? I think I'll stand by the doorway and have a smoke. See if I can get a little breeze."

"Go ahead then," he said solicitously. "You could use a little breather. Everything all right now?"

She smiled. "Everything is just fine. Just a nicotine fit."

"The one vice that escaped me. I'll have to give it some thought before it's too late."

"Be cheated out of one thing." She grinned.

"True, true," he said. "Then I won't have to plead guilty to gluttony. Well, I'm off to the horseshoes set."

As he walked toward the table, Sissy vowed to get to know him better. Though his remark had been light, she didn't like the "too late" reference. It was all too rare that they talked as they had today. She wouldn't waste so much time in the future trying to charm him with banter. He had a depth she wanted to touch before it was, indeed, too late.

SHE MADE her way toward the door along the wall across from the table. She wouldn't even look in that direction. She didn't want to be trapped. It wasn't so much Nellie and Catherine as the others. They'd devour a cop's widow quicker than the pastries.

Besides, she was thinking about taking another half-Valium. She felt as if she was waiting for a test to begin at school. The pressure was getting to her. But she'd see if a cigarette worked first. She didn't want to be on her ear during the ceremony.

Then she spotted him and froze. He was watching her with that supercilious smile. His professional look. Sissy knew he had more than one look. She had made the wimp drop his composure.

When it came to Gordon Groves, Deputy Commissioner for Public Relations for the NYPD, she and Eddie reached a rare oneness. Groves was a fourteen-carat shit. His daddy and all his airs couldn't disguise that. Daddy, a professor, taught a course on The Criminal in Culture and Literature at NYU and was a regular member of the Mayor's think tank. Sissy had heard him being interviewed on television, with his references to Dostoevski, Stendhal, Genet, and Cleaver. He was rather impressive with his analogies of literature's outlaws and current criminals. Eddie wasn't so moved. "I never read these guys, but I guarantee you those quiffs couldn't hold on to their typewriters in the South Bronx."

Regardless of the father's merits, the son was a cipher, a joke.

Before Sissy had confronted him, she checked him out in a back issue of the *Times*. The story had appeared when he was appointed to the PR post for the NYPD. He had bounced from college to college until he finally got a degree from someplace she had never heard of in the Berkshires. His work record was no better. As a PR flack, he was nomadic—"wide-ranging experience," the *Times* man called it. When Sissy met him, she knew the reason for the shoe leather resumé. The schmuck couldn't sell Kool-Aid at a day camp.

He was still looking at her and now, for effect, he pulled out a pipe and started to finger the bowl. The pipe only made him look more ludicrous. With his gangly body and his baby face, he looked like a teenage nerd trying to play a sophisticated lead in a high school production.

He kept adjusting his body, trying to look nonchalant. If he could have, he would have carried a fireplace with him to lean on, Sissy thought. And of course, there was the open jacket to display his hand-tooled holster and snub-nosed .38. That touch was the joke of the force. Sissy had heard him ridiculed hundreds of times for carrying (and *always* displaying) a gun.

Eddie said it all. "I'd like to see that jerkoff blow his nuts off with it—if he had any."

Yet, for today, he was threatening, he was the obstacle Sissy wasn't sure she would clear. She had his word, and so much depended on it. But it was the word of a petulant little play actor. To think he held the key. She could see herself going across the room, picking his holster, and blowing that smirk right off his face.

It had started with the manila envelope Sal brought from Property. It contained the things Eddie was carrying on him the day he died. Sissy could feel various items through the paper—watch, ring, coins, wallet. She thought of checking the contents, but she imagined they had an unearthly quality to them. Instead, with two fingers, she fished out Eddie's wallet, not touching anything else. That was her sacrifice to being a functioning widow. There were credit cards and whatever cash Eddie had been carrying. Sissy had to pay for a burial. She sealed up the rest, and after a small debate, placed the envelope in Eddie's chest of drawers, not her own. She felt the dead shouldn't mingle with the living.

Both Nellie and Catherine suggested she bury Eddie wearing

his wedding ring. Catherine said she had always found the custom touching. "It's like carrying the marriage beyond 'til death do you part."

Sissy thought Eddie had a tough enough time with that burden in Brooklyn, never mind eternity. Besides, she had given him the ring, it was part of their special time. It was a talisman against total despair, a reminder that they, too, once upon a time, had a Camelot. Also, it was valuable. One never knew when push would come to shove. Four years of college wouldn't come cheap. Better his daughter than a *gonif* gravedigger.

She would get to the envelope in due time. After the burial. That was when she would start to function bravely. That was when the neighborhood would say in awe, "It's amazing how well she's adjusted. Who would have ever thought? One thing tragedy does, it brings out the worst or the best in people. Well, if Eddie is looking down, he can be proud of that one." Sissy never minded the clichés if they were used to gild her.

But her ascendance to local grace was delayed. The envelope had remained untouched. Finally, that piece of unfinished business began to loom larger and larger. Sissy decided to open it before the act reached frightening proportions.

One night after a hot bath accompanied by a few glasses of red wine, she emptied the contents on her bed. The gold chain struck her immediately. She thought she knew all of Eddie's accessories, but the chain was a stranger. Maybe he had made another one of his deals—a jeweler with some violation or another. Or perhaps the jeweler had asked for a little special protection from the precinct.

Sissy turned on her bed lamp to examine the chain more closely. It was real gold! Always her first reaction when it came to jewelry. Long ago, she'd developed an eye for the McCoy. But it was the pendant hanging from the chain that mesmerized her. There were two interlocking circles with an initial etched in each, E and T. Sissy lifted the chain directly under the tensor lamp. There was no mistake: E and T—Eddie and Theresa.

On even closer examination she realized the circles were, in fact, handcuffs. E and T cuffed together. It was such a sweet sentiment. Sissy thought of her ring in the pretzel bowl. She started to cry. What occasion was on the horizon—her birthday? Their anniversary? Neither was even close. But for sure, it was a gift for her. Where was the gift box, she wondered?

She peered harder at the chain. The gold didn't seem new. It was scratched and dulled by skin, dulled by wearing. Eddie's skin. Of course, he was wearing it like her ring. She turned clammy all over. Her sweat glands released an awful odor, as if she needed a bath. But she had just had one.

She had never given Eddie such a gift. Or had she? Maybe when she was going through her bad time? A gift of forgiveness? Sure, that was it. Some part of memory must have been erased. Though not entirely. Wispy traces remained, like a scrubbed blackboard. She concentrated. The ghost of the chain was back there somewhere, as if on tracing paper. All she had to do was apply pressure and its shape would come clear. She pressed mentally. She drew a blank.

Her hands began to shake. She swung out of bed, went down to the bar, and poured a large tumbler of red wine. On second thought, she brought the bottle back up the stairs with her. She sat on the bed and gulped the tumbler. Her hands still shook, and her breathing became very rapid. She was about to hyperventilate. She reached into the night table and took out a bottle of Valium. She could hear Eddie's admonition when she had done this in the past. "Not with booze, for chrissake. Do you want to end up a vegetable?" It used to frighten her. Now a serene, dreamless coma seemed less menacing.

After taking the pill, she put down the chain and closed her eyes, lying back against the pillow. After a few minutes, she could hear her breath come at more measured intervals. The smell coming from her body was awful. Christ, she stank. She looked at the clock and thought of waking Eileen. The girl would remember when she had given Eddie the chain. That heartened her. Then she realized she couldn't shake the child from her sleep at this hour. She would be alarmed seeing her mother, stinking of booze and sweat. That would just about put the two of them around the bend. Her logic calmed her. She was back thinking rationally again.

With deliberate effort, she rose and walked to her night table. She held the chain before the mirror. Maybe a reflected image would trigger the blurred memory in her brain. She looked absurd in the mirror. Standing there holding the chain spread out with a clasp in each hand, she looked like an unholy one about to decorate her wall-eyed clone. She was going to crack, to shatter in the mirror before her own eyes. If not Eileen, she'd better get someone. Who? Not the family. Who? Lynn. God, yes, Lynn, to come and hold her. Hold her together. But that brought back the memory she couldn't handle. Then scream, dammit, scream into the pillow. She was about to run for the pillow when she noticed how small the chain was.

Deliberately, with steady hands, she tried to fasten the chain around her neck. The ends failed to meet by two inches. It was not a gift for her. And certainly it didn't belong to Eddie. Eddie wore a sixteen-and-a-half inch shirt collar. A thirty-five inch sleeve. The numbers gave her confidence. People about to break couldn't muster such information. Her mind started to click. She had been a cop's wife long enough to sort facts. Organize them. Chalk facts up on that blackboard, Sissy.

The first came. Eddie never called her Theresa. It was always Sissy. His Irish gamin when they were beach royalty. Then T was someone else. Eddie was bringing it to someone else. Nice detective work.

But it wasn't a gift. No box. Chalk that in, Sissy. It had been worn. Chalk that, too.

Yet it was in his possession. She fumbled for the next step, then she hit on it. He was bringing it to be repaired for someone. She went back to the bed lamp. There was no trace of repair on the chain.

She scattered the remaining contents of the envelope on the bed. No receipt, no repair claim check. She checked the chain again, tugged at it. It didn't need repair. But it had been found on Eddie.

Why? Why? It was someone else's, and it was found on him. Come on, Sissy, it's in front of you waiting to be chalked in. The process of deductive reasoning excited her. The thought of another human being on the other end of an inanimate object. She thought how heart-stopping it must be when you were trying to trace a gun or a knife. She could understand how civilians could never match such an experience. Eddie was right—there was another world out there.

She was close to it. Not hers, not his, not a gift, not to be repaired. Yet he had it on him, it was found on him. Or near him? The thought made her dizzy. One of the junkies he was chasing. It would have to have been a dwarf with that neck size. Possibly a kid, a punk druggie?

But why the handcuffs? A felon using handcuffs as the hallmark of affection. Hardly, unless he was a dark humorist. Lenny Bruce was the only junkie she could think of who might float such a sentiment.

No, the handcuffs were a cop's touch. A macho surrender. A cop's fey idea of a joke. A woman would never give a man a gift of handcuffs. It smacked of possession. Ball-and-chain and all that drag. No, it was a cop's idea of romance. You have my balls in your slammer. My cock in solitary. It was a cop's gift.

Eddie's gift? To whom? Found on him. But where was the box? Was someone else near him? Someone small? A woman. A woman grieving over his body. Erase that. Someone near him when it happened. Someone who wasn't supposed to be there. Not supposed to be there for the outside world, she amended. Her world.

There when he took his heart attack. From what, if not chasing junkies? Something tolled in the distance. Something Sal said, or was it another cop? Something someone said to her. At the wake, at the funeral, at the house afterward? Something that bothered her. Something she had dismissed as confusion. It was too distant. Get back to hard evidence, Sissy.

A heart attack. That was sure. Stress, strain, someone else, a woman. God, that was too dark to believe. Lenny Bruce again. If it was so, why would the cops send Sissy the chain, the evidence? They'd be meticulous about that. They'd fine-tooth comb everything. But damn, she was confused. Why not them? Of course, it was the T. How would they know it was the wrong T? E and T.— Eddie and Theresa.

What else would they, could they think, if it was lying next to him? E and T is solid evidence. Eddie and Theresa. They would never have checked his neck size. E and T. Airtight logic.

But the chain wasn't broken. It had to have been taken off. In a casual, relaxed situation. It was possible. Jesus, maybe it wasn't a sick joke.

Damn, what was the thing, or things, nagging her? Things that were said to her. There was a connection. It was where Eddie was found. Voices she could only identify as cops said different things. On the stairs, on the landing, in the hallway, in a room. Nothing major, but cops usually were consistent about such things.

She decided on the acid test. She put the chain into her mouth and sucked it. There were traces of sweat and perfume. Even if there weren't, she would have known it wasn't Eddie's. She had feasted often enough on her husband's skin to know its taste. Even now, with an imaginary lick or suck, she could bring back his essence.

She ran to the bathroom off their bedroom, fell to her knees and hugged the bowl as she threw up.

She thought about taking another Valium to help her sleep, but she decided against it. The vomiting had exhausted her enough. Along with the vigorous mental exercise. She was beat. Good beat. It felt satisfying to go through such an exercise. Like the first time she fathomed that algebra was more than an abstract. Besides, she didn't want another pill.

The last thing she wanted was to wake up a vegetable. There was work to do in the morning. Enough for one night. She'd start with Sal. He would be easy enough to crack. No sweat. She always could blow him out of the water. The thought of that facile process was enough to get her to sleep.

*N*OTHING COULD be accomplished the next day. When she finally reached Sal, he told her he was on the last leg of a seventy-two-hour shift. So she invited him to dinner the following night. The excuse was that she wanted to show her thanks for his kindness and support. He told Sissy her gesture was unnecessary and delivered an encomium to what Eddie, she, Billy, and Eileen meant to him. George M. Cohan was no less enthusiastic about the flag. But the promise of home-cooked lasagna ended his drivel.

At first, she was disappointed at the delay. But thinking it over, Sissy came to feel the one-day wait was beneficial. It would make her less anxious, give her time to think. It would be a test of her discipline. The wait would steel her resolve. She thought of it as being on twenty-four-hour stakeout.

One of the first things to be done was to insure Eileen's absence. Easy enough. When she told Eileen about the dinner, she gave the girl an out. Perhaps Eileen would like to stay at a friend's house? The girl, out of guilt, wavered. Sissy knew what she was thinking. Sal and her mother would get mellow on dinner wine and parade her father's ghost over the long stretch of the evening. Wouldn't Sal be hurt by her absence?

"Of course not," answered Sissy. "Besides, we have a lot of shop talk to do. Your Dad's pension fund and insurance. I need some advice. We'll bore you to tears."

"Well, if you're sure," the kid said, looking as if she had won a reprieve.

With that out of the way, Sissy concentrated on the dinner. Nothing fancy, just substantial. Food as fuel. Sal had the appetite of a jock. She used her big pan for the lasagna. Enough for an infantry. Plus a huge salad and a couple of loaves of garlic bread. End up with spumoni, espresso, and anisette. No wonder the Romans had a thing for vomitoriums, she thought.

And of course, there would be plenty of wine. That would be a pain. To please him, Sissy would have to buy Ruffino instead of French. But it was preferable to hearing him go on all night, pontificating that French wine couldn't stand up to Italian food. "It just don't have the body." So Ruffino it would be. Straw-covered bottles, too. She'd make him feel like it was his prom night.

She set the table with her best linen and silver and crowned it with candles. Momentarily, she had an impulse to empty two of the Ruffino bottles into a decanter and use the bottles as candle-holders. She laughed at her cunning but rejected the notion. He would love it, but she'd be damned if her home would look like a spaghetti joint in *My Sister Eileen*.

Sal arrived, scrubbed and awkward, carrying a safe box of mints. "I thought Eileen would probably like them, too. You know, most kids have a sweet tooth. I hope I guessed right." His concern was so sad that she reassured him profusely. She recognized the neighborhood need for shuffling on social occasions. That lack of sureness in taste that is handed down from parents. An apology came with every gift. It would resurface later in the evening, it always did. A dismal game in which the receiver had to reinforce the giver repeatedly. If the gift-bearing wise men were neighborhood, Jesus would still be in the manger, explaining that he'd always longed for gold, frankincense, and myrrh.

Through most of the dinner Sal's conversation was limited to compliments for her cooking. Sissy didn't press him. She was content to ferry in the food from the kitchen and coquettishly dismiss his elaborate compliments. She watched him relax under the caloric onslaught. She would wait for the coffee and anisette on the couch, when his competitive body was glutted into repose. His senses, too, she hoped.

When Sal sank into the couch, he exclaimed, "You might need a crane to get me out of here."

"Do you want to relax while I do the dishes?" Sissy asked.

"No way, you did enough tonight. Dishes are mine. Great chefs shouldn't muck with soapy water. You enjoy your coffee, and when I catch a second wind, I'll hit the sink."

"Come on, you make it sound like I'm worked to death. I'm not breakable china, you know."

Sal looked at her with concern. "I know, but we worry about you. You had a terrible kick in the pants. A couple of kicks in the last few years. I haven't been around as much as I should. You know. The wacky hours of the job and everything. But has it been going all right?"

Sissy smiled bravely, rose and took Sal's cup to the table where she filled it three-quarters full of espresso, the rest with anisette. When she returned to the couch, Sal took the cup and sipped. "Wow, I'll be flying out of here tonight."

"Oh, come on. I've seen you and Eddie do a bottle of anisette with a pot of coffee."

Sal grinned. "Sometimes we were working on the second."

"That's what I mean. And you're worrying if you're going to be all right."

Sal took her hand and patted it. "No, I was worrying about if you were all right. We all miss the hell out of him, Sissy, but we have to keep living."

Sissy was tempted to ask, "What for?" She'd always wanted to ask that whenever she heard that particular cliché. She had heard it since she was a girl. She often wondered what the answer would be—"to eat," "to sleep," "to weep"? As if life were some sort of endurance contest. Hang in against the forces of the cosmos as long as possible. Win a pyrrhic victory drooling in a nursing home. But she checked all that. She had Sal where she wanted him.

She put her other hand over his and patted him back. She softened her voice. "I'm all right most of the time. And Eileen seems pretty good. Kids have so much to keep them busy. It's all right most of the time, but . . ." she lowered her head.

Sal picked up her chin with a strong index finger. "But what?" he asked.

"I'm a Catholic, you know."

Sal seemed perplexed. He clearly didn't know where she was going with this nonsequitur. "Well, we all are, I guess," he said. "I mean, even if we don't practice like we used to, it's always there. It's like your mother. I mean, if you don't get on with her, she's still your mother."

"I know, I know," said Sissy. "That's why I'm so worried about Eddie not having a priest."

"But he did," Sal consoled. "I told you that. The precinct rushed one over there."

"But not before he died."

Sal was getting uncomfortable. Spiritual semantics were not his strong suit. "Yeah, but it's supposed to work anyway. The last rites, I mean."

"Normally, I guess, yes." She fought to keep her voice even. "But not the way Eddie died."

Sal panicked. He reached for the coffee and gulped at it. He nearly shouted at her, "He died in the line of duty."

Her fish was about to bolt. She eased off. "Sal, please don't be upset. I've come to terms with the way he died. It's all right. That's part of life. I just wish he had a priest in those circumstances."

"What circumstances?"

"Sal, I'm going to be all right. I've adjusted. Except for the priest." She was impressed by the monotone of her voice. "You should have a priest when you die in bed with a prostitute."

He stood up and shouted down at her, "Who told you that? Who told you that shit? That craziness?"

"Sal, will you please sit down and calm yourself." She took his hand and pulled him down to the couch. "Now have your coffee and try to relax. I'm not upset." He obeyed. She granted him the gratis of one sip. "Don't you think cops' wives talk among each other?"

"You mean a *friend* called you and told you that?"

Sissy was like a metronome. "And why not? You guys tell each other everything. Do you think we're any different? Besides, everyone knew Eddie played around for years. But God—a hooker!"

Sal was recovering. "And where did this so-called friend get that story?"

"Why, from her husband, of course."

"You mean some scumbag told his old lady that? One of our own snitched on Eddie?" The last was what he found incredible. She only heard the word "snitched."

"Oh, Sal, it was husband-and-wife talk. Married people do

that, you know. Besides, Eddie had the reputation years ago."
She took his hand. "Who knows that better than us?" Sal
snatched back his hand and turned crimson. He didn't want to
be reminded that he, too, was once a scum to Eddie.

"Anyway," she let drop, "when I heard it, I had my doctor
call the M.E." She knew the inside jargon would impress him.

"Yeah," he said belligerently.

She dismissed him, "Oh, why get graphic, Sal?"

"I don't know what you mean. I don't know what any of this
means."

She thought of how to phrase it: come, scum, gism. No, cops
were most formal when the going got sleazy. "The M.E. found
traces of semen." She wondered if she should have said "alleged
semen."

Sal rose. "I got to use the john."

Sissy looked at him. He was sweating. It wasn't the liqueur and
the coffee. He looked like a kid who knew the teacher was about
to question him next and leaving the room was his only solution.
She held him with a stare.

"I really do," he pleaded.

"You go ahead, Sal. Believe me, I'm all right. It's just that I
wish it wasn't a prostitute. A cheap whore he died with, and no
priest."

Her eyes released him. She sat chilly, not moving. He stayed
away as long as he could. She could guess at what he was thinking. When he returned, he looked better. He had washed his face.
He didn't sit.

"Do you want some more coffee?" she asked.

He now suspected her every kindness, her invitation, the whole
evening. "No, I don't want anymore. I had too much, my stomach
feels lousy."

"I'm sorry," she said.

"It ain't your fault, I just overdid it. But what about you?"

"What about me?"

"You know. This whole thing."

"Sal, I was never naive. I knew Eddie went his separate way
years ago. He didn't even try too hard to hide it. But a whore!
Some two-bit slut. That shocks and saddens me. To die like that
without a priest."

"Is that it?"

"Is what it?"

"The whore business."

"If it wasn't for that, I could deal with it. My daughter's father in mortal sin, dead with a common slut."

"Are you sure that's it? All of it? Just the hooker?"

"Sal, with Eddie's history, what else would shock me?"

"Well, I don't know where you got your information, or what idiot gave it to you, but it wasn't a hooker."

She resisted the urge to flop him in her boat. She took his hand and reeled him down on to the couch again. "Sweet, sweet Sal. Such a loving friend. You'd do anything to spare my feelings. You're a lovely man."

"I'm telling you, it wasn't a prostitute."

"That's sweet of you, Sal, but I know better. Who was it then?"

"I can't tell you that."

"See what I mean? It's lovely of you, but I know." She paused dramatically. "I'll always know. I'll die knowing."

"Goddamn, it wasn't a prostitute."

She patronized him by shaking her head. "Please, please don't, Sal. I understand. You're Eddie's loyal friend."

"What would you do with it if I gave it to you?"

"What?"

"Her name."

"If it was logical, I would believe it. And it would be a horrible stigma removed from me and my daughter."

"Is that all?"

"Is what all?"

"You wouldn't confront the woman and make a horrible scene and just cause more misery for everyone?"

She paused. This had to be good. She phrased it carefully. To her, a promise was meant to be kept. "I would never confront the woman and tell her I'm Eddie's wife. I would never, never mention—on the grave of my father—that she was in bed with my husband."

Sal studied her. The parental grave had weight. Sissy knew that with an Italian a maternal crypt would carry more weight, but what could she do? And he knew about her special relationship with Mickey.

"It was a cop's widow. A good cop's widow. The furthest you could get from a prostitute."

"Who is she? Do I know her?"

"No."

"Well?"

"Is a name necessary?"

"I don't think you're a liar, Sal, but I know you would do anything to protect Eddie. And me," she amended.

"Are you sure?"

"Of what?"

"You know. You won't do anything about it?"

"Are you insulting my reverence for my father?" She could tell that sunk him. Some things you don't question.

"It was Ray Fernandez's widow."

"What's the widow's name?" she asked evenly.

"Toni. Toni Fernandez."

She could have squealed aloud when she heard the T. "Oh," is all she managed.

"Oh what?"

"Who is she?"

"I told you, it wouldn't mean anything to you."

"Well?"

Frustrated, he blew out air. "Ray Fernandez worked out of Flatbush for years. He died a few years ago from a bleeding ulcer."

"That doesn't tell me anything."

"He had a boy who was starting to become a badass. Pushing pot and some street shit. When Eddie heard about it, he came down on the kid. You know, disgracing Ray's name and everything. You know Eddie."

"Yeah, I know Eddie," she said flatly.

"Well, Eddie had a hook into some local congressman's office, and he got the kid shipped out west into one of the Job Corps programs to study welding before he got his ass busted on the street. The kid's doing fine. Building bridges somewhere out there."

"Yeah?"

"Well, naturally Toni was grateful. Wait, I don't mean it that way. That sounds terrible. It wasn't what you think. You see, they were just comfortable together."

Sissy would never forgive him for that. "And she was with him when he died?"

"Yeah."

She had to check her rage. "Yeah, what?"

"She was with him."

"How did the story of him making a drug bust come about?"

"The guys engineered it."

"And how did he end up on a stairway?"

"The guys."

Jesus, all Flatbush knew of her husband's farewell fuck! "What state was he in?"

"What state? He was dead."

"What state?"

"For chrissake, Sissy, this isn't doing anyone any good. The guys took care of that. Let the thing go, willya? He wasn't with a hooker."

She thought of the cops pulling on his underwear, looking at his wet privates. She couldn't handle it. "So the guys did everything?"

"It's not as rare as you think. Similar things have happened in other precincts. I heard of it before. Especially when a guy is supposed to be working the streets. Cooping out like that could blow his pension to his family."

"Only the guys know?"

"Only the guys who took the call. And the captain. They called me right away. I warned them to button up. I should have added, to their wives."

Sissy couldn't quite believe it. She couldn't understand the cop credo, even in death! They were so archaic, they were beyond corruption. Her marriage, the foundation of her life, came down to covering up cooping and saving a pension. They were so pure they should be preserved. The lot of them should be put into the Museum of Natural History. "What does the widow do—collect a pension?" Sissy asked.

"She works," Sal said defensively.

"At *what*?"

"She runs a social club in the precinct."

"That sounds like a whorehouse to me."

"Jesus, will you get off that tack? It's a social club."

"What kind?"

"A pig, if you must know."

"A pig?"

"Yeah, a pig. An after-hours joint. People go there to drink and play cards after the bars close."

"Isn't that illegal?"

"Jesus, Sissy, she's a cop's widow. What do you want us to do—bust her? We go there ourselves. It's just a good clean joint where you can go for a drink and have a little blackjack action. Good neighborhood people go there. We keep an eye on it. No trash comes in off the street. What do you want—the woman on welfare?"

Never, the poor dear. Welfare. More cop bathos. Besides her husband's pension, the bitch probably had a score of benefit dances thrown for her. Plus chance books in every open door in the precinct. Sissy had seen Eddie orchestrate more than one widow's annuity.

"It still sounds like a cathouse," she said.

"Oh, Mother of God!"

"She's a whore. My friend was right."

"Sissy, I swear to God, she isn't."

"Then let me meet her."

"Oh, no. Oh, no, you don't. You swore you wouldn't pull this. You swore on your father's grave."

"I swore I wouldn't confront her."

"What's the difference?"

"I won't believe she is what you say she is until I meet her."

"You can't."

She screamed to frighten him. "I was right. She is a whore, and my husband is burning in hell because of her."

He backed off. "Even if I could, how would I do it?"

"Just bring me around."

"The guys in the precinct will see you and think I'm bats."

"Do it off-hours. The daytime. I just want to look at her. One look, and I'll be satisfied. On my father, on my God, I won't say a word to her."

"Supposing I bring you around. In the day. When she's setting up. She'll ask who you are. What the hell am I going to say?"

"Say I work with you."

"As what? She knows all the cops."

Sissy paused. "As a clerk. A clerk in the precinct. Don't tell me she knows every clerk and typist, too?"

He was wavering and she moved in. "I'll tell you, Sal, if you don't do this for me, I'll die thinking my husband is in hell. Condemned there by a whore. If you don't do this, I'll know you're covering up and you're no different from all the rest. The cops who looked down on me. Eddie's other friends." She put her head in her hands to play for time.

"Jesus, Sissy, don't cry. Please don't do that."

Through her hands, she said, "You have my solemn oath. I always thought you were somebody special. Not like the rest. If you don't do this, I never want to look at you again." She buried her face deeper. To get what she wanted, she was beyond shame. She used her final lure. "I thought your specialness might mean something in the future. For the rest of my life." She let the euphemism "my life" dangle.

She felt his hands on her shoulders. "I guess I can understand," he said. "It must be terrible for you to live with a thought like this. I'd like to kill the person who put it there. I'll see what I can do. No promises."

Sissy hoped her smile didn't beam through the cracks in her fingers.

She wasn't long waiting. She had figured on that. Sal presumed she was in a wild state, and that was dangerous. Not dangerous to her, of course, but to his own fraternity. Sissy could pull down the whole structure, the whole image of New York's Finest. Men put stock in such things. In group image. In the history of the Marine Corps there never was a faggot.

Sal was tense over the phone. He laid down marching orders. He would pick her up by car Wednesday afternoon. They would arrive at the social club a little before four o'clock. Precisely between the change of shifts—eight to four and four to midnight —at the precinct. That way, no one who knew them should be at the club. She would wait in the car while he checked through the window, just in case. If anyone, but *anyone*, except Toni was at the club, it was a no-go. Sissy would be introduced as a clerk on loan from East New York, who was helping Sal's house with the current paper load. She should decide on what name she was going to use. And the visit was a drop-in, not to exceed ten minutes. Preferably shorter. And Sal would be monitoring her every word. If anything fancy came out of her mouth, he would personally drag her out of the club as he muffled her. Sissy agreed to the behavioral code as eagerly as a child receiving the ground rules for a trip to the circus.

Choosing a name provoked more of a dilemma than Sissy had expected. She had to fight her penchant for intrigue. Plus, she thought, an "inside" name would be a private mockery of that bitch. She thought of "Nora Charles," but decided that the low-bred probably spent her hours in front of a television set and surely would connect Nora with *The Thin Man*.

For the life of her, she couldn't remember Miss Marple's first name. That would be a hoot, but only if she wore Red Cross shoes. Maybe her creator, Agatha Christie? But Sal could be a problem there. Cops were notorious mystery-watchers, even though they loved to badmouth the shows. And the Christie mysteries were always on rerun. Sal had probably spent some evenings sneering at the "limey asshole." Sal was Eddie's acolyte, and Eddie bestowed rectum rank on anyone who fictitiously fought crime.

No, as much as it pained her, she would keep the name simple. If Sal sniffed any hint of play, he might call off the meet. Simple, with a root to match her looks. It was still difficult. She thought of Taylor, but Liz immediately came to mind. She'd always loved the name Liz and wished she could use it. Then it came. One of Liz's married names. Liz Todd—it was simple, and it fit. Todd sounded Irish. Still, the Liz was risky.

She compromised to the point of humility. When she told Sal in the car, Mary Todd, he seemed pleased at its lack of adornment. It wasn't until they were underway that she realized she had chosen the name of a demented wife.

Sissy could determine the degree of Sal's discomfort from the way he held the steering wheel. He was normally a graceful driver, weaving a car through traffic with fingertip ease. Today, he gripped the wheel as if it were a lifesaver. Or her neck, Sissy thought. She tried to ease him off. "I made a promise," she reminded him.

"Yeah," he acknowledged.

"More than a promise," she explained, "a sacred oath."

That helped some, but it wasn't a clincher. "Remember," he said, staring hard at her. "In and out in a couple minutes."

Just like a quickie, she thought. She nodded obediently.

When he pulled the car to the curb, she wasn't expecting it. She could feel her color rise and her pulse throb. She wanted to tell him to move on. Why didn't he give her some warning? Did he think this was really a social call?

"You wait here," he commanded as he left the car.

She watched him approach a storefront and peer in. From the outside, the club didn't look any different from the ones where

she had seen old men congregating in Little Italy. She saw him
reach into his pocket and take out something—she thought it
was a key—and tap at the window. After a minute, he gave an
animated wave. He was smiling.

When he turned toward Sissy to motion her from the car, his
smile disappeared. She walked toward the storefront, trying to
look composed, but she felt as if her legs would fail to support
her. Oddly enough, it was the same unstable feeling she had had
on her wedding day when she tried to negotiate the aisle.

A woman opened the door. Sissy watched Sal embrace her.
Sissy couldn't discern anything about her, except that she was
wearing a housedress. Sal turned toward Sissy and said, "Toni,
this is Mary. Mary . . ."

"Todd," Sissy added, extending her hand.

She was staring at the woman when she heard Sal. "Yeah,
Todd. She's over from East New York, giving us a hand with
our paperwork. She's a clerk. I was giving her a lift home. You
know that neighborhood. And I just felt like saying hello."

Toni was looking at Sal, amused at the way he blurted everything out. Sissy was furious. The woman suspected. Why did
he have to introduce Sissy as if she were a dossier? Then she
checked the woman's bemused smile. The suspicion was for
something else.

"Well, then, come in and say hello," she invited, smiling.

She turned to Sissy. "Does he always explain you?" She
winked at Sal. "With her looks, you don't need to make excuses."
She broke out laughing as she led them into the club.

The bitch thought she and Sal were lovers. She probably
thought everyone was making it in bed with everyone else. A
summer memory followed by embarrassment made Sissy calm
her fury.

"How about a drink?" asked Toni. "I'm just setting up, but I'm
sure I can find a couple of clean glasses."

"No, no, we have to run," Sal said. "We just dropped in to say
hello."

Toni was amused by what she perceived as Sal's ardor to spirit
Sissy off. "Then say hello with a drink. I'm sure Mary could use
one after a tough day."

Sissy found her voice. "I'd love one. Scotch-on-the-rocks."

Sal glared at her.

"Scotch, rocks. A cop through and through," Toni said.

"She's only a clerk," Sal corrected.

"So is that a crime?" asked Toni teasingly.

"In the Property Department," Sissy explained. "Be careful. You know these guys with their sense of priority."

When Toni laughed, Sal took the cue and grinned. For the first time, he looked pleased with Sissy. "Yeah, don't be elevating anyone to the force. We have a union, you know."

"All male," Sissy said lightly.

The banter put everyone at ease. Sissy was delighted with herself, doubly delighted she had had the opportunity to get her rehearsed line in early. Sal never noticed. No wonder he had never gotten out of uniform. As a detective, he would be worthless.

The front of the club was unlighted, and the blinds over the main window were half-drawn. As they followed Toni toward the back, Sissy spotted a coffee urn, a pinball machine, and a few tables placed in random order. Very much like the clubs in Little Italy.

With Sal's nervousness and the poor light, Sissy hadn't had a chance to appraise Toni. Her impression was that she was dumpy. Dumpy and older than Sissy had suspected. Not Eddie's type. Maybe it was the housedress.

Toni opened the door into a back room that was, surprisingly, bigger than the one they had left. Sissy's eyes fell first on the green felt of the card tables and then on the small but elaborately stocked bar. Toni moved behind the bar and poured scotch all around. Her face was pleasant, no more. Sissy had the aid of lights now. Toni's body, with the exception of full breasts, was concealed by the bar. "The house's round," she announced, and they all clinked glasses.

Sissy made a move. "You'll be working behind there all night," she said. "Come on out and join us."

Toni smiled at Sissy. Begrudgingly, Sissy had to admit it was a lovely smile. One stoked by genuine warmth.

"Now I can tell you're not a cop," said Toni. "Manners and concern. You'd never make it on the force."

When she came out from behind the bar, Sissy took her in. She wasn't fat, but she certainly was plump. And short. Her legs seemed rather stubby. That pleased Sissy. Hell, she couldn't walk in Sissy's shoes. Sissy tried to imagine what she looked like naked. The breasts were full, but they would sag. The legs had shape, but they ended abruptly. Still, her ripeness didn't obscure her curves. And her face, rising from a surprisingly slim neck, was what carried her. A soft brown face with darker brown eyes and wonderful white teeth. For sure, she wasn't a smoker. Her very short-cropped black hair also worked to her advantage.

Sissy ran her up and down again. Picked her apart zone by zone. No way she could match Sissy in the buff. Still, there was something about her. The browns and black made her look like good furniture. If you took the complete view, she had something. She was a chair a man would like to sink into. Unlike Sissy, she had no hard edges. Sal was right. She was comfortable.

Sal became wary of Sissy's staring. "Well, let's drink up. We have a drive to go, and Toni has work to do."

Toni was still amused. "Christ, there's no holding cops. They're the jumpiest people in the world. My guy was the same way."

"Your guy?" asked Sissy.

"Yeah," Toni said, "my husband. He's been dead a few years."

"Oh, I'm sorry," said Sissy. "I didn't know."

"That's all right, sugar, it was a while ago. But they're all the same. Always on the move. Sitting still is like a death sentence to a cop. Right, Sal?"

Sal grinned uneasily.

"You know, darling," Toni said to Sissy, "if I could ever figure out what was out there on the streets, I'd bottle it and sell it to cops' women as perfume."

Sissy was moved. Jesus, she could like this woman. "The secret ingredient, hey?"

"I'd be a millionaire."

Sal injected, "How's Richie doing?"

"Oh, building bridges in Colorado. My son," she explained to Sissy. "He's taken up skiing. Now, Puerto Rican surfboarders I heard of, but a skier! Those cowboys out there will swear he's practicing quick getaways for winter purse-snatching."

It was becoming sickeningly clear to Sissy why Eddie would like Toni. She wanted to leave. Sal's broad laughter confirmed Toni's special charm. Sissy gulped her drink and turned to Sal. "I'm ready."

Toni stood up. "Well, I guess there's no holding you two. But Mary, you come back and see me again without Twitchy Ass."

Sal froze. Sissy handled it. "Oh, I doubt they'll need me much longer in the precinct. As soon as we straighten out Property, it will be back to home base."

"Well, whenever." Toni nudged Sal toward the door. "And do yourself a favor, Mary. Stay away from cops. Get yourself a nice regular guy."

Sissy smiled. "I got one."

Sal grabbed her arm in panic, but Sissy held her ground. "I take care of my father." She didn't know why she said that.

"Good for you, honey. These guys will bring you nothing but grief." She laughed.

Sissy took Toni's hand and shook it. "I can well imagine."

Outside, Sal was so nervous he could hardly get the key into the ignition. Sissy held his hand to quiet it. "I want to thank you very much. You did a very special thing for me and Eileen."

"Is it all right now?" he begged.

"It's perfect," she assured him.

"Home?" he asked.

"You know something? I'm starving."

Sal beamed. "Hell, me too. Where to?"

Sissy had to calm his fears. His fear that she might return behind his back. She needed the proper ambiance to lull him. "Let's go to Vincent's for scungilli."

"Jesus, what a great idea. I haven't been there in so long I can't remember."

"Well, Little Italy it is then. The works—shrimp, mussels, scungilli with hot sauce. And lots of dago red."

"Then Ferrara's for pastry," he added.

"Perfect, just perfect. And it's all on me," Sissy declared.

"No way, lady."

She knew the thought of a woman buying him a meal secretly pleased him. "If I don't buy, it's a no-go. You dropped a big one on me today."

He blushed with pleasure. "Well, I'll get the cappuccino and dessert then," he compromised.

"It's a deal." They shook on it.

"Geez. Vincent's. What a great idea," he said wistfully.

Sissy thought so, too. The restaurant with its street-smart style would put him right at ease. Cops and hoods were always on tap there. A precinct house with a menu.

"You were something," he enthused. "You were wonderful in there, just wonderful."

"Oh, stop flattering me," she joked. "I said I was buying."

"Just super," he said, starting the car.

You bet your ass, thought Sissy.

VINCENT'S WAS only the opening salvo in Sissy's campaign to numb Sal's senses. Though he was no genius, he had a cop's sixth sense. That was always dangerous on a percentage basis. If you constantly thought poorly of people, your batting average would be respectable.

So in June, Sissy put her major objective aside while she skirmished with Sal. If she could hold him safe during June, then she would be able to move in July when he traditionally rented a cabin at Lake George for three weeks with some single friends. Early on in their marriage, Eddie had taken Sissy there for a few days in the summer. She abhorred it, and much to Eddie's chagrin, refused ever to go back.

The place was a pastoral precinct. The entire town seemed to be overrun with vacationing New York cops. The talk was endless shop, accompanied by heavy drinking. And God, the flashy outfits they wore always came with one accessory—the piece on the hip. When they went swimming, Sissy wasn't sure if the bulges in their trunks were their genitals or their service revolvers secured in Saran Wrap.

They never could get off it. Their profession was all they had. In restaurants there was always the identifying phrase to the waitresses, "Honey, if that blouse was cut any lower, I'd bust you on a morals rap." Or "I have handcuffs back at the room. You're not into S&M, are you, sweetheart?"

It wasn't only the crude remarks to the equally crude local girls that disgusted Sissy. In truth, it had nothing to do with sex at all, but with a pathetic need to identify themselves. Sad occupational flashers.

But for now, she was glad the place existed. With sun, booze, fishing, and boiler room talk, Sal would be distracted from Brooklyn. For the present, Sissy had to prepare him, like a child for camp; she had to obliterate any fears he might have.

The quickest way to Sal's heart was through his muscles. It was easy to set up. Sissy told him she felt lethargic since Eddie's death. Too much sitting around with compulsive eating and smoking and, of course, marathon brooding. She needed to shake up her blood. Get the system going again. Sal couldn't have agreed more. To him, sweat was chicken soup.

They started easy with the nine-hole Pitch and Putt course at Riis Park, which was enough to give Sissy pain in the lower back and stiffness behind the knees in the hamstrings. She immediately took to doing floor exercises at home to loosen up. She had a vigorous regimen planned.

She tried desperately to cut down on her smoking and attempted some light jogging to open up her lungs. She even went so far as buying a book on the subject by a doctor with an Irish name. She shucked it quickly when she got to his passage on the cleansing joys of physical punishment. If she wanted to wade into that, she could have gone back to reading *The Lives of the Saints.*

But in her fashion, she stuck to it. Indeed, she even began to feel a little better. At least, her color rose. Good thing. Sal graduated her to bowling. She didn't know which was tougher to swallow, the strain on her muscles and the broken fingernails, or the social implications. She'd always figured bowling dates were for duds from Paramus.

But there was the enjoyment of minor achievements. One par on a round of golf, one strike in a frame. Over beer at the alley one night, when Sal was enthusing over her improvement, she decided to chance it. She used her pat casual lead-in. "By the way . . ." What followed was that she had spilled coffee over the property receipt for Eddie's belongings she was supposed to sign, and she could use a blank. She would type in the list. Sal said that could be done at the precinct, but she said she didn't want to put someone through extra work because of her carelessness. Besides, she added, she was a crackerjack typist. She said she'd watched Eddie hunt and peck and figured he was the police standard. Sal's grin told her he couldn't deny that.

"Anyway," she'd continued, "I'd like to get all that behind me. I've delayed enough. You understand that, don't you?"

"No sweat," he said. "I'll get a blank tomorrow."

He seemed pleased she was dispatching her former life. She had counted on that. But before he could find any implications in her request, she added with gusto, "You know, I think I have one more good line left in me tonight, unless you're chicken."

"You're on. No mercy," he said joyously, pulling on his bowling glove.

Sissy found she wasn't anxious to fulfill her plan. The various activities, at least some of them, began to please her. Golf was fun, the bowling wasn't so bad once her legs got used to it, and she showed some flair at paddleball. The few trips to the BAT-A-WAY in Coney Island frightened her. Even the slow pitching machines were terrifying, and all the bats were too heavy. Though it gave her an appreciation of what it must be like to face major league pitching.

In a fit of exuberance one night, Sissy even swung the heavy mallet and tried to ring the bell on the test of strength. Her fantasy of ringing it and being oohed and aahed by an adoring crowd (was that in *State Fair*?) fizzled when the rubber cylinder climbed pitiably, like tired blood. Sal, of course, came to the rescue.

But even the failures were fun. She hadn't felt this alive since Lynn. Not only in body but in mind. She was on to something, something private, something uniquely hers. It had been hers since conception, and the step-by-step preparation for delivery was thrilling. In a melancholy way she didn't want it to end. She wanted to keep refining it, filigreeing it. Completion would mean sharing. It would be sullied by the inclusion of others. She finally understood the dilemma of the procrastinating artist.

But the time had come. Sal delivered the property receipt without a sign of suspicion. He figured in only one more turn. That would come at dinner on the eve of his departure for Lake George. Where he was concerned, she had to add her final touch. Considering what she was up to, the artistic metaphor seemed grandiose. Eddie would have put it more succinctly—she had to get off the pot.

Sal gave her the lead-in after dinner over coffee and drinks. She knew early it would be easy when he suggested a French restaurant in the Village. To Sal, French food was effete torture. So what he was about to say was already established by his abdication. He held her hand in a way that didn't suggest immediate demands but futuristic longing. "You know," he said, "I'll be a little sorry to go on vacation. These last few weeks have been special to me." Thinking he might have gone too far, he added, "You know what I mean."

She patted his hand reassuringly. "Sure I do. It has been fun, hasn't it?"

"A great time, really a great time."

"I want to thank you for pulling me out of my doldrums."

"Ah-h, come on. I had a ball."

"I bet," she said. "Watching me make a fool out of myself. I'd win the Olympic medal for incompetence in all events. The drip's decathlon."

"Get off it. You did pretty good. You know you haven't tried anything in a long time. You can't expect the moon. You did damn good, considering."

"Promising rookie, hey?"

"The trick is to keep at it. And I notice you did pretty good cutting down on those cigarettes. Now don't let everything slip while I'm away. You know, you were really good at paddleball. I mean it."

"That was my early tennis lessons showing." She remembered how her tanned legs had once looked in white shorts. When Eddie was in the Marines. So long ago.

"Well, you should work on that. You don't need a partner. Just hit off the handball court wall every day. That tightens everything up. And it will get your legs in shape for skiing in the winter."

"Skiing?"

"Well, I mean, I go up to the mountains on weekends. I thought you and Eileen could come. I'm pretty good at it. I could show you. I mean, only if Eileen came along, of course. She'd love it. It's like a Christmas card up there."

"It sounds nice."

"Do you think we could all try it?" Jesus, he was begging. His face looked so beseeching. The meal suddenly didn't sit well on her stomach.

"It sounds like a ball," she said.

"Great. I'll check out weekends and everything when I get back."

She hated him for being such a gentle mark. She wished she were dealing with a bona fide bastard. He was making her feel dirty. Yet . . .

"You do so much."

"Come on."

"No, you do. You have concerns of your own."

"Hey, since when haven't the Sullivans been one of my concerns?"

"No, you go out of your way. You're a generous guy."

"Hey, would I do it if I didn't enjoy?"

"You're too good. That's why I hate to ask you . . ." She paused and lowered her head.

"No, it's too much." "Ask what?"

He was yearning to please. "Name it. Name it. Come on. Anything."

She spoke, her head lowered like a contrite monk's. "I couldn't. I've imposed on your life enough. I just couldn't ask more."

"Sissy, please. What am I here for?"

"It's just that . . . I've got a problem."

"With who? With what? With me?"

"No. It's that woman."

He was stunned. "I thought that was over. This isn't fair." He was whining.

"Oh, that part of it is over."

"Then what? You swore."

"I have no right to ask this."

"You're going to, though."

"You seeing her, and seeing me and Eileen. It brings up memories. Bad memories. I have no right to ask. But it doesn't make me feel right. It's like—I know this is crazy—like you're being disloyal."

He let out a sigh of relief. "Is that the extent of it?"

"Yes. But I have no right. You have your life."

"Look, look," he pleaded. "I understand. I understand. I should have thought of it myself. It was dumb of me, damn dumb. I put you in a helluva position."

"No, you didn't. I can't tell you how to live and who to see."

"It's no big deal. I never really enjoyed the place anyway. I only went there to meet Eddie . . . I'm sorry."

"Don't be silly. Please forget I ever brought it up."

"Forget, nothing. It's done."

"You mean you won't go there anymore?"

"It's done. It's over. I should have had the brains myself."

"But won't it be awkward? With the guys, I mean?"

"What awkward? I was no big deal there. Eddie was the . . ."

"Are you sure? I don't want to embarrass you with your friends."

He was preening. "Look, I'm off on vacation for three weeks. They won't be used to seeing me. Besides, I only drop in now and then anyway. What's to miss? The joint's always mobbed."

"You don't mind?"

"Mind, hell. It's the right thing to do. I'm a schmuck. I'll tell them I'm on the wagon. Getting ready for ski season."

"Won't you have to go back to explain?"

"Never. The joint's seen the last of me."

"Never?" she asked, hardening the question slightly.

"Never. On my mother," he added for solemnity.

"You're unbelievably kind and understanding," she said.

"Aw, can it. I should have done it in the first place." He picked up the check. He was jubilant. He was born to serve her. "Let's get some air and check out the weirdos."

She rose and took his arm. "You are unbelievably sweet and gentle."

"Yeah, wait 'til you see me as a ski instructor. You'll change your mind. A real tyrant."

"I can't wait."

As he paid the check up front, she checked herself in the back bar mirror. She didn't want to know the woman who looked back at her.

The day after Sal left for vacation, Sissy made a disciplined decision. She wasn't going to blow everything on impulse. She couldn't be too careful. Supposing Sal was playing her along as she was fiddling him? That was one of the problems when you started to work people over. You could never be sure that they weren't just waiting for their turn at bat. Sal could be sandbagging.

For two days and nights Sissy rang his phone at home, getting no answer. On both days she called the precinct to be told he was on vacation. Her calls to Sal's house after midnight strangely excited her. There was something delicious about calling someone's number in the middle of the night, knowing that if he answered, you were going to hang up and strand him to supposition. The feeling was sexual. Not nice warm sexual, but tingling sleazy sexual. It had to do with control. Power. Co-option. She had never realized that charge was accessible for a dime.

But two days and nights were enough. Anymore would shuttle caution across into paranoia. It was time to move. Time and time again, she rechecked the property receipt she had typed against the chain. Her description and jargon seemed detailed enough to pass for bureaucratic. The next day, at 3:30, she hailed a cab by waving the manila envelope in her hand.

She had the cab stop a block away from the social club. It was 3:45, right in the time frame of hers and Sal's visit. She walked slowly along the block, checking for familiar faces or anyone entering the club. On both counts, she was clear. She took her keys out of her bag and approached the window, ready to duplicate Sal's routine. It was a needless effort. Toni was mopping the floor in the front room and spotted her through the window. She waved her in.

As she opened the door, Toni said, "Hi. Where's that twitchy boyfriend of yours?"

Sissy involuntarily snapped, "He's not my boyfriend."

Toni held up a hand. "Whoa, I'm not indicting you."

Sissy cursed her stupidity. "I'm sorry. God, that did sound harsh and priggish."

"Well, is he parking his car, or should I close the door?"

"He's on vacation. He left the beginning of this week."

"Oh, hell, I knew that. Lake George. I envy him. Ray and I had some great times up there."

Sissy thought Eddie had really changed colors with this one. "Yes," she said. "I've heard it's a lot of fun."

"Fun. A ball. From sunup to sundown. And with our kind of people."

Sissy looked at her, dumbfounded. Did she mean Puerto Ricans?

"You know," Toni said. "Cops."

"Oh, sure," said Sissy. She smiled at her. "You really admire cops, don't you?"

Toni looked at her strangely. "Look, sweetheart, I have a terrible confession to make. I'm lousy with names. I don't remember anyone till they become regulars in here. I'm sorry. It's really lousy. Rude."

Sissy was relieved. For a moment she thought Toni's confession was going to be truly terrible. Also, she was pleased Toni had forgotten her name. There wasn't even a mental murmur of Eddie. "Mary. Don't be embarrassed. I do it all the time myself."

"Next time I won't forget."

"Don't count on it. It might be a long time. I'm wrapping up over here in a few days."

"Well, I'll remember whenever you come back. I have a feeling you won't be such a stranger." She gave Sissy a knowing wink.

Sissy wasn't about to argue with her mythical notion of a romance. "We'll see."

"Now, how about a cup of coffee? Or a scotch. See, I got that right."

"Coffee would be fine."

Toni went into the back room and returned with two cups of coffee. "I keep a small pot going back there. I don't use the urn till night. You want cream?"

"No, black."

Toni went back and returned with a bottle of scotch. Without asking, she topped both cups. "It's better than cream," she said, hoisting her cup toward Sissy. "Are you getting off or going on?"

"Off," Sissy replied. "I broke a little early."

"Well, good. Nice to see you again."

Sissy knew she was waiting for an explanation. "Oh, before I forget why I'm here. Before he went on vacation, Sal asked me to drop this off. He said you'd be anxious to have it." Sissy held out the envelope.

Toni opened the string on the envelope, reached in, and pulled out the chain. She smiled as she fondled it in her hands. "God, I love that Sal. He would think of this."

"Something you lost?"

"Yeah. A gift from a friend. It's kinda special."

"You lost it?"

Toni cased her, then tried to sound matter-of-fact. "I think one of the guys picked it up here by mistake. Probably turned it in when he sobered up."

"Oh."

Toni started to put it on. Sissy couldn't watch the sacrilege.

"Damn, it's good to have it back."

"Special friend, huh?"

"Yeah. He was great to my family."

"Was?"

Toni became alert and stared hard at Sissy. Sissy was sorry she had said it.

"Did I say was? I meant is. Especially to my boy. I didn't know how I would face him if I lost it."

Sissy helped engineer her escape. "I know what you mean. I lost a pin my dad gave me on a birthday, and I searched all over town to find where he bought it. I finally tracked it down and replaced it. He never found out."

"See, you should have been a cop."

Sissy laughed. "I doubt it. It took me three weeks, and all the time it was in Macy's. I never figured he'd shop in New York."

"Macy's window," Toni laughed.

"Yeah," grinned Sissy. She reached for the envelope and pulled out the receipt. "By the way, Sal asked for you to sign this. He said your jewelry was checked into Property. You'd understand." Sissy squeezed her knees together as Toni read the receipt. Suddenly, she had to go to the bathroom. "Do you understand?" Sissy asked. She knew it was an insult to Toni's insider's knowledge.

Toni looked up, grinning. "Hell, do I understand procedures? Honey, I lived with them all my life. Some day the city will be burning, and all the cops will be able to do is throw their paperwork on the blaze."

Sissy had a pen at the ready. Toni took it and signed the receipt with a flair. She was cop all right, thought Sissy. Bluff it when you're not sure. She took the receipt and put it back in the envelope, fastening the string. She moved it under the table as if to put it on her lap but secured it instead under her butt.

Toni was fingering the chain lovingly. "It would take Sal to look out for this."

"You really do admire them, don't you?"

Toni looked puzzled. "You asked that before. Don't you?"

"Oh, sure. But I mean you're really close to them."

"I was married to one for over seventeen years. But you're right, I like being around them."

"Well, I don't get much of a chance, with dad and everything. He's not well. He needs a lot of attention. I was just curious."

"That's all right. I guess if I hadn't been married to one, I'd be called a buff. They're the only ones in this city that have a bottom line."

"I just started clerking a few years ago. I took the job to be closer to my dad. My old job was in Manhattan. So I guess I just don't understand."

"What?"

"The bottom line."

"Oh, it's a saying we have. When it comes down to it, these guys have a bottom line."

"I'm afraid I'm still a rookie at this."

"It's nothing so difficult. Look at it this way. Civilians don't know what goes on out there. One time they want this, next year they want that. They don't know which side is up, so they don't have a bottom line."

"I get you a little bit."

"Simply, what it means, honey, is if it really gets tough, you can count on a cop. There's a line where they cut off the shit. These guys live on the edge. That's why they're so exciting and so screwed up. This job knocks the hell out of them."

"And civilians have no bottom line?"

"Okay, how would a civilian cure crime?"

Sissy felt as if Toni had her in a trap. "Why, with more social programs, naturally," she said proudly.

"You're not a liberal, are you?" asked Toni incredulously.

"Why? Is there something wrong with that?"

"Well, it's just that every one of them says that. It's knee jerk, bleeding-heart newspapers, television, John Q. Public. More money, more public housing, more understanding. It's like pissing in the wind."

"Well, some of it works," Sissy said defensively.

"Yeah, but it's a lousy return on your buck. Look, every do-gooder thinks the disadvantaged are noble. Or they hope they are, since they're scared of them. If you ever lived with them, you'd get rid of romance in a hurry."

"You have? Lived with them, I mean?"

"In Puerto Rico when I was a kid and in Red Hook till I married Ray. Believe me, I don't make pilgrimages."

"But they're your people."

"Don't saddle me with that, honey. My people are people who like to live like me. What am I supposed to do, embrace some guy who smacks his lips at me and says, 'I want to eat your pussy,' just because he comes from my hometown, Ponce?"

Sissy had the same sinking feeling she used to get when she tried to convert Eddie. "But everyone can use a little help, can't they?" Dammit, she was begging Toni to give an inch.

"Sure. And some get it and use it to good advantage, bless them. They get their ass in gear. The rest you can forget."

"I'm sure your folks could have used a hand. Back then, I mean."

"Many a night at the dinner table, honey, many a night. But my dad made it on his own. He came to this country alone. Left us all behind and worked four years as a janitor till he had enough to start a business and bring us here. He got himself a little beer distributorship in Red Hook. He left when I was three. I saw him again when I was seven."

"He must be a wonderful man. But everyone can't be that strong." Sissy knew she was going to lose this.

"You bet he's wonderful. He raised five kids, and every one of them turned out all right. You know what his *amigos*, his *compañeros*, did for him? They stuck him up fourteen times. Fourteen fucking times over the years."

"Puerto Ricans?" Sissy exclaimed.

"Not Nelson Rockefeller, honey."

"That's hard to . . ."

"No, it ain't. You know where the highest crime rates in the city are? The poor neighborhoods. Bed-Stuy, Harlem, the South Bronx. And do you know who gets it? The poor, from their own people. Rap Brown liked to say to the whites, 'Civilize your own.' That little shit should have started in his own backyard."

"But people do pull together for their own kind."

Toni laughed. Laughed right in her face! "Your father don't let you out too much, does he?"

Sissy yearned to slap her. It was an old feeling, just a different face.

"Now you don't believe all the bro, *amigo* shit. Hell, honey, that's for the man. For whitey and television. This city is full of people ripping off their own."

"But these people have had a terrible history." Sissy would drown her in philosophical waters.

Toni became mockingly gentle. "Ah, honey, everybody has a terrible history. The world is one big crying towel, if you want to use it."

"But society could do more. Everyone knows that." (Eddie used to say, "Who the fuck is everyone?")

"Society could, their parents could, Santa Claus could, Christ could. And it would help some. No denying. But who picks up the tab? More money, more schools, more housing. And still there'd be people who'd rip off the money, vandalize the schools, and wreck the housing. My sister lived for a while in public housing. Her girls had to ring the bell so she could come down and ride up in the elevator with them, so some punk didn't grab their tits in the elevator. There will always be night hawks who poach on the nine-to-fivers."

"But society—we—have to try," protested Sissy.

Toni looked at her with exasperation. "You are a case, aren't you? What is your daddy—a preacher? Society! Society don't know what they want. One year the cops are pigs, the next they want them to lock up the whole city. Drugs were hip, now they're the cancer of the city. Everyone yelled too much police brutality, now they want to give cops back the use of the nightstick and throw in the death penalty as a bonus. Society, my ass! You know what society is? Ride the subways. Some wino is waving his prick under a nun's nose, and society got their heads in the *New York Times* reading recipes."

"That's unfair. Some people help."

"Name them. You know who I think of when I hear society? Kitty Genovese. Remember her? Screaming and banging on doors in Queens while she was getting murdered, and the people inside checking their locks and putting out their lights. Ask Kitty Genovese about society."

Sissy felt assaulted, mugged. She hated this woman. Goddamn it, she had lived with her in a different guise all her married life. "Are you going to tell me all cops are so forthright?" Sissy challenged.

"No, but they got a bottom line. Are you about to give me crooked cops? Christ, there's a ton of them. Plus crooked judges, DAs, and politicians. But that's money. And not as much as you think. How do you make out your income tax, huh?"

Oh, Christ! It was like hearing the anvil chorus. Sissy wondered if there were cynical choir practices held around the city.

"Hell, I'm crooked," Toni continued. "By law, I shouldn't be operating this place. I used a hook to get my kid off a felony. Who doesn't? You think society hands their kids over to the law when they break it? Honey, everybody finagles when it hits close to home. Tell me about all those wonderful citizens who try to fix traffic tickets and scheme out of jury duty, and then go out and get buzzed at a party and talk about the breakdown of the criminal justice system.

"Everybody plays, but cops know where to draw the line. With the exception of a few psychotics, and they get booted out eventually. But you can bet on one thing. If there was one cop, even one old retired cop behind one of those doors in Queens, Kitty Genovese would be alive today. And honey, that's the bottom line."

"It's an awfully limited vision, isn't it? If it's that bad, why bother—any of us—going on?"

Toni rose. She looked tired. She was bored with Sissy. Sissy knew the look well.

"You play in the ballpark that's out there. If you know of a better one, I'll change uniforms. I hate to rush you, honey, but I have to get my work done. There are enough slackers in society already." She put out her hand. "Say hello to Sal for me when you see him and tell him he's a sweetheart. A real prince."

Sissy just nodded and left with her envelope. She noticed there was no invitation to return another time. She was glad. She wanted to be thought of as the enemy.

She felt violated. Gangbanged by practicality. Eddie hadn't had an affair. Love had nothing to do with this. He was in bed with himself, whether he knew it or not. Eddie, who scorned jerkoffs, had settled for onanism.

More's the pity. He didn't realize what he once had at home. She might be street dumb, but she hadn't gone numb. She still naively dreamed. Her thoughts didn't end at the bottom line.

She wanted her tub. Her hot, scalding tub. If she had to come by a philosophy secondhand, she preferred it to be Mickey's. His airy legacy of ducks, tall stories, Technicolor, and Saratoga trunks—at this terrible time—had the foundation of Tara.

*I*T WAS Sissy's battering by Toni that made her decide to deal with Gordon Groves. She just couldn't go head to head again with a pure cop mentality. Not if she was going to pull this off.

Originally, she had considered contacting the precinct commander, but now she knew that was impossible. Besides, he probably didn't have the clout to deliver what she wanted. The Mayor was a titillating possibility, but access was a problem. And if that could be overcome, there were his reputed morals.

Indeed, that was going to be his major problem in his re-election bid. He seemed so pure and rigid that, with the exception of the reform base that had fostered him, he had alienated most of the city. City workers, the cops in particular, couldn't stomach him. His prissiness had won him the title "The Virgin Queen" in the city's precinct houses.

It had to be someone in between the careerist cynicism of the cops and the pristine platitudes of Hizzoner. To Sissy, Groves seemed to fill that gap. He was hip enough to the cops' world, yet not truly part of it. Sissy knew that for a fact from the conversation of Eddie and his friends. To her, Groves's reputed "assholeism" translated into "civilian," thus the possibility of bendable humanity. The bonus was that he was a career PR man. The twentieth-century alchemist—if there was shit, there must be a pony. It was just the kind of mentality Sissy was depending on.

Also in her favor was that this was an election year. Groves's hook, his rabbi, Starched Shorts himself, was due to face the electorate, and the results of all the current polls showed him up for grabs. If the election were confined to Manhattan wine and cheese bars, he would be a shoo-in. Among Eddie's people in the ball-and-beer joints in the boroughs, he wasn't even a contender. Though Sissy had turned her back on such places, she had never forgotten how those people, her people actually, thought. Early on, Mickey had schooled her in this mentality, and like a glass stain on a bar, it was never entirely obliterated.

She read everything she could find on Groves in the back newspaper and magazine files in the library. Also on record was a series of lectures on police work he had given at the New School for Social Research, which had been collected in a clothbound book by some obscure publishing house. Sissy smelled his prestigious father behind the imprint. It figured. The kid had all the earmarks of a family remittance man.

The essays were reassuring to Sissy. Though young Gordon—modern man that he was—acknowledged "isolated" cases of police corruption and brutality ("the sad hazards of an imperfect system"), the book in toto was a valentine to the force: "the beleaguered blue line which stands between civilization and chaos." Perfect. Purple prose for the boys in blue. Sissy thought she knew her man.

Her approach to him had to be flawless. She had to rock him beyond recovery at their first meeting. She didn't have much time. Her plan had to go down quickly—while Sal was on vacation. She wanted to establish a siege mentality. The mayoral primary was coming up in early September. That was in her favor. By mid-July the contenders were cranking up in earnest, and the Mayor—if the polls were right—would be scurrying with the lowliest of them. Resting on his laurels would be thorny business.

Also, the Mayor was vulnerable in an area that heightened Sissy's scheme: Law and Order. His main competition seemed to be coming from a conservative Italian Catholic congressman from Staten Island who had declared for the race. His background was perfect: World War II combat infantryman and a sojourn as a correction officer in the state prison system before he went into politics. Plus he had a family so large he could win a fertility contest. Abortion was abhorrent to him, and birth control was obviously something practiced by those who had no faith in God or society. He had sired a well-scrubbed legion of Christian soldiers willing to do battle with the Beelzebubs of the big town, while the Mayor had a solitary son ensconced in an Episcopal prep school in Connecticut.

The congressman's home base of Staten Island didn't hurt him either. It was a blue-collar and uniformed-services haven that brooked no nonsense or disruption. If invaded by the unruly hordes from the other boroughs, it was safe to say there were enough guns on the island to stop the marauders at the connecting Verrazano Bridge with the congressman leading the contingent, evoking his triumph at the span at Remagen.

The Mayor, on the other hand, was not only identified by Manhattan but by the strange parameters of the city's chic and downtrodden. Lincoln Center and Lincoln's legacy. The congressman ruled the roost in the whitest of all boroughs, and his association with minorities dealt with incarceration. It would be a tough contest for the incumbent. A liberal reactor vs. an Old Testament god. Sissy had plenty to work with.

It was fear she had to play on, but how she wasn't yet sure. She had to place Groves in an irrational state, where he would be open to a proposition. Fear and embarrassment. What she had was that her husband's death had been covered up by his colleagues. But as ugly as that seemed, it could be perceived as a gracious gesture to a fallen comrade's family. Much like the government reporting a drug-induced death in Vietnam as a combat casualty. And since Eddie's fall reflected more on the family, her and Eileen, than on the force, it was a gambit she might have to abort if she were challenged to play it through.

So Toni herself wasn't an ironclad issue. Even the specter of her raised open legs. It was a man's world. Speculations would be introduced. On the precinct level it would be that Eddie probably wasn't getting it at home. On a higher philosophical plateau, Eddie would be viewed as the beleaguered warrior finding succor in the combat zone. The bitch could come off like Lili Marlene. A Latin lamppost lover. It was a gambit that had societal bias against it.

But Toni's cottage industry was another matter. An illegal pig operating with the cooperation of the law. God knew how many of them and of what rank. Certainly the precinct commander. Sissy knew enough to know that very little went down without sanction from the top. As Eddie had often said, there was little free-lancing on the job. The pecking order, even in the clandestine reaches, was maintained. And the collaboration could, and probably did, reach outside the precinct. Cops were notorious fraternizers. If a joint was in, it would pull from bordering precincts. And Toni was a cop's widow, which enhanced the draw. That mawkish clannishness that came with the beat. Christ, at one time or another, a large percentage of the Brooklyn command might have walked through her doors.

And not just for a drink. That might float. There was the gambling, and Sal had told her Toni skimmed a cut from each pot. Sissy wondered how much unreported income that was. Unreported, illegal income in a city straining to stay alive. Better yet, for Sissy's purposes, unreported, illegal income for a minority to whom the cream of Brooklyn's crime fighters gave their benediction. It smacked of the Mayor's indulgence, his "coddling" of such groups. Sissy smiled at what the savior from Staten Island could do with that one. He could walk across the water on it right to City Hall.

Her presentation had to be like a rocket launching. Something to startle Groves. Something so dramatic it would take his breath away. But it must be drama with substance. It had to have cop content. A frightening logic. She spent time on this, editing out her fanciful flourishes. She became aware of her weaknesses. She replayed Eddie's attacks on her dreamy nature in her mind, letting his voice snip away like shears.

She went over her scenario again and again in grainy black and white. This wasn't a time for Technicolor. It wasn't MGM, but all the marbles.

She took a trip to One Police Plaza and lingered outside, hoping to catch a live glimpse of Groves. That might help in dealing with him. Though she didn't see him, she hit on a bonus. An offbeat opening. Down the street on the corner of Worth, she checked the working order of a bank of public phones. She copied down the number of the third one, third from either end of the bank of five. She didn't want any foul-ups.

The next morning at home she dialed his office. She handled the phone without smoking. She couldn't remember the last time she had done that. Before she took up cigarettes, she supposed. But the lack of a crutch was a new discipline she was testing. If she couldn't deal with him over a phone without a pacifier, he'd crack her in person.

If he was at work, she knew she'd get through to him. She asked for him, and the operator switched her to a female in his office. "May I ask who is calling, please?"

"Theresa Sullivan. The widow of officer Edward Sullivan."

After a short pause, Groves picked up. Sissy was right. Being a widow was invaluable in public relations.

"Ah, Mrs. Sullivan, how are you?"

"You know of my husband, of course."

There was a pause. She could feel his discomfort. He should have known. That was his job. "Of course, it's ringing a bell, but we're swamped here today. I feel like such a muddled fool."

"Officer Edward Sullivan who died in the 67th in Brooklyn. A drug case. About four months ago."

"Yes, of course. I was out of town. But I understand someone from my office attended the funeral. That's my standard direction. I hope there wasn't a slipup. That would be shameful. Totally anathema to my directives. But please, let me take this opportunity to offer you my personal condolences. The city and we, all of us, have lost a valuable officer."

What shit! He didn't come to his profession by accident, thought Sissy. "Thank you" is what she said.

"Now can I do anything for you? Anything? You must have some problems the department can help you sort out."

Sissy kept her reply as neat as a surgical probe. "Is your phone clean?" she asked.

He stammered. "I beg your pardon. The connection. I missed that."

"I said, is your phone clean? Not bugged?"

His voice was strange, but he forced a laugh. "Now, Mrs. Sullivan, why would my phone be bugged?"

"Why not?"

From his pause, she realized he had never considered the proposition before, but was now giving it a moment of merit. Sissy wanted to induce paranoia.

"Why should it be, for heaven's sakes? We have no secrets around here." He was assuaging, talking down to her, as one addresses a potentially dangerous person on the subway.

"Well, I have. Secrets, that is. And I have to tell someone not directly in the department. You (she let it hang for a moment for absorption) or the newspapers or the television."

She heard his gulp. The deadly duet of the media had had the effect she desired. "Now I don't think all that's necessary," he said. "Do you? Let's air whatever little problems we have right here. I assure you, you have a sympathetic ear. You can ask anyone on the force about my loyalty to the line officers and their families."

"I'm not airing anything over the phone."

"Then why don't you come in to my office? I'll make time today or whenever you would find it convenient. I'm sure we don't have a major problem."

"I'm not coming to your office either. I'm not discussing this in any official police surroundings. I won't know who'll be listening."

He was panicking. Sissy knew he was seeing imagined headlines and revealing interviews on the evening news. "Mrs. Sullivan, I assure you . . ."

She cut him off. "Are you leaving your office for lunch?" she asked.

"Yes, I normally walk out for a bite. Do you want to meet someplace? Would that please you?"

"No. At twelve o'clock be at the bank of public phones on the corner of Worth Street. Do you know the place?"

"Yes, of course. I guess so. I mean, it's down the block. I can find it. But is this . . . ?"

"Go to the third phone. Its number is 350–4231. I'll ring you at noon."

"Mrs. Sullivan, I can't believe this is necessary. Please, let's meet for a nice lunch and iron out this misunderstanding, whatever it is. God, these extremes just can't be necessary."

"I assure you they are," she said. "Necessary for the future of everyone concerned. Me, you, the Police Department, the current administration, the City of New York. It goes that deep. What I have to say about my husband's death is that grave. Noon." She hung up before he could respond and hungrily searched the room for her cigarettes.

It was 10:45 A.M. when Sissy hung up. Just as she had planned it. The hour and fifteen minute interlude would give Groves just enough time to deepen his concern. In such a short period the checking he could do would come up only with perfunctory results. The precinct would give him the same story (the drug bust) they had given her. But that wouldn't calm him. He was sure to ask for suspects in the case and recovered evidence, a drug cache, and there would be neither. She was sure of that. The precinct wouldn't have fleshed out their scenario in such depth. After all, why would a distraught widow question her husband's death by heart attack in the line of duty? No, no such care would have been taken. After all, Sissy was a civilian. Fourteen-carat assholes only got the surface line.

So the sketchy account of Eddie's death would slightly irritate Groves's nose hair. Even he had to suspect that the real business of the force was withheld from him. The way Sissy saw it, the only difference between her and him was that he had the illusion his box seat gave him access to the field and the players. She knew better.

But he would find out one fact that was elementary. Elementary. Sissy's hospital stay. Eddie's medical insurance had paid for it. It was also common precinct knowledge. The flowers and basket of fruit from "the guys" was testimony to that. When Groves reported that he'd had a strange call from Eddie Sullivan's widow, that would be the precinct's reply. She had a history. A dossier of dottiness. Play her along, they'd say. She's probably a little around the bend after her husband's death. Groves could check all this out against Eddie's medical insurance file. This, Sissy assumed, would give him small solace.

Indeed, Sissy saw it as her edge. A crazy cop's wife could give no comfort to anyone. It was accepted knowledge that every cop's wife was in collusion with her husband in accepting the vow of the Blue Wall. The vow of silence. No different really from the mob's code of "omerta." Another comfy parallel between presumably warring factions.

And Groves had to know that cops' wives know their share. Certainly not all, but enough. There was loose talk under the influence of alcohol or revelations spurred by anger. Divulgences that normally wouldn't surface. And of course, there were always finances. The cops' wives' great sin of omission. Never question too deeply the color Sony, the second car, the wall-to-wall carpeting, the summer bungalow. Just how many tips on a good horse, hits on a number, or bargains that were steals can one believe?

Sissy didn't even want half of the junk in her house. But "half" told all. She had played D&D to the extravagances. Never questioned the offered story, the endless streaks of good luck and good fortune, the relatives of some guy on the force who let something go at an unbelievable price. Tooth fairy economics. She didn't want to question. She wanted to believe. The claustrophobia of Mickey and Nellie's railroad flat had never left her.

She rationalized she owed something to her kids, didn't she? Something more than she'd had. Wasn't that the eternal rule for parents—to eclipse your own history? She didn't know for sure. Really sure, she meant. But that was morally glib. She had committed the punk's sin of going along for the joyride. At least, Eddie had had the guts to take what he wanted. She wondered to what circle the craven were consigned.

Maybe if she'd interceded back then, it all would have been different. Their whole life. Even Billy might still be with them. After all, Eddie had once had a sense of humor about the absurdities of war. He was never macho about his own time in Korea. Never once had she heard him brag. She remembered those sweet, sweet letters with the mocking cigarette burns in them. The gentleness of them. In those letters, he even omitted mention of the enemy. There was only them and the future. The menace of her future was reduced to cigarette burns. Bullets were really flaming cupid's arrows.

Back then, whenever that lost time was, Eddie had never used racial slurs. Well, far less than the other guys. The coarseness would come into his—their—lives later. AC—After the Cops. She should have made a move back then.

But what? Ask him to be a different kind of cop? She wondered if that would have been possible. Was there another kind of cop? Not in this city. She could have asked him to leave the job, but after he was indoctrinated, that was like asking a junkie to kick the habit. He was hooked. Even when they retired, they needed the methadone of past memories.

She could have demanded he leave the job, but she knew that was steeped in risk. Her or the job. She didn't want to chance that. Sissy's sex appeal or the streets. Toni gave her the answer to that one. The female smell wasn't a match for the stench of the squadroom.

So she went along. Faking blissful ignorance like her sisters, the tin wives all over the city. She couldn't imagine how many of them on this hot July day were sunning themselves in some clandestinely floated cabana, charring in their own sins of omission.

Groves had to have some feel for this. He couldn't be so dumb as to think cops' wives were oblivious to what went down. It was her edge. Plus her certified hospital stay. That put her in the "unmanageable" realm. Though he couldn't afford to pass her off as a loon. At least, she hoped not. She was counting on it.

She'd bluff that she would take her story public. That would corner him. Even if he thought he could dismiss her as a head case, he couldn't afford to go that way. That would open another sewer. As a college boy loaded with sociological fodder, he could figure that one out. He wouldn't want all those devastating statistics to surface. Especially in an election year. The rate of nervous breakdowns, alcoholism, divorces, and suicides in police families. The rate that dwarfed that of the civilian population. No, he couldn't be sure someone wouldn't pick up on her "ravings"—if he saw them as such. Especially in this time of female consciousness. His sense of PR would back him off that tack. Some liberated reporter straight out of Bryn Mawr laying it all out in a three-part series in the *Times*. The troubled lot of the cop's wife. With all those damaging statistics that would lead the public to ask, what kind of people are we entrusting with guns and our safety?

So when she rang the number at noon, she wasn't surprised that he answered. He was slightly truculent. She knew why. She was calling the shots. She had taken the play from his turf. He didn't realize that the fact that he was on the street waiting for a phone to ring was an irretrievable mistake.

"Look, Mrs. Sullivan," he began, "the only reason I'm going along with this is because of your recent hardships. I feel I owe it to one of my officer's widows. Otherwise, I find this whole goddamn charade ludicrous."

Sissy gave him points for his opening. Not bad. Junior had a temper. And the use of "goddamn" and "charade" wasn't bad either. Slap her back to her senses. Always be firm and realistic with emotional cases. Standard pop psych. Logic will level lunacy. He had a little more bottom than she had suspected. But she didn't bite. She blandly played cop.

"I feel it behooves you to listen to me. For all concerned."

He backed off slightly in tone. Sissy figured it was the "behooves."

"Why? Can you please explain to me what all this mystery is about?"

"My husband's death."

"Mrs. Sullivan, I know you're suffering terrible grief, but there is no mystery to your husband's death. He died of a heart attack in the line of duty. There's a report to attest to that."

"A cop's report."

"A medical examiner's report, Mrs. Sullivan."

"Same thing. A cop's report."

"Okay, do you want to tell me how *you* think your husband died?"

"I think he was murdered." He took that even better than she'd expected. "Mrs. Sullivan, we all feel he was murdered in a way. And half of Brooklyn is looking for the two dealers who caused his death, and we'll get them. I can see how you can perceive it as real murder, but that doesn't account for these zany machinations you're putting me, and the department, through."

"There were no drug dealers," she said calmly.

"Mrs. Sullivan, this is leading nowhere. We have his fellow officers' testimony."

"More cop testimony."

"Well, dammit, just how do you think your husband died?"

"He wasn't investigating drugs. He was investigating police corruption." She waited.

He tried to recover. "We have no evidence of that."

"I do. Something belonging to a woman, the source of the corruption, was found next to my husband's body."

"This is insane." He caught himself. That wasn't good PR. "Illogical, I mean," he amended.

"It's logical as hell, and I have hard evidence to prove it."

"What evidence?"

"Not over the phone. It has to be seen."

"Can't you tell me more? This is irrational."

"Just this. This person, this woman, was running an illegal gambling parlor frequented by cops. Plenty of cops. Not only cops in my husband's precinct, but all of Brooklyn. Not only street cops but higher-ups. This is very big, Mr. Groves."

"You can prove this wild charge?"

"Most definitely. This woman was present at my husband's death, and a cover-up story was concocted. It had nothing to do with drugs. Where's the evidence for that, besides corrupt cops' testimony? Were drugs confiscated? What are the names of the alleged dealers? Why would Eddie try to crack it alone? That is total anathema to police procedure." She was happy he had lent her the word.

Groves was deeply shaken. "Look, I don't know the answers to those questions, but I'll find them for you. Please curtail your wild charges until I do. Would you do that, please?"

"These are not wild. They're substantiated."

"By you?"

"I said I have hard evidence."

"Will I be shown this evidence?"

"Soon, I hope. Something must be done soon."

"Just slow down, please. Let's not rush foolishly into anything. The department has always been capable of cleaning its own house."

"I doubt if that applies this time."

"And you feel this woman, whoever she is, killed your husband?"

"I didn't say that."

"Well, had him killed by her gambling associates?"

"I didn't say that either."

"Then just who do you believe killed your husband?"

"Simple and logical. The cops he was trying to expose."

She was surprised his wail was so primal. She thought him too proper for that. "My God! You mean his fellow officers?"

"Exactly."

"His fellow officers!"

"My husband didn't consider dirty cops his fellow officers."

He was regrouping. Such a story couldn't even be wafted as a rumor. "Mrs. Sullivan, can we talk this over in detail?"

"That's why I called you—first."

"Good, good. No need to carry this further. Please don't even think of such a thing."

"That's difficult to do."

"Can we meet this afternoon? I'll come to you."

"That's impossible."

"Tomorrow then. First thing."

"I'm afraid that won't do. I'm going to the cemetery. My

husband's stone just went up and there's landscaping to do. Flowers and shrubs."

"Of course. I understand. I understand. But will you be all right?"

She knew what that meant. Could she sit on it for a day? "How about at my home at ten the next morning?" she offered.

"Fine, fine. Brooklyn, right?" She gave him the address.

"I'll be there. For sure at ten. Are you sure you don't want to meet earlier than that?"

"No. I've got things to do," she replied cryptically.

"All right. But please assure me you won't mention this to anyone until we talk."

"I guess that will be okay."

"Are you sure?"

"I promise."

"Good. Fine. Ten o'clock at your home the day after tomorrow."

"Right. And Mr. Groves, will you make me a promise?"

"Anything."

"Don't discuss this over your phone. Trust no one." She hung up while he was searching for the answer that would temporarily sedate her.

Sissy had wanted to grant Groves the day and a half. It would give him a chance to probe her charges, and she was betting he would find out just enough. Enough to let him stew in a pot of partial truths. He certainly wouldn't confront the brass at Eddie's precinct with the charge of killing a fellow officer. Groves wasn't secure enough in his relations with the cops to even suggest such a thing. A suggestion like that would put him in professional limbo forever. He might even have his gun lifted. Groves couldn't bear such a castration.

What he would do, Sissy surmised, was to use Sissy's history as entrée. "Eddie Sullivan's old lady has been wigging out over the phone to my office." That would guarantee him a handout. A few tidbits here and there, and then he would have to draw his own conclusions. She was sure no one would give him the ugly story straight and unadorned. This was a society that stonewalled its own shoo-fly squad and numerous political investigation panels. It wasn't likely to roll over for a publicity flack. It would give him just enough to clam up the mad widow.

He would be able to establish the existence of Toni's club.

That fact was safe enough to grant him. Groves knew better than to blow the whistle on a cop's widow's piece of action. Especially since it was visited by his own people. And he would be able to sniff out something about the relationship between Toni and Eddie. Indeed, perhaps that Eddie had checked out in her presence—if he pressed it. If he stressed that he needed the information to squelch scandal, he could get that much. But that info would be prettied up. Eddie at the bar of the club or at the blackjack table, keeling over from cardiac arrest. The trauma of whiskey and a nine busting his sixteen had sent him south. But the seizure in bed would be denied Groves. Covering up his death in an illegal club was one thing; that was understandable. Face-saving for everyone concerned: Eddie, his family, Toni, the precinct for letting the pig operate. After all, if an executive keeled over in a topless bar on Eighth Avenue, the family in Larchmont would be told he fell on the street on the way to a business meeting. All that was good form. No one wanted to evoke tassels and G-strings when the organ struck up the requiem music.

But dying in the crib, during the actual act, was another matter. Look at poor John Garfield. You would think that was the only performance he ever gave. Besides, the smarmy implications and the mechanics were endless. When? How? At what moment? Pre-, post-, or during climax? And what were the problems dressing the body? Did rigor mortis set in before help arrived, and if so, in what area? The great sympathetic barroom speculation would reach its normal humane heights: a perpetual hard-on and the problem of closing the coffin lid. That was not the information you burdened a PR man with.

Besides, the collusion would be bottomless. Not only who dressed Eddie, but the cover-up from the medical examiner to everyone who had heard about the incident in the precinct. And Sissy bet that was everyone. It was just too good a story for them not to share it. It ranked in cops' classics. What good was it unless the boys knew?

No, on this, she and Groves were on equal footing. Each was on the edge of the circle, unable to penetrate the sanctum. He would be given a little more than she, in order to dispel her charges, but what he would be given would also be a lie. And he had to know he was working with half-baked material, unless he was a terminal schmuck. Sissy couldn't believe his dumbness was that pure. So they would square off with the bottom line belonging to Sissy on both ends. She knew what she wanted, and she also knew what he didn't want.

After the phone call, Sissy refused to answer the phone for the rest of the day. If Groves was calling in to reassure her in order to reassure himself, Sissy wasn't going to be an accessory. The next day, her "cemetery" day, she left the house early and went to the handball courts with her racquet and balls and rallied endlessly off the wall. The workout felt super, as if it were priming her for the following morning. While the sun baked her, and she dripped healthy sweat, she thought of Groves in clammy fear, dialing her silent phone, conjuring up Sissy sitting at a reporter's desk or in a television studio and slinging her rocks at the Goliath of the department.

After the workout, she stopped for lunch on Flatbush Avenue and then did some shopping before she returned home at dusk. Eileen was already taken care of. Sissy told her to see if she could arrange to have dinner at a friend's house and sleep over, since she was going to ransack the house to prepare for the exterminator's visit the next morning. Sissy knew the child hated both the smell of the fumigating spray and the sight of a roach. Eileen wangled an invite pronto. Sissy also liked the symbolism of the ruse.

Around ten that evening the phone rang, and Sissy answered it. It was Groves. He tried to sound nonchalant, but he tipped his hand immediately. "Hi. Just checking in to see if we're on for tomorrow."

"We're on."

"I tried to get you earlier a few times."

Sissy figured he'd be a lousy poker player. "I told you I had personal business to attend to."

"Personal?"

"The cemetery."

"Oh, yes, of course. Is everything all right?"

"As good as could be expected."

"Yes. It must have been a trying day."

"All my days have been trying lately."

"Yes. Of course, of course. Tomorrow then?"

"That's what we arranged, didn't we?"

"Yes, certainly. Of course."

She wanted to humiliate him even on the most minute point.

"Tomorrow," he reiterated.

"As planned," she confirmed.

"Yes. Good night. Till then."

"Till then," she said and hung up.

She set her clock for eight the next morning. She had things to prepare. Two hours should be sufficient. A Valium would insure a good night's sleep, but also a residue of cobwebs in the morning. She decided instead on a cup of hot milk, which she sipped in bed with her last cigarette of the evening. It was a nauseating combination. She abandoned the milk.

She got up and brushed her teeth, gargling with mouthwash to remove the filmy taste from her mouth. Freshening her mouth made her crave another cigarette. She would have one more, a last one, before she put the lights out. One last cigarette and one last mental rehearsal. She wished it were all over. Even life, sometimes. More often than she presumed was healthy. But maybe not. She wasn't privy to other people's macabre musings. No figures were published on such stuff. It might frighten the general populace.

But it was always on her own terms that she wanted life to be over. Total memoryless darkness for everyone. She could never believe in a happy family reunion, a celestial clambake, in heaven. Just where would all the joyous participants park their memories? Maybe there would be lordly lobotomies before everyone gathered at the heavenly table, but she doubted it. The pleasant memories, the achingly lovable ones would be the worst. She and Eddie shimmering in specialness back then, the young, vibrant, beguiling Mickey of her childhood, and Billy. Billy, the beautiful child who for a while cemented their dividing lives, until he became the ugly contents of a body bag. A war he was suckered into believing in with the aid of his father. But then, Eddie and Billy weren't really an aberrant case. They did love each other deeply. That was evidence, hard evidence. There had to be hundreds of thousands of fathers and sons who had played out the same Asian tragedy with the public opinion polls cheering them on. No, Eddie and Billy were in the blessed womb of the commonality. They weren't isolated. That was the problem. There were no tragedies. Multiplication transmuted tragedy to the commonplace.

What Sissy longed for was a simple shining faith. That of a country priest. Not the priests she had known who had to keep an eye meant for heaven on the oil level in the school boiler. There were no tragedies in a world that had to keep God aloft on bingo games and special collections.

A simple faith with pure, definable tragedies. But it seemed to her God left no room for that. His death for our sins was the only accredited tragedy. Three hours on one Friday afternoon would never be atoned by the blood of lambs like Billy. What unspeakable vigorish, she thought. She was crying. Crying not for her singular sadnesses, but for the mundane, everyday, commonplace slaughter of souls.

She broke her promise and lit another cigarette. There was no damned sense in crying over spilled milk or spilled blood. Futile. Beyond her scope. She had the immediate to deal with. She had to secure her family, maintain her orbit. With Eddie's death, it was now up to her. Only she had the brains and the energy to look out for them. The old ones couldn't be expected to do it. They had enough, with their chronicle of woes, just to keep going. Eddie had bequeathed this to her, and she wouldn't fail.

At first, she had simply wanted revenge. To wreak havoc on the forces that had dirtied her family. To beat the bastards at their own game. Then Eileen's financial security entered in. Now it was beyond that, too. Her cause was much richer. She saw it as spiritual without a trace of irony in that designation. She had a family to protect. All of them. Eileen, Nellie, Christy, Catherine.

After all, Eddie had been integral to all of them, to their happiness. Moreover, there was Eddie. Eddie had to be protected in death, if they were all to move on. She owed him this. She didn't owe him for not adopting his philosophy, for not becoming another Toni. There were enough bingo games in life. Bottom line boiler-watchers. She owed him because she had been an accomplice. She owed him because she didn't insist he live the life that should have been his. Owed him for muffling her conscience. She had to redeem her silence.

If she could get Eddie officially enshrined, the family might survive. She knew the way of cops—hell, the world—and without an official seal his ugly end would always be there ready to surface and drown the family in bilge. But with the Mayor's seal, he would be placed in the realm of neighborhood myth. Untouchable. It would be sacrilegious to move against him. Canonization did that. The saints were testimony to that. Their very lunacy was now sanctified.

Besides, there was Eddie personally. For all Sissy's attraction to the silver screen, it was her husband who was the slave to image. At some level Sissy always knew the real from the reel. Eddie, right down to his hand-laundered khakis on the beach, was the lover of illusion. He had played to an audience all his life. It turned his head. So much so that he had never examined his life. Appearances made all things palatable. A little sugar. Much like Mickey. She helped neither. She only played the adoring cheerleader to their flashy game plans.

So she would coat his exit. A final teaspoon of sweetness. She would do it partially out of her own guilt, partially out of necessity, but most for bygone love. She would secure his image eternally. No one would lay a glove on her husband in death. If she had her way tomorrow, all the waiting, harsh hands would be forced into applauding approval. The weight of her project sank her into sleep.

She rose with the alarm and put on a pot of coffee to perc while she showered. She ran the shower as hot as she could bear it, and when the steam loosened her tight muscles, she did stretching exercises under the water. Gradually, she tempered the water to cool, and finally hit herself with a blast of cold as she sang snatches of songs from the fifties to assure herself her breath wouldn't cease. Her skin glowed in the bathroom mirror, bespoke fighting trim. Now, if she could only corral the damned butterflies in her stomach.

She went to the kitchen naked except for her slippers and poured a cup of black coffee. That certainly wouldn't help her stomach, and she pondered making some toast but decided against it. Food early in the morning deflated her, made her sluggish. It was like working on a good buzz at a party and then having a plate of food and feeling the glinting edge disappear. She compromised and put a heaping teaspoon of honey in the coffee cup. It gave her a rush, and when she inhaled the first drag of her cigarette, she knew she had made the right choice.

She took the coffee into the bedroom to sip while she chose her costume. The temptation was to turn herself out with deadly sophistication—the black sheath intrigue of the Dragon Lady. But that wouldn't fly. She had to dress to Groves's perceptions. His perceptions of a distraught, crazy Brooklyn cop's wife.

Prejudice was a street with a U-turn in it. She had learned that from the civil rights movement. The object of prejudice often uses the stereotypical concept he's railing against to advantage.

Sissy had seen mannerly, middle-class black kids transformed, when they weren't getting their way, into foul-mouthed street dudes. And though she had heard blacks scream racism at reports of their diminutive cranial cavity, she had never seen one dispel the rumors of their ruler-length dicks. Her sober, socially aware sisters, waving burning bras for the television cameras like crazed harridans, also came to mind. You hustled what you had. With this in mind, she chose an old housedress.

The dress was small from constant machine washing, which made it even better. It accented every curve in her full body. After checking herself out in the full-length mirror, she took off the dress and removed her bra. She put on the dress again. The effect was devastating. She was right out of *Tom Jones*. She wished she had a tankard to serve Groves's coffee in.

From Eddie, she knew that when you were working over someone, you tried to break his concentration, never let your subject gain control. Eddie had explained the art of interrogation when they were watching a cop movie. "None of that hokey light-in-the-eyes shit. The trick is to destroy his balance. Anything to keep him from concentrating. The best guy I ever saw is Lenny Fried. He has the worst case of acne you ever saw. Christ, it must be terminal. While his partner is shooting questions, he just sits there squeezing these Mount Vesuviuses of pus. It's disgusting, but it mesmerizes the guy. They always catch the guy they're working on in a slipup."

Sissy walked back and forth in front of the mirror and watched her breasts shift with each stride. Let Groves ignore those eruptions. She added her makeup. She didn't overdo it grotesquely, but the applications would have been better suited for a night on the town than a morning kaffeeklatsch. She also put on the highest heels she owned, forgoing nylons. It was a look she personally hated, but she had often watched its effect on men. Bare legs rising from formal pumps. It reeked of ignorance of the dress code, that was its allure. It had the earthy tone of a barefoot Erskine Caldwell farm girl dressing from the trunk of a city cousin. She checked out the total effect. It was dynamite. She looked like every milkman's dream of a housewife.

In the kitchen she finished another cup of coffee and poured the remains of the pot into the sink. That was by design. If he wanted coffee—and she was sure he would—it would be instant. That bilious slop would put anyone at a disadvantage. Besides, instant coffee bespoke a hostess too out of sync to observe the amenities. Just the aura she wanted to create.

She arranged the kitchen—her chosen site for this talk—to add to that mood. Some stray dirty dishes left in the sink, two dirty ashtrays on the table, a dish towel slung over the chair, a stack of old newspapers on the floor. She secured one place on the kitchen table for her heavy arsenal. There, she marshalled a collection of drug bottles. A battery of various vitamins and, prominently in what would be his view, facing his chair, prescriptions for Thorazine and Valium. In the Thorazine bottle, a nonrenewable prescription she had used sparingly during her sickness, she placed vitamin C tablets. The Valium prescription was still valid, so she emptied the contents into an egg cup in the wall closet and replaced the pills with saccharin. The tableau was the picture of a soul under stress—drugs to fend off breakdown, vitamins to speed up repair.

Her problem of the night before remained. She still couldn't find a way to hide her ace, her edge. The best she could come up with was to place it inside a covered bowl, but she feared that would compromise its effectiveness. She searched in the cabinets for something that wouldn't have the density of a bowl. Maybe she could put it on the floor under the table, but he might drop something accidentally and see it when he bent over. Then again, the floor might be too far away. She knew next to nothing about such things, except the operational basics Eddie had shown her.

She stood on a kitchen chair to check the far reaches of the cabinets. The damn dress nearly cut off her flow of blood. There, ignored in a corner of the top shelf, was a monstrosity Catherine had given her. A toaster cover her mother-in-law had found on one of her bargain tours or pried from her own stack of unused gifts. Catherine was a great one for fobbing off on Sissy things she had received which she deemed below her taste. Over the years Sissy had gotten such a collection of grotesques she could have opened a curiosity shop.

She took down the cover, fluffed it out, and set it on the table. She had to laugh. She couldn't have commissioned a better prop. The cover was quilted aquamarine vinyl. Pasted on one side were two cut-out black poodles with stick-on, hard plastic eyes. The poodles were connected by a small chain between their collars. A brace of schlock, thought Sissy. It would take Catherine to find something beyond fag camp. But it was perfect. For her purposes, it was blue ribbon.

The material was thin enough to offer little interference. The size was right, too. And it looked tasteless Brooklyn proletarian. Groves would be secure with such an item placed near him. The only suspicion he would have was the one he already held—the working class desperately needed him to do public relations for them.

Sissy couldn't figure out why she had held on to such a thing over the years. She believed Eileen was in her dog period then, and anything canine was to be treated with reverence. Either that, or the Good Will collector had rejected it as beneath his standards. Either way, she was in Catherine's debt. The poodles were priceless.

She was ready. But not ready for the phone when it rang. It was Groves, she knew, calling her to cancel, to tell her to stuff it, to peddle her papers elsewhere. She picked up the receiver with defeat draining her body.

"Are you still alive?" asked the voice on the other end of the line.

"What?"

"Are you still alive? From the fumes. When will it be safe to come home?"

It was Eileen. "Oh, not for a while," Sissy said. "He's still at it. The place is a wreck. But I'll air everything out before dinner-time. Can you stay out that long?"

"Sure. We'll find something to do. What's for dinner?"

"It depends on my mood. If the burial detail of our four-legged friends isn't too severe, it will be something special."

"Yuck. Don't spell it out."

"I'll try to have everything in shape."

"Well, don't knock yourself out in those fumes."

"Worried about your old lady?"

"You'll have to do 'til my Prince Charming comes along."

"Eileen?"

"Yes?"

"I love you very much."

"Mom, is everything okay?"

"Can't I say 'I love you' to my daughter?"

"You bet you can. It goes double for me. Double with topping and nuts."

Sissy's eyes filled. "Let's shoot for something special."

"Around five, okay?"

"Five will be fine. So long, cupcake."

"So long, double dip sundae," the child replied.

Sissy gave a final check. She poured a bottle of chilled Bloody Mary mix into a pitcher and put it into the refrigerator. She didn't add booze. She went to the bar. The vodka wouldn't work. Not enough aroma. Instead, she took a bottle of gin and walked back to the kitchen. She ran a glass of water at the sink for a chaser and hoisted the bottle to her lips. She held the gin in her mouth, added a little water, gargled, and spit the mixture into the sink without swallowing. She then replaced the gin behind the bar and blew on her hand. Her breath ricocheting off her hand made her pull her head back. The perfect perfume for a psychotic. The bell rang. It was 9:45. She'd figured he would be early. The toaster cover needed a final adjustment before she went to the door.

Standing in the doorway, he was the height of officialdom. With his light gray suit, his shirt of muted peach, his pale green tie, his cordovan attaché case, he signified the new breed in government. No basic blue suit and starched white shirt for this administration. Groves was a stranger to the ethnic clubhouses of the city. He sprang fresh from a designer's sketchpad, not immigrant loins.

"Mrs. Sullivan," he said, putting out his hand.

"Yes?"

"Gordon Groves. So nice to meet you."

Sissy returned his handshake. "Won't you come in?" she invited breathily. From the wary shift in his eyes, she knew he had caught the waft of gin.

"Of course. Thank you."

"This way." Sissy led him to the kitchen, deliberately making her backside undulate under her dress. She gestured toward a chair, but when he made a move to sit down, she grabbed him, halting his descent, startling him. She removed a dish towel from the chair with an apologetic smile. "Things have been a little chaotic around here."

"Yes, of course. Don't explain. I understand." His empathy didn't stop him from making a perfunctory swipe at the chair with his hand.

He placed his attaché case on the table and opened it. He started to pull out papers. "Now, let's see if we can straighten out this little misunderstanding," he said.

Sissy knew the act well. The props of authority. "Little to you, maybe," she said.

"I didn't mean to trivialize your concerns. It's just not as dire as you suppose. So shall we get on with it?" he added cheerfully.

"Would you care for some coffee first?" she asked.

He didn't really, but he was trying to please her. "Sure. Yes, that would be real nice. A cup of hot coffee."

Sissy felt as if she had offered him the aurora borealis in a mug. She heated a small amount of water in a Turkish warmer. It came to the boil within minutes. He tried small talk as she watched it.

"You have a daughter, don't you?"

He had done his research. "Yes," Sissy replied.

"How old is she?"

"Eighteen."

"Out of high school yet?"

"Yes."

"What is she working at?"

Sissy bristled at his implication. "Four years of college. Her father insisted on it. One lousy career is enough for a family."

He flushed. "Of course. I wasn't thinking. All the kids go on to college these days, don't they?"

"Even the blacks and the working class," Sissy noted.

He was very uncomfortable. "Is she at home? I would love to meet her!"

Sissy didn't answer immediately. She took a pot holder off a hook to pick up the pot of boiling water. She let it drop to the floor near his feet. Before he could uncross his legs to retrieve it, she bent down in front of him. Her dress rode up over her knees and strained at the unbuttoned bodice. She could feel his stare as she reached for the pot holder, slowly. She straightened up and poured the water into a cup, then stirred in a spoonful of instant coffee. The stirring brought a whitish foam to the top. Sissy never knew how Eddie could drink the stuff. It looked like polluted water. She placed the cup on the table in front of Groves heavily, and he scampered to remove his papers, sensing a splash.

"I hope you don't use milk," she said. "I have none. I just haven't been with it lately."

"No. Black is fine. That's the way I always take it," he said, looking glumly at the contents of the cup.

"Fine. She isn't home."

"Pardon?"

"My daughter. She isn't home."

"Oh."

"I don't want this thing to touch her."

"Can we sit down and talk this thing over?"

"That's why you're here, isn't it?" Sissy asked.

"Sure. Why don't you get your coffee and sit down, so that we can iron this out?"

"I don't feel like coffee," Sissy said, opening the refrigerator door and removing the pitcher of Bloody Mary mix. She took a glass from the cupboard, filled it with ice, and poured the red mix over the cubes. "I guess I should have offered you some of this."

Groves looked glummer. She could tell this wasn't going the way he had planned. "No, it's a little . . . I mean, I haven't had breakfast yet. The coffee is fine."

"You don't mind me?"

"Not at all. Go right ahead."

Sissy flashed him a seductive smile and hoisted the glass toward him. He responded by meekly raising his coffee cup a couple of inches off the table. She sat down opposite him.

Eyeing her directly, he took a firm tack. "Look, let's clear the deck first on one matter. Regardless of what you suspect, or what you may have heard through some malicious, insidious rumor mill, your husband didn't meet with foul play. Certainly not at the hands of fellow officers, nor by anyone else. Do we have that established?"

"No," she said.

"No?" He looked incredulous.

"No, Mr. Groves, that is not established. Maybe it's established in your mind, or in the mind of the department, which is probably the same thing, but it is not established in my mind."

"I see."

"Do you really?" she asked. She had the feeling he hadn't thought out his presentation beyond his opening remarks.

"Mrs. Sullivan," he said patiently, "can you tell me concretely, not through innuendo, not through hearsay or rumor, but concretely, why you think your husband was murdered?"

"Because I know he died under other circumstances than I was told. Why else would I—his wife—be lied to, unless there was something horrible to cover up?"

"And you know for a fact that he didn't die the way you were told?"

"During a drug bust?"

"Yes."

"Are you telling me, Mr. Groves, for certain that that is the way he died?"

"I didn't ascertain that," he said.

There was a crack. "Well, I'm telling you he didn't. There was a woman involved. A woman who ran illegal activities."

"And you know this for certain?"

"Yes," she said, sipping her drink.

"May I ask how?"

"You may." This time, she took a hearty slug out of the drink.

"Well?"

"Well, what?"

"Well, I'm asking you."

Sissy slowly slid an envelope out from under her pill bottles. She held the bottles firm as she did so, Groves watching the process and scanning the bottles. Sissy took her time so that he could zero in on the labels of the tranquilizers. She pushed the envelope toward him. "Open it," she said.

He pulled out two sheets of paper. They were Xerox copies of the property receipts—Eddie's belongings and the one she had had Toni sign. Groves scanned them without comprehension.

"Check the item I have underlined."

He read. "The gold chain?"

"It was found near my husband at the time of his death."

"Yes. All right."

"Check the other receipt."

He read again. He was shaky, but unsure of what she was driving at. "Okay, but I don't make a connection."

"You're the only one who doesn't. The chain found near my

husband's body was this woman's property. She identified it and signed for it. Are you going to tell me this woman was working on a drug bust with my husband? That she was chasing pushers up flights of stairs with Eddie? Is that your story, Mr. Groves?"

"Can I ask you how you came by this receipt?"

"Eddie has lots of loyal friends in the department. Some of them are looking out for me."

"How do I know this receipt for . . . Mrs. Fernandez is valid?"

"We could test it in court if you doubt it. Or let the newspapers run it down."

"I didn't dismiss it," he jumped. "I was just positing a doubt."

"Believe me, Mr. Groves, there is no doubt. That woman was at the scene of the crime. The crime committed against my husband."

He was so nervous he started to drink the coffee. He was rummaging. Sissy knew she had him wavering. He nervously started to play with the chain on the toaster cover. Sissy hoped it was his nerves.

"Eddie's mother gave it to us. An anniversary present."

"What?"

"The toaster cover."

He stared at it. He couldn't hide his distaste. "Yes, it's lovely."

Sissy was delighted. She had the little bastard lying about everything. She got up, went to the refrigerator, and took out the pitcher of Bloody Mary mix again. She stood above him, her breasts inches from his nose. "Can I interest you in some?" she asked.

Flushing, he stared at her tits. "I beg your pardon."

"Some of this," she said, waving the pitcher.

"Oh. No, no. I want to conclude this. And I have other business in the city."

Sissy filled her own glass and sat down again.

"Okay, Mrs. Sullivan, let's say, for argument's sake, that the signature is valid. And let's say, hypothetically, that this woman was in the vicinity of your husband's body. Okay, let's say we grant all that. Why would these facts, hypothetical facts, bring you to such a wild conclusion as murder?"

"Why would they lie if there wasn't something to cover up?"

"Mrs. Sullivan, don't be so rote. We're going around in circles."

"Okay," she said. "Let's add, hypothetically, that this woman was involved in illegal activities. And let's say, hypothetically, that corrupt cops were covering up her activities. And let's say my husband was about to expose this. Hypothetically, what conclusion would you draw?"

"Can I ask where you found out about these alleged illegal activities? The woman's, I mean."

"I told you. Eddie has many, many friends on the force. Many cops haven't liked what has happened to the force in the last four years. The morale and all."

He sat there, stunned. He couldn't believe it. Surely, the Mayor had made enemies on the force, but not to this extent. Not to the extent of a cabal against him. A plot to humiliate him, disgrace him personally. The younger officers were with him right down the line—Civilian Review Board, community relations, the whole program.

But what about those beer-bellied neanderthals? The old guard. The comic strip "Pottsies" with their big guts and red noses, who longed for the old regime. The Irish Mafia running the force. All chastisement done internally. The hush-hush. The gravy days of giving them a chance to throw in their papers when they got caught with their hands in the till to protect their pensions. They could be behind this. Using this woman. After all, she was one of their own. A Mick. A Brooklyn Mick with a slovenly house and vulgar taste. They wouldn't be beyond using her. A morning lush, a certified head case. He didn't know what he was into here. He had presumed Sullivan was diddling Fernandez's widow, that he was with her when he died. They indicated that much, that something was going on between them anyway. He presumed Sullivan bought it when he was cooping in the club. They had hinted at that, too. Just a standard cover-up to protect all parties.

But signed property receipts, loose talk of gambling at the pig with cops present, and murder, for Jesus's sake! Someone, a group, was trying to overturn the administration. The administration of which he and his dad were an integral part. Those fucking corrupt relics! So that was their game. God, this poor sad woman probably didn't even realize what she was abetting. He had to win her over.

He began slowly. Patiently. "Mrs. Sullivan, I'm going to be open with you. As honest as I know how to be. But first, I want you to consider one thing. And that one thing is this: Sometimes those who pose as our friends are not friends at all. They use us to grind a personal axe. I believe this is true in your case.

"Certain people have come to you, certain people with their nasty, bloody axes, and given you a smidgen of truth in trying to reach their devious objectives. They are cynically, evilly using you to do great harm. They have no real concern for you, or anyone else for that matter, or for anything, including the City of New York. Their concern is to solidify their archaic, discredited, corrupt little fiefdom. And they are using your real and understandable grief brutally to achieve their nefarious goals. Can't you see that?"

Sissy didn't know what the hell he was talking about. She felt she had lost control of the situation. The whole thing was about to collapse around her ears. "I'm not sure," she said warily.

He continued in the same soothing tone. "You shouldn't be. Only a mind trained in such matters would see the real purpose in this. Some people in the department told you this woman was present at your husband's death, right?"

"Yes," she said. Too quickly. Dammit, he was carrying the ball.

"And what else did they tell you about the woman?"

"That she ran an illegal gambling operation."

"With the sanction of corrupt cops, correct?"

"Yes." She couldn't check her automatic responses.

"And that this woman and these so-called corrupt cops might have been instrumental in your husband's death?"

This time Sissy nodded. It was no better. She was still being led.

"Did they tell you anything else about this woman?"

Sissy shook her head.

"Of course not. They gave you just enough rope. Not only to hang you, but this administration."

Sissy felt that everything was getting away from her. She wanted to get back to her rehearsed scenario. This was unfair. She had worked so hard, planned so thoroughly. What was he getting at?

"Do you know who the woman is?"

She lied. "No."

"Well, I'll tell you. She, unfortunately, is like you—the widow of a police officer. A career officer. Ray Fernandez. Who gave his all to the job. Like your Eddie."

"But she runs gambling."

"Yes, but that's another skeleton of truth. Do you know what the big gaming syndicate is? Of course not. Eddie's so-called friends wouldn't tell you that. This woman, this cop's widow, Toni Fernandez, runs a social club where locals play penny-ante card games. Neighborhood people. Hard-working neighborhood people. People looking to come down after a tough day's work. A little drinking and a little cards."

"But . . ." she began.

"But it was illegal. But the cops knew about it. Sure, they did. And yes, they frequented the place, too. Ill-advised, to be sure, but a criminal hangout? By whose lights? Only to those who have something to gain by saying so. Not by your husband's standards or any other honest cop's. It was a way for a widow to make a modest living for herself and her son. I'm not saying the officers who frequented the place were discreet. No way. I'm not an apologist for the force.

"But their abandonment of duty—let's call a spade a spade— was not based on hard corruption. It was the softness of their hearts for a fallen comrade's widow. Would you indict a police force for that, Mrs. Sullivan? I think not.

"And if I read Eddie's file right, with his numerous citations, I don't think he would either. Eddie was interested in the real criminal element in the city, not in cracking down on a cop's widow who served an after-hours drink and let a few cards be dealt in her place. Don't you know what we're into here, Mrs. Sullivan?"

Her silence said she didn't.

"These so-called friends of Eddie are trying to take this indiscriminate, but really innocent, incident and blow it out of all proportion. They don't even have the guts to do it themselves. They're using a comrade's widow to do their dirty work for them. That should tell you something about their character."

Sissy was so enraptured by his scenario that she forgot her own. "For what purpose?" she asked.

"The worst possible one, I'm afraid," he said gravely. "They're trying to embarrass the department, to scandalize it to get at the Mayor. The Mayor is no friend of cops like these, and they know it. They have resisted every advanced program he's proposed. They know that if the Mayor continues in office, their days are numbered. They, and every other antiquated cop, will be purged from the job. Don't you get it?"

She was fascinated. She shook her head.

He switched his voice into dramatic overdrive. "What we're

talking about here, Mrs. Sullivan, plain and simple, is a plot to overthrow the Mayor of New York. Ugly, isn't it? But the only word for it is insurrection. Insurrection within the ranks. It's not unheard of. After all, the force is not unlike an army. These people, and God knows how many more are in on it, are looking to overthrow a duly elected official.

"Mrs. Sullivan, we might be dealing with an isolated incident or the tip of an iceberg. For all we know, this could be an orchestrated effort by malcontents throughout the city, or at least the Brooklyn command. They have probably been waiting for such an opening. Doesn't it strike you as odd that this should surface now—during a crucial election? Believe me, Mrs. Sullivan, it took me a little time to sort out, but I'm convinced we are dealing with anarchy, and you are an innocent instrument."

Sissy checked his face to see if he was trying to snow her. But his look was one of smug satisfaction. He looked as pompous as Sherlock Holmes after he delineated the depths of devilish deeds to the dim-witted Watson. She had only used "friends of Eddie's" to protect Sal for unwittingly bringing her to Toni. Now this wonderful whacked-out paranoid had raised her an army! A mutinous army that opposed his Mayor's police programs. Her surge of confidence returned, rushing from her feet to the top of her head, where she thought it would spring forth as a geyser. His paranoia transformed her from a widow working on a wing and a prayer to St. Joan leading a legion of dissident blue. She couldn't blow it now. She commanded the marching forces of her blood to turn cold. She stared at him intently.

"Mr. Groves, earlier on you said I was drawing wild conclusions, conclusions I had come to based on some very solid facts. Now you turn around and want me to believe an outrageous plot by the police? Eddie's fellow workers? I was accusing some corrupt cops of trying to protect their careers. Protecting themselves by harming my husband. And you dismissed me. Now you present me with this—I don't know what—a cop underground, and you want me to believe you?"

"Mrs. Sullivan, believe me. I can feel it. Anyone who brought you the kind of information you received was not looking out for you. They had bigger fish to fry. And logic dictates that can mean only one place."

"Logic!" she scoffed. It was delicious to have him defend his credibility. She hadn't expected such a turn.

"Yes, logic. Why bring you Xeroxes of property receipts? Why fill your head with rumors of a mystery woman when there is none? Simply to move you in your grief to be a catalyst of their contemptible mischief."

"Aren't we forgetting one thing, Mr. Groves?"

"That being?"

"If the woman is who you say she is, why was she chasing drug dealers up a flight of stairs with my husband? Where does logic come into that?"

He took a deep breath. He had been expecting this. "All right, Mrs. Sullivan, you're finally going to get the truth. Yes, you have been deceived. But not for the reasons you think, or that you were told. The woman in question was in proximity to your husband's death."

"On a stairwell?"

"No, your husband didn't die chasing drug dealers. Your husband didn't die at the location you were told. Your husband died in Mrs. Fernandez's club, where he was a regular."

"I don't believe you. Why hide that? You're accusing others of scheming and plotting, and you're doing the very same thing."

"I'm not. Believe me, I'm telling you the truth."

She shouted, "Everyone is looking out for everyone else, but no one is looking out for me."

"Please, Mrs. Sullivan. I'm concerned about you. It's me, me alone, who is looking out for you. I wish you would believe that."

"Then explain," she shouted. "Make me believe. Why cover up my husband's death in the presence of that woman, if everything was innocent?"

He began reluctantly. "You see, Mrs. Sullivan, a cop's life on the street is a lonely one. A life immersed in pressures. Sometimes, in this pressure cooker he gravitates to others, others outside his family, for solace."

She felt like laughing in his face. "Gravitates for solace." A PR euphemism for fucking. Orwell was an early arrival. She decided to chance it all. She stood up, hovering over him, and screamed, "Get out of my house. Just what are you trying to imply? Don't answer that. I don't want that dirt in my house. The nerve, the impudent nerve of you! Coming in here and spitting on my marriage, on my dead husband who's not here to defend himself. If he was, you wouldn't dare."

She looked up at the ceiling, imploring, "Eddie, Eddie, come down for a minute and protect me. They're trying to destroy me."

Groves stood and took her shoulders. He looked as if he were going to be sick. "Mrs. Sullivan . . ."

"Don't you dare touch me," she screamed. "Don't you dare put your hands on me. Get out of this house."

He sat down, trembling. She stood threateningly above him as he rubbed his forehead with the fingers of both hands. She knew he was trying to regroup. She eased off, not wanting to send him running at this moment when she thought she had him.

"I'm sorry, Mrs. Sullivan," he said. "Please sit down. I'm sorry. I didn't mean to imply that at all. It just came out wrong. Please sit down and give me a chance to explain."

Sissy picked up her glass and went to the refrigerator. She put in fresh ice and poured in some mix. She returned to the table and picked up the Valium bottle, shaking out two saccharin tablets.

He looked horrified. "Are you sure you want to take those? At least, take just one—with water."

She put the two pills in her mouth and washed them down with the mix. "It's all right," she said. "If I don't, I'll . . . Give me a moment."

She sat down and placed her arms on the table with her head resting on them. "Just a moment. I need a moment. I feel very strange."

She made a game of waiting him out. After a couple of minutes, he tentatively asked, "Mrs. Sullivan?"

She didn't answer. This time, there was urgency in his voice. "Mrs. Sullivan? Are you all right? Are you okay?"

She grunted.

"Oh, thank God. You have to be careful with medication. Please remember that."

"Okay," she agreed, drowsily picking up her head.

"Can we talk now?" he asked.

She nodded her head dopily.

"All I was trying to say," he began, "was that your husband was a regular at the club, and that he was a friend of the woman. After all, she is a fellow officer's widow. Many of the local guys are friendly with her. Most of them. I've even heard your husband helped her boy out of a scrape.

"You see, Mrs. Sullivan, your husband was on duty, and he had no business being in that club at that hour. Plus *we* know, strictly speaking, that the club is not legal. Now how would that look in the wrong hands? An on-duty cop hanging out on gambling premises? Premises owned by a cop's widow? We know it was innocent, but surely you can understand what some enterprising politician or some grubby reporter could turn that into. You see, that's why his fellow officers, his true friends on the job, covered it up. Surely, you can see that."

"I can't 'surely' see anything," she said. "One side tells me one thing, and you tell me another. I'm being pulled apart."

"Mrs. Sullivan, I know a way of settling this. You contact the people who have been feeding you this scandal, and I'll confront them here and now. I'll wait all day for them, if necessary. I'll clear my calendar."

She hadn't expected this turn. She pulled her response out of the air. "I'm afraid that's not possible. I don't know who they are."

"I don't follow you."

"The information. The phone calls. They wouldn't give their names, except to say they were friends of Eddie's."

"You mean they have been feeding you this tale anonymously over the phone?"

"Yes."

"And what about the receipt with Mrs. Fernandez's name on it?"

"The same thing. But through the mail. With a letter explaining it, signed 'Friends of Eddie's.' "

He couldn't have been more pleased. His suspicions about a coup were validated. He brought the fingers of both hands together in an A-frame, which he opened and closed repeatedly. "Now doesn't that say it all? Gutless and clandestine. Tell me, would a true friend of your husband, of your family, operate that way? Tormenting a distraught woman with anonymous innuendo? Come, Mrs. Sullivan, logic and decency dictates otherwise." He sat back, like an attorney contented with his summation.

"Perhaps they were afraid of reprisals?" she suggested.

"From whom?"

"Other cops. The department. I don't know."

"Well, I do. The only reprisal they feared was the truth."

"But they were right about the woman. You admitted that."

"Right as far as they went. Yes, she was there, but I explained that to you."

"How do I know that's true? You have a stake in this, too. You want to smooth this over. Don't tell me you don't have a vested interest. The department. The Mayor. They're your concern. Aren't you working from a bias yourself? The only reason we're getting near the truth about my husband's death is that I challenged you with information. You didn't come in here on your own offering me anything. I don't know where to turn. Perhaps somebody outside should look into this. Someone with no axe to grind."

His smugness crumbled. "Now, let's not be hasty. All anyone on the outside would do is parade the dirty laundry."

"What do you mean by that?" she snapped. "I don't have any dirty laundry. You're making inferences again, Mr. Groves. Inferences that there is something unwholesome about my husband's death. I won't hear any more of that. I have a daughter to raise, and she isn't going to go through life with the stigma of scandal on her. Do you have a family, Mr. Groves?"

"No, I don't. I'm not married."

"You're not, huh?" she said accusingly. "How old are you?"

He bristled at her question, but he was used to the innuendo. The Mayor with his goddamn championing of gay rights. Every single aide was suspect. "I'm thirty-one. But I don't see that as pertinent."

"Well, you have to admit that is a little old not to be married," Sissy said. "Most men your age have a wife and family. But maybe I'm prying where I shouldn't."

"You're not prying," he said defensively. "I have every intention of getting married."

"I'm sure you'll find someone someday," she said patronizingly.

"Single or not, Mrs. Sullivan, I have warm feelings for families. I assure you that your future, and your daughter's, concern me."

"The difference is that to me it's life and death, Mr. Groves."

He paused for a moment. Sissy felt he was formulating his final argument. He leaned across the table to give his words the intimate weight of sincerity. "Mrs. Sullivan, do you have a parish priest in whom you and your family confide?"

Sissy couldn't figure out what he was about to suggest—a

round-robin confession for all concerned parties to determine who was telling the truth? A Roman *Rashomon*? "Naturally," she declared in a tone that said, how could it be otherwise?

"Good," he said. "Why don't you ask this trusted man to check it out, to ascertain if Mrs. Fernandez is who I say she is, and if she runs this club? A man beyond reproach. A man with no axe to grind. Wouldn't that settle everything?"

The little shit must have gotten his view of Catholicism from Barry Fitzgerald movies, Sissy thought. "It's normal to hire a lawyer for that kind of work," she said.

There was no deterring him. "Fine, better yet. Have your family lawyer check out Mrs. Fernandez's background. I'll tell you what. I personally will pay his fee."

"What would that prove?"

He was exasperated by her stupidity. "My God, it would prove everything. That your husband expired in innocent circumstances. And the quote-unquote cover-up was the most understandable thing in the world. That it was done out of generosity for him and his family."

She paused. She decided to give him a glimmer of hope. "I might."

"Good."

"But it doesn't solve my real problem."

He was crestfallen again. "And what's that?"

"Let's say that what you said proves out. That my attorney verifies it. There are still those who know my husband died in a way that wasn't the way it was reported. Ugly rumors would still be floating around out there. Fact distortion. For instance, that my husband died in the company of a strange woman. You know what people could do with that. Malicious gossip is hard to put to rest, Mr. Groves, and conceivably it could reach my daughter. That would destroy her, and me with her. I can't leave it like this. I owe it to my husband not to leave his death in shadowy whispers."

"But the public word is that your husband died a hero—trying to bust drug dealers. That should be more than sufficient. If Mrs. Fernandez checks out properly, you certainly could live with that account."

"We know it's a lie, Mr. Groves, and so do others. Suppose my daughter begins to get anonymous phone calls and letters?"

"Certainly they wouldn't do that."

"You just told me they're trying to topple the Mayor of New

York. If that's true, why would these people, these anonymous people, give my daughter special consideration?"

She had given him a thorny problem he couldn't solve. "I don't know what else I can suggest," he said gloomily.

"If Eddie could only be seen as a hero in death," she said wistfully.

"But he already is."

"I don't mean local word of mouth. Precinct stuff. If there was some way—I mean if what you say about that woman is true— that the department could officially honor him."

"I just don't know . . ."

"I'm always so moved when I watch official ceremonies on television. You know, cops getting medals or promotions from the Mayor, with all those reporters and television cameras. And the families in attendance with the Mayor shaking everyone's hand. It's always so beautiful. Nobody would dare gossip about a cop after such a ceremony. It's like looking at a priest getting ordained."

She had watched him closely during her discourse, had seen his eyes glisten over when she got to the press and the television. He looked horny.

"Yes, something like that might do it. A medal of some sort," he said.

"Or a posthumous promotion," she suggested.

He looked at her warily. His nose was working. Sissy dampened the thought with her tears. "Eddie was such a good cop. So many citations for bravery. Did you know that?"

"Yes, of course. He had a reputation of being fearless."

"And you did say the force was like an army, didn't you?"

"I did."

"That's what I mean. I always thought it was so touching in the movies when a fallen soldier was given a posthumous battle-field commission. Wouldn't that be something? Edward Sullivan. Lieutenant Edward Sullivan. Would his daughter ever break her buttons over that!

"But I guess that's just silly. That only happens in movies. This Mayor doesn't really care for cops, does he?"

"That's unfair. Grossly unfair. The Mayor has an intense feeling for the force." Groves thought of the television cameras picking up the faces of all those misty-eyed, well-scrubbed, working-class families. That would be better than several hundred thousand dollars in campaign spots and maybe a like number of bodies at the polls.

"Lieutenant Edward Sullivan," he mused. "A battlefield commission. You're right, it has a nice feel to it."

"Yes," she said. "But the Mayor would never do that. All the facts. Too messy. But it's a nice dream anyway."

"Not really," he said. "The Mayor doesn't have to know anything more than the precinct report. He needn't be involved in all this."

"But surely *you* don't have the authority . . ."

"The Mayor," he said archly, "takes all my suggestions on police matters." He was thinking how he would present his brain child. Why just one cop—Sullivan? Several being cited would be better, with Sullivan's promotion the pièce de résistance. A cop of each ethnic persuasion. Or at least one from each ethnic group with whom the Mayor was running weak. An Italian, a Pole. Sullivan would cover the Irish. He had to check the demographics when he got back. There were bound to be other hostile groups. The Swedes in Bay Ridge, for sure. He'd work through the borough commanders for recommendations. All the boroughs should be represented. A lily-white show. There had been too much identification with the blacks and Puerto Ricans. The polls showed that. Thank Christ, his department didn't have to worry about the gays.

What an extravaganza! It would be a personal coup for his office. All the networks, the local channels, the major dailies, and any little jerkwater paper out in the boroughs with a printing press. They'd all come. He'd plan refreshments afterward. An open bar down in the press room. That would secure every ink-stained sonnuvabitch in the city. He wanted to get back to his office to draw up the proposal. He'd deal directly with the Mayor and his reelection team. This would make them all sit up and take notice. His dad included. This mad, maudlin, trashy woman was a blessing in disguise. A veritable Cinderella.

He swallowed his enthusiasm. "It's within the realm of possibility, Mrs. Sullivan. Would this—if it can be accomplished, it won't be easy, of course—put all your worries to rest?"

Sissy didn't want to seem overanxious. "Mine, and my daughter's. That is, if that woman checks out."

"Of course, of course. She will, Mrs. Sullivan."

"I hope so. I hope to God what you say is true. You would lift a terrible cross from my family's shoulders."

He stood up and gathered his papers back into his case. He held one of her hands in both of his. "We're going to try. Try like hell, believe me, to ease your burden."

"I do hope you can. I'm beginning to feel glad it was you I contacted first."

"You did the right thing. And if those filth peddlers call, tell them nothing. Is that a promise?"

"It's a promise," she said demurely.

"You can offer them my number though. I'd love to deal with them."

"I will," she said.

"Do that. And I know what you and your lawyer will find will put your mind to rest."

She let the tears flow down her face. "Can I ask you just one more thing?"

He smiled at her warmly. "Certainly."

"If Mrs. . . . the woman . . ."

"Fernandez."

"Yes, Mrs. Fernandez is a cop's widow. I don't want you to do anything about her club. Please. Cops' widows suffer enough. Will you promise?"

"I agree. It's a promise."

If that wasn't paying her dues to feminism, Sissy didn't know what was. She doubted if even Susan B. Anthony would demand such a tariff. "Good," she said.

"Now, as you can imagine, I have lots of work to do."

"Of course." She walked him to the door. "Thank you for coming."

"And you," he said, "go easy on those pills. If I can work things out, you'll have no need for them. I'll give you a progress report daily. Okay?"

"Okay."

"And remember to tell those gutless phantoms to peddle their trash elsewhere. Namely, at my office."

"I will," she said. "And thank you."

He went down the stairs by twos he was so pleased with himself. Which irritated Sissy a bit—he was under the illusion he had conned her. Another dumb peacock male. He'd get the news soon enough. For now, she had to whip the house into shape before Eileen's return. But to hell with cooking. It was a night to celebrate. She and her college-bound daughter would stuff themselves out on Chinese.

Groves was as good as his word. He checked in daily with progress reports, plans in formulation, and such. She knew he'd be working his ambitious little tail off. The quicker he put the lid on her and this business, the better. The Mayor's polls remained stagnant. They could use a goose.

After five days, she told him that her lawyer, using discreet contacts, had reported back favorably on Toni Fernandez. She was everything he had said she was (except a piece of ass, naturally). Sissy reminded Groves of his hands-off promise. He reaffirmed his word.

To keep the fires burning, she told him she had received another phone call, but this time she had demanded that the caller identify himself. She told Groves she had even proposed a meeting, and the caller immediately hung up. She hadn't had a call since. He granted her an accolade: "Good girl." That was one more she owed him.

After a week, he told her the ceremony was in the works. Near the end of the following week, she received notification and an invitation in the mail. It wasn't to be only Eddie. Groves was pulling out all the stops. As she suspected, it was going to be a media bash. A parade of honorees with the Mayor and a "host of dignitaries" presiding. Sissy grinned at the invitation. The fuzz version of the Academy Awards. Christ, she was proud of herself!

*S*ISSY'S ANXIETY over the Mayor's arrival was percolating toward anger. She thought it unwise to approach Groves in view of other members of the Mayor's staff. That might single out her relationship with him. Possibly set tongues wagging. It was too late in the game for such a gaffe, though she was longing for reassurance. Though he had given it verbally, there was nothing in the letter or invitation specifically stating that Eddie would be promoted. He could simply be honored like the rest. Some worthless medallion to trot out for the grandkids. That and a token would get you on the subway.

She just didn't trust the people she was up against. Perhaps on further checking, Groves had found out something? What if he had decided she was bluffing? Groves was close enough to the cops' mentality to doublebank her, if he thought he could get away with it.

Why wasn't the invitation more specific about Eddie's promotion? It could be that Groves was reserving her comeuppance for the surprise of the ceremony, the smasheroo curtain. It would be his style.

His smile was not encouraging. Not reassuring. The cat who ate the canary. She didn't like that imagery. Her as the canary ready to sing about the force.

She decided to saunter closer to him to see if he would make a move toward her. Drop her an A-OK sign perhaps? But as she edged along the wall, someone else approached him and whispered in his ear. Groves nodded to the man, and both left the room, heading toward the outer corridor. She would be in suspense still longer. But now the path was clear to find a water fountain and drop a pill.

She looked over at the family. To hell with it. If the day didn't pan out, she wanted to remember it. She wasn't coy. Never had been. Not like those twerps who used to feign passing out in the back seat of a car from beer, so that their boyfriends could feel them up. If Sissy was going to be screwed over, she wanted to remember it. She made her way toward her family.

Before she reached them, she heard a hubbub of noise behind her. She turned and saw the Mayor entering the room with Groves and a covey of aides running interference for him. Two of the aides, the male and female who had greeted Sissy initially, were shuffling index cards and whispering to the Mayor as he stopped at various groups and greeted them. From the sincerity of his hand-clutching and the time spent with each group, Sissy knew he was being fed names. And from the slavish smiles he was winning, Sissy presumed the cards contained facts. Nice little personal tidbits. Not unlike the Queen of England remembering your region was famous for its smashing plum pudding. She had better get to Nellie's and Catherine's side before they started to practice curtsys.

When Christy saw the Mayor come within earshot, he turned to Catherine and Nellie and said, "Now remember, you don't have to kiss his ring. That's the fellow uptown in St. Patrick's."

Catherine glared at him. "Haven't you sobered up yet? There's a time and a place."

"Yes, my dear, and you always know it," he said drily, "much to your unending credit."

Sissy winked at Christy and took command. "Well, I guess the show is about to get on the road."

"Yes, the star has arrived," declared Christy. Catherine only glared, not wanting to give him a chance at rebuttal.

Eileen looked at the Mayor making his way toward them. "Wow, he's a doll," she said.

Sissy had to give her daughter's estimate merit. In her day he could have stood Breezy Point on its ear with that blond hair and that tan. His outfit didn't hurt either: cavalry twill slacks, black loafers, and a blue blazer. The only incongruous thing was that his shirt was open at the neck. It seemed terribly raffish for such an occasion. "The Prince playing the Pauper," Christy whispered to Sissy. But his looks could stand up anywhere. In the field of politics, they were astonishing.

Sissy could see Groves coaching him as they approached. The Mayor centered his smile on Sissy. "Mrs. Sullivan, so nice to meet you. I wish it were under happier circumstances. One of the terrible tasks of this job is that it seems you only get to meet those— the families who are so invaluable to the city—when it's too late to really say thank you."

Sissy could only manage to shake his hand and say, "Thank you."

He turned away from Sissy to Nellie and Catherine. "Can you two lovely ladies tell me how you manage to keep so fresh and cool-looking in this weather, when I'm running around wilted, even without a tie?"

Sissy couldn't make out their muted replies, other than something about the terrible heat. He was really good, she thought.

It was more telling when he turned to Sal and Christy. He went through quick, perfunctory motions, never even showing a glimmer of recognition for Christy who had met him before. Men obviously bored him. Dull, male, prismless faces incapable of reflecting his glory. He quickly moved on to Eileen. "So this is the college girl?"

Sissy was stunned. She stared at Groves, who looked as if he were about to crow. Sissy was impressed. Even if it was bullshit, it was well-researched bullshit. The Gordon Groveses of the world had their place. If he had been a steward on the Titanic, he would have made sure you went down in your own deck chair.

Eileen answered, "Well, in the fall. Columbia."

The Mayor bent toward Eileen confidentially. "They couldn't afford to pass you over. It's a fine school. Many of its sons and daughters have made immeasurable contributions to the city.

"I want to see a super report on you at the end of the semester. You hear? I'm going to look forward to seeing it. And don't you be shy. That door down the hall is always open to the daughter of one of my special officers. You just come down and bang on it. Good and loud. Even if I'm working on the fiscal budget."

He pulled back and incorporated them all in his glow and grinned. "*Especially* if I'm working on the budget." He turned toward Groves.

"Now, Gordon, you get everything ready. I've been keeping all these wonderful people waiting here long enough." Groves nodded.

The Mayor turned back to Nellie and Catherine. "Now I have to freshen up a bit and get a tie on. I wish I had you ladies' secret." He was off.

Sissy swore she heard Christy groan. She thought it slightly unfair. He wouldn't have been so critical if the routine were delivered by a woman. She ventured he would have been smitten. It was all surface, to be sure, but it was done to a turn. When he was finished, Sissy had watched his pale blues go blank. She was sure he hadn't another line in his head. He exited before a comment could be made, since that would force him into an unrehearsed response. Sissy had seen similar performances by girls in the bars of her youth. The girls always flitted off, with the boys still open-mouthed in admiration. Like the Mayor, they lacked the longevity of substance. They were made for the lacy interludes. Like them, the Mayor would make a gorgeous one-night stand.

Groves turned to Sissy's group. "Would you folks please go outside now? Your seats will be somewhere in the first three rows with the other families. There'll be someone there to seat you."

They started to make their way to the door, but Groves interrupted. "Not you, Mrs. Sullivan. You come with me." Sissy numbly followed him, inwardly begging for a sign that was not forthcoming. Either her tune was about to be played, or the jig was up.

As she watched her family recede, she experienced the same sinking feeling she had had on her first day of school, when her mother abandoned her to the nuns with the instruction that if she acted up, the good sister had Nellie's permission to "kill" her. She had often wondered how many volumes Spock could have gotten out of that.

Groves led her outside. She watched her family descend the steps and go to their seats in the first row. Sal and Christy flanked Nellie, Eileen, and Catherine. Only Philly was missing. Sissy was concerned about that. In his obnoxious way he had been protective during the morning. If he ever reported to Carmela that he had been snubbed, Mama would put the horns on the Sullivans for life.

Groves led her toward the podium. Chairs were lined up on

each side. The school analogy sickeningly struck again. It looked like a graduation. Groves showed her to the last seat on the left and motioned for her to sit. She anchored a row of spiffed-up cops. She looked up at Groves for guidance. All he offered was, "Pay attention. Listen for your name." He was gone again inside City Hall.

Sissy smiled at the cop sitting next to her, and he awkwardly grinned back. She leaned forward in her seat and looked down the line. On the other side of the podium was another line of cops, sitting decorously. But there was no female counterbalance at the other end. She must look ludicrous in this setting. Like a transvestite in a shapeup of teamsters. One glance at Nellie with her head down, sneakily peering up, convinced her of that. Her daughter was about to mortify her again. God love her. At least she had a fixed view of things. The galaxy was a maze conceived to trap mothers.

Christy was staring at her and made a "What's up?" sign with his hand. Sissy shrugged and Christy stared back coldly at her. Old negotiators didn't like last-minute rabbits pulled out of the hat. Only Eileen was beaming. Sissy looked straight at her, un-smiling, and made a discreet motion with her index finger to her lips. The child happily nodded.

The sun filtered through the trees in the park behind the audience. Shards of it were hitting Sissy in the eyes. She wished she had brought her sunglasses. But that would make her look worse. A moll in a lineup of cops. As she blinked her eyes, she felt the vessels in her head contract. The pain was dizzying. Thank God she hadn't taken the other pill. She might have keeled over, right off the chair, as if she'd been shot. Come to think of it, the rigid lineup looked like a row of condemned prisoners— Belle Starr (was it Yvonne DeCarlo?) and her gang mowed down at high noon. Whoa, girl. Even that damned first pill was too much.

She heard some fussing at the podium but didn't want to break the symmetry of the line by bending over to look. Instead, she tilted her head slightly forward so that no one could see she was closing her eyes. If she kept staring into that sun, she knew she would puke. The thought made her smile: Cop's Wife Spills All at Mayor's Feet. Groves's greatest fear realized.

She heard an introduction and a summons to the gathered to bow their heads. For once, she had been ahead of the pack. She heard a prayer begin. When it was over, she raised her head and heard the introductory voice again. Then a new voice began another prayer. She wondered how many more invocations she would have to sit through before the ecumenical equal time was fulfilled. The FCC even had a shingle in heaven.

She recognized Groves's voice take over, and she strained to hear him. It wasn't what she was waiting for. He was introducing someone else. Some commander or another. She could feel the sweat gather in the crevice of her breasts and between her thighs. If they ever did get around to her, her rear would be stuck to the chair.

The commander came on like thunder. The old refrain. A blue boy singing the blues: holding back the jungle, civilization crumbling, chaos on every corner. A real upper. He'd be a great warm-up act on Judgment Day. A doomsday Ed McMahon: "And herr-r-e's Eternity."

His gas bag finally deflated, and Sissy shifted into alertness. The Mayor surely had to be next. But Sissy should have remembered it was an election year. Next up were the borough presidents. Each of them was a Baedeker to the glory of his fiefdom. It made no damn sense. Everything was blended together. Favorite sons with landmarks, temples with opera tenors, the Bronx Zoo with prize-winning chemists, movie stars and museums, sacred churches with the hallowed memory of Ebbets Field, and the cops being honored today joining the pantheon of parochialism. Sissy figured the Mayor had to be in desperate shape to let this boosterism run on. The shaky polls had to have deep, dire underpinnings.

Finally, he rose. He opened with a tapeworm of thank yous. Never had one man owed so much to so many. Nonetheless, Sissy hung on every name. Eddie's and hers were not among them. Finally, the Mayor declared it was "time to get down to the main business of the day." After a brief recounting of each of their deeds—stopping a robbery in progress, foiling a rape, breaking up a numbers operation, thwarting a suicide, saving a child drowning in the Hudson—the cops rose individually to receive their citations and the applause of the gathering. The Mayor seemed to be picking them off one by one, until Sissy was painfully isolated. She stared out at her family for some connective solace, only to see Nellie muttering to herself as she shifted her hands. She was saying her rosary! But what the hell had Sissy expected? She had seen her do the same thing on buses, at the kids' graduations, and during movies. It was as automatic as a child in a crib moving play beads endlessly and aimlessly back and forth on a steel shaft. Sissy stifled her embarrassment. Maybe that was the simple faith she could never attain.

As she watched Nellie, she heard the name Edward Sullivan. Sissy nearly bolted from her seat and shouted "Here!" But the Mayor was just warming up. He talked of Eddie's family and his endless network of friends, his immense popularity in any precinct he worked. Sissy could find no argument. At odd moments she wondered if Eddie had gone on the take to avoid offending the offerer of the bribe. It was possible. Wanting to be loved was a bottomless thing. How well she knew.

But she was happy the Mayor had centered on Eddie's popularity. Eddie would have liked that. He would have been pleased with this day. Too bad it wasn't being recorded, piped into every neighborhood joint where he ever reigned. They too would like that. A videotape they could play back over and over, like the deciding touchdown in the Super Bowl. The legend of Eddie Sullivan in stop action and slow-mo. Something to show the young pretenders to his throne. Something to shoot at. The neighborhood's Nobel prize.

Nellie and Catherine were crying. The handkerchiefs moving to their eyes with the cadence of the Mayor's words told Sissy that. But they were doing it with great dignity. No sobbing. Just a dab here and there, like punctuation. Eileen was keyed, leaning forward in expectation.

When Sissy heard the words "a fallen comrade" and "battlefield commission," she knew she was home free. Her eyes started to flood in relief. She squeezed back the tears. The Mayor called her name. She braced herself. There would be none of that. No mawkish slop to sully Eddie's day. The day she had conceived. The byword would be dignity and valor. She had rehearsed this moment repeatedly in her mind. They would all be looking at her. Looking for the trite, conventional act. Something they could empathize with, nudge each other with in collaboration.

But this was hers alone. She had been there at the beginning. Conceived it out of dust. She strode toward the Mayor as if the part were destined for her.

He bent and kissed her on both cheeks. She couldn't help thinking of the "Marseillaise." The Mayor pronounced, "For his unstinting valor, we, the City of New York, in our heartfelt appreciation, today elevate Officer Edward Sullivan to the rank of Lieutenant."

Groves handed the Mayor a small open box, holding lieutenant's bars. "If I may," said the Mayor. Sissy could sense the photographers and the TV men edging closer. She nodded her assent, though she didn't know what he meant. He took the bars from the box and pinned them on Sissy's dress. She hadn't counted on that. She glanced over to see Eileen crying. With the bars in place, the Mayor kissed her again, stepped back, and smiled.

It was overwhelming. She dearly wanted to say something appropriate but didn't trust her voice. She was afraid she was about to slobber until she heard a piercing whistle. It repeated itself. The sound froze everyone. She looked out to see where it was coming from.

It was Philly, standing behind the last row of chairs. He did it again, and Sissy laughed in relief. Spotting Sissy's smile, Philly whistled again, shot his arm in the air, and shouted, "Right on!"

Involuntarily, Sissy waved back. The Mayor seized her hand aloft, and they waved in tandem to the now standing, applauding crowd while the cameras had a field day. As a team, they could run this city! Sissy thought triumphantly.

When the cheering subsided, the Mayor lowered her arm but held her hand at his side as the police band on the fringe of the park played the national anthem. When it ended, Sissy made her way to her family. She had never felt lighter. She had done it. She alone. A solo. She against the odds. A lonely aviatrix. Indeed, she felt as if she *could* fly.

Eileen rose to meet her. "Mama, mama, you were right."

They hugged each other, and Sissy spun her daughter around in her embrace.

"And you were so good. So great up there. I was so proud of you. No kidding, you were dynamite."

For the first time, Sissy allowed a tear. She went first to Catherine, who was now in shambles. "Shush, this is a day to be proud," she said. "That was your son they were talking about up there."

"I know, I know," said Catherine. "It's just that I am so proud."

Sissy hugged Nellie next.

"You were wonderful," her mother said in admiration and astonishment.

"It was that rosary you were working on," countered Sissy, laughing.

"Three," said Nellie. "I said three during the ceremony."

"Then it was the overtime that did it. Thanks, Mom."

She turned to Christy who looked delighted but quizzical. She hung on his neck and whispered into his ear, "You were right, Pop. A lot of people loved him. More than I ever imagined. I'm so happy for him. The department really showed their colors today. They must have put a lot of pressure on the Mayor to do something as grand as that."

She pulled away from him before he could reply, turned to Sal. "And Sal. Dear Sal," she said. "Thanks for being such a good friend. Such a loyal, good friend to Eddie." She grasped both his hands.

"Whatta day! Whatta day! I just gotta talk to the guys for a minute." Sal excitedly walked toward Groves, who was happily mingling with a group of cops.

Philly came up behind her. "Hey, I hope I wasn't out of order back there. But man, it just blew my mind."

"Mine, too," she said, feeling him stiffen under her embrace. "You were just perfect. Real class. Eddie would have dug you."

He beamed at her. "Well, if you don't mind, I'd like to get the folks back. You know, traffic building up and everything."

"Yes, Theresa, I'd like to get Catherine home," Christy concurred. "She's had a big day. I think she could use a rest."

Sissy looked at her mother-in-law. She looked vanquished. "Sure, Pop, we'll get you on the road."

"Well, don't let us dampen your day if you and your mom and Eileen want to do something. You know, something special."

"No," Nellie said. "I'll go with you. But Eileen love, here's a little something to take up to the college with you." She took an envelope out of her pocketbook and handed it to the girl.

Eileen opened it. It held savings bonds. Those $18.75 bonds Mickey used to claim Nellie stashed away. Eileen protested, "Grandma, I can't."

"You can, and you will. How many pleasures do you think an old lady has left? You're my pleasure, young lady."

Like a little girl, Eileen looked to Sissy for help. All Sissy could think of were the floors that had been scrubbed, the other people's dirt that had been cleaned to accumulate that small cache. The diligence it took keeping it from Mickey.

"Oh, Mom. Dear Mom. That's so sweet it's heartbreaking." She nestled in her mother's arms. She had forgotten how nice it once felt.

Christy whispered, "Why don't you take your mother with you? I think she'd love it."

"Well, who's ever going, I think we should get started," Philly said. "Besides, I can't wait to get back to the neighborhood. Wait till the guys hear about this. *Marron!* Just wait till Mom hears. Man, the neighborhood will be jumping tonight."

"You take Mr. and Mrs. Sullivan," Sissy said. "I'll handle the rest, Philly."

Philly turned to Eileen and chucked her under the chin. "And you don't forget we have a date in four years. A limo for prom night."

"Sure," she said.

"On me," he said.

"It's a date."

He led Christy and Catherine toward the car.

Sal was involved with his cronies. He was settled in. That was good. He would have to get used to being outside her orbit. Nothing blunt. Nothing cruel. Just gradual attrition until she phased him out completely.

Groves saw the group dispersing and walked toward Sissy. She separated herself from Eileen and Nellie to confront him. It was such a day she'd let it drop. Forget about it. He had more than held to their bargain.

"Well, what did you think?" he asked.

"It was wonderful. Thank you."

"I told you I'd handle it." She wished he wouldn't crow. Not now. Let it rest.

"The Mayor is delighted. Did you see the coverage?"

"It was impressive," she said.

"More than that. Amazing. Didn't I tell you? Now wasn't it right to leave it in my hands?"

She wished he'd stop. He didn't.

"I always tell my people to come to me first. Bring your problems through my door. I say it time and again."

Why couldn't the fool have quit while he was ahead?

"I tell them I don't care what level their problem is on. It can be settled inside. Bring it to someone who looks out for you. Don't air it outside.

"For instance, we never would have had this day. Just imagine you in the papers tomorrow with the Mayor, waving to the crowd. Did you ever think you'd see such a day? I mean, the Mayor of New York holding your hand up. What a shot that will make! The evening news guys loved it. I bet you'll be on the phone alerting the neighbors tonight. Did you ever imagine it? Did you?"

"From the very beginning," she said.

"Huh?"

You wouldn't, she thought. You vain, silly, patronizing male. She'd be damned if she would let him get away with it. She'd gag him on the feather he was sticking in his hat. She thought of reaching into her bag and taking out the tape cassette. The one that had silently spun under the toaster cover. But that would put her back in their league. Those days were over. "I always knew. From the beginning," she said.

She turned away from him and walked back, purified.

Life might never be the same for her, but she was as close to even as she could get. She could start again. She was capable. She had dealt in the real world. The toughest damn segment of it. And by doing it, she had held her own world together. The looks on the faces of her family proved that. She had paid the last installment of Eddie's dues. She hadn't let them crumble.

Now her daughter was off to college.

Then Lynn. She would call her. Eileen's starting college would be a perfect excuse. Lynn was too valuable to lose over some isolated emotional binge. Lynn had been kind enough to console her on a night she desperately needed it.

Enough damned sniveling. No more blaming others No more one-way mirrors. By God, she'd even find a way to get those snooty sisters of hers into the hinterlands. It wasn't a fresh deck, but she still held some cards. She wasn't ready to fold yet.

In her exuberance, she walked up to Nellie and Eileen and put her arms around them. "Come on," she said. "Let's go register the family star and then have a ritzy lunch."

"No kidding? Where?" Eileen asked excitedly.

Sissy gave each of them a resounding thwack on the butt. "You can bet your gorgeous Irish asses it won't be Schrafft's."

Eileen squealed, "Mom, you're gross."

Sissy rolled her eyes and extended her arms like a movie monster. The girl squealed again and ran off, with Sissy in stiff-legged Karloffian pursuit.

"Mom, you are. You're terrible. You are gross. Everyone's watching. Stop it," Eileen said, laughing helplessly as she ran.

Nellie lagged behind, joining the girl in laughter.

Sissy's soul was singing. In pursuit, she couldn't help noting that her daughter was leaving them all in her wake, distancing mother and grandmother, jettisoning generations as she ran in the direction of uptown.